BEYOND THE RIVER

A POST-APOCALYPTIC JOYRIDE

Book One

C. R. WRIGHT

First paperback, hardback, and eBook editions published November 2024

Book design by C. R. Wright

ISBN 979-8-9918666-0-6 (hardback edition)

ISBN 979-8-9918666-1-3 (paperback edition)

ISBN 979-8-9918666-3-7 (paperback edition)

ISBN 979-8-9918666-2-0 (eBook edition)

www.thewrightswrite.com

Special Acknowledgement

To Marilyn Boake, Indie Publishing Group, Inc., our copyeditor who not only showed an abundance of patience and willingness to teach but also had to fix the same mistakes over and over and over again.

C. - To my wife, my love, my greatest supporter.

R. - To my husband, the forever creative, whose ideas keep me intrigued and boundless passion requires me to extend my own artistic abilities.

CHAPTER ONE

(Major Oliver White—U.S. Marines)

Wednesday, January 8, 2048

Location: Omaha, Nebraska—Joint Base Eppley, Lookout Tower

The dark purple and red streaks painting the evening sky remind me that soon, the ground will be stained in the same way. A landscape that not even Bob Ross would paint if he were alive. What should be a picturesque scene of a peaceful winter evening overlooking a meadow of smooth, glistening, snowcapped trees and a gently flowing bend of the Missouri River isn't what it seems. It's a mirage that covers the ugly horrors hiding underneath. This godforsaken land smells of blood—metallic and dirty. Its stench lingers even in the dead of winter. A land absorbed with the souls of our fallen brothers and sisters. It's like we're all sitting on death row, waiting for our final moment that'll devour what's left of humanity. The vicious battles have infected my memory with endless heartache. There'll be no "happy fucking accident" here anytime soon.

For twenty-seven years now, our lives have been spinning in chaos. Not even a speck of light can be seen at the end of the proverbial tunnel. I don't know how much longer we'll be able to defend our position because "they" are getting more daring as each year passes. Within the past three years, attacks along our border have become more frequent and more strategic than random. "They" knew precisely where our weak spots were located, and "they'd" wait for our maintenance crews to arrive, then ambush them as they attempted to repair affected areas within our territory.

Anyone who's stepped foot on a battlefield with an enemy knew what "they" were doing: testing our defenses, our reactions, and how we counter each of their offensives. We're always playing defense in this barbaric chess game, and that needs to change. We haven't figured out for certain if it's from their own desperation to survive or if they want total domination. Maybe it's a mixture of both. After all this time, their motivation is still unclear.

We've come a long way since running from town to town, scavenging whatever food was left on already-looted store shelves. And if it weren't for the cold Nebraska winters, I doubt any of us would still be here. The harsh climate, one of only a few frailties our adversary employs, keeps "them" at bay for the time being. Even though winters are short-lived, it's just enough time to harden our defenses, improve upon our weaknesses, and get us ready for war when warmer weather moves in.

Once winter has passed, the only other saving grace we have that separates us from "them" is a man-made river we built years back as a triumphant testament to the new times we lived in. We call it simply "The River." It stretches one thousand miles in total length with a width of at least forty feet in its narrowest spots. From Omaha, where our main operating base is located, it extends east five hundred miles to the southern tip of Lake Michigan. Then, heading north from Omaha, it's another five hundred miles into what was once Canada.

It truly was an engineering feat. We used more explosives to help carve out the channel than what I had witnessed when stationed in Iraq and Afghanistan. It took thousands of tireless men and women working year-round for almost fifteen years to get it completed. Is it perfect? No, but like the freezing temps, it does a damn good job of keeping "them" out.

I stand up from leaning on the lookout tower railing and cup my hands to my mouth, blowing warmth into my worn leather gloves. I rub my hands together even though they aren't cold. Just a habit, I guess. When I clench my fists, the pop of my knuckles and the whine of the leather cracking are the only sounds that fill the desolate space. My hands have always felt filthy. No amount of soap can wash away the pain they carry: the sadness of those just out of reach and the gut-wrenching pain of robbing someone of life. So many that I've lost count. They aren't people. Not anymore.

I used to think it's what helped me sleep, but honestly, I've lost interest in the soul I once had. Numb. Unaffected anymore by this purgatory. This is where we used to live and thrive as a nation. What a fucking joke. Sometimes I wonder if this country will ever flourish like it once did.

I had an optimistic future in the Marines, achieving the rank of Major before all this bullshit. Now, nearly four million people have put their trust in me. And never in my life would I have thought I would be in this position, leading what's left of America in a ravaged world.

Through the wall-to-wall glass windows of the lookout tower office, I look to the southwest, toward the remnants of Omaha City. I can still picture a buzzing metropolitan and wonder how it would have changed had the Turning never happened. Twenty-seven years might not have changed the landscape much, other than a new skyscraper here and there, but life would still be moving forward. At this time of day, I imagine that office lights would be flickering off with people heading home to be with their families. Streets full of flashing red taillights from the stop-and-go traffic. The annoying honk of some idiot driver who's in a hurry, cutting people off. People just living their normal, mundane lives.

It's a useless thought, though, and an unwelcome blast of cold air hits me, and I see it for what it is now—a wasteland stripped of all its value. Unlike an ancient Greek ruin we used to read about in magazines, no one will be flocking here to admire its history. The city is crumbling from all angles, stained with decay no matter where you look. Now, the windows are as dark as night. No over-achieving worker staying up late to impress their boss come morning. The streets are empty of life. Feels like we don't belong here at all.

The remainder of my life will be spent fighting this endless war. Deep daggers of depression hook into my thoughts, taking center stage. Sometimes I think I want to be alone, but that's when my demons make themselves especially known.

I push aside the periling thoughts long enough to distract myself with an old, circular analog thermometer with a cracked plastic face cover that's hanging slightly off-center from a rusted nail. A mild cold front blew in last night—a twenty-seven-year record low— causing the temperature to dip into the negatives for a few short hours before the sun came up. Just plain fucking cold if you ask me, but good to know someone is keeping track of these statistics in a time like this. The uselessness of it makes me draw in a deep, stinging breath only to watch the white foggy plume rise and dissipate into the surrounding air like a ghost. If only this was an indication that winter, a temporary solace within this hell, would stick around longer than normal.

For the hundredth time today, the gray digital readout on my well-worn Casio G-SHOCK watch reminds me of the date. Where has the time gone? I can't believe another year is behind us, but how many more are ahead? That question haunts us all.

This lookout tower is the perfect hideout during the winter months, and I come here as much as possible. It's never occupied during this time; there's no need, really. When the temperature starts to rise, though, it holds a full complement of military personnel, teaming with eagle-eyed soldiers looking for anything that would wreak havoc on our sanctuary and communicating with the other outposts along The River to get status updates. Outposts have been strategically positioned every twenty-five miles along our side of The River, each named after the city they are located in. The outposts are constructed of metal and concrete, towering one hundred feet in the air, offering 360 degrees of unobstructed view, and loaded with plenty of firepower.

This one is located at the southern tip of what was once Eppley Airport in Omaha, Nebraska, along the Missouri River, now our main military base, renamed Joint Base Eppley. I find it relaxing. It gives me enough space to analyze my next move. A place to get away from it all and think. No one bothering me. No one bringing me another issue to resolve.

As of late, my time here has me thinking more and more about a mission I once brought up years back, but it wasn't popular with the other officers. However, now I think it's warranted. We're at a crossroads, and we need to venture out beyond The River. Only a handful of missions have ever been conducted outside the confines of our territory. I'm tired of playing defense. We need to recon farther south to help us understand our situation and the enemy better. Maybe give us a leg up for once. We could explore the area for intel and see what remaining supplies would help repair or even replace our dilapidating assets.

The mission would take us down into unknown territory: Texas. The once-largest state in the contiguous US was one of the last states to fall victim to the uprising of a new being and what was left of our shattered military at the time. The remaining survivors transported everything they could get their hands on down there in hopes of outlasting whatever was terrorizing the world. A two-decade old report stated that Fort Hood, Fort Bliss, and Lackland Airforce Base still had most of their weapons stockpiled and vehicles stored untouched and intact. We haven't stepped foot that far south in twenty years, and no one really knows the condition of the vehicles. Sitting that long will take its toll on anything.

But, if the supplies are in good condition, any one of those bases, Fort Hood specifically, since it is the largest and closest of the three, could provide us with much-needed parts for our vehicles. Half of what's left in our fleet—helicopters, aircraft, tanks—is battered beyond repair. Machine shops are doing everything they can, but with materials hard to come by, they can't keep up with the demand. All the bases within our boundary were picked clean years ago. I can't help but smirk at the ammo boxes and crates full of a variety of weapons stacked around me. Thank God we have plenty of weapons and ammo, probably the only items we'll never run out of.

It will take some serious convincing with the other leaders, but I don't think we have any other option. I know as soon as I say the word "Texas" for a mission, they'll all wonder if I've lost my mind. Texas is Their primary migration route into Mexico. When winter temps start moving in, they hightail it south for the warmer climate, like old folks retiring to Florida. If I ever find that shit hole they hide in, I'll bomb it to kingdom come, leaving it plastered with more craters than the moon. What I would give to call in that air strike.

Considering all our needs, I grab a set of binoculars sitting on a nearby table to inspect what I can of The River and catch weak spots even from up here. *How have we not figured this shit out by now?* Lowering the binoculars, I spy a patrol boat with the River Guard speeding away east, leaving a tall wake in its path. I wonder if something has happened. Maybe others have Turned? It's been a couple of years since we last recorded a Turning within our territory, but it wouldn't be impossible. They're probably just going to check something out. We get alerts all the time from drone operators flying over The River, but we can never be too safe these days. My watch shows 17:15 hours. I have too much to do to be up here thinking about the world, and besides, it's starting to get dark.

I could stand up here all night—sometimes it's better than sleep—letting my brain remind me why I am standing here today in the most twisted of ways, reminders I do not need. I take my eyes off The River for a moment and glare south toward Texas. What secrets is it hiding? My gut tells me it's something I need to know. Twenty-seven years ago, I would have been able to see their every move. I miss the technology we once possessed, especially since intel is hard to come by these days without putting lives and resources at stake. Satellites went offline over a decade ago, and my two-way radio just isn't quite the same.

I jerk my head toward the rumble of an engine fast approaching my location. The headlights from the oncoming vehicle bounce up and down on the two-track path, glimmering between the trees, and soon, the faded green M1109 Humvee comes into view. As it fishtails back and forth, the tires create a wave of mud and snow.

"What the fuck is this all about?" I grumble.

The Humvee pulls up at the base of the tower, and the two passenger-side doors fly open before the vehicle comes to a complete stop. *This can't be good.* Better not be another ridiculous problem that a ten-year-old could fix in five minutes with a paper clip and a roll of duct tape. I watch as two Privates exit the vehicle and make their way to the north-side staircase.

I'm facing east, away from the stairwell, so I won't be staring directly at whoever chooses to visit me when they reach the top. I know ignoring them won't stop them from interfering; however, it does let them know I'm annoyed by their presence. In my position, I am brought the most tedious of matters, and I can feel my mood change.

I slip my right hand into my coat pocket and search for my OTF knife, a habit leftover from when people were still turning. I grip its smooth handle so tightly that my knuckles ache. With a push of a button, the concealed blade can extend out in less than a second to reveal five inches of the sharpest metal man's eyes have ever seen. I wouldn't hesitate to take their life at the first sign: the twitch of their head, pupils enlarged beyond the whites of their eyes, or any violent aggression.

Anyone could become one of them at any moment, and that first phase of the Turning is quick. Once they Turn, there is no reversing it. The person only has a few moments before it is too late, and they're consumed by overpowering rage. The second phase of the transformation is a bit more extensive, taking up to six months to complete, depending on how healthy the person is. This is where their hunger kicks into overdrive, and they eat constantly, feeding the muscles that will add another two to three hundred pounds to their original body weight.

I've become paranoid and untrusting over the years since. It feels healthy. I close my eyes to listen, and my heart beats hard in rhythm with the sound of their boots on the metal stairs. The ringing grows louder like a gong being pounded over and over. The two Privates stop abruptly at the top of the stairs.

"Major White, sir!" one of them announces, breathing hard, as they stand at attention at the top deck of the tower. I'd be out of breath, too, from running up ten flights of stairs in that short amount of time.

I take one last good look toward the horizon, along with one last breath full of cold country air. It stings as it goes deeper into my lungs. Guess I do feel things.

One of them clears their throat.

"Major White, sir!" another voice announces, but a little louder this time.

It's obvious from their pained faces that being here is not for pleasantries. Two twenty-something males in woodland cammies salute and stand at attention. Though some aspects of the military are not as formal as they once were, discipline is still very much foundational. I examine each one, trying to gauge the importance of what they have come all the way down here to tell me. Then it dawns on me. *Fuck.* I left my radio in my jeep down below, and they probably tried contacting me. Before he can deliver the message, I hear the faint sound of turbines winding up in the background. *Fucking great!*

Even in youth, the war sits on these worn, young soldiers like a giant cloud of exhaust; it's all they've ever known. Their innocence was stolen long before they ever entered this world. I don't let the sadness of that thought linger for too long, and I certainly don't let it show on my face.

I must look intimidating to them, looking all of my fifty-six years. A crooked nose from too many punches, sunken gray eyes, and bags underneath them from years of stress and chaos. I walk in front of the one to my left, holding the message. I stand so close my breath hits him in his face as he stays deathly still. At six foot four inches, I'm looking down at him, and he stares into my chest. After a moment of eyeing them, I back up and release the tense grip on my knife.

"At ease, men." I salute back. "What's your message, Private"— I strain to look at his name tag in the quickening darkness, the overhead light hitting it just right— "Baker?" There are too many men to remember everyone's name, but I took a shot at what I thought I saw, though he probably wouldn't have corrected me if I was wrong.

"Sir, one has got loose. Possibly from the research facility," Baker replies with hesitation.

"THE RESEARCH FACILITY? What the fuck do you mean 'one' has got loose? Dr. Anderson hasn't been operating there for two fucking years. You sure you got your message correct, Private?" I spit angrily just inches away from his face, eyeing him hard.

"The Post Captain from Atlantic Outpost called it in just a few minutes ago, sir. He has a team currently en route. We tried contacting you on your radio, but you never answered, sir," the private replies nervously but with callousness.

"If the doctor is there, why the hell wasn't I notified he was back and doing more research? That motherfucker knows better than to be doing any work without my knowledge or consent. And where on God's green earth has that man been? Did the Captain mention any of that?"

The men stare at me with blank looks on their faces as my boots echo like rapid military drumbeats as I pace across the metal grating. I knew they wouldn't have been able to answer any of these questions. I just needed to vent my frustration. This will be the last time that piece-of-shit "doctor" does any more work in my territory.

I can't help but sigh loudly and clench my fists over and over as I make another pass in front of the pair waiting to be dismissed, giving me time to think.

The research facility was once an old prison just outside Atlantic, Iowa, around seventy-five miles from here but a few miles north of the outpost, right off The River. The earlier River Guard's boat must have been heading there. Prior to this location, and unknowingly to us, Dr. Anderson was secretly doing research out of an abandoned building in Michigan with minimal security. I can't quite understand how he has survived all these years with the type of patients he's been dealing with. Figured he was dead since we hadn't seen or heard from him in so long.

Since moving locations, he's continued studying the enemy to get a better understanding of what we're dealing with and sharing his research with us. That was the one compromise we made—we would help protect him and allow him to conduct his research if he provided us with information. His research has been somewhat successful over the years as he sliced them open to study their innards. Which reminds me.

I stop in front of Private Baker. "Was it a Mod?" I ask more calmly. Mods, originally called Modifieras, were named after some Italian doctor who identified them way back in the beginning. They are small, dumb and mindless, but their sheer power in groups can cause complications when trying to facilitate them or even take them down. Since setting up the research facility, we've been able to trap and study them. We didn't think this was a problem anymore, especially since they are slow on their own. Can't be a Mod; they wouldn't have come all this way to tell me this. Of course not. I'm not that lucky.

"No, sir." His voice is shaky. "It was a Josco, sir." His eyes widen and dilate, likely concerned, as he should be.

I scoff under my breath. Now I'm fucking pissed. The two young men take a step back. The Joscos are a different breed altogether: intelligent, strong, fast, and with well-managed leadership. One Josco alone could take out a small group of fully armed men in a well-armored vehicle. They often feed on what's left of the Mods during the winter months. It keeps them satisfied until they launch their attacks on us come spring; then we're the food if they are lucky enough to get their hands on us. Oddly enough, we've only seen males within the past fifteen years. We have no idea what happened to the female Joscos. Maybe all the males killed them. Ate them. Died off from an unknown disease. Who the fuck knows? I'll be hitting up Dr. Anderson for some answers if I don't kill his dumbass first.

Joscos have been known to harvest us, keeping us alive until they're ready to eat. We've located some of their holding facilities down south when out on missions, but our rescue attempts were nothing but blood baths. It's known that if you're captured by one of them, you're on your own. If you get captured by your own misdoing, then you pay the price. Not my men. In the last facility we were able to infiltrate, the people's arms and legs were broken so they couldn't crawl away to escape. *Tell me again that Joscos aren't smart.*

I can still smell the maggot-infested bodies that were strewn across the grounds like someone had a food fight with the captives' entrails. Without a doubt, it was the most gruesome scene I had ever seen, and being in the military all these years, that says something. Most had died from starvation, infection, or wounds they suffered during their initial capture. The ones we saved wished they were dead and that we should've shot them out of mercy. Can't imagine sitting there in a building waiting to be someone else's meal.

Joscos are not the humane type. They don't kindly kill you before they start gnawing on your body parts like fucking corn on the cob. Not something you want to dwell on. Several of the survivors told us stories of being forced to watch a loved one being eaten alive, with parts of the victim being spat out as they cried and reached out for help. And then knowing they would eventually be next. Fuck that. Give me a dull spoon to slit my wrist any day before having to go through that.

For the ones that we did save, that life-altering event haunted them every day up until the end. We did everything we could to counsel them and comfort them. But in the end, having lived through that ordeal, they just couldn't carry on, and unfortunately, most of them took their own life.

I turn to face the Privates. "Thanks for the message. Now let's go fuck up this Josco's day!"

CHAPTER TWO

(Major Oliver White—U.S. Marines)

Wednesday, January 8, 2048

My mind must have switched to autopilot because I don't remember the short, five-minute drive from the tower to hangar four. I've made the trip so many times the route must be burned inside my brain, and when anger floods my system, it takes control. All I can think of is, why now? Is it just a lone Josco, an outcast from its pack that somehow found itself roaming on our side of The River, or are there more? Is this another one of their tactics, trying to gauge our response during the winter months? Maybe they are getting desperate.

As I pull up to the hangar, my head starts pounding, causing me to brake harder than I should. The jeep slides across the snow-covered tarmac, stopping shy of the threshold. I clutch the cold shifter and shove it into park, almost forgetting to turn off the engine before slamming the door shut.

Forty yards out, a small group of Marines stands by one of the two Sikorsky UH-60 Black Hawks that are warming up, awaiting my arrival, ready for the hunt. Everyone has their own way of dealing with pre-mission jitters, and for this rowdy group, clowning around is evident. The moment one of them spots me heading in their direction, their horseplay comes to an abrupt halt, and they alert the others. Two of them turn on their heels and start walking in my direction.

Lance Corporal Adam Jones, a recent graduate of the Marine Corps Scout Sniper School who completed the program with some of the highest marks for helo operations, and Corporal James Wicker, an

15

outstanding Marine and our top sniper, greet me as I approach the nearest chopper. They sport matching gray beanies with the Marine logo: a fouled anchor that resembles our strong ties to the U.S. Navy, a globe, and the oh-so-familiar eagle on top with a ribbon stating our motto "Semper Fidelis" front and center.

Wicker's mid-twenties stalky frame has him striding ahead like a pit bull who's ready to charge the moment he's given the order. A two-month-old cleanly trimmed beard only covers a portion of the colorful tattoos peeking out from what's exposed of his thick neck. Jones, on the other hand, has a shine to his face like he'd just finished shaving. He still has the luxury of youth, being in his early twenties. Standing taller than Wicker, though not quite the same mass, he's still shorter than me.

"The Josco was last seen heading south toward The River but staying east of the Atlantic Outpost! We've alerted the other outposts nearby, sir!" Wicker yells in a deep, throaty voice to keep from being drowned out by the engine noise.

His intense face says "Let's get this fucker," and he relaxes his bolt-action M40A5 sniper rifle on his shoulder as we walk.

I remove my favorite Nebraska football cap, gripping it tightly so the downwash from the rotor blades doesn't blow it away.

"Is it just the one?" I ask, eyeing Wicker and hoping he says yes.

"We believe so," Wicker replies. "The patrol en route only advised of the one, sir. They were three klicks northeast of the Atlantic Outpost when they spotted it. Damn thing darted across their vehicle, scared the shit out of them. They engaged but lost track of it in the woods."

"Do we know why the hell there's a lone Josco north of my River this time of year?" I ask, shaking my head in continued disbelief. "What the fuck? Do they now have scouts performing reconnaissance in our territory?" We crouch in unison as we approach the bird. The warmth of the helicopter's exhaust blankets my face, and despite the acrid smell, it's soothing in contrast to the freezing air.

"Hope not, sir!" Jones smirks. "If they have scouts running missions now, that would be a game changer!" Jones muses, clasping his M110. "We have two four-man teams from Atlantic Outpost already in pursuit, but as Wicker just stated, they lost track of it. The footprints in the snow disappeared. The area is heavily wooded with lots of alcoves, so there are a number of places for it to hide. The River Guard has a boat in the water and should be in the area shortly to assist just in case the thing tries to jump across if it hasn't already."

I nod in response. "Has Nolan been informed?"

"He's been sent a message, sir. We received word back that he'll return sometime in the morning. He's still out with the Special Ops guys doing some training up north," Wicker replies.

"Roger that."

The Josco must be trekking along The River, trying to find a suitable place to cross, which will be difficult since the water level is up from the snow melting a few weeks ago when the temperature rose into the fifties. Maybe it'll find a floating ice patch to jump across and get the hell out of here. It certainly won't head north; that's too risky for a single Josco.

Wicker slides open the door to the Black Hawk, and I take a seat in the middle where I'm facing the backs of the pilots' heads as they go through their pre-flight checks. The two door gunners jump in next and get into position, checking over their M240 machine guns. Wicker jumps in last and sits closest to the door, facing me. Jones jumps in the other bird along with their gunners.

"Thanks for the lift!" I nod to Warrant Officers Ryan Martin and Anna Hardy, both helicopter pilots with the U.S. Army.

I swirl a finger in the air, signaling them to get going. It'll be pitch black soon, and I want that thing dead before then. The pilots waste no time getting off the ground, and as soon as they change the pitch of the rotor blades, the delicate snow whips up in a frenzy. The entire helicopter is blanketed in white as if we're sitting inside a tornado. Brief images of the outside world flicker through tiny cracks.

I sit back and enjoy the ride as we climb fast, and my body sinks into the frayed bench. The snow dwindles away as our altitude rises, and I'm staring at the tarmac due to the forward angle the chopper takes off at. I glance out the port-side window as the other chopper climbs alongside us, their nose pointed toward the ground as well. We then head east in formation, ascending to five-hundred feet, just below the clouds.

I grab the headset hanging in front of me and place it over my ears. The coldness of the earpieces sends icy waves down my spine.

"Good afternoon, sir." Hardy's smooth, formal voice comes over the comms. "ETA twenty minutes. Once we get on location, we'll provide air support to the two teams currently tracking the Josco. Hopefully we can hunt this thing down quickly and have you back in time for dinner, sir."

"Roger that." I follow up with a thumbs-up.

Several black-colored M27s are mounted in front of me; I grab the one with a vertical grip with an Advanced Combat Optical

Gunsight (ACOG) scope. Chances are I won't need it, but there's no telling what will happen when coming face to face with a Josco. I take off my warm glove, exposing my hand to the elements, and grip the handle. It feels like home. Being in command, sitting behind a desk most days, I haven't felt the cold metal of a rifle in some time, and I must admit, it feels good.

I go through the motions of checking the rifle, making sure it's ready. The first time I ever held one was shortly after I joined the Marines. I'd shot plenty of rifles before joining, hunting rifles like a Winchester Model 70, but not one like this. Damn, that was so long ago. My nerves got the better of me that day, which I soon learned to control. Looking back, I was just a kid trying to follow in my father's footsteps. He enlisted the very day he turned eighteen. Seems to be a family tradition, Whites in the military. Both his father and my father-in-law were soldiers, though one was in the Air Force and the other in the Army. Holiday gatherings were comical once the alcohol started flowing and jokes were being hurled back and forth. I miss those days.

The click of the magazine releasing catapults me back to the present. Making sure the rifle has a full metal jacket, I slide it back in and pull the charging handle ensuring the chamber is clear. I peek through the scope toward the darkening sky. *Damn, we need to hurry.* I let out the breath I'd been holding then locate the safety to make sure I'm good. I eye Wicker, who's watching me and probably curious about the last time I held a rifle. I nod, and he nods back, then looks away with a slight smirk. Some of us really do live for this shit.

"ETA five minutes," Hardy announces.

Both gunners slide open their doors. My ass puckers tight from the incoming assault of cold air. They move into position and ready their machine guns. I shake off the cold and stare dead ahead, barely able to make out the flickering lights from one of the vehicles in pursuit. The sun is almost tucked away for the night, but we still have a few minutes of soft, orange glow left on the horizon.

We catch up to the easterly moving vehicle of Team 1 and closely hug the north side of The River. The pilot throttles back, slowing to twenty knots while descending several hundred feet. We fly slightly above the thick forest, just ahead of the ground unit. Wicker repositions himself to the starboard side while connecting his safety strap. He then places his rifle on a strap that stretches across the doorway to help reduce the vibrations from the helicopter when he engages. He takes a seat with one leg dangling outside the cabin like he's done a thousand times before. The cold doesn't bother him one bit. We trained him well.

The other bird heads west to provide air support for Team 2 in the off chance the Josco circled back in that direction. Not likely, but we need to cover all potentials.

Hardy changes our radio frequency so we can communicate with the men on the ground. As soon as it switches, we hear their chatter. They're an uncensored bunch. The River Guard is also on, and the two groups are in the middle of arguing about who will be the one to kill it. They make several bets among each other before the berating ensues.

"You fucking river pirates couldn't hit the riverbank if you were standing on it," mocks one of the Marines in the Humvee below. Laughter fills the airways.

Hardy makes our presence known, which couldn't have come at a better time. Any more jabbering between the two and they might start shooting at each other.

Team 1 quickly gives us a situational report or SITREP. They think the Josco is continuing east, as they've come across several more massive foot imprints. Just to be sure, though, Team 2 will continue heading west. Joscos can be devious when they know you're tracking them. It's a game to them, and that's when they surprise you—when you least expect it. You think you're onto them and the next thing you know, you're face down, dead, having fallen victim to their trap. However, this Josco isn't playing a game, not this time. It's trying to survive, and as with any living thing, survival can make it an even greater threat.

My leg bounces impatiently with every second that passes. No signs of the beast send my blood pressure and frustration to new heights. Our constant delays circling above the Humvee as it struggles to push through the deep snow make matters worse. Patrols have established routes along The River, but this one doesn't appear to be one of them. The tall pine trees lining the snow-covered dirt road provide all the cover the Josco needs, making it difficult for us to see anything. The Humvee's powerful spotlights illuminate the trees, causing deceptive shadows to creep along the ground.

I switch views to one of the twelve-inch monitors in front of me, eagerly watching the vehicle crawl forward. The Black Hawk is equipped with several thermal infrared cameras mounted to the bottom exterior of the fuselage and can be controlled by either of the pilots. Joscos emit a brighter heat signature than normal human beings or animals, so they light up like a ball of fire on our screens. The sun has finally gone down for the night, so both pilots don their night vision goggles, sparking us to do the same.

Wicker scours the area through his scope. Even though it's cold, my hands are sweating with anticipation, while my stomach aches with anxiety. I want this thing dead, and the longer it's out here, the harder it'll be to find. They're fast and capable of running a mile in under two minutes, given the right circumstances. The cold will slow it down but not by much.

We continue onward, scouting just ahead of the ground unit, but nothing is coming up. Wicker's face hints at the irritation I'm also feeling. The men on the ground talk as though it may have crossed already, but there's no way of knowing for sure. The River Guard searches the riverbanks for any sign, but they don't see anything that indicates it has crossed. We'll search all night if we must. I want to know for certain that the Josco is no longer north of The River. No longer a threat to my people.

Depending on the physical condition of this Josco, which I have to assume is great, even a team of heavily armed men in a well-armored vehicle would still be an underdog in the fight. We've all seen the devastation and destruction just one can do, like the time a single Josco ripped through a Bradley tank in a matter of minutes, prying open the hatch, then ripping it off the hinges from the frame, bending the steel back just enough to grab a few of the soldiers inside. It didn't end well for them. So, in this particular situation, our air superiority will help even the playing field.

"Twelve o'clock! I have a visual," Martin announces, bringing my focus back to the monitor in front of me.

A speck of white about four hundred yards dead ahead lights up on the thermal display. It's faint, but it's something. Adrenaline courses through my veins.

"Team 1, keep your distance while we recon the area," I communicate to the Marines on the ground.

They trudge along and wait for our orders. The pilot throttles up, and we accelerate forward.

I fidget with my scope, squinting hard. It's difficult to make anything out at this distance. It could be an animal since there are plenty of them running around these parts. Ever since we made this our territory, we've seen more animals migrating up this way. It's safer up here. Even the animals know where to seek refuge.

As we approach the object, not even the sound of our helicopter hovering over top scares whatever it is away. It stays motionless; the unrecognizable outline on the screen cuts in and out from the tree branches as we circle above. Hardy turns on the helicopter's bright spotlight and directs it right on top of the target, but it's still not a good visual.

"Whatever it is, it's not moving," she announces, echoing my thoughts.

Joscos hate helicopters, anything that flies, so this probably isn't it. They usually scatter the moment we show up in one, which makes for fun target practice.

We circle several times, but with the trees in the way, we're still unable to identify what it is. We advise the ground unit to proceed with caution and scan their sectors.

My heart pounds as we wait for their report. I steady my breath as the vehicle inches forward, now within yards of the target. They focus their lights in the direction of the mystery creature. I watch the monitor as a single Marine steps out from the vehicle, weapon raised, and inches toward it.

"We have movement," Martin confirms.

"I can hear it," the Marine whispers into his mic. The light mounted to his rifle highlights the way. "It's struggling," the Marine continues.

Seconds feel like minutes as he takes slow, cautious steps, now within feet of it just behind a tree. He pauses, then side steps to the right, peering around the thick tree trunk, his weapon aligned on the target.

"It's a fucking hog!" the Marine reports back.

"Damn it!" I punch the hard metal side of the helicopter. My hands are so numb I can't even feel it. The Marine walks forward to stand over top of the wild boar.

"It's severely wounded," he advises. I lean in closer to the screen as he kneels right beside it.

My back stiffens; they've tricked us before, using animals as bait.

"That Josco was here, though. There are signs of a fight, and I think we all know who won," the Marine says. "Looks as though it just happened. Not even five minutes ago. The Josco tore this shit up. Rear leg is missing, completely ripped off, and a chunk has been carved out of the middle like a turkey on Thanksgiving Day. We do have a trail of blood leading east, though." The Marine points his rifle with light in the direction.

Good! We're on his trail, and since all signs indicate it's heading east, Martin makes a prompt radio call to Team 2 and orders them to turn back around. They're ten minutes from our location, but we'll continue moving east until they've caught up with us.

We survey the adjacent area, and out of nowhere, the Humvee's lights flicker, shaking violently in all directions, followed by men shouting and yelling over their mics in horror. Panic spreads through the bird as we try to discern what's happening on the ground. On the monitor, I watch the soldier behind the tree unload his weapon back toward the Humvee. The monitor flashes with every bullet expelled from his rifle. We hear the crashing whine of metal through our headsets, wincing at the sound. I realize that the Josco, in full force, sideswiped the Humvee. All I can do is watch as the vehicle rolls over onto its side, throwing the Marine stationed at the .50 cal. on top into a cluster of trees.

"It's the Josco!" The port-side gunner's eagerness explodes as he squeezes the butterfly trigger grip on his M240.

"Hold your fire, gunner! You don't have a clear shot," I snap at him.

The monitor now shows the Josco charging toward the Marine by the hog. With the approaching sound of the helicopter, it could only last so long, especially by itself. The stupid fucker knew this was going to be its last stand so why not create some collateral damage. The hog was more than likely a meal to give it a boost of energy before the big showdown. Joscos must constantly feed to keep up with their extremely high metabolism.

The Marine gets a few body shots, but not before succumbing to the wrath of the Josco's grip. Its hands wrap around the Marine like he's a loaf of bread and repeatedly slams him against the surrounding trees. He goes limp, and the Josco tosses his body as though he's garbage to be discarded. The Marine falls to the ground awkwardly, lying motionless, face up. The Josco doesn't wait around, but I continue to watch the monitor in horror.

"Get up! Marine, please get up!" I urge him in desperation, but I know better.

Martin adjusts positions, maneuvering the helicopter to follow the Josco. The camera that was on the fallen Marine pans out, and I lose sight of him. "Fuck!"

This Josco is a fast son-of-a-bitch, and it returns to the Humvee with wrecking-ball force. It strikes hard, rocking the vehicle on its side, then pushing it back into a tree.

Another Marine emerges from the rear door window and comes face to face with the Josco, who is ripping away at the undercarriage. Twisted metal parts fly in all directions. The Marine engages his rifle point blank with the Josco. The bullets whiz all around it, none of them making contact. The Josco swipes violently at the Marine, causing him to fall back inside the Humvee. The Josco leaps up and slams his body on the elevated side of the Humvee, ripping the door off and throwing it up at us, but gets blocked by the tree branches.

"Come on!" I yell. We just need one good head shot. I hate being helpless. All we can do is circle above and wait for the Josco to get clear of our men.

The pilots attempt to radio the ground unit, but they don't respond. We see rounds exiting the side of the Humvee, shooting straight up into the air. Wicker switches to the port side to get a better look, but his barrel gets tangled in his support strap before he recovers into his new position. The Josco is still too close to our men for the gunner to release hell. Wicker, on the other hand, lets out a grunt of anger, and he gets on his scope.

"I'm taking a shot!" he yells out.

Even with the small chance of hitting one of our men, he fires a single shot and strikes the Josco in the back of the right arm.

"Damn it!" Wicker says.

The Josco falls forward, landing on his back, flat on the ground. The Josco pauses for a brief moment to rub the arm that got hit. As it looks up, its oversized facial features cover the entirety of the monitor. Even though we're one hundred feet in the air, my legs shiver with fear from the menacing look it gives back, like it knows exactly where the camera is pointed. It's as if it's staring at me and only me. I'm frozen like a deer in headlights. Wicker fires another shot, breaking my concentration from the monitor, but he misses to the left.

The Josco rolls over and darts off, running west along the shoreline. The River Guard is quick to engage but stops when it retreats inland. Martin informs the others that it's heading their way while simultaneously swinging the helicopter back around. My body jerks from the momentum. Wicker grabs ahold of a rope above his head to keep from falling backward. We're now flying sideways so the gunner can get his angle, making sure to keep the Josco positioned between us and The River. Even at forty knots, The Josco pulls away through the thick trees, and the pilot throttles the engines to keep pace.

Courtesy of our gunner, the unrelenting M240 machine gun spits out 650 rounds per minute in the direction of the fleeing beast. Trees take the bulk of the hits, shredding bark to sawdust confetti. The hot bullets glow on the monitor, looking like a meteor shower raining down. Multiple rounds hit the Josco's backside, red clouds of blood showering out one after another in the spotlight, but it's still on the move. It leaps from spot to spot, doing everything it can to avoid another hit. The trees provide it with much-needed cover as it switches direction multiple times in an attempt to evade us, leaving a trail of red blotches in the snow. This Josco has strength. It's massive, which I can tell even from up here.

The pilots adjust and respond to its every move, keeping the helicopter situated perfectly so that one of the gunners can continue firing at all times and keep it as close to The River as possible.

Within minutes, the headlights of Team 2's Humvee come into view. They are directly in front of us, approximately one hundred yards. The Josco doesn't hesitate and does a one-eighty, running back east.

We circle around, staying north of The River while the other helicopter stays to the south. Team 2's men engage, shooting from their roof-mounted .50 cal.

"Careful, Team 2. You have friendlies up ahead," Martin advises.

Wicker once again switches back to the starboard side of the helicopter and fires several shots. One hits directly in the back of the Josco's right leg, forcing it to stumble and fall to the ground and causing a wave of snow to cascade through the air. It jolts back to life faster than the blink of an eye and gets moving again with only a small stagger.

Fucking shit. To have that level of strength to keep going after all that must be an empowering feeling.

The Josco, with the help of a tree, makes another one-eighty and heads straight for Team 2's ground unit once again, zigzagging to avoid the onslaught of glowing hot bullets screaming its way. The Josco slams fearlessly into the front of the Humvee, smashing the front grill, lifting it off the two front wheels, and then slamming it back down. It rips off the front guard and throws it at the windshield, shattering the passenger-side glass. The men pause, stunned, but with no severe damage to the vehicle, they rush back to the chase.

Wicker fires another shot and hits it right above the buttocks. It limps. Jones fires from the other helicopter, hitting it in the other leg. Damn thing has been hit at least twenty times, but the Josco finally comes down in a heavy heap, now too injured to keep moving. Team 2 pulls up in their Humvee, and Marines pour out of it as if it were a clown car. The Josco drags its body along the ground, swiping at the closest soldier. Jones and Wicker put two more bullets in it, striking its neck. Blood spurts out in an angry torrent. The Josco grabs hold of its neck but still flails about violently. The Marines surround the downed beast with weapons drawn but make sure to keep their distance.

"Shit. How is this thing still alive?" one of the Marines shouts into his mic.

"Because no one shot the fucker in the head. That's why," another one says. "You guys need to work on your aim." He snickers.

Damn, that Josco is one tough bastard. One of the bigger ones.

"Quit jabbering and kill the son-of-a-bitch already!" I reply, anxious that it's still breathing.

We hover over the scene, watching the muzzle flashes light up the surrounding area like a strobe light in a nightclub. The men put another fifty bullets into it just to be safe. A spectacular sight to see from the air.

"Good job, men. Make sure to burn the body after you help the others. I want a full report on my desk by morning."

As we make several passes overhead to ensure the scene is secure, we're advised that the Marine who got out to check the hog didn't make it. I punch the monitor and the screen cracks in a spiderweb of broken glass.

CHAPTER THREE
(Major Oliver White—U.S. Marines)

Wednesday, January 8, 2048

My mind whirls on the quiet ride back to Eppley as I process the death of Private Peter McKenzie. What should have been high fives and jovial smiles from our victory was anything but. Winter is supposed to be a time of calm and peace. No worries except for the rare slipping on ice, breaking someone's leg or an alcohol-induced accident.

We lost a good soldier tonight, and unfortunately, the night isn't over. Not for me. The second-worst part of this is yet to come. Soldiers dread the possibility that one day their loved ones will get a knock on their doors from the Notification Officer delivering the worst news of their lives. It gnaws at your soul. We've all spent plenty of sleepless nights wide awake in our hot, muggy bunks, thinking about the family of someone we lost in war and what they're about to go through. And tonight, I must break the news to the deceased Private's wife that she'll never see the love of her life again. I could easily make someone else do it, but it just wouldn't be right. It's something I must do, a responsibility to my men. It's going to be tough explaining why he was killed in the most brutal of ways by the hands of a Josco at this time of year.

As I stand in front of my closet, staring at my Service Alpha uniform, thirty years of war-ridden memories invade my mind. Memories both good and bad, and both from a time before the Turning and after. The faces of all our brothers and sisters we've lost along the way flash through like a timelapse video, one after another, in a Rolodex of thoughts. God, there were so many. Only a handful of the soldiers I served with before the Turning are still alive today.

I grab my uniform and hold it up next to me in front of my mirror. I haven't put it on since God knows when, but it feels appropriate tonight. The perfectly pressed creases still have an edge that would slice through an apple. The clear plastic cover has protected it all these years. Not a single fleck of dust has penetrated the sheet. I put it on, one layer at a time. To my surprise, it still fits, though a little loose around the waist, which is quite the opposite of what I thought would be the case.

Staring at myself in the mirror, I come to the realization that I can't do this by myself. There's someone I need to visit that I haven't seen in quite some time. I'm not sure what he's going to say or if he'll have anything to say to me at all, but the widow can't go through this alone. I need him to speak the words that I cannot and comfort her in ways that have been lost on me over the years.

I park in front of his house and stare at a crack in my windshield. It didn't always extend the entire length of the glass, but slamming the door earlier must have pushed it past its breaking point. I'm close myself. The events of tonight play over and over in my head. The image of his body being continually battered…the pain he must have felt just before the end.

Guilt creeps up and sits in a tight ball in my throat. Forcing a cough doesn't change the fact that I wish I could have done more. But what else was there? There is always a different way, but would the outcome be any better, worse, or the same?

The old church on the serene property remains unchanged, giving me a false sense of security that nothing is different. Damaged off-white paneling still hangs in disrepair just below the roofline, and the stained-glass window remains intact, creating colorful patches on the snow like a kaleidoscope.

My neck aches as my body stiffens. The last time I visited this place was well over five years ago when Pastor Stuart, my minister and confidant, passed away. Shook my faith in the good Lord, which was already on a slippery slope after Lily was taken from me. His son, Jr., as we call him, took over and continued with the sermons. I couldn't bring myself to attend but one or two more Sundays after that. The last thing I wanted to hear at the time was someone telling me to forgive, especially myself. He did seem to have his father's passion, though.

The Post Captain was kind enough to inform me that Private McKenzie and his wife attended Pastor Stuart's church every Sunday when Peter was in town. He also told me they had just welcomed their first child. The sting of that knowledge makes me want to vomit. I close my eyes and bang my head on the cold steering wheel to get my head straight. I need to stop stalling; it's getting late, and I know he has several kids who are probably already asleep.

A soft flicker of light turns on from inside the pastor's house, a small three-bedroom colonial that sits at the back of the church's property. I take a deep breath, psyching myself up. *Why does this time feel so much more difficult?*

The driver's side door makes an obnoxious creak when I open it. "That's fucking new," I mutter.

As the door shuts, the same noise echoes through the quietness as if there is nothing around for miles, and the two short echoes are the only sounds that remain. The snow is thick with five-foot-high drifts around the driveway, and the yard is a placid white plain yet to be agitated by children.

A sign hangs from the door: "Prayer changes perspective." I prayed for so long, for so many years, but nothing changed. What's the use?

I lightly knock on the bright red door. I don't want to wake any of their kids, so I wait a moment before knocking a little harder. Byron swings open the door with his eyes wide open. I hesitate for a moment. I don't remember him looking that much like his father, but standing here now, he's a spitting image. Olive complexion and dark, commanding eyebrows that squeeze together with the onset of wrinkles. Shaved head and all, just like his dad.

"Major, is that you?" He squints his already narrow eyes. I give him one sharp nod as the shock of his appearance wears off. "It's good to see you, sir," he says as he leans his head out the door and peers around.

"It's just me. Sorry to bother you this late. Please, call me Oliver."

"No bother at all. What can I do for you?"

Byron's wife, with her small brown eyes and head full of blonde curls, walks up from behind, peeking her head over his shoulder. "Everything okay, honey?" she asks.

"I'm not sure." Byron shrugs while maintaining my gaze.

"May I come in?" I ask, trying to break the awkwardness with a forced half-smile.

"Yes, of course. Sorry, please come in. I was finishing up this Sunday's sermon, discussing Acts. You remember Philip, the one who was chosen to care for the poor?" Bryon nods in approval.

"It's been a while, but I remember."

"Would you like something to drink? Do you need me to make some coffee?" Mrs. Stuart offers, wrapping a red and green tartan blanket around her shoulders. She must have been getting ready for bed before I showed up.

"Thank you. Coffee would be fine if it's not too much trouble." My face and demeanor probably give way to the idea that something is very wrong. Shit, just my presence does that. The ultimate bearer of bad news.

"No trouble. I'll go make some." Mrs. Stuart darts out of the room like a caged animal set free.

"Please have a seat, Maj…eh, Oliver."

"Thank you." I take in the small room, committing to an old leather recliner that dips further down than expected and lets out a small huff of air in protest as I sink deeper into the seat.

The room is dimly lit by a frilly white lamp on a single side table covered in bibles and open notebooks next to a pink-striped recliner. Dark shadows make it almost impossible to make out framed family photos that cover the tattered floral wallpaper. The adjacent wall has nothing but photos from the previous owner's family.

Byron caught me looking before saying, "For some reason, it didn't feel right to take them down. We couldn't bring ourselves to box them up, never to be seen again." He answered the question I hadn't asked. "It sure was a different time back then." We both stayed silent for a moment. "So, what can I help you with, Oliver? It's been a while since we last spoke. We sure miss you on Sundays."

"Um, yeah, I know." I refuse to address that. "Do you know a man by the name of Private Peter McKenzie? I believe he attends your church." I get straight to the point and successfully sidestep my presence or lack thereof from church.

"I do know him, as a matter of fact. Our congregation is growing, and lately, there hasn't been an empty pew. Though, there'll always be a seat available for anyone wanting to hear God's word." I felt as though that comment was more of an invitation than anything else. "I still know every member. Is everything okay?" His voice trails with concern.

"Unfortunately, there was a terrible incident this evening, and he was killed."

Byron leans back in his chair. He takes a deep breath, covering his face with both hands and shaking his head. "What happened? Can you say?" He eyes me up and down. "The uniform you're wearing didn't even register with me."

"It's late, and visits like this shouldn't be occurring, especially at this time of year." I pause for a moment, considering whether I should say it. "It was a Josco."

"A Josco!" he screams in his high-pitched nasal voice.

"Private McKenzie and several others tracked it down earlier this evening after it was spotted during a routine patrol."

We sit in silence as I watch his eyes dart back and forth across the floor as if he's replaying my words in his head and still can't figure out what I just said. Mrs. Stuart returns with two bright blue cups of coffee in hand.

"What happened? I heard you yelp all the way in the kitchen. Careful or you'll wake the kids," she scolds her husband as she hands each of us a mug. Mine says "World's Greatest Dad!" "Sugar?" she offers with a kind smile.

"Honey, Oliver has some terrible news. Peter McKenzie was killed earlier today by one of those Joscos." Byron's last word comes out slowly, as if the word itself tastes bad.

Her eyes shoot straight to mine as if seeking confirmation. "But it's winter, Major. I thought they stayed away when it was cold. Are we not safe?"

"Rest assured, it was an isolated case. We have the security in place to take care of these matters, so I wouldn't worry too much." I may have been stretching it a bit, but I couldn't bring myself to tell her that we didn't know if the doctor was back doing more research or if there were more Joscos out there. The news will get around fast enough as is. Not many secrets around here.

"Oh, thank goodness. But Byron"—she brings her hands to her mouth—"you just baptized their daughter, just before he went on hitch." Mrs. Stuart turns as white as a sheet and tears well in her eyes.

"Does his family know?" Byron brings the focus back to me.

I shake my head. "No, and that's actually why I'm here. I think you being there would be very helpful during this time."

"Yes, of course. I'll get dressed right away and grab my things." Byron looks up at his distressed wife before continuing. "It might be a long night, honey, so please, don't wait up for me." He kisses her forehead as she just nods.

I finish my coffee in one big gulp, and I thank Mrs. Stuart for her hospitality. She does her best to smile, wiping away a few escaped tears. Byron walks me to the door, gives me directions, and says he'll meet me at the couple's home. It's not too far from here, and I'm thankful we won't be riding together.

With effort, I keep my mind numb as I drive through the winding streets. After the Turning, this neighborhood was bleak and lifeless; not a single soul occupied any of the homes. We were all beaten down, near the point of giving up. However, the fortitude of the American spirit wasn't dead. Seeing the snowmen in the front yards as I pass by does give me hope. Our population continues to grow, and our last census two years ago put us at just over four million. People have been repopulating, settling in places we haven't inhabited for over two and a half decades.

I pull up to the quaint house, turn off my lights, and wait for Byron. The lapse in time makes me anxious. I stop tapping the steering wheel long enough to allow myself to think about what to say. It's never easy finding the words; they usually end up spilling out in a nervous rant.

Private McKenzie only had a few more days left to go on his stint before coming home. He was only twenty years old. He didn't deserve to die that way. His wife doesn't deserve to live the rest of her life without him, and his child doesn't deserve to grow up without a father, to truly never know him.

It's like Groundhog Day, and I'm plagued with the duty of telling another family that their husband or wife or daughter or son will never come home again. My chest aches and my head pounds with waves of pain, weighed down by a horrible feeling of dread I can't describe, one I've never got used to, but it keeps me sober to the importance of each life I command and what I ask of these men and women every day—of course, only things that I would be willing to do myself a hundred times over.

My watch tells me it's almost midnight. Byron pulls up right behind me, and just in time too. My stomach is churning, and bile burns my throat. His father had been on many of these visits with me before he passed. I remember each of them.

Several interior lights shine through the front windows as we walk in tandem to the door, so someone must be up. Then again, she could leave the lights on for security while Peter is away. Lily used to do that.

After lightly knocking, the silhouette of a body appears through the glass. My heart pounds so hard it feels like it might burst through my ribcage. Someone pushes a side-window curtain aside for a moment, then the click of the dead bolt unlocking vibrates in my head like a gunshot. I let out a deep breath as the door swings open.

A young, beautiful woman with sandy blonde hair and dark blue eyes stands just beyond the threshold of the doorway. She greets us with a concerning hello. She's wrapped in a silky white robe.

"Ms. McKenzie, I'm sorry to bother you so late, but I have—" My voice cracks as the words escape me. I attempt to clear my throat, but it's no use. I look down at my hands, which are holding my dress cap, my thumb grazing across the logo.

"Yes, Major, what's going on? What is it? Please tell me." She starts to cry, darting her eyes between Byron and me.

"I'm sorry, Ms. McKenzie, but your husband is no longer with us. There was an accident earlier today, and Peter passed away. I'm terribly sorry for your loss." I get it out as fast as I can and wince like someone sucker punched me in the stomach.

My words cut her down at the knees, and she drops to the ground, her hands covering her face as she gasps for air. Both Byron and I reach down to comfort her, but there is nothing we can say or do at this point. All we can do is be here for her.

"Let's go inside," Byron says in his kind, gentle voice, cradling her while she nods through a sob.

We move inside, and I direct her toward the couch. She slumps over onto Byron's shoulder. He places a hand on her head, and I take a seat on the other side.

The room is very plain, likely kept in the same manner as its previous residents. Many places remained undisturbed when new families moved in. Most folks took the photos and boxed them up just in case the families ever returned. I don't even need one hand to count how many times that has happened. This place is just another reminder of that.

She takes a deep, shaky breath, then frantically gets up to grab the landline phone in the kitchen. She calls her mother to announce the horrible news and pleads for her to come over as soon as possible. I can only sit on the edge of her tan, pleather couch and listen, staring at the frayed edges of the green rug in the living room and remain numb. Little knickknacks and family photos sit on the white brick fireplace mantle. One in particular hits me hard. It shows Peter with the biggest grin, one only a new father could don. He's holding his newborn daughter, likely just moments after she was born, wrapped in one of those blue-and-pink-striped blankets the nurses put them in. *Fuck me. Breathe.*

Tears try to burst from my eyes like an open floodgate. That picture reinforced the fact that Peter would never get to hold his daughter again, hear the cheerful laughter of being woken up way too early in the mornings, or feel the tight grip of her hand wrapped around his finger as they walked to the park, not pulling away until she's ready to let go.

After a few minutes, Ms. McKenzie's mother burst in wearing floral pajamas with a long heavy coat and striped beanie with one of those fluffy balls on top. She makes a beeline for her daughter on the couch and holds her tight, both now in tears. She got a quick glance of me and seemed surprised. I stand and nod my head to show my respect. I then replay the events of the night with the mother. I always get asked, "Why?"

It should be an easy answer, but it never is. I can't explain to them why this Josco was there, as that might create more panic. I let them know that Peter was strong and that his sacrifice will never be forgotten.

I learn that Peter's father passed away several years ago from cancer. They have countless stories to tell, a sadness attached to each of them. I have done what I came to do, though. Byron stays at his position between the two widows as I wave in thanks to him and step toward the door. He jumps up and walks with me the rest of the short distance, putting a hand on my shoulder.

"Maybe we'll see you one of these Sundays?" His thick eyebrows raise in encouragement.

I just turn and walk away, unable and unwilling to respond.

CHAPTER FOUR

(Major Oliver White—U.S. Marines)

Thursday, January 9, 2048

Half-dazed from a late, restless night, I head straight for the coffee—black with a half teaspoon of sugar. With the bold, slightly sweet taste to my liking, I make my way to my office. Karen Harris, my fearless assistant of ten years, greets me as I pass by her desk, which is clean and tidy as usual.

"Late night?" Her curt tone agitates me. It shouldn't, but after yesterday's events, I doubt anything could brighten my spirits.

"Unfortunately," I mutter back, sounding as gritty as I feel.

Karen was a JAG Officer in the Navy for twenty-eight years before retiring from the military and becoming a very successful prosecutorial lawyer for some big corporate firm before the Turning. Even in her early seventies, she has more energy and fight in her than I see in some of the young recruits. She's stern and orderly with a no-nonsense attitude, keeping me in check from time to time. I keep telling her that she needs to retire for good and live out the rest of her life with her husband, who was a Lieutenant Colonel in the Marines, somewhere far north of here. They've both earned it as far as I'm concerned, but she's quick to remind me that she already lived that life of isolation and wants no part of it ever again.

Taking a seat at my desk, I thumb through the daily reports that came in overnight, looking for one in particular. Only half of the forty outposts along The River are occupied by skeleton crews this time of year. That may have to change after last night. Each outpost is required to submit a daily report by 05:00 the following morning. Most state "nothing to report" or list routine maintenance that's being performed. Rarely do we have sightings of Joscos or wandering Mods. Paperwork sucks, but the mundane task has to be done.

The folder from Atlantic Outpost is a little thicker than the others, as it should be. Captain Teagan must have stayed up all night to get this prepared, with photographs and a map with two distinct colors highlighting the exact route the Josco traveled before and after contact. I read through it in detail until I get toward the end, where it mentions the Marines finding tracks from the Josco that came from the north, where Dr. Anderson's research facility is located. My jaw aches from the constant tension. I haphazardly toss the report on the desk. As it thuds, I swivel around and stare out the eight-foot-tall window to a snow-covered runway.

"Karen?"

"Yes, Major." She leans back and tilts her head in the doorway.

"Can you please get Captain Teagan from Atlantic Outpost on the line for me?"

"Yes, sir. Anything else?"

"No, ma'am."

My phone rings the moment I turn back to my desk. That was fast. He must have been camped out by the phone, waiting for me to call.

"Good morning, Major. I was wondering when this call was going to come in. Any additional information regarding last night?"

"Nothing yet, but I think we'll find out soon enough. Just finished up with your report. I appreciate you working late to get this to me, but I need you to send a team over to the research facility ASAP!"

"Yes, sir! I was thinking the same thing. I debated sending some men up there after we retraced the Josco's steps but thought I would wait to hear from you before doing so."

"Good work. I'm glad you didn't. We need to proceed with caution," I reply.

"Dr. Anderson has strict orders to contact this outpost if he is up here conducting research, but I haven't received any news that he was back, nor have my men been given any such message."

"Well, knowing that man, you probably wouldn't have. When has he ever followed orders? He lives by his own set of rules." The jaw pain creeps up my ear, forming the beginnings of a headache.

"I will get a team put together immediately. They should be there within twenty minutes, and we'll report back."

"Thank you. Oh, and one more thing. Just have your men drive by and scope out the place. Under no circumstances are they to enter the building or communicate with Dr. Anderson in any way. They need to keep their distance. He'll probably have a vehicle sitting outside if he is there. I don't want any issues stirring up before I arrive."

"Understood, sir."

With our business complete, I slam the phone down without saying bye. I suppose I'm nothing if not direct.

My foot taps impatiently as I review several other reports while I wait for the Captain to return with news. Peoria Outpost has a Humvee that is dead in its tracks and looks like it may have been sabotaged. Probably those damn kids again. *Just wait until you're of age and have to join the military, you little shits.* Another outpost is requesting an excavator to help dig out debris that is piling up in a bend, almost bridging the two sides of The River together. That'd be a top priority if it were summertime. Heater out at another. Looks like they're going to be roughing it for a while. Another list that never ends.

My phone rings, and a glance at my watch confirms it's right at twenty minutes.

"Major, bad news. It does appear that Dr. Anderson is back and more than likely the cause of last night's fiasco." I grip the cold plastic, taking my frustration out on the phone. "My team spotted a vehicle outside the facility. They're headed back now. Is there anything else you would like us to do?"

"No, I will be there shortly. I'll advise you when I'm in the air so you and your team can meet me there. Make sure you're well-armed and ready for the worst."

"Roger that, sir. I'll get everyone ready and wait for your orders."

I rush over to Captain Nolan Wilkinson's office, my second-in-command with the U.S. Navy. He stands six foot five inches and is as broad as a bull. It's comical seeing him sit there behind that tiny desk, typing away on his computer with his giant sausage fingers. I swear he lives in a gym with the Josco Brothers.

He and I have been a team since the Turning. Nolan commands the Navy personnel and special forces in addition to leading training for new recruits. He helps evaluate everyone who's required to join the military when they turn eighteen and places personnel where they fit best, including which branch of the military. A little different than it once was when people had a choice, but not everyone is cut out for post duty or going out on missions. There's a certain level of mental *and* physical conditioning one needs to get assigned to those positions.

We happened upon each other a year after Pandora's box exploded. Nolan was holed up in a little town in northern California with a small group of civilians and a few others who were serving at the time, fighting for their lives. He might argue otherwise, but they wouldn't have survived the night had we not heard their firefight as we were passing through. They lost a large chunk of their crew that evening. We busted in like white knights, taking out the pack of hungry Joscos clawing at their ankles. If not, they'd have been entrées on the Joscos' menu that night.

Nolan was in Basic Underwater Demolition (BUD/S) training, having already been in the Navy six years prior to changing direction to become a SEAL. He was in the final phase with only a week or so left, but unfortunately, he never got to officially finish. Little did we know we would be fighting a completely different monster. But, with time and a lot of help from others, he was able to reinstate the programs and requirements to become a SEAL, now in its third year.

"Hey, squid, you have anything pressing the next hour? Want to take a quick field trip?" I ask, leaning against the inside of his doorway.

"Back to name-calling, I see." He smirks. We're always giving each other shit. "Good morning to you too, sir." He leans over, opens a drawer from his desk, and tosses something at me, which I catch just before it smacks me in the face. The moment the small, yellow and green cardboard box left his hands, I knew what it was.

"Nice." I couldn't help but chuckle at the half-used box of crayons.

"I took this off some Marines the other day. They were gnawing on them while swinging at the playground."

I shake my head. "How long have you been waiting to pull these out?"

"A while, actually." He lets out a grizzly bear chuckle. "But no, wish I could go. I have some rowdy new recruits to deal with in a few minutes. You Marines just don't quite get it sometimes." His eyebrow raises and another smirk creeps across his face. "Anything you need me to do?" He looks back at his computer and continues to type.

"Not at the moment. About to head over to the research facility. Just got off the phone with Captain Teagan. In typical fashion, the doc failed to inform us of his return."

"I heard about last night. How the fuck did he get across The River without us knowing it? We need to button that up." He leans back in his chair, placing his hands behind his nicely combed hair, his face switching from jovial to serious in the blink of an eye.

"Good question, and yes, we need to get something put together ASAP. I don't want that to be an issue come summertime. Maybe I'll ask the little fucker if I don't kill him first."

"We lost a good guy last night. Sad to hear that," Nolan says, casting his eyes down.

I could only nod my head in agreement.

"Where the hell has the doc been, anyway?

"Who the fuck knows." I can hear the sourness in my tone.

"Well, sorry, Oliver. I don't think I can make this one unless you want to postpone it another hour?"

"I already have choppers warming up as we speak. I want to get this shit over with. If anything changes"—I look at my watch—"I'll be at hangar four in the next ten minutes. Try not to miss me."

"Roger that."

At hangar four, a group of Marines, dressed and ready for battle, stand at attention, awaiting my arrival. This squad should be enough to keep us safe in case things go south. Plus, Captain Teagan will be there with an additional twenty soldiers. There's no telling what Dr. Anderson brought back with him.

"You men ready?" I yell out.

"YES, SIR!" Thirteen deep, raspy voices reply in unison. We load up between the two choppers and fly out as the rising sun hits our faces.

The doctor and I have never seen eye to eye from the day we met. He's in his late forties or early fifties. Never asked his age. He's full of arrogance, entitlement, and bullshit. His mousy brown hair in a bowl cut sits atop his large head and tiny frame. One punch and he'd go down. From what I can tell, he's somewhat of a hermit. I've never seen him with a woman, or a man for that matter. As far as I'm aware, he doesn't have kids either. Can't imagine anyone wanting to be around him long enough to produce offspring. When he's here, he's held up with his "research."

Even though Dr. Anderson is an awful human being, and I would love to see him gone, he has provided us with some good intel over the past decade. We need to find out if they have any other weaknesses; that information is more crucial than ever.

He's free to deal with the Joscos as he pleases with an understanding that he shares whatever valuable information he obtains about them: their weaknesses, their strengths, and so on. It's how we found out about their quicker healing capabilities and that they have a leader-and-pack mentality, like wolves. He told us he caught one of the leaders a while back. All the other Joscos that were being held were submissive to the one. The Joscos never spoke one word, so we think they might communicate telepathically. Not sure how we can determine that for sure. Autopsies showed they still have all the normal internal body parts for speech, but for some reason, we've never heard them say words. Only grunts and groans ever come out, and they only seem to exert those sounds with physical activity, not to signal others.

Dr. Anderson's the only one who works at the facility, and it frightens me. Because of his minimal security measures, I lost a good man last night, one of eighteen in total, to his carelessness. It could have been much worse. I'm shutting him down for good to put an end to all his so-called research. We need intel, but at what cost? I'm tired of having to tell him to upgrade security protocols. We didn't even know he was here, or I would've considered wasting my valuable soldiers' time babysitting him to prevent such a disaster.

We land near an open field, just east of the facility. If he wasn't awake, he should be now. Upon meeting Captain Teagan and his men, I order them to set up a perimeter and be at the ready.

The thirteen Marines march behind me in a smooth procession to the solemn structure. It's a small prison, maybe twenty thousand square feet in total. Dead, overgrown ivy left imprinted black stripes along the gray cinder-block-and-concrete exterior walls. The dreary sky and snow do nothing for the dreadful building.

The busted front door we enter is weathered beyond readability. It was once painted white with faded black lettering. Now it hangs in disrepair by a few broken hinges. We pass through a dark hallway, then march straight back toward his office. My men scan every angle as we proceed. Lights mounted to their M4s illuminate the dark crevices and corners causing shadows to dance across the room. We reach the cell blocks; the stench smacks us square in the face like a cartoon character stepping on a rake.

"Oh fuck!" one of the Marines up ahead huffs.

I stop dead in my tracks and cover my nose with my undershirt, trying not to gag. The hairs on my neck stand on end. Several Marines rush around me, gripping their weapons even tighter, each of them pointing a rifle at one of the four Joscos that fill up each of the undersized cells. They perk up at our presence, but they remain calm and observant. I figured they would be smashing at the bars acting like taunted apes at the sight of us. Perhaps the doc has them drugged; the entire scene makes me uneasy. I can't shake the eerie feeling I have traipsing up to one, but I am curious. The thick reinforced metal and concrete hinder them from reaching out past the cell's threshold. Twelve inches is all that separates us from them. I've never been this close to one that wasn't dead or that I wasn't in the process of killing.

"Holy shit, Major. That's one big fucker," another Marine barks out, but I don't break eye contact with it.

The thing wears pre-Turning leftovers, shreds of a shirt and stretched-out shorts that were once pants. Their stench is overshadowed by their stature. I see an unrecognizable rotting carcass draped haphazardly on a chair in the corner of the cell. A pool of blood sits underneath with the occasional slow drip sending ripples across it.

It stares back at me, its black eyes dark and intense like the evil it is. Standing nine feet tall and carrying well over four hundred and fifty pounds of pure muscle, the Josco is dense. This one is bigger than any Josco I have ever seen. Its muscle definition is incredible with veins winding around its body like a pulsing road map. Watching its blood pumping makes mine keep pace. Deep gashes, still inflamed around the edges, run up and down its long, exaggerated facial features, while purple bruises litter large portions of its torso and appendages. Patches of its hair are missing from its skull, likely ripped out in a violent rage or fight with another. These things are animals. Its condition proves it.

I notice a health chart in a pouch hanging next to its cell. "Adam? Seriously? You have names?" Pretty fucking ridiculous, but hey, if Dr. Anderson wants to name his lab rats, that's his business.

The beast breathes deeply. Its lips twitch open, revealing black voids from missing teeth. The others are as ugly yellow as a dehydrated man's piss.

"Well, Adam, let me tell you something. I have a bullet for you and all your friends out there. Your kind has ruined my life and destroyed my family. I have no idea what Dr. Anderson has planned for you,"—I bang my fist on the cell—"but you will no longer be my problem." It glares at me with a menacing look that makes me feel even more uncomfortable, almost as if it understands what I'm saying.

I step back, turn, and walk toward the doctor's office. The other three Joscos pound on the cells with their fists as we move along unaffected by their behavior but wary of the possibility of what they're capable of. The Marines hold tight in their positions along the hallway, each still pointing their weapons at one of the Joscos.

The door to the last cell is busted. Nothing left but twisted metal and shattered concrete. This must have been the holding cell for the one that escaped last night. Red stains cover the corner of the floor where I assume its food sat. Must've taken it to go, I guess.

If that one busted out of this cell, what's keeping the others from doing the same right now? That thought sends a nervous shiver down my body, from the hairs on my neck to the tip of my toes. I crack my neck to shake off the feeling and continue my walk.

The office, with its door wide open, is just around the corner and feet away from the Joscos. Dr. Anderson, looking all professional in his white lab coat, sits there as if nothing happened. He knew we were here and didn't even have the decency to greet us. He leans back into his worn-out leather chair and peers at us through his black, square glasses.

"Major, how are you? To what do I owe the pleasure?" His tone is as smug as his shitty demeanor. He's an egotistical son-of-a-bitch. In an instant, he annoys me more than I thought possible.

"Well, doc, I lost a good man last night. We didn't even know you were here because you failed to let us know and besides, I've told you too many damn times to beef up the security and you've done jack shit. I'm about to personally bulldoze this entire facility to the ground with you and your lab rats in it," I say with a slight smile. He puts his feet on the desk, mocking me. "You've been gone for the last two years with not one damn person knowing where you've been, and one day you decide to show back up, and what do you know? This shit happens, *again*!"

He raises a finger to interrupt me, but I don't give him the opportunity. "Your last two security upgrades were shit, and I haven't seen squat from your research besides what we learned in the beginning! I'm ordering you to cease and desist immediately. If not, I'll be more than happy to personally escort you and your research to the other side of The River. We will be back to exterminate the problem at zero-eight hundred hours tomorrow. Don't try anything stupid. We'll be babysitting your every move. Gather whatever you need because you're officially shut down as of this moment. Time to find another occupation!"

The doc's right eye twitched, but then he brightened back to his usual irritating self. Beads of sweat start to form on my forehead. Time to go before I decide to jump across his desk and beat him to a pulp.

"Oliver..." He stands up and removes his glasses.

"NO!" I shout, moving closer and pointing my finger directly in his face. "I'm not going to stand here and listen to your bullshit. We lost a good Marine, so you don't get a say unless you have new findings!" I pause. He looks down letting out a deep breath, but he says nothing. "Didn't think so. You let one of those fuckers escape here and you didn't do a damned thing about it. Not one notification." My clenched fist was ready, just inches from his face. *Please just say one word. Give me one more reason to come over to your side of the desk.* It was all I could do to hold back my punch.

The look on his face, twisted with hate, was quite satisfying. He had kept it together while I spoke, but now I could see he was feeling the impact of the conversation. Good.

Sixty seconds. That's all the time I needed to say my peace before I saw myself out of his office. I place my right hand onto my sidearm, thinking I should kill them all right now, but I don't want to start a frenzy without more backup. There are four of them and we all know too damn well what one can do, so we need to be prepared. As I continue toward the exit, I turn my head to look over at Adam, the Josco, for one last look. Our eyes meet, and its stare makes my knees quibble. Is it perhaps studying me? It all feels wrong.

I never understood how Dr. Anderson was able to acquire his subjects. I know he goes down south, beyond The River, which I don't like, but it has never been clear how he does it. I had contemplated sending men to tail him, but I never wanted to risk good soldiers. Guess I figured he wouldn't ever be coming back. If he leaves again, I should prohibit him from re-entering. He's nothing but a pain in my ass.

I continue my walk, stopping just shy of exiting the facility, and pause. With my back to the doctor, I yell, "Zero-eight hundred, Doc!"

I'm the last one to leave after my men exit the building. Captain Teagan is waiting for me just outside the facility.

"Listen, I need you to keep a close watch on the doctor," I inform him of the four Joscos inside. "If he does anything out of the ordinary, I want to be contacted immediately. He knows that tomorrow, we'll be back to terminate all the Joscos under his care. As much as I'd like to handle them now, we don't have the manpower. I'll update you later today with a plan to move forward."

I start toward the helicopter before turning back. "Oh," I say to the Captain. "You have full authority to do whatever is needed and use whatever force you deem necessary. Grenade the place if you have to." His eyes light up with delight.

"Yes, sir! I'll get a team to stand watch starting now and rotate them throughout the night."

"Roger that, Captain. Call in whoever or whatever you need."

And with that, we head back to HQ.

CHAPTER FIVE

(Major Oliver White—U.S. Marines)

Thursday, January 9, 2048

Back in my office, a surge of exhaustion overcomes me, bringing me to my knees and consuming me with a lightheadedness that causes tunnel vision with black and white specks that dance around.

What the fuck is happening to me?

I blink a few times, hoping my vision returns to normal. I do my best to shake whatever this is, hoping it's just the effects of a long day's work.

Am I that stressed?

Today was full of answering other Officers' questions about what measures would be implemented to ensure what happened the other night never happens again. They're fucking Joscos. No one knows what the hell they are going to do or when. The discussion quickly turned to Dr. Anderson and what the hell to do with him. Arresting him was high on everyone's list. After all, he is under strict orders to inform us when he's doing work. There needs to be consequences.

I was glad to hear the Officers have all had enough, making a solid case for discontinuing his work. We questioned what more we could learn from his research and came up blank, including myself. Just like we'd done for any other decision we've ever made, we outlined the benefits of him continuing his research versus the risks. His fuck up column is longer than The River itself. It was an easy choice to make, and we unanimously decided that Dr. Anderson must

56

be shut down for good. Tomorrow will be a day that Dr. Anderson will never forget.

Even I have to answer to others, so a vote is required for decisions such as this. I'm no evil dictator and my position isn't set in stone. It never has been and never will be. The population could easily decide to replace me with someone else. The idea of bringing back a partial government floated around when a few surviving politicians drafted legal documents outlining the necessity of their jobs. They were damn near burned at the stake for even bringing it up. Politicians and lobbyists were what started this mess in the first place, pushing for the creation of these so-called wonder drugs to try and eliminate all the autoimmune diseases.

It was at Dr. Roger Josco's research center, founder of Josco Genetics, where his breakthrough drug, Autoimmune Vaccine (AIV), was formulated. The goal was to somehow alter a person's genetic code in order for the body to suppress its own immune system to slow and eventually reverse whichever autoimmune disease the patient suffered from. Josco Genetics had already been in clinical trials for years prior to the public knowing anything about it—before it was leaked, that is. Josco Genetics touted the greatness of the news like a dandelion being blown in the breeze. When foreign governments saw the positive news, which did not include the laundry list of side effects, they all wanted a piece of the pie. The Josco Genetics database was hacked on multiple occasions, and several foreign governments were able to retrieve bits and pieces of the formula. These governments then created their own versions, which ended up being inferior to the AIV of Josco Genetics. We believe these inferior drugs are what created the mindless Mods.

Needless to say, we haven't had a working government since the Turning, and people seem to like that. Maybe one day, there will be a government, but right now is not the time for bureaucracy to get in the way of our survival.

Feeling somewhat normal again, I swipe my keys and bag from the dingy floor and head straight for the jeep to avoid confrontation with anyone else who might be here this late. The engine roars to life, and I let it warm up while taking a moment longer to relax. I close my eyes and lean my head back, trying to clear my thoughts. The second I do that, mild chest pain creeps up, as if a giant rubber band is contracting around my torso. I take slow, intentional breaths in and out. I don't have time for this. Has to be from the stress of everything that has happened in the last twenty-four hours.

"What will tomorrow bring?" I grumble, then throw my jeep into drive before shit goes south again.

The streets are desolate with only a few other drivers this late at night, likely police officers patrolling the roads. We established a police force five years ago. There was a definite need with the growth of our population and the increase of activity. The military had Joscos to handle; cops could deal with disputes between two drunken neighbors or other domestic issues.

This neighborhood, in the dilapidated town just east of downtown Omaha on the Iowa side, hasn't been inhabited since it burned to the ground decades ago. Neighborhoods like this are pocketed all over our side of The River. Most have sat black and singed since the last ember flickered out. Others were cleaned up as much as possible while also being picked clean of anything useful.

We've been trying to redevelop sections in the surrounding area, but like a lot of things, it's slow going.

West Broadway is lined with miles of abandoned buildings. Oddly enough, some still have business signs on their front awnings. Can't believe they're still hanging after all they've endured. We use a few of the buildings for when one-off items come in, kind of like a mini flea market. People are even bringing vintage cars of all types from the 1950s, '60s and '70s back. Heard a story years ago about a group who goes out looking for these cars, not to sell or trade but to preserve them so that maybe one day they can be used for something historical. I haven't seen it, but word is that they've filled several parking garages full of these cars. Since then, various picking groups have formed to go out and collect just about everything: clothing, electronics, Pez dispensers, you name it.

An old abandoned Sonic Drive-In catches my eye, and my stomach starts to growl. Perhaps my body is telling me to eat. I can't say I remember eating today other than inhaling a glazed donut and drinking a few cups of coffee early this morning. I take a right at the next intersection to head toward the twenty-four-hour grocery store that's located a little farther outside of town. They should still have a decent selection of products at this time of night.

I gaze through the store's solid glass front and see several workers bustling around. The glass is covered in a handwritten list of newly arrived items. Some have already been crossed out, meaning they're out of stock. The chicken hasn't been, so that's good.

Farmers and hunters sell their goods to those who prep and cook it then sell it to the local grocery stores. Currency is still a work in progress, but we have marked bills that we use to pay for items. People still attempt to counterfeit, just like old times.

Items are usually fresh and damn good, like the jalapeno-stuffed sausages, but at times, it can be slim pickings if you're the last to get in. On days when fresh shipments arrive, the lineup of people will stretch half a mile down the road. All the food is evenly distributed among the many stores that are strategically set up across our area, but small local businesses can also sell directly to the stores.

After wandering the aisles, I grab some precooked chicken and a bag of whole potatoes. When I get home, I'll just sprinkle some salt and pepper on it and throw it into the oven. It'll be ready in no time.

"Ma'am," I say to the clerk at the checkout counter, who is probably in her early fifties. Bags weigh down her hazel eyes and a few wrinkles stretch along her forehead. I've seen her here before, but I've never spoken to her; I talk enough during the day.

I pick up a small bottle of moonshine that's sitting at the front of the counter. After a quick investigation, I slide it into my pile of goods. The lady watches me as her lips creep into a small smile.

"How are you, Major? Late evening for you?"

"Unfortunately. It's been a long day, to say the least."

"I'm sorry to hear that. I heard about the Josco."

I nod. "One of our men was killed last night." It hurt even to say it.

"Is that doctor back doing his experiments like the last time?" she asks with a hint of hatred. His sins will forever haunt him.

I stood there quietly, staring at her longer than I should have. There are no secrets about the doctor's research, and most remain unhappy about it. Not because of the experimenting, though. People couldn't care less about torturing a Josco. It's the wake of destruction he's left behind in our community that no one will forgive him for.

Fifteen years ago, he had a facility, unknown to any of us, where several Joscos escaped from. They went on a killing rampage, wreaking havoc on the population until they were finally hunted down and killed.

"Eh…He's been shut down permanently."

She nods and finishes up, putting my groceries in the worn fabric sack I brought in with me. I give her the best fake smile I can muster, pay, then grab my items and walk away.

"Thank you for all you've done for us."

I catch a glimpse of adoration in her eyes before she turns and walks away, leaving me no chance to say anything in return. I appreciate the sentiment, but I don't feel like I deserve a thank you.

As I pull into the parking lot of my apartment complex, the crunch of the snow echoes through the cab of the jeep. I put it in park and take a moment before exiting. It's peaceful watching the snow float gently down from the dark void of night. There's just something about the quietness that's relaxing, unlike the rest of my life. The gentle taps of the larger snowflakes hitting the windshield put me at ease. It makes me temporarily forget about the hunger scratching at my stomach.

Walking up the three flights of stairs, I nod to a few others who are smoking cigarettes, conversing, and drinking. I'm pretty sure it's an alcoholic drink by large, square ice cube showing through their glasses. *Mm, Old Fashions I bet.* I'll soon be partaking in the same, though not with this group. This complex is full of military officials without families. Those with families have taken over the neighborhoods where there's a lot more freedom for kids to jump and play.

The unit opens to boring white walls, beige furniture, and bright white curtains that make it feel sterile. A few scenic paintings hang on the wall in an attempt to liven up the place, from when Ann, my girlfriend, for lack of a better term, visited a month ago. The place is small, one bedroom, but adequate for my needs. I couldn't care less about these accommodations; it's just a place to lay my head. My real home is in the woods, up in Michigan. Wish I was there right now.

Thoughts of Ann flood my mind as I walk through the threshold of the lonely apartment and stare at a cityscape painting she'd hung. She's the perfect distraction. I need to get away from this place, even if it's only for a few days. *Maybe go to the cabin.* Perhaps she could meet me up there. She lives in Mackinaw City, Michigan, which isn't too far. I don't feel as much guilt about her as I used to. We've never officially labeled ourselves a couple, but for all intents and purposes, we are.

The idea of Ann flits away as I spark the gas oven to heat the chicken. I drop the potatoes in a pot of boiling water after cutting them into perfect square blocks so they cook faster and evenly, something Ann taught me.

While the food cooks, I jump in a hot shower. The warmth of the water running down my body clears my head from the day's activities and directs my focus back to my cabin. I let my mind drift. I haven't had some good eatin' in a while, and Ann sure knows how to grill some juicy venison, among her other talents. All I can envision now is being with her, a bottle of whiskey and smoking some wild game in a wood-burning pit. I can already smell the mesquite smoke and tall pine trees.

It's nearly midnight as I get out of the shower. The smell of roasting chicken hits me as I round the corner to the kitchen with the damp towel around my waist. Good, it's just about done. I hand-mash the potatoes and remove the chicken from the oven with a hand towel, burning the tips of my fingers in the process. I shake a little salt and pepper on everything and smother the potatoes with butter. *The simple things in life.*

Still in my towel, I sit down and look at my accomplishment with satisfaction. Ann would be disappointed with the lack of sophistication the meal offers, but it pleases me. The table is laid out with every utensil in its proper place, with a glass of cold water and my little bottle of moonshine. It's quiet. Lonesome. I start thinking about the curves of Ann's body as I cut into the tender chicken and take a bite along with a heaping pile of potatoes. I miss the touch of her soft skin. The smell of her hair and that seductive smile gets me every time.

I never thought I could love after my wife, Lily, died. Maybe what I have with Ann is love. The jury is still out on that. We met up north one night when I was checking up on a project we'd been working on for a while—one that's still ongoing to this day. The team and I had gone to a nearby town for some food, and she was at the restaurant with seven friends. Didn't find out until later that she operated the fine dining establishment we had enjoyed. She and her group of friends were squawking like hens while we were trying to get some work done, reviewing plans, the schedule, and diagrams.

I could feel their excitement from across the room. It was a nice interruption. The big smile on her face woke something inside of me that I hadn't allowed for so long, and I wanted to know more about this woman. At that moment, I realized life was looking up, and we were doing our job. People weren't afraid anymore. They were relaxing and could go about their business without having to worry. They were living again.

When we finished our meeting, Ann and her friends were still sitting there having a good ol' time. Empty wine bottles littered the long walnut table, along with empty trays where food once sat. She looked amazing in a snug, black, long-sleeved shirt and jeans, with her hair and makeup expertly done, minus a wedding ring, to my hopeful excitement. I walked over to their table to ask them how everything was going, almost unable to contain my stupid smile. Just small talk. All I wanted was to get her name. One of them knew who I was, which made it a little easier to talk to them. The other ladies kept chatting with me, but Ann didn't say much, even though I saw her looking.

She had a confidence about her as I stood there like an intoxicated dope. After a few minutes, completely discouraged, I said my goodbyes. My nerves got the better of me, which is hardly ever the case. It had been much too long since I'd had to do anything like that, but to my surprise, Ann came running out of the restaurant after me, something I'm pretty sure her friends harassed her to do. Either she liked me, or it was the alcohol, but she had no reserve. She wasn't afraid to state the obvious, unlike me, commenting with a smile, "For someone in your position, you really missed the very obvious hints I was sending your way."

The other guys started making inappropriate comments, so I motioned them away, and fortunately, they took my command. I'd be sure to repay them for their improper remarks.

"Fuck! That hurt." Biting my cheek distracts me from the memory.

I throw the fork on the table as if it were the culprit. An empty plate stares back at me. It didn't take long for me to scarf it down. I suppose I'd always been a fast eater. It didn't help that the first two years after the Turning was eat and run, eat and run, if you were fortunate enough to eat at all.

I wash the plate and utensils then place everything in the drying rack before walking back to the table and taking a big swig of my smooth, homemade moonshine. I try to remember the last time I had a drink. Must've been when Ann was here. I pick up the bottle of "Mary's Moonshine" and realize that Mary was the clerk at the grocery store. Guess we've all had to find things to make the time go by.

I need to get some rest. It's going to be bliss seeing Dr. Andersons face when we terminate the remaining Joscos and tell him he's no longer in business.

A recurring dream torments me for the thousandth time. The darkest of blacks in her eyes paralyze me into submission, controlling me. She wants me to do something, something horrible. My body stays deathly still, trying to fight the urge. We stand there in slow motion while the world speeds up all around us. I can feel the gun in my hand and grip it tighter and tighter. A stabbing electric pain shoots up my arm and throughout my entire body as though it were one giant funny bone. Her face goes from a calm, peaceful smile to horror, anger, then violence in a matter of seconds. I raise the gun. The handle crushes under the pressure of my grip, and a single bullet finds its way perfectly between her tar-colored eyes. A lonely drip of blood travels down the bridge of her nose until it reaches the tip. I wait for the drip to fall, but it never does, making me even more angry. Her face morphs to that of a deer's head, antlers spread wide, and the glowing bright white wall behind her turns a dark red. I blink, and she's gone in an instant. Now I'm standing in the middle of nowhere, looking up at the stars in the night sky.

In what feels like moments later, my alarm goes off at 06:00. I know that I must've slept a few hours, but I have one thing on my mind. Shut down that facility.

CHAPTER SIX

(Major Oliver White—U.S. Marines)

Friday, January 10, 2048

The slow rise of the sun turns the snow on the tarmac into a blanket of shimmering diamonds, a beautiful view when I actually get to stop and look at it. Even the obnoxious squeak from my office chair as I rock back and forth doesn't bother me. The constant sound is somewhat soothing, to be honest. My first cup of morning coffee warms my hands, creating a perfect setting for the morning. Maybe it's just the fact that today will be Dr. Anderson's last day of being a pain in my ass? One less thing we'll have to worry about going forward.

As I begin to appreciate the peace, my phone rings, with its annoying tone made more irritating by the fact that I was enjoying myself—and it's too fucking early. I barely got the receiver to my ear before hearing the penetrating voice of Captain Teagan on the other end.

"Sir! We have a situation. Something's gone wrong at the research facility!"

My mind struggles to keep up, going numb as the trembling words come out of his mouth: "A team is already there and has secured the premises...multiple casualties...ground and air patrols are canvassing the area."

The phone goes quiet for a moment. I glance at the note beside the phone, with a stick figure drawing of Dr. Anderson with a noose around his neck and "08:00" written below. It's not even 07:00 yet.

"We're on our way," I reply. It's the only thing I could muster before placing the phone back in its cradle.

The words "Something's gone wrong at the research facility" keep playing over and over in my mind. The anger builds inside like a piston from an engine cylinder compressing the fuel and air mixture just waiting for that next revolution to spark and explode. The next person to speak to me will be on the receiving end of a violent wrath that hasn't shown itself in a long while.

I lean back in the chair to compose my thoughts. The obnoxious creak that was soothing only moments ago might as well be fingernails on a chalkboard. The view out the window doesn't have the same allure, nor does the coffee have the same bold flavor. I was stupid to think this was going to go as planned.

After informing Nolan of the mess now sitting on our laps, we ready the team for an earlier-than-scheduled departure to the research facility; the only difference now is we won't be terminating the problems. This will be more of a clean-up situation if I understood everything the Captain said. This will be the absolute last visit because that building will no longer be standing after today.

As we pull up to hangar four, Nolan and I meet the team of Marines and SEALs who are loading up between the two choppers. My cheeks flush with an unwelcome warmth. My greeting is short and direct with the soldiers. I wasn't in the mood for chatting. I just want to get going.

Not one word is uttered on the journey aside from the pilots advising ETAs and other flight information. Not even Nolan, who chose the seat across from me, tries to spark up a conversation. He knows me all too well.

Palpable tension makes the thirty-minute ride feel like thirty hours. We already lost one good man not even forty-eight hours ago and now this bullshit. I blame myself. I should have just taken care of them yesterday and suffered whatever consequence arose at the time.

The pilots circle the facility a few times before landing, giving us a good aerial view of the personnel scattered around the premises collecting evidence, taking notes and photos. Goosebumps race down my spine in anticipation of the horrors I'm about to see. If Dr. Anderson isn't dead in this heap of shit, I'm going to personally put two in his chest and one between his eyes.

Post Captain Teagan greets us the moment we touch down. No niceties are exchanged, only a salute and a shallow hello muttered between the three of us. Nolan and I follow him, making our way toward the facility entrance. Nolan orders the team of soldiers to stand watch, and they snap into position around the perimeter, accompanying the other Marines already standing guard or canvasing the area.

Several staff members exit the building wearing hazmat-like suits. I wonder if we should be wearing them too. It's all I can do to keep from punching something.

"Is that smoke, Captain?" My nose starts burning with a slight tingle as we stand just outside the building's entrance.

"Yes, sir." He steps aside, allowing Nolan and me to enter the building first.

What the fuck are we getting into? Dark red streaks are smeared along the floors, and blood spatters on the walls and ceiling answers one of my many questions. In unison, we cover our noses and mouths. For me, it wasn't so much the smell but the image of what happened playing like a major motion picture in my mind. The movie only gets worse as we head toward the holding cells.

All four cell doors that once held back a Josco have been ripped from their hinges. Those, along with chunks of concrete and bent rebar litter the crimson-stained floor.

"Clearly these were fucking useless." I shudder, picturing myself here the day before. Could've been my limbs torn from my body.

I pick up a bullet casing sitting on one of the two-ton concrete reinforced steel doors lying on the ground.

"I guess whatever drug he had them on to keep them calm wore off?" It wasn't necessarily a question, but if anyone had an answer, they were free to speak up.

"The Marines standing guard here put up one hell of a fight, sir," the Captain comments as I examine the bloody bullet casing, rolling it between my fingers.

Looking at the broken bodies of the Marines and the pile of brass surrounding them makes me sick to my stomach, but I'm also proud of their fight. As young Marines, we all had our own heroic image of when it was our time to go—like going out in a blaze of glory, so to speak—and what it would look like. My image was much like this scene: a mountain of spent casings piled around me and making sure the enemy felt my rage before I took my last breath.

"How many men did you have posted here?" Nolan asks, looking at Captain Teagan.

He hesitates. I could see in his eyes that he was processing the question a little deeper.

"Three, sir." His voice trails off as he winces.

He must have known that question would be asked, and he's got to be thinking it wasn't enough men. *Would more have helped, or would there have been more dead Marines?*

"I should have had more," he adds. His facial muscles flex as he grinds his teeth.

There's plenty of fault to go around, but in the end, it rests with me.

"We could have had a platoon here, and it may not have made a difference. We should have brought enough men back yesterday to end it right then and there," I mutter to myself. Hell, now I'm doubtful that the team we had prepared would have been enough.

There's one dead Josco that didn't even make it out of the cell from the looks of it. Brain matter is plastered on the opposite wall, and what's left is dripping out of a softball-sized cavity from the side of its head as it lays face down, its body dangling over the busted steel bed. *Do they even sleep? What a weird question right now.*

I stand up and toss the casing to the ground. We carefully maneuver the scene, making sure not to step on our fallen brothers. We make our way to the doctor's office. My eyes are drawn to an opening in the far corner of the office that I don't remember being there. The cinder-block wall surrounding the opening is blackened with soot that climbs to the ceiling.

"This is where we think the fire started." Captain Teagan points to the hidden room that is roughly ten feet by ten feet.

Different scenarios start flooding through my mind. The first one is that a fire accidentally started and sent the Joscos into a frenzy, and they did everything they could to survive and smashed out of their cells. The Marines came in to see what was going on, possibly to help out but were caught in the middle, and the Joscos ended up killing everyone. It seems logical, but where is the doctor's body? Maybe the Joscos took him as a travel snack for their journey back to wherever it was they came from, which brings another question to mind.

"There were four Joscos here last night. I only see two dead ones. Do we have two Joscos running around?" I ask, looking directly at the Captain. Things aren't making any sense here.

"We're unsure at the moment, sir. I have patrols on the ground and in the air searching." He shakes his head. "It's the oddest thing, though. There are no tracks that lead us to believe they ever left the area."

"We need to find out ASAP. I don't need any more running wild up here."

"Absolutely, sir." The Captain changes our focus. "Take a look at this."

I walk up to the opening where Captain Teagan kneels and shuffles through a burned stack of what looks to be old boxes and folders.

He hands me some charred papers which still have some visible markings on them. It wasn't much, but I know what I'm looking at. It's one of the medical charts the doctor kept for his subjects. This one is blank, though.

"What do you think this room was used for?" the Captain asks.

"Just looks like a storage room to me. Too small to be anything else. Unfortunately, it doesn't look as if any of this will be useful," I reply, peeking my head in deeper toward the empty soot-covered shelves. "It's more than likely too damaged, but let's get all this stuff back to the base. I want every piece analyzed thoroughly."

"Looks to me like the doc may have been hiding some research he didn't want us to know about, and he stored his documents in here," Nolan says. "But why would he need to do that? There are no laws to keep him from doing whatever the hell he wants to. Something's not right here."

The doctor had no reason to hide any of the work he was conducting unless he was doing experiments he didn't want us to know about, which brings me to the next scenario. He started the fire on purpose, and it got out of control. Whatever the situation was, the room is burned to a crisp. All that remains is a heaping pile of ash.

We complete the tour with a quick look inside his lab. Nothing appears to be out of the ordinary, and honestly, it doesn't look like it has been used since he was here years ago. We exit the facility with more questions than answers. Captain Teagan informs us that the last message received from the Marines standing guard this morning was in order. This incident appears to have happened right after that SITREP.

Nolan and I say our goodbyes to the Captain, and he gets back to taking control of his crime scene. He has a lot of work to do, but before we leave, Nolan and I take a minute to stroll around the perimeter to discuss our thoughts.

"What the hell happened here, Nolan?"

"I have no answers, sir."

"You think he was conducting other forms of experiments here?" I question.

"I'm no doctor, but the lab didn't appear any different than normal. Hell, to be honest though, I have no idea what all the equipment is used for."

"Yeah, me neither. I guess we should have paid more attention in science class." We share a short-lived smile. "Well, if I ever see Dr. Anderson again, I'm putting a bullet between his eyes." We both nod in agreement.

We come upon the doctor's incinerator to the north of the building and inspect the inside. Doesn't seem like it's been used for a long time.

"No dead Joscos in here," Nolan says. Being who he is, he checks that it's working properly. "Incinerator works fine." He then looks around curiously and points out what we all should have noticed earlier. It gives us a big piece of the puzzle.

"Wait, where's the doctor's van? Didn't you say he had one of those big transport vans here?" Nolan asks.

I look around. "Damn right, he did. Big enough to carry five nine-foot, five-hundred-pound Joscos in."

We surveyed the entire facility once more, and sure enough, there is no van in sight.

"I doubt the Joscos learned to drive in the last couple of years, but you would think someone would have seen the van driving around," Nolan says.

"You think he's still here?" I'm hopeful, as I want to kill him personally.

"There's one way to find out. Let's get Bridge Post 1 on the radio. I want to talk to them right now. Let's start there." Nolan darts off to grab a handheld radio from the helicopter and hurries back.

We have nine bridges that allow access to the other side. Bridge Post 1 is our main bridge just south of Eppley. Four bridges connect the eastern side of The River, and four connect to the north. We have several unmanned bridges that go into Canada, but they haven't been occupied since Joscos have never been spotted up there. That will change today.

"Bridge 1, do you copy? This is Nolan. Over."

A few seconds pass. "Go ahead, sir. This is Bridge 1."

"You didn't happen to see Dr. Anderson in a white, serial-killer-type van within the last hour or so, did you?"

"I have not, sir, but I just got on shift a few minutes ago. We're reviewing notes now with the nightshift but let me check. Over."

"Thanks."

"You don't think he booked it, do you?" Nolan asks, leaning against one of the parked vehicles. "Maybe with the two remaining Joscos?"

"Who the fuck knows what that guy does with those Joscos when we're not looking." I reply. Nolan let out a small laugh. "If I were him, and with the events that took place here recently, I would have high-tailed it out of here too. And never return."

The radio interrupts. "Hey, Nolan. You copy?"

"Yes, sir, go ahead."

"Dr. Anderson departed at zero-six twenty-three. The other guys here said he was going to dump several Josco bodies and that he would return within the hour, but that's it. There's no record of him returning, sir. Over."

"Thanks." We give each other an ominous stare. Nolan jumps back on the radio. "Oh, and if he does return, you hold him there at gunpoint and notify me immediately! I don't care what time it is. You do not let him go. You shoot him in the knees if you must. That is an order. You understand me?"

"Yes, sir! Understood, sir! I'll let everyone here know."

"What the fuck?" I throw my hands up in exhaustion.

We contact the other bridge posts with the same instructions and to make them aware of the situation.

"He's been gone for almost two hours now based on the last message from the Marines standing watch. You want to send a team down to look for him?" Nolan knew the answer but asked it anyway.

"Fuck no! I'm not wasting any more resources or risking any more lives for that piece of shit. Why the hell would he need to dispose of the bodies down there? And why is it taking so long for him to return? This doesn't add up, Nolan. Let's head back and let these guys finish up here. We'll eventually figure out what he's been up to. It may take some time, but we'll find out."

CHAPTER SEVEN
(Lieutenant Scott Dodson—U.S. Marines)

Thursday, January 16, 2048

Remnants from an overnight blizzard taper off, and by the looks of it, it dumped at least a foot of snow on an already packed layer.

The drive in this morning should be a fun treat. I let go of the slat from the blinds then open them completely. Hopefully, the snow-plowing crew will clear the road before I head out in a few minutes, but I doubt it. *Lazy fucks.*

I continue to gaze out the wall-to-wall window in the family room where a large elm tree's fragile branches sway back and forth. There's just something soothing about the sound of gusting winds whipping and the snow thrashing through the leafless trees this time of year. I could stand here all day staring out the window with a warm mug of coffee.

I yawn as I think about the unwelcome guest who crawled into bed in the middle of the night. Every time a storm pounds through, we can expect a visit from Abigail, our two-year-old daughter, cold feet and all. You would think the cause of my insomnia would have been the tree branches wrestling against the roof, Abigail snuggled between Maggie and I, or the wind howling, but none of those things kept me up. The Major called for a meeting late yesterday evening but left out the important details. My mind has been racing, and I'm curious as to what the hell it's about. He has always provided a high-level mission overview, but not this time. He only indicated that our presence was required at 0800.

I have eighteen minutes to get there, with one stop along the way. Lieutenant Sean McCauley better be ready this time or his ass is getting left behind. I don't need another butt-chewing from Major White or Captain Wilkinson because he has poor time management.

The hissing of the coffee maker grabs my attention as it drips the last of the perfect dark liquid into the pot.

"Got to get going," I mutter, chastising my own time management.

I inspect my uniform piece by piece for possible flaws. Convinced I'm up to standard, I tiptoe back into the bedroom to grab the rest of my things. Abigail is sprawled out on my side of the bed, her brown curly hair covering most of her freckled face. The two of them look so peaceful. The whole scene makes me want to jump back in bed and forget about the rest of the day.

I'm hesitant to disturb Maggie by giving her a kiss on the cheek before heading out, as I always do. Knowing that she loves it, I go in, thankful she remains still. I tread softly to the other side, doing the same with Abigail. She shuffles in response to the bed creaking when I lean on the headboard. Panic strikes me for a moment, making me freeze. I hope she doesn't wake up and ruin the peaceful morning for them both. She rolls over, clutching a green stuffed doll, a pickle with a funny face. Abigail refused to part with the weird thing after we found it in the prior homeowner's leftover boxes. Thankfully, she snuggles into Maggie's back and settles down once again.

I step out of the bedroom and release a big breath before another clumsy accident has me begging for forgiveness later. The nutty aroma of coffee puts a little pep in my step as I head to the kitchen. I grab a red thermos from the cupboard and let the deep brown brew flow to the brim. The sound of it pouring entices my taste buds into overdrive, salivating for that familiar dark roast.

"What would I do without you?" I take a sip off the top with a slurp.

A small wedding photo of Maggie and me sits on the counter. The unrest I'm feeling makes me pick it up, something I haven't done in a long time. Can't help but laugh because we look like babies. I even see a sprinkling of hair still on my head long before I started shaving it. Jeez, we were barely into our twenties; it was only our Pastor and us the day we said our "I do's."

I was two years old during the Turning. I never got to know my mother like Maggie got to know hers. Any memory of her that I may have had stored away has been long forgotten. All I know of her are the pictures my father left me. She was at work when everything went down, and it just so happened my dad was using some vacation time and kept me home from daycare that week to hang out. He worked for one of the larger airlines at the time. It wasn't until his health started deteriorating near the end of his life that he told me the story of my mother. I guess he felt like it was important to tell me before his time was up.

For three weeks, he searched every day for any indication that my mom was still out there. I can still see his red, puffy face as he told me the story, the scars still fresh after so much time. Tears ran down in small streams as he went through every detail he could remember, some of which had clearly faded with age. He had a difficult choice to make: Stay and keep looking with the risk of both of us getting killed or leave to a safer place if one even existed. He had no choice but to get the hell out, and quite frankly, I don't blame him for his decision. He carried a photo of her until the day he died in hopes that one day he might run into someone who would recognize her and tell him she was alive and well, even if she had found someone else. Just knowing that she was alive was all he wanted.

He passed away of a heart attack a few months before Maggie and I got married. I kept it together but was devastated he wasn't by my side. Maggie's hair is still the same sunshine yellow with large curls that cascade down her shoulders. Her sweet face doesn't look like it's aged a bit, just slimmed slightly through the jaw. I love that girl more now than I ever have.

Man, last year in my twenties. Fucking war has aged me, confirmed by my reflection in the glass staring back at me with dark brown, bloodshot eyes set deep into my skull. I put the photo down and suck in my stomach. I haven't gained too much weight, but the picture's honesty gets to me.

With my coffee in one hand and my bag in the other, I exit the house and climb into my Humvee, hightailing it out of there to pick up Sean. He lives around the corner from me, and fortunately, it's on the way, only a few miles west of Joint Base Eppley.

"Nice weather we're having today, huh, baldy? I see you shaved the wrong part of your head again," Sean quips. His full head of obnoxiously luxurious red hair curls up underneath his beanie.

"Just get in and shut the fuck up, ma'am! Don't need your lip this early in the morning." I inch forward the moment he tries to step foot inside.

"You think you're funny, cupcake!" he says as he leaps in, overcompensating the jump should I decide to lurch ahead again. He slaps his boots together, knocking chunks of bright white snow onto my floorboard.

"Dude! Let's show some respect to Miss Mod-vee. She's been through a lot over the years." I give the steering wheel some kisses and gently rub the dash, knowing Sean hates it when I do.

I named her after plowing through a small pack of Mods years back after they wandered into our territory. At forty-five miles per hour, the heavy-duty bumper was like a battering ram when it contacted their skinny, weak bodies. Their heads were like water balloons, popping and spraying brain matter all over the windshield. Some of the best fun I ever had until it was time to clean it up. Ugh, they smelled like shit, vomit, and body odor mixed together and left out for a week in ninety-degree weather. A few months later, I found an eye wedged under some wiring in the engine bay.

"Don't dude me." He reaches down and swipes more snow off the tops of his boots just to irritate me more, which works.

Sean's pure American, but somewhere along the way, he got some Irish genes—pale skin, freckles, all the traits of an Irishman and my favorite way to pick at him.

"You ready to shave that hideous, red pirate beard off your ugly face?" Miss Mod-vee's tires spin as I give her some gas.

We have a three-month-old bet to see who will shave their beard first. I'm not even sure how this stupid bet got started in the first place, but I'll die before I cave. He's always the first to give up, coming up with some lame-ass excuse every year.

"In your dirtiest wet dreams," he replies, smirking.

"So, what do you think the Major wants with us this morning?" I switch topics before we argue this bet like a bunch of sixteen-year-old girls for the next three hours like we did yesterday.

"Probably to have you shave that pathetic, poor man's beard. God, that thing is horrendous. Just a few pubes that crawled up onto your face one night." He leans over and takes a closer look, cringing. "Can you even grow a full beard? Bunch of patches like an unwatered lawn in the summer." He laughs alone.

"Ha, ha. Fuck you! Want to walk?" I start to slow, only half joking.

"Yeah, yeah, yeah, keep drivin'. If he wants to see us, I'm sure it's about a mission. I hope it's someplace fun this time. The last mission was a bust and not a damn thing we could use other than that box of tampons we found for you." He cracks himself up again.

"That really was a fun trip. Tampons were for you after screaming like a little girl in that hotel. Remember when that Mod popped out and you peed your whittle pants," I say in my best baby talk.

"That wasn't me, dude."

"Damn sure was you!" I yell. "The entire platoon was a witness and called you Peed Myself McCauley for months." He wasn't going to deny this one on my watch.

"That was a manly bellow," he whispers back, glancing out the window with a frown.

"Uh-huh. Sure it was, lil buddy."

"Maybe Hawaii?" He quickly changes the subject. "I've always wanted to go there. Think he'll ever send us to someplace warm like that? There was a lot of military shit there at one time." Sean's eyes widened.

"Keep dreaming." I take the next right. The vehicle fishtails, pushing through the snow that has yet to be plowed. "Fuckers need to get their happy asses out of bed and clear these damn roads." Laziness is a pet peeve of mine, and there are plenty of them around here, unfortunately.

Sean bringing up Hawaii is going to make my mind think about island life all day long now. I've never even seen the ocean, but Maggie and I have had serious discussions about this after we commandeered a forty-eight-foot MTI pleasure boat a while back with twin, eleven hundred horsepower TCI Mercury engines. We'd taken a drive up north one day and found it stashed away in a large metal building on a nice piece of property with a massive castle-like house. It was in pristine condition, minus the rat's nests and some needed engine work, but it barely had one hundred hours on it. I made some modifications to the fuel tank, adding an additional two hundred and fifty gallons for when we do make the decision to bug out. We have it stored over in Two Rivers, Wisconsin. All we would need to do is hook it up on the way out and book it.

The hardest part would be getting the boat to the Atlantic Coast and then taking it down to either the Florida Keys or the Bahamas. We could eat MREs, or meals ready to eat, until I got the fishing rig up and running. With hundreds of islands down that way, there's gotta be at least one that is uninhabited with Joscos. The damn things should have starved to death by now, being on an island for so long and afraid of water.

Damn, I can picture it now. Find a little cottage on the beach, fix it up, and then spend all day fishing while taking in the sun's rays while Maggie works on her tan and Abigail plays in the sand. The only bad part about being alone is just that—we would be alone. No doctors or grocery stores, none of the luxuries we have now. I guess we'd get used to the body odor.

Sean punches my shoulder, grabbing my attention. "Earth to Scott. Hello? Anybody there?"

"Sorry, what? I was daydreaming until you ruined it, asshole."

"Daydreaming?" He gives me a side-eye. "What the fuck are you daydreaming about, facial hair?"

"Ha-ha. You mentioned Hawaii and had me thinking about a conversation Maggie and I had a while back about getting the fuck out of here and heading to some island out in the middle of nowhere."

"Thinking about going AWOL, huh? Please do, so when the Major asks who wants to go hunt down Scott, I'll be the first to sign up!" He laughs by himself again for the third time in less than ten minutes.

"Dude, you couldn't find a dingleberry forming on one of your own ass hairs. Plus"—I hold up my middle finger—"I've served my time."

Sean lets out the most ridiculous laugh I have ever heard, then wipes the tears from his eyes. "I love you, Scott! I really do. You crack me up. Fucking dingleberries. I love it!"

I roll my eyes, resulting in him hitting me in the arm hard.

"You better watch yourself," I warn him with an evil smile and raised eyebrows.

Everyone is in good spirits during the winter months. It's the only time we can afford to laugh and fuck around, probably a little more than we should.

We make it to base and head straight for the Operations room a little before 0800 hours, stopping by the coffee pot so Sean can fill up, then find our usual seats in the front row. Major White likes us front and center. If there are any open seats in the first two rows when he walks in, he'll go ape shit. And when he calls a meeting, we'd better be there on time or he'll make an example out of the delayed party. He's old-school military. He doesn't butter things up; the tougher, the better, and the stronger we'll become, according to him.

The Operations room was once a small first class lounge at Eppley Airport. The older guys told us they used to have comfy leather chairs and TVs and an endless supply of beer. Most of us have only ever seen it staged as it is now, with off-white painted wooden tables and uncomfortable mismatched chairs. There are a few TVs, but they only project mission-related details on them. The tables have years of handcrafted art sketched into them by all our brothers and sisters before us, and most are obscene. My view is of a naked, busty lady in a cowboy hat riding a missile shooting toward a Josco's ass, an original piece signed by GSX-R. He was a motorcycle guy who was into Suzuki's. Had a collection of them, something like twenty-plus bikes. He died on a mission ten years ago.

There are also lists in remembrance of people who sat here before us, names with the date they died. I've carved out a few myself. "The Wall" has photos of old friends, a reminder that when we go out, we may not return.

As I sit here waiting for the Major to show up and enlighten us on why we're here, a cold downdraft blows through and rattles my bones. A third of the ceiling tiles are missing, allowing a cold draft to come through during winter. I keep my jacket on for the time being, but I'm not sure which is worse, the constant coldness the building stays in or the sweaty summer months. It's by no means a dump, and the new recruits keep it spotless, but maintenance is lacking.

A group of about sixty or so sits behind Sean and me. A lot of familiar faces, most of whom I haven't seen since last winter. During the summer months, we all work post duty, and so we're scattered along The River in alternating months. Most live on the outskirts or near other bases within our territory, so running into them is rare. Only a few in this room, like Sean and myself, actually live near the base.

Conversations break out behind us. Jokes are being cracked, and harassing comments are being made, which is the typical banter when we all get into a room. Corporals Frank Roberts and Bryan Tindale sit in the back on their comfy love seats, as they're too big for these cheap plastic chairs. We lovingly refer to the unrelated dynamic duo as the Josco Brothers. One could easily confuse the two as actual Joscos, just a tad smaller version at seven feet and close to four hundred pounds. All the real estate, from their extra-thick necks to their size 30-something feet, is inked in gory scenes. Frank's back piece consists of a field of spiked Josco heads being feasted upon by black crows and a naked, well-endowed lady wielding a bloody machete. Those explicit scenes make my meager religious tattoos look like child's play.

The two guys are inseparable—born with all the strengths of a Josco but not bat-shit crazy. Well, not in the traditional murder-cannibal way of the real thing. Coincidentally, they were born within a month of each other, and unfortunately, neither of their mothers survived their births. The poor bastards spent the first half of their lives being poked and prodded like lab rats to figure out why the little mutants were born that way. There was no conclusive answer at the time because neither mother advised the doctors during their prenatal checkups that they received the first series of AIV shots that led to this bullshit in the first place.

The testosterone-fueled pair spend most of their time in the gym to burn off the extra energy, at least when they aren't eating like teenagers. These asshats love to irritate the Major by clowning around when he's talking. You would think after being demoted three times and having to mop up the tarmac in the pouring rain, they would have learned their lesson, but they'll always be smart-asses. They keep us entertained, though it's a damned good thing we aren't still in Basic because I wouldn't hesitate to make them into blanket burritos and beat the shit out of them for making us do extra laps or clean the latrines.

There's an ongoing bet that they'll Turn—when it will happen and who will be the first to get a bullet between their eyes. Frank even placed a bet on himself. Not sure how he'll receive the winnings, though. I wagered that they'd Turn a year ago. Even though I lost that one, I'm still hopeful that I'll get to shoot at least one of them. Nothing makes this crowd more rambunctious on missions than running through the possibilities.

Riley, the only female in our platoon, sits behind Sean with her muscular arms crossed and her headphones blaring some kind of heavy metal that causes a pounding buzz to penetrate the chatter. Her fiery red hair is tucked away in a ponytail that barely peeks out under a tropical pink beanie printed with palm trees. Damn, the good Lord is really planting the seeds of island life.

She's one of the shortest team members at a staggering five foot ten, but she can squat as much weight as the men sitting in this room. She gets shit just like everyone else, but she never backs down and puts them in their place on occasion if they get carried away.

"You…got…to…be…shittin' me," I whisper to Sean, nudging his arm. "Look who it is. Staff Sergeant Jared Jones." Sean couldn't have been more noticeable, staring directly at him; he doesn't seem to care one bit. Jared catches his stare and drops his head.

As per usual, Jared has that drunk, sleepy look going on. Must've been up late last night drinking again. He lost his wife a few months ago. Drowning his sorrows with alcohol is his favorite past time. He hasn't worked his post since, which none of us blame him for, but I don't see him being an asset for any upcoming mission if that *is* what this gathering is about. He would be a liability, for sure. His presence makes me even more nervous. *Are we so desperate that we have to ask for anyone's help?*

The room goes quiet as Major White enters with his normal air of confidence, followed by six members of his staff. We stand and salute him. I notice, as I'm sure everyone else did, that Nolan isn't with him as he typically is with mission meetings. Maybe it's not a mission then.

"At ease." His deep voice vibrates the room. We all take a seat in one fluid motion. He walks straight to the podium and starts talking. "Alright, everyone—"

"Is it movie time, sir?" Frank blurts out in a childlike voice, clapping his hands as one of the staff members starts hooking up a computer to the projector.

What a fucking idiot. I shake my head exchanging a look with Sean. That guy will never learn. A few quiet laughs echo throughout the room. Major White shoots him a glare that says don't fuck with me right now. His stare is short and direct, and then he takes the same opportunity to survey the room. I catch a glimpse of a painful grimace as he lets out a sigh.

"Men, I know you all are wondering why I have you here this morning. So, I'll get right to it. We're going on a mission." There were a few cheers, mostly from the Josco Brothers. The Major eyes them both. "You won't be cheering here in a minute. Look, I know last year we only had the one, and it was a bust, but this one will be different. Unlike any we've been on in the past, so listen up carefully."

"It's a little later than usual, sir." I state. I didn't mean to say it out loud, but normally, if we're going on a mission, we'd have already been at least a week deep into reviewing details.

Embarrassed at my outburst, I sit back in my chair as a move of submission. Sean nudges me with an elbow while the staff unrolls several large maps, hanging them on the wall one by one with magnets and laying out other documents along a table off to the side. The projector clicks into action.

"Yes, Lieutenant Dodson," he replies. "This is a later start than usual, but there's a place we need to check out. As you all know, we need supplies and various equipment to keep our fleet in rough condition, to say the least. And"—he goes quiet for a moment—"attacks were up over the past three years. More strategic as you all know." He looks around the room. "I want to know where these bastards are coming from. We need intel, so it's time we start venturing out a little farther. The staff and I have been discussing where to go." He pauses again and looks around. His face says it all. He didn't have to continue; we all know where this is going. He's been saying for years where he wants to go, but it just never ended up formulating into anything but awkward conversations.

One of his top staff members jumps in, saying, "We have a squadron heading out tonight to do a little reconnaissance."

"A recon mission?" someone in the back asks. "Where exactly are we going, sir?" They asked the question we all wanted to but were afraid of the answer. My right leg shakes uncontrollably.

"We're going to Texas. Fort Hood to be exact."

What the fuck? All the air in the room got sucked out in one moment. Sean and I look at each other in disbelief. No one followed up with a smart-ass comment. My eyes instinctively shoot to the "Wall," and I find their group picture. On the last run made to Texas, only one guy out of sixty came back. Fucking one! He died several days later. Internal organs were beaten to shit. He was so messed up, we don't even know what happened to the guy. It's a mystery as to how in the hell he made it back, but they didn't have all the fun toys we have today to protect us.

Another staff member jumps in and starts talking, going into detail regarding the two C-130s heading down to collect data, while another puts a map of Fort Hood on the screen and talks high-level through what they think is furnished at the base and what we'll be grabbing when we're there. He also put up some aerial pictures taken right around the time of the Turning. Rows of equipment sit in the massive parking lots, and that's just what we can see. Who knows what else is stored in all the hangars and warehouses scattered over the massive base?

Clearly, the Major has been planning and researching this for a while as they all talk through the potential travel routes and other details. They mention there will be two teams but have yet to determine who's with who. My mind travels elsewhere during the rest of the meeting. My baby girl's face, hugging my wife, everything I would miss if I never returned. What would they do if I was gone?

This shit is suicide. What the hell am I going to tell them? Oh, hey honey, the Major has decided to send us all to our deaths. I'm pissed. My heart races and my stomach is in so many knots that I don't know if I need to scream or puke. I've given my entire life to getting rid of Joscos, and we aren't any closer now than we were eleven years ago when I joined. I blink hard to clear my head. Looking around, I could see it in everybody's eyes. Their demeanors were grave. I peer over at Jared, the only one who seems to be happy. Not even the Josco Brothers showed hints of a smile.

"Lieutenant McCauley, your mission objective will be focused on locating and safely loading and securing all the good equipment you can find. There is a wish list of what we're looking to collect being developed as we speak and will be provided to you in the coming days. Lieutenant Dodson, you will provide security for McCauley's team, scanning the area for any threats, collecting intel, and writing up an inventory list of everything you see while driving down there and while on location. If this is successful, we may want to return in the future…"

If this is successful? The words echo in my head, bouncing around my brain.

Sean leans over as the Major keeps talking and whispers, "Bitch duty" in my ear.

I can't formulate a thought let alone control the physical aspect of my tense body, aside from sitting with my arms crossed tightly across my body so I don't jump out of my skin.

"...you guys need to get your shit together. We don't do this, we might not survive another decade. One day we will be rid of them and be free again like it used to be."

Some perk right up with that comment, but for others like me, the Major's speech doesn't resonate. I don't remember that life, the freedom he speaks of. I don't even know what that means. What I have now with my wife and kid isn't terrible. Of course, I want to be rid of those bastards, but I can't envision a life without the Joscos, either. The stories the Major tells us are just fairy tales to put kids to sleep. Sometimes I feel like the Major has this impossible feat that he wants me to fix personally, and I don't see how I can or if I even want to.

We spent the rest of the morning listening to the Major and his staff drone on about the mission before he releases us for lunch, and then he ends up dismissing us for the rest of the day. The ride is a deep contrast from our normal drive; no jokes or harassing comments are exchanged. It was probably the quietest time the two of us have ever had together. Neither of us even say goodbye when I drop Sean off at home.

The rest of the drive home is a blur as I try to process everything the Major said, at least what I heard of it. Maggie met me at the door, surprised to see me home so early, but one look at my face and she knew. Her sweet face turns red, and she breaks down in tears, as she's done for my other missions, but this time, even I have doubts that I don't express to her. I have nothing to say to comfort her, so I don't say much at all. Abigail doesn't quite understand but knows when her mom is sad, that she should be too. She starts tearing up, mimicking her actions. Maggie comments that we should just make a run for it. No way that'll happen. There is nowhere to hide, although the thought of going to Hawaii did briefly cross my mind—you know, if I was a pilot and had a plane.

The rest of the day I spend playing with Abigail, taking in every detail of her small face and embracing my wife more than normal. It may be the last few days I get to do either.

CHAPTER EIGHT

(Lieutenant Scott Dodson—U.S. Marines)

Friday, January 17, 2048

The next morning comes too soon after another restless night of tossing and turning. Maggie didn't sleep well either, which is typical before missions. She won't rest until I've returned, knowing I'm back safe and sound.

For sanity's sake, I stick to my regular morning routine: get dressed, kiss the wife and kid, pour a large thermos of coffee and then pick up Sean on the way in. Our conversation is a little more jovial as we chat about the events of yesterday. We can cry all we want, but that won't change the fact that it's going to happen. We have five short days to get everything ready, so we better have our minds focused on the mission. We must ensure every nut and bolt is checked, rechecked, and then checked once more, and depending on how I'm feeling that day, a fourth time, as we can't leave anything to chance.

The parking lot is damn near empty as we roll in. I figured this place would be packed by now with all the team members who couldn't sleep like me. The parking lot has a fresh coat of white powder. I can't let all this white fluffy snow go to waste. It's taunting me, calling my name, whispering soft payback in my ear.

Sean exits first with his belongings in hand.

"I'll catch up to you in a minute. Gonna grab my things out of the back seat. Meet you inside," I say as he shuts the door to Miss Mod-vee.

Sean walks ahead, waving a hand in the air. "Wasn't gonna wait for your slow ass anyway."

I duck down behind the rear door, allowing it to conceal me in the off chance Sean looks back to grin, proud of his comment. I grab a handful of snow from the ground and pack it nice and tight. Sean is about fifteen feet in front of the Humvee, the perfect distance, so I ready the pitch, wind it up, and hurl the snow baseball at him. It arches perfectly, straight for him. A head shot would be glorious. The white powder pelts him right on the back of his neck before exploding into a beautiful, circular halo around his head, with the scene made even better by snow falling down his shirt.

My laughter explodes, loud and hysterical.

"You shithead!" he yells as he wipes the leftover snow that's clinging to his beanie.

"That was for yesterday, punk."

"You motherfucker! Yeah, let's see you do that when I'm facing you." The raspberry shade of his face said it all.

Not a problem. I have another waiting for him. As he looks down, using both hands to brush the rest of the snow off his back, the second snowball smacks him in the forehead. I fall to my knees with tears welling in my eyes. The pain from laughing so hard hurts my stomach. That one may have been packed a little tighter than the first.

"Really! You son-of-a-bitch!" He throws up double middle fingers, while glaring at me as the snow trickles down his face. He then untucks his shirt, which I know he hates.

"You okay, Buddy?" I continue to taunt, staying a few feet away from his reach as I pass by him.

"You'd better watch yourself, fucker! I might just leave your ass in Fort Hood."

Sean takes a few minutes to clean off and readjust his outfit, then we walk toward the hall to the Operations room, still maintaining a safe distance and keeping a watchful eye. I can't help but smirk the entire way, holding onto the little joy I still have.

"Keep laughing, chuckles."

We turn a corner, feet away from the Operations room, so I try to change tunes, but the image of the snowball hitting his face won't go away. The last thing I need is to roll up with a stupid smile on my face with the Major being all serious.

I slow down and let Sean enter the room first. I purse my lips together to stifle the grin threatening my face. The Major is already in the room with Nolan and several of his staff members, all in deep discussion over a map. The bulletin board on the far wall is covered with enlarged aerial photographs of Fort Hood. If the pictures are accurate, it's going to be like Christmas morning when we show up. Every parking lot looks to be full of equipment: tanks, helicopters, Humvees, you name it. Some even look like they are covered with massive tarps.

On the other wall, a projector illuminates a map highlighting potential routes. Damn, that is one long yellow line, the longest we've ever seen. A bird's eye view shows one main route, but there are other routes off the main line around several of the larger cities. The guys must have been up all night reviewing the data after it came in.

Major White glances toward us. "Gentleman. Come in."

"Good morning, sir." We both salute.

Nolan looks at Sean and, after a double take, says, "You alright, Lieutenant?"

"Yes, sir!" I could feel Sean eyeing me. "A little snowball incident that will work itself out later. All good, sir."

The Major didn't smile, but Nolan and the others sure did.

"Well, gentlemen, we have a lot to discuss today. Let's get to it, shall we?" It wasn't really a question.

A high-quality, bird's-eye view map of Fort Hood, a smaller version than the one on the bulletin board, sits on the table, with the name Operation Texas Bandit written on top. I like it as it gives me a Wild West image of a group of outlaws strolling into Fort Hood with weapons drawn.

A multitude of buildings, along with some parking lots, are highlighted in either red, yellow, or green, indicating their importance. Red's a no-go, probably too damaged from what they were able to see. Yellow could be worth it if we have room or time to load up, but green means we'd better get it unless it's not in good shape once we put closer eyes on it. Handwritten notes are scrawled next to each location.

We follow Nolan to the bulletin board where there's a list of team members posted for Sean and me. We already knew our mission objectives, but we didn't yet know who would be with us. Sean's team makes sense. Most know their way around an engine block, so they can determine which equipment is of good quality or at least better than the next.

I couldn't help but read ahead regarding my team and noticed one name that gave me heartburn. Damn! Staff Sergeant Jared Jones is assigned to my team. With what he's been through lately, I don't think he is in any shape to be going on a mission of this caliber.

Nolan then reads my team, but I interject.

"Sorry to interrupt, sir, but Jared? I'm not sure about him being back in the field. This mission may be too much for him."

"I'm aware of his current situation. I discussed it with him yesterday. He is ready." Nolan says confidently.

The fuck he is. He may say he's good to go, but that doesn't give me the warm fuzzies about it. The last thing I need is someone who's not all there watching my six. He's been trustworthy before, but he could also end up being a mental case. I push my concern, but I should bite my tongue and move on. My stubbornness refuses to let it go.

"Sir, I just don't know. I don't feel comfortable with him being a part of this. Not this mission. If it were any other—"

"Lieutenant," the Major interrupts. "He will be on your team, and that is final. Understood?"

No. I don't understand, but what choice do I have? I understand he needs to get back into the swing of things, but why does it have to be on this mission under my command? I let it go, but I'm going to have a nice chat with Jared when we're done here.

"Yes, sir." I nod and keep quiet so we can move on.

We review more information than I can soak up in a single sitting, studying the potential travel routes in detail and identifying the checkpoints along the way. Which buildings to recon when we get down there, extraction points, backup extraction points, and setting up new repeater locations for comms, the list goes on. The rule of engagement is always the same—shoot to kill—and then we discuss every possible scenario we can think of and how to respond to each.

The hours slowly float away. My mind drifts in and out like at most mission briefings, but this one had me way out in the middle of nowhere. Maggie would pop into my head, then Abigail. Island living came to the forefront more than once and really had me thinking hard about it. I've been doing this for eleven years. We're only required to serve eight, so technically, I've fulfilled my requirement. What would happen if I were to just walk out, right now, without saying a word and be done with all this? I'm sure the wife and kid would be all for it, and I would get some serious brownie points for it, but I probably wouldn't make it to the building's exit without getting a beatdown, mostly from Sean. But at this moment, it might be fueled more by the snowballs.

But that's not me. I can't leave everyone hanging like that—or Sean. Well, maybe Sean, but after this mission, I'm seriously going to have a heart-to-heart discussion again with Maggie about that life we dream about. Even if it's just to the north around the Great Lakes, I could leave this place and never look back. Not many could since this is the safest place on Earth, as far as I know. This place has drained every bit of life out of me, and I'm tired of fighting. I want what the Major has spoken about all these years: the peace and quiet, the freedom, the calm. I want to hear the wind, the waves hitting the sandy beach. The happy laughter of Abigail playing in the ocean and running away from the water or screaming due to a fish swimming too close. We can't have that life here.

Sean nudges me; he must have noticed that I was elsewhere, and after five grueling hours, the Major releases the two of us.

We both say formal goodbyes and exit the room.

"Where the fuck were you?" Sean asks, pushing me.

"Fuck, that was long. My brain is dead."

"Yeah, the Major sure knows how to put people to sleep."

"I need him to come tuck me in and tell me a bedtime story tonight. I could sure use the sleep."

"I hear that."

Sean and I meet with our respective teams out in one of the hangars, where all our gear and equipment are being prepped for our departure. They should already have a few vehicles sourced by now and had better not be fucking around.

Sean busts through the door with a swagger in his step. "All right, ladies and Riley!"

"Hey, asshole!" Riley yells out from the far end of the hangar.

"Sorry, Riley, I had to."

"Dick!" Riley replies.

"Let's go get some chow." Sean claps his hands as though that was the signal for people to get their asses moving.

We break for lunch and collectively head over to the chow hall. Sean and I grab a seat apart from the rest of the group. It wasn't because we didn't want to sit with them; I just had a few things I wanted to get off my chest, and I didn't want word getting out. I scarf down my meal while Sean takes his sweet-ass time, which is fine because he can finish eating while I bitch.

"What the fuck am I going to do?" I ask him, throwing down my fork on the plate. I stare at Sean, who is clearly in another world of his own making. After two minutes, the awkward silence finally makes him look up from eating his perfectly cut chicken.

"Oh. What?" he says with a mouth full of potatoes and carrots.

"Welcome back." I shake my head. "Jared, dumbass. I can't believe they put Jared on my team. I feel sorry for the guy and all that he's been through, but really? He's not ready. Not for this magnitude of a mission."

"Oh, yeah." Sean laughs. "That was awesome, watching you flounder like a fish out of water! You got to work on that."

"Yeah, thanks for the help back there. You think he's ready?"

"I don't know. He probably needs to start getting back to a routine. Just give him some dinky job. It doesn't matter what I think. It's Nolan's and the Major's call."

"There are only sixty of us, fucker. A dinky job? Really. Going to Texas. Were you paying attention at all? All of them are important jobs. We're only as strong as the weakest link. Remember that?" I clear my throat intentionally.

"Well, give him the one with the least amount of responsibility. Have him count ammo." He laughs at his own joke.

"Have him count ammo? Who the fuck does that? Seriously, do you listen to anything I say? Or better yet, do you listen to the words that come out of your own mouth?" I look up at a clock hanging from the middle of the room. It's been thirty minutes. Thank goodness.

"We need to start heading back." I let my face fall into my hands. "Fuck me. Hell, maybe next, the Major will give me a toilet plunger to fight off the Joscos." I act like I'm poking Sean with a pretend plunger.

"You've lost it, man. Seriously." Sean gives me a look between disgust and having a bowel movement.

"You take Jared, then."

We finish eating and make our way back to spend the rest of the day checking off each piece of equipment as our teams bring them to us for inspection. I requested the big guns for this one. If they want us on this mission, they're gonna provide the good stuff. Night is going to be our most vulnerable time, and we'll need every ounce of firepower we can muster into a sixty-man platoon. I requested four mobile close-in weapon systems, called M-CIWS, semi-trucks with modified forty-foot trailers, each outfitted with two systems that fire a 102 mm armor-piercing round that'll explode a Josco upon impact. The system has been reconfigured to identify the thermal heat signatures from a Josco. Each trailer holds fifty thousand rounds, so that'll give us two hundred thousand rounds total. I smile at that. The sight and sound of one of those going off gives me a hard-on every time. It's quite the sight to watch a Josco be obliterated to a bloody mist in less than a second by one of these pushing out thousands of rounds every second. Each outpost's watchtower is furnished with one, and if you're lucky enough to be on shift when one goes off, you'd be in awe of the power it possesses.

By the end of the day, we were able to locate and collect half of what was on our inventory list for the mission. And with little luck, we should have everything collected by the end of day tomorrow. With Sean and I satisfied with the work performed, we call it a day and let everyone go home.

After dropping off Mr. No-Help, I go straight to Jared's house. I just hope he's there and didn't go to some bar. I need to make sure for myself that he's ready to go. I need to see it in his eyes and hear it in his voice. If he's not, I'm gluing his ass to a seat, handcuffed and duct-taped until the mission's over. He wouldn't be the first guy we've had to tie up out there from going bat-shit crazy. These missions sure as hell ain't for the weak of heart.

The snow hasn't been cleared from his walkway or drive. Trash is piled up on the side of the house, and it looks like there's some busted furniture as well. At least it's stacked up in a pile and not strewn across the yard. I think about what I'm going to say to this broken man. I sure hope he doesn't take it the wrong way and go crazy on me. He could rip me apart in seconds, as he's a few inches taller but at least fifty pounds of muscle heavier.

I step out into nine inches of snow. Before I'm halfway to his front door, to my surprise, the door opens, and Jared greets me with a friendly, "Hey, Scott."

He was quiet today, but he seemed focused, so that was good. I just hope it continues. I give him a curt wave. He looks okay, like a typical, regulated human being.

"Hey, Jared, how's everything going?" I respond as casually as I can.

"Sorry I haven't shoveled. Been working on the inside, and I guess I neglected the outside."

"It's okay, man," I say while knocking the snow off my boots and pants onto his porch. We shake hands.

Inside it's a lot cleaner than it had been. A few of us stopped by a month or so ago to see if there was anything we could do for him. Needless to say, he told us in a drunken rage to get the fuck out. I try to look inconspicuous as I eye a few additional holes in the wall about chest-high near the front door. We've all lost loved ones, and everyone deals with it in their own way.

"Um, things are better, I guess. I just needed some time to grieve. She was the love of my life, Scott. I know I reacted badly when she died, shutting everyone out. She was all that I had in this fucked-up world."

"I hear you, man. It's difficult to have to go through that alone, but we're all here for you. We know a thing or two about tough times."

I take a seat on his brown, worn-out couch, and he sits in a rickety old rocking chair across from me. I can tell he's searching for words to say something.

"It was tough watching her in all that pain and what she went through the last two months she was alive. I prayed every day for her to get better and wished that it was me lying in that hospital bed and not her. It just happened so fast. One day, she was fine and healthy, and the next, she was sick." He chokes up and pauses for a moment. "Did you know we were trying to have a baby?" His eyes start tearing up.

"I can't say that I did." Goosebumps cover my arms as I recall those days when it was Maggie and I and how different it could have turned out.

"Two years we tried. It wasn't until after she died that I found out she was pregnant. The doctors didn't even know until afterward. We had no idea. I don't think she did, either. With her being sick, her body wasn't the same. That was the hardest part of it all. That was the one thing she wanted most in this world: to have a little baby and watch him or her grow up. That was what pushed me over the edge. She wanted so much to have a family. I mean, what are the fucking chances that after two years of trying, she finally gets pregnant, but neither of us knows, and she gets an aggressive form of cancer and dies?" He leans forward, and his head falls into his hands.

I swallow hard, forcing the lump back down, and I blink to keep the tears from bursting out. It makes me want to run home right now and wrap my arms around Maggie and Abigail and never let them go. I couldn't imagine going through all that.

"I don't know what to say, Jared. I don't think any of us knew that part of it. I sure didn't. I'm so sorry, man. It's difficult to find words that make sense of all this, and I wish I had some comforting words to tell you other than we're here for you. I don't know what God's plan is for us, but my prayer is that we find peace with what's happened."

"Thanks, Scott." He pauses for a minute, wipes away the tears, and then lets out a small laugh. "Look at me." He throws his arms up. "A two-hundred-and-thirty pound Marine crying in front of my CO."

"Trust me when I say we've all been there. You aren't the first, and you won't be the last. We Marines are probably some of the biggest crybabies out there." We both have a short-lived laugh together.

"Well, I just want you to know that I'm better now, Scott. I-I've mourned long enough, and it's time to get back into it. I need this. I know you have your doubts about me, and I get that. I was wondering if you were going to stop by and have a talk. But you can trust me to be there."

I take a long pause before speaking. There's a lot you can tell by looking in someone's eyes. It took me a minute, but I could see it and hear it. But I still have to ask.

"Are you one hundred percent good to go?"

He sits back in the rocker, which creaks as he leans back. "A week ago, I wouldn't have been, but I'm good now. Nolan and the

Major came by yesterday, and we had a good long talk. I've spent the last five months drinking myself into a coma almost every day, and the other night was the first time I didn't have a single drop. Haven't touched it in three days now."

"That's good to hear."

I *can* see it in his eyes and hear it in his voice that he wants to come back and be a part of society again.

"I need someone that I can count on and trust to be there to support us in case the shit hits the fan. This mission is unlike any other we've been on, and it's going to test us. I need to know you'll have our backs and won't choke. If you show any signs of jeopardizing our team or the mission, I'll personally take you down. I don't care how much bigger you are than me!" I smirked to show him I was joking, but only a little.

He knows how I operate, having been on many assignments with me. He nods his head, and I know he understands. We shoot the shit for a while longer before I stand up and walk to the door. A few nights of sobriety aren't much, but it's a start, and we have a little time before we leave.

"Thanks, Scott. You can count on me."

"See you at hangar seven tomorrow at zero-eight hundred hours. We have a lot of vehicles to prep and make ready before Wednesday. I want everything quadruple-checked before we head out."

"I'll be the first one there, sir."

CHAPTER NINE

(Major Oliver White—U.S. Marines)

Saturday, January 18, 2048

As I walk past Karen's desk with a fresh cup of coffee, she reminds me that today is the quarterly meeting with the department heads. With everything else that's happened the past few days and Operation Texas Bandit just days away from heading out, this wasn't even on my radar. *Damn!* It's going to be a long and exhausting number-filled day, reviewing the previous quarterly stats to see if we met our target goals and then ensuring we're on track to meet future numbers. It's important to know we're moving in the right direction, and if not, I just hope there's some good news coming because I could really go for some right now.

With that reminder seeping in, I ask Nolan to take the reins on Operation Texas Bandit for the time being, which he gladly accepts. This is what he lives for. His passion. It's like a chess game to him. Thinking ahead. Contemplating each potential move or scenario and then moving his pieces to get a particular outcome. And with the added bonus of bossing my Marines around, what Navy guy wouldn't love that?

While I wait for my first arrival, a stack of perfectly aligned folders sits parallel to the corner of my desk, stacked in the exact order of when each department head will show up, fourteen in total. *I'd be lost without Karen.* I grab the top folder and open it up to brief myself before Mr. Paddock, who manages all the cattle farms located in our territory, arrives to discuss agriculture. I lean back to relax, taking in a deep breath and then releasing it slowly. I'm starting to think I should have pushed these meetings back a few days or at least until after Operation Texas Bandit was either underway or maybe upon their return because I can't seem to think of anything else. Chest pains kept me up most of last night, and the occasional nauseous feeling made me visit the restroom a few more times than usual. *What the fuck is wrong with me?* I pound my chest a few times, hoping it'll jostle whatever it is that's not cooperating. *Was it something I ate that was giving me heartburn?* I sure hope it's nothing serious. If it continues, I may have to visit a physician, which I hate and don't have time for.

While my chest tightens a bit, I continue to read through Mr. Paddock's short synopsis. Rather than spending hours reading through a fifty-page report, I've asked them to be summarized into a few pages. Some things I'm particular about and want to read every little detail, but others, give me the bullet points and call it a day.

After digesting the report, I switch gears to another folder that's been eyeing me from the other side of the desk. I still have a little bit of time before Mr. Paddock shows up, so I open the report from the incident that took place out at the research facility a few days ago. I dive in, hoping it takes my mind off the mission and whatever my body is going through. The open folder reveals a single, clear plastic sleeve with a burned sheet of paper within. I pick it up and inspect it for anything obvious, but nothing. It's a sheet of paper, something a doctor would write notes on, but nothing conclusive as to what Dr. Anderson was doing there. I read through the report and flip between the photographs, which triggers a flood of anger at first, then frustration, and then sadness. Losing those men hurts deeply.

"Sir." Karen's voice startles me, and I look up from the report to see her head tilting in the doorway, with a gentleman standing just out of sight past her. "Jerry Paddock is here to see you for your nine o'clock."

I toss the report on the desk and stand up.

"Thanks, Karen. Please send him on in."

On time, like his father. Always punctual. His father, John Paddock, was someone you could count on and trust to get things done and done correctly. Jerry took over two years ago after his passing. If it weren't for his father, we wouldn't have one percent of the cattle and other livestock we have today. In the beginning, we set up farms all over our territory, some even on islands in the Great Lakes, just in case something was to happen and whoever was left could pack up and move on and hopefully continue to live.

John's the reason we have meat in our grocery stores and on our tables. Once The River construction began, he took it upon himself to start farming and raising cattle, knowing we would have a safe place to do so. He was a farmer before the Turning, and without a doubt, he knew what he was doing, passing all that knowledge down the line to his one and only son.

"Jerry, it's a pleasure." I walk around my desk to shake his hand. His face is on the thinner side, even with his full beard. He looks more fit, even though he's a thick man. "How have you been the past few months? You're looking healthy."

"I've been well, sir." He pats his belly with both hands. "Damn boys are keeping me busy. They have me running around more than ever."

"I bet. You have them working the farms yet? How old are they now?" I walk back behind my desk and gesture him to sit. "They must love it on the farm, all that open land to run wild."

"Thank you, sir." He removes his black Stetson with a tan band and lays it on the corner of my desk. "Let's see. Luke is eight and Alex just turned five. Damn, I can't believe how fast they are growing up. They love every bit of the farm, especially riding on the equipment, but for some gosh darn reason, when it comes time to do the actual work, they get lazy on me and go running back home to their mom." He throws his hand up in the air. "Go figure." We both enjoy a short laugh. "Luckily, I have a lot of hands out there to help me."

"The work you guys do out there is vital, and if not for your father, we wouldn't be in such a great position."

"Well, I appreciate those words, sir. And, as always, the feeling is mutual." He tips his head in appreciation.

I can tell there's more he wants to share. "Ok, what's the grin for?" I ask.

"Well, we recently found out we'll be having another child."

"Really! Congratulations, Jerry!"

"Yeah, the wife is hoping for a daughter this time, especially with us three boys running around the place. I guess we'll find out here shortly."

"That's great news. Congratulations, and yes, hopefully Mrs. Paddock will get her wish. Look, I know you had a long drive down here, so let's get to it, shall we?

We spend the next thirty minutes going over the current and projected numbers for the coming years to make sure we stay on track as our population continues to hopefully grow. Cattle is up over a percent, which is great news, considering last year's misfortune. Blackleg set us back and killed off a large chunk of our young cattle at one farm. The livestock are vaccinated and healthy. It's a good thing we still had the capability to develop medicine and act on what would have been a devastating blow to our cattle.

After the meeting, Nolan butts into my office. "How's everything looking? We going to have enough meat to last us the rest of the year?" He rubs his hands together, while licking his chops.

"I think we'll have enough beef ribs and filet mignons to last you the year," I say making Nolan smile. "Numbers are up, and the livestock looks healthy. Jerry's doing a great job."

"That's good to hear. You know I like my filets."

"Yep, medium rare," I reply.

Nolan gives me a questioning look after I grimace from a sharp pain deep within my chest. My right hand involuntarily leaps to my shirt, putting some pressure on the area. I fall back in my chair, hoping for relief, but the stabbing remains.

Seeing my distress, Nolan speaks up. "You okay, sir?"

His voice is muffled in my ringing ears. I gasp as if the air is being sucked out of my lungs, making me panic. I lean forward in another attempt to gain control but fall out of my chair onto my side. *Fuck! Is this a heart attack?* Tiny, white patches cover my vision and grow by the second. I barely see Nolan's face as he rushes around the desk to my side. I hear the faint sound of Nolan yelling for Karen to get the doctor before everything goes black.

***

Squinting through the glow of halos caused by the lights above, I make out what I assume to be white curtains surrounding me. My eyes take a minute to focus. I'm in a hospital gown connected to monitors that maniacally beep when I start to pull them from my chest. The doctor, three nurses, and Nolan come running in with horrified faces. They look both irritated and perhaps relieved when they see me sitting up, wires in hand.

"Good God, Major. You just scared the shit out of me," Nolan declares, rubbing his forehead.

"Why the hell am I here, and how the fuck did you get me into this gown?"

"You passed out in your office," Nolan says.

"Passed out? You mean I had a heart attack?"

"No, sir," Doctor Ferris interjects more cheerfully than I would have expected, his green eyes wide.

"Hypotension or low blood pressure. In fact, it's really low. More than likely caused by dehydration. Have you been experiencing any vomiting or diarrhea? Stressed out lately?" He walks closer to me while grabbing for his stethoscope.

I look down at my socked feet and can still feel the pressure as I raise my hands and lay them on my chest.

"D, all of the above," I reply to the doctor. I take another deep breath and let it out slowly, leaning back. "Low blood pressure. I thought I was having a heart attack."

"Chest pain can be associated with low blood pressure, and in your case, it seemed to be a little more painful. We did an EKG, and as far as we can tell, your heart is in good condition." The doctor leans forward and puts his freezing cold stethoscope on my chest while the nurses attempt to reattach the cords I pulled out.

"Well, that's good to hear, I guess."

"You've been under a lot of pressure lately, and the doctor thinks it would help if you tried to get away, just for a little while. You've been going nonstop," Nolan says, adding facial expressions to sell it even more.

"If I wanted your opinion, Nolan, I would have asked for it."

I'm not going to lie; the idea of getting away excites me, and I can feel my face light up more than what is probably acceptable in my situation. Then reality takes over, and that initial feeling is replaced with a grimace. I can't leave now. There's still much I need to do: the research facility, Operation Texas Bandit, and the rest of the day's meetings. I sit up, refusing to let the dizziness get the better of me, waving the nurses off.

"Major White, I insist that you let us continue monitoring you for at least a few more—"

"I'm not going to lay around in a hospital bed, Doc," I interrupt. "I have work to do so more people don't die." It came out as ugly as I felt. All that burden bubbles up and flows right out of my mouth sometimes. I know the guy is trying to do his job, but I have to do mine, and right now, mine's more important.

"Well." The doctor throws his arms up. "What the fuck do I know? I'm just a doctor." Both the doctor and Nolan look at me in disappointment. The doctor signals the nurses to leave the room.

"Don't look at me like that." I glare at Nolan.

"Well, if you're not going to stick around here and let us look after you for a bit..." The doctor reaches into his coat pocket and tosses me a medicine bottle. "Take these. The directions are on the bottle, but I'm sure you'll do whatever you want. It's fludrocortisone, which increases the sodium levels and blood volume in the body. Drink plenty of water. No alcohol." The doctor points to a glass of water on a stand next to the bed. "That clear, liquid stuff right there." He walks toward the door. "I'll be right back."

Nolan shakes his head and gives me a disapproving look. He crosses his arms over his chest, which I return with defiance, daring him to speak as I slip on my pants. I couldn't care less that he's worried about me. Rolling his eyes in defeat, he storms out, leaving the curtains dancing in his wake. The doctor returns, holding a device in his hand.

"Here. It's a blood pressure monitor. Use it first thing in the morning, then around lunchtime, and then again before bed. If it gets low, you get your ass back here." He looks straight into my eyes. "I'm serious! I guess you're free to go."

"Yes, sir, Doc." And with that, I'm left there all alone, just the way I like it.

CHAPTER TEN

(Lieutenant Scott Dodson—U.S. Marines)

Saturday, January 18, 2048

By mid-morning, we've collected everything we think we need for Operation Texas Bandit to be successful. Forty vehicles, their respective equipment spread out in an orderly fashion around each, occupy two large hangars. Seeing weapons of all calibers with their ammo boxes perfectly arranged, along with our food, drones, and a bunch of other fun gadgets sitting nice and snug in their crates, is impressive.

Nolan and the Major approved every request Sean and I put in front of them, but only time will tell if we planned this out appropriately. The array of vehicles sitting before me is quite a sight to see, made even more impressive by the addition of the Phalanx M-CIWSs with their bay doors open, exposing their components. We use them on location to form a protective shield around base camp and configure each one to a certain firing grid so no two systems get confused and shoot at the same target.

We start the grueling inspection process to make sure all forty vehicles are in pristine condition, ready to tackle any obstacle that gets in our way. We'll check every nut and bolt a hundred times over, leaving nothing to chance. If a major component like an engine were to fail, it would be unfortunate because those vehicles would be left behind—unless we have room on our way back to load it up. Being that this will undoubtedly be the largest convoy we've ever assembled, it's going to sound like a damned freight train plowing through. Any Josco within ten miles of us is likely going to hear us coming, so we have to be ready.

"Dodson! Finish up what you're doing," Nolan calls from across the hangar. "I need you and McCauley in the Operations room ASAP."

"Yes, sir!" The door shuts behind him before the last syllable leaves my mouth.

I turn back around to my team, who are dirty, sweaty and covered in grease. "Alright, listen up. You know what to do. Everything is to be triple checked by the time we leave for the day. Any issues come up, I need to know about it. If something isn't working, let's repair it, and if we can't, replace it. Brad, start collecting spares. Tires, batteries, whatever you think we'll need. If something breaks while we're out there, we only have minutes to fix it or it's getting left behind. I don't want to be sitting ducks for any long periods of time."

"Yes, sir!" the group collectively sounds off.

I shimmy over to Sean's hangar so we can go over to the Operations room together.

"How's it coming along on your side of things?" I ask as we walk.

"So far, so good. But we just started getting into it. We'll know soon enough if we come across any issues. You?"

"Nothing too serious. We have a few vehicles that have some brake issues, but nothing major."

"Well, if it comes down to it, the vehicle in front of you will help you stop." Sean snickers.

"Wouldn't be the first time," I retort, recalling a few memorable missions.

We make it to the main office building and then to the Operations room.

"You wanted to see us, sir?" I beat Sean to the punch, and I can feel his glare. We enter a semi-dark room, where the only light sneaking in is through slits in the blinds. The projector illuminates images of Fort Hood and the surrounding area on the wall opposite the windows.

"Yes, in here." Nolan and the Major walk over to the screen, and we meet them there, standing off to the side to keep from blocking the image.

"After further review of the information from the recon, it didn't show a single Josco sighting en route or while on location. They circled the area for an hour, scouring the surrounding areas, but didn't pick up one single hit on the thermals or any other system. It's still mildly cold, but the most likely explanation is that the sound of the planes scared them into hiding, if there were any nearby. And upon further review, Fort Hood is stockpiled with equipment and materials throughout the base." Nolan points to several areas on the screen. "A few things have changed, but don't get excited, gents. It's nothing that will deter the mission. It appears that a fire broke out here." He points to another area on the screen. "We believe it was contained to this area, but most of the vehicles look to be destroyed. We've scratched that section from our plans."

Nolan steps back before continuing. "We have a more detailed map that we'll review here in just a minute, but regarding the travel route,"—a staff member changes the images on the screen—"the primary travel itinerary still looks better than I thought it would be. Somehow the more direct route is ninety percent free from obstructions. We can only assume these roads were cleared before it got bad out there. You'll hit blockades at a few places, mostly the big cities, but again, we'll go into detail regarding alternative routes."

I start running through scenarios of what could go wrong. I tend to be an optimist, but in this case, there are hundreds of ways we could fail. I'm sure Sean is doing the same.

"So, thermals picked up nothing?" Sean sounds depressed, but I'm feeling skeptical.

"Correct, which surprises me. Usually, we see small groups, but maybe they haven't migrated north just yet. You two know what to do if you come across them. I'm sure there are a few groups lurking somewhere," Nolan says.

We spent the next several hours reviewing the additional data collected from the recon mission. We memorize as much as we can, taking notes because we'll be giving our teams the same briefing once they are finished and ready to go.

"I think that just about does it," Nolan says. He must have seen that Sean and I have had enough information shoved down our throats. Anymore and I'm pretty sure I would have turned into a Mod myself.

"Any questions?" the Major asks.

"Not at the moment, sir. It's just the unknowns that always give me the shakes," I say, crossing my arms.

"Just remember your training, and you'll do fine." Nolan nods at me with confidence.

The Major follows up by giving us Sunday off to be with our families or do whatever the hell it is we do on our time off, so long as we have everything in order. He also informs us that he's heading out tomorrow to go up to his cabin, under strict "orders" from his doctor—and Nolan, apparently.

A bit surprised to hear that, I suppress a chuckle. Never heard of the Major being told what to do or that he'd admit a medical issue or take a vacation during such an important mission.

We stick around a few more minutes to talk about some last-minute questions that popped into Sean's brain, then head back to the hangars to check on our team's progress. We'll return bright and early Monday morning to complete our final checks and do one last inspection before we bug out Tuesday morning.

***

As with every Sunday that I'm in town, after a hearty breakfast of bacon and eggs, Maggie, Abigail, and I attend church to hear Pastor Byron's sermon. We spot the McCauleys and Maggie gives them a quick wave as we make our way to a few open seats. I just nod. We sit off to the right and converse with a few others. I worked post duty with one guy in particular when I first joined the Marines.

He is no longer serving since he lost a leg one winter evening when a rogue group of outcasts attacked the outpost where he was stationed. There are still scavengers out there who don't want to be a part of a normal society, roaming the Earth wherever their feet lead them. Though rare, they attack in an attempt to grab supplies. We talk about life and what we've been up to before taking a seat, and Pastor Byron walks up to the podium.

I gaze around the room; the medium-sized building just isn't working out anymore. It's starting to feel cramped. Byron needs to start thinking about finding a bigger place if this keeps up.

His sermon couldn't have been more suited for this Sunday, about a young Israelite named David, who later becomes the King of Israel, and his fight with the Philistine, Goliath. Ultimately, David defeats Goliath by hurling a stone from his sling, followed by David cutting off his head. Sounds like my kind of guy. A lot of similarities with us being the underdog in the fight against the Joscos. Along with Jesus by our side, we have heavy artillery and .50 cals, not slings or spears.

Once the sermon is over, we say our goodbyes and head back home. Normally, we'd meet up afterward and have a BBQ lunch with a few of our friends, but seeing that we'll be leaving in two days, we stay home and enjoy each other's company.

I still BBQ some burgers after wiping the foot of snow off the top of the grill, then I play with Abigail before her nap. I snooze a little on the couch while Maggie replays the first season of *Friends* on the DVD player. I'm sure she will have gone through the entire series by the time I get back.

I will, however, meet up at the local bar later tonight and have a few beers with the Team. Everyone should be there. Though Jared may, and probably should, sit this one out. It's a tradition to get together before a mission and let loose, and since it's our only day off, we'll make the best of it.

"You sure you don't want to go? I'm sure we can get a babysitter for Abigail." I tried to coax Maggie one last time.

"No, you guys go have your fun. It's y'all's thing. You know how I am with babysitters. Plus, I have something I've been itching to do for a while anyway."

"I've heard that before." I smack her ass on my way to the kitchen to drop off my dirty cup.

"As a matter of fact, it's sitting on the table, ready to go as we speak."

"Really?" I peek around the corner.

She's a very talented painter. Painted up until the time Abigail was born, but once she popped out, time away from her just wasn't worth it. Maggie wanted to spend every second of her day with her. And when she went down for a nap, Maggie did the same. Her painting took a back seat to everything else, stored in a closet collecting dust.

"Maybe you should paint a self-nude portrait for me, you know for the road." I give her a wink and a look that says, "I very much want you naked right now." She looks hot in her tight jeans and a snug sweater that hangs off her left shoulder, exposing a red bra strap.

"I'm glad you think that I'm talented enough to paint that much detail on something you could fit in your back pocket." She wraps her arms around me, teasing me like she's going to kiss me.

I swing her around so Abigail doesn't see my hands grabbing Maggie's ass. "Abigail is right there," she scolds.

I could take her to bed right now, rip her clothes off, and be done in two minutes. Something is happening below, thanks to her seductive eyes.

"I love you," she says as she stares into my eyes, bringing her hands down to the very delicate area that is already on the rise.

"Girl," I whisper into her ear. "You keep that up, and I'm going to personally go out there right now and find a babysitter so I can finish what you're starting."

She lets out a quiet, breathy laugh and continues searching with her hands in all the right places. I glance back, trying to keep it together, but mostly to ensure Abigail isn't paying attention to what her mother is doing.

Maggie only makes it worse with her hands gripping me tight. Seeing that Abigail is distracted with a toy, I shimmy the two of us over into the kitchen, picking her up and placing her on the counter. I lift her sweater just above the tops of her perfectly round breasts, revealing the full front view of her red bra. I lean in, my mouth salivating for the taste of her skin. My tongue dances across her breast, leaving a shiny, wet streak. I unbutton her pants, and just as I start to slide my fingers underneath the lace of her underwear, a little voice screams from the living room.

"Mommy, where are you?"

I attempt to pull my hand away, but Maggie grabs my hand, forcing it back to where I was going initially. I stroke one finger over her soft folds that reveal she's already wet for me. She bites my bottom lip, keeping me close. I remove my hand and thrust my hips into hers. She wraps her legs around me.

"What's wrong, big boy?"

"You really want her to see us in this position?"

I'm one of the most inappropriate people out there, but there are some things that maybe I won't do with a kid in the other room. She leans farther back on the counter, raising her hands and grabbing her breasts, pushing them together erotically.

"I guess we'll just have to wait then." Maggie then pulls her bra down just enough to show her hardened nipples, raising an eyebrow.

"You're going to make me explode right here, right now, if you keep this up."

"Mommy, come play with me," Abigail yells out.

"Coming, babe. Give me a second." Maggie releases her bra, and it folds back up over her budded nipples, but before she can lower her sweater, I catch one in my mouth and suck gently, making her gasp. "Feels like daddy may only need a second," Maggie softly whispers into my ear.

"Okay," Abigail replies cheerfully.

Maggie grabs my chin to bring me to her lips in a crushing kiss while unraveling her legs from around my waist. I take a step back, taking her in, wanting her. She climbs off the counter, and we both adjust ourselves, but Maggie pulls me back in.

"I'm so wet right now. My panties are soaked." Her warm whispers makes my bones shake. She licks my ear to finish off the exchange.

"You're killing me." I take a few steps back. I have to walk away. She continues her tempting smile as I keep walking back, still facing her. "Love you, babe!"

After another moment and another adjustment, I give Abigail a kiss on the head, grab my jacket, and head toward the door. Maggie follows me, making sure to get one last grab before I leave. I could only let out a deep grumble and do my best to keep it together.

I try not to get any more excited than I already am. "You want me to bring you back anything?" I ask, and after hearing it out loud, I probably should have been clearer with my choice of words.

With her hand back on my package, she says, "All I want is this," as she rubs me hard.

"Offer still stands to take it to the bathroom?" She shakes her head and motions toward Abigail. "Fine, you're missing out. You can get your fill later. No, you WILL get your fill later." I love the tease.

"Call out to the bar if you need anything." I kiss her hard, then run out of there as fast as I can so I don't get stuck again.

***

It's a blistering ten-minute walk from my house to the Just North of Hell bar, which is great since it gives me the time to get things settled down. The bar is nothing fancy, but they have some of the best locally crafted beers this side of The River. Their food isn't bad either. I clutch my light jacket and speed up, realizing I should have worn a much thicker coat. I was too distracted to realize I was an idiot.

The warmth of the inside blasts my face as I open the door. I take in the room to see who's shown up. I remove my beanie and let my ears adjust to the awful music playing from the jukebox. Several of the guys are playing a game of pool in the back. It's much livelier than I would have thought for a Sunday night.

The guys notice me, and I give them a nod and hold up one finger, letting them know I'll be over in a minute. I head for the bar and wedge myself between a couple of barstool commandos reminiscing about the good ol' days, then spot Max, the owner. He's always tormenting me with his new beers or liquors or whatever the hell he's concocted. Last time I tried one, I was sick for three days. It may have been the beer, not quite sure, but I blame him every time, regardless. It gets me free beers.

"Dodson, my man, you gotta try this new one," he yells, eyeing me from the far end of the bar. His slinky frame runs back and forth between the customers. For someone who's not in shape, he sure can move. He's younger than he looks, with a head full of long gray hair.

"No. I don't have to try anything," I yell back, shaking my head.

"But I've been perfecting it for two months now."

"Really? Have you forgotten what happened to me the last time I tried one of your crazy concoctions? I was shittin' liquids for three days. The wife wasn't too happy about having to babysit my ass either."

"Yeah, I'm still not so sure that was my beer that did it. Anyway, this one is much, much better. Better ingredients. I have a new farmer providing me with some new barley." He makes it sound like there should be a guarantee along with it.

"My stomach still churns every time I drive by this shithole, Max."

"I promise you'll like it. It has a hint of apple," he says as he pinches his fingers together like he's some kind of chef.

"What's it called?" I'm unconvinced.

"Ah...I don't know. I don't have a name for this one just yet. Still working on it."

"You don't have a name for it? What kind of beer crafter are you?"

"The best there is."

"I doubt that. I've yet to try any other places." He pours me a small glass from the tap. "I didn't say I wanted anything."

He slides the glass closer. I lean in to smell it and pucker.

"Max, I swear, if this fucks me up, you're going to be eating food from a tube the rest of your life. I'm leaving in two days, and if this keeps me from going, you better get used to drinking your meals." I look up and happen to notice a stage reflected in the mirrors behind the bar. I turn around and raise my glass. "What is this setup?" I do everything I can to delay the inevitable.

"A band is going to play in a little bit."

"No shit! When did you start this?"

"Trying something new. Attract some new customers."

"Customers? You're the only bar around here for like two hundred miles. What, are you trying to get the angry housewives in here?" He just laughs. I'm pretty sure he's single and loving that lifestyle.

I take another look around. There are some new faces here tonight, a lot of women in particular. Ones I haven't even seen around town.

"Seems to be working. Just don't advertise your crappy beer or whatever the hell it is that you call it, and I'm sure you'll do just fine." I take another sniff.

"You'll be fine. You're a big, strong man," Max says.

"Damn right, I'm strong!" I say with a little sarcasm. "Okay, I'm only taking one sip." I tilt the glass just enough to wet my lips and spit out what little came out.

"Are you fucking kidding me, Max? Give me my usual. Have people actually been drinking this crap? It's...too fruity."

"You don't like it? I told you it had a hint of apple. It's very popular with the ladies."

"Do I look like a fucking lady to you? Jesus, Max. Just go get me my usual, will you? And I have a name for it. Shitty Apple Cider."

I look down at the end of the bar and see my old friend Charlie standing there with a group of people. I walk up from behind, removing his cap and revealing his shaggy hair, then pinch his ass. I say in my best girly-man voice, "Charlie, why haven't you called?"

He whips around. "Well, shit! Look who it is," he says with his country twang. He's one of those guys who likes the party life.

"How have you been? Where do they have you stationed these days?" I ask. "It sure has been a long time."

We met years ago when the two of us were stationed at the same outpost. We've been through some tough shit. Nearly lost the post from an attack in the middle of the night one summer. The night crew wasn't keeping watch as they should have been, and we woke up to gunfire. Half of the men were dead by the time we rushed out the door of the barracks.

"Man, I can't complain. They've got my ass way out in BFE, the Fargo outpost in North Dakota. We barely see any action way up there."

"Damn. Who'd you piss off?"

"I know, right." We both laugh. "I actually prefer that post to some of the others." We both give each other a look of agreement. Several posts out there see nonstop action in the summer months. So much so that rarely does anyone ever go back after their hitch. "Is Maggie with you?" He looks around.

"No, not tonight. She never really liked coming to these things. Not her scene, and since we still have a few days until we head out, she decided to pass."

"That's why I'm single." He smiles and raises his beers, one in each hand. "That's right. I heard you guys are about to go on a run. I sure would hate to be you right now." He takes a long swig.

"Yeah, thanks. The Major wants us to check out Fort Hood before winter's gone. See what's down there and maybe head back next winter if we like what we see. I'll put in a good word for you and maybe you can go on the next trip."

"Fuck that." He takes another long swig, shaking his head.

"Hey, not to move off the subject, but are you guys playing tonight?"

I did want to change the subject, though. The last thing I want to think or talk about right now is this damn mission. I'm here to let loose, relax, then go home and take care of my wife.

"Yeah, we call ourselves Better Days. We're going to jump on here in a few minutes. We have some new material we've been working on. Just getting some drinks in before we take the stage."

"I remember you saying something about having a band a while back. Are we going to see a tour coming up soon?" He laughed.

I glance at the small stage, somewhat impressed. They must have raided an old theater or something with the equipment they have stacked.

"Like a true rock star, Charlie." He lifts his glass and nods his head. "I'll catch you later before I head out. It was good seeing you, man."

"Same. You guys be safe down there. Oh, make sure you do see me before you leave. We have CDs on the stage," he says, overly excited. "Give you something to listen to on the way down. Maybe it'll frighten away those fucking Joscos."

"If it's anything like the previous music I've heard you play, I don't doubt that one bit."

I leave Charlie with the groupies and meet up with the guys playing pool, all hanging on tight to their girls. Makes me bummed that Maggie didn't come. They see me coming, and before I reach them, they raise their empty glasses up in the air, screaming and yelling, signaling me to bring them more beers. I walk to the bar and order a round of Max's shitty apple cider before going over. This will be the last time those fuckers ask me for more drinks. As the night progresses, more and more people pour into the bar. Sean shows up shortly after and gets a chance to try out Max's beer as well. He damn near spewed chunks across the pool table to my delight.

I stay for several hours and get a good buzz before going home to fuck my wife—twice.

CHAPTER ELEVEN

(Major Oliver White—U.S. Marines)

Sunday, January 19, 2048

The brutal seventeen-hour drive to Wetmore, Michigan has left my aging body feeling defeated. My body aches in places I didn't even know possible, like the muscles in my fingers and knuckles. I had to loosen my death grip from around the jostling steering wheel after turning off onto the dirt road that leads to my cabin. The bumps and dips are too much for these old, beaten-down hands. It didn't help that halfway through the snow-covered icy roads of Wisconsin, I had to change out the chained tires for a set of tracks due to the deep snow, four torturous hours I'll never get back.

Every mile after that felt like something was telling me to turn around, like a posted warning sign saying, "Do Not Enter." Maybe it was the fact that if I got stuck out here, there'd be no one to rescue me in a timely manner. I'd be a frozen meat-sicle before someone came across my lifeless body that had been partially devoured by wildlife.

Not too many people live this far north, so road maintenance isn't quite up to speed with what we have back in Omaha. Small groups have settled in nearby towns along the way, and they help keep most of the main roads passable during the winter months. If I let them know ahead of time, they're usually good about clearing the roads all the way to my cabin, a nice bonus of being in this position. I didn't hassle them this time since it was such short notice.

A tall, white pine marks the final turn of the long stretch leading up to the cabin, and a wave of relief swoops over me. It's amazing

130

how quickly your mind can rejuvenate your body when your destination is within grasp. My back and fingers almost feel normal again as the engine muscles the four-thousand-pound jeep forward, my headlights leading the way through the narrow turns, the overgrowth scraping the vehicle all around me.

Minutes later, the quaint, two-bedroom, thousand-square-foot log cabin comes into view. It needs some work, as the porch awning droops slightly in the middle from the weight of the snow over the years, but even the sight of the distressed cabin recharges me even more. Seclusion is exactly what I need. It's nestled just a few short miles from Lake Superior, where trout fishing is second to none, and with the hopes of Ann visiting in the morning, this should be the perfect getaway for both of us.

The snow crunches beneath the tracks as the jeep comes to a stop. I leave it running to power the roof-mounted LED light bar that'll illuminate the front until I can get the generator running and turn on the few lights within the cabin. I step outside, pausing to take in the pine-filled air, stretch for a long minute with my arms far above my head, and let a sigh escape in relief. I let it all soak in, the sharp, fresh air clearing my lungs in another lengthy breath. There's not a cloud in the sky. The stars shine bright, with little halos surrounding each one. The black void around them is deeper and darker than I remember. Without the brightness of tainted light pollution, it's an appreciated view that will always be number one in my book. It's quiet, aside from a gentle wind that rustles a few tree branches together. Cold, but not the bone chilling cold that hurts your face.

My relaxing moment is short lived. The covered porch—where two rocking chairs just peek through—is blanketed in four feet of snow blocking the front door.

I drudge through the thick snow to a shed off to the side of the cabin where my generators are stored. First things first, I need to get these generators warmed up and going, then I can start clearing the snow from around the cabin. With Ann getting here sometime in the morning, having the place warm and cozy for her arrival will be welcoming. When I advised her of my intentions, she was quick to close her restaurant for a few days to be here with me. With her up here in this neck of the woods and me being down in Omaha, we don't get to see each other as often as we would like. It's a conversation I know is coming my way.

It takes an hour to get the surrounding area cleared to where I can come and go freely between the cabin, the shed, and the jeep. Next up are space heaters as well as a fire in the living room fireplace. I found this place fifteen years ago, and because whoever built it had country living in mind, they put a fireplace in the master bedroom, something I hope will spark a fiery passion between the two of us during our short stay here. Ann's favorite pastime is lying snuggled up in a soft, comfortable blanket next to a cozy fire with a glass of wine and a romantic novel in her hand. She loves the sound of crackling wood, and if the mood hits her just right, she could read an entire novel in one sitting.

Even though some of the elements of living out here would be considered rough, I have some luxuries in place. I check the propane tank at the rear making sure it's still full from my last visit, as well as the plumbing to ensure the cold hasn't damaged any of the pipes. The last thing I want is to have to repair broken hoses when I should be relaxing per the doc's order. It's not a complex system, but everything looks to be in order. I light the pilot to start heating up the one-hundred-gallon water tank. The first thing Ann is going to want to do is to soak in the oversized clawfoot bathtub, another fine feature built into the cabin. Twenty-five years ago, this place would have been on the cover of some opulent, country living magazine with all the fancy elements and extravagance that Ann and I are reaping the benefits of.

I take a seat in front of the fire in a rustic, dark brown leather chair that has been perfectly formed to my body. With the lack of distractions, it doesn't take long for the guilt to set in as I watch the small embers flutter in the air when the wood pops. In two days, sixty of our best soldiers will be heading to Texas on the biggest mission ever conducted post-Turning. McCauley and Dodson are two of the finest Marines I've ever had the pleasure of commanding. I trust them. I have to. I hate that damn doctor for telling me I needed to get away, which reminds me. I grab my backpack and reach for my meds, and in doing so, my hand grazes the bottle of Mary's Moonshine. I pop in a few pills and take a swig, closing my eyes as the warm burn travels down my throat and feeling damn good.

I continue to drink, keeping my mind occupied by grabbing my hunting rifle from a custom walnut cabinet that was here when I commandeered this place. For as long as I can remember, before every hunt I've ever been on, I would meticulously clean my rifle, verifying everything was aligned and functioning properly. It's a tradition that dates back to my very first hunt with my father when he was home. For several years now, I've been eyeing a massive whitetail whom I've affectionately named Bucky. I've never had a clean shot to take him down. Maybe he's still around, but maybe not. Seeing as I didn't bring that much food with me, I hope I see something.

***

The moment the sun peeks over the horizon, and after getting the coffee going, I saunter over to the wooden shed, and for better lighting, I push the snowmobile out to an area that I had cleared the night before. After a visual inspection of everything, checking the gas and oil, and doing routine maintenance stuff, I then prime it, turn the key, and throttle the trigger.

"Hot damn, would you look at that! Started right up." I patted the seat like a dog that did as it was told.

While it warms up, I slide out a cargo sled, hook it up, and load it with bags of corn along with some tools, making sure it's secure. I also add several weapons and plenty of ammo; one can never be too safe out here. Wolves, mountain lions, and bears are just a few predators that roam these parts and would love nothing more than to make me their meal. Back inside, I put on base layers and thicker clothes then grab a thermal tumbler, filling it to the max with black coffee and placing it in my backpack along with a few pre-made snacks.

After donning a helmet and a pair of gloves, I head to a couple of clearings about three miles from the cabin. Three hundred yards of open land expands about fifty feet wide. It's a clear path for hunting anything that comes walking by. This is exactly what I need. The sights, the smell of open land. Not a soul in sight. This is relaxation.

At the first hunting spot, I clear out the snow before spreading the corn out in a small area, then check a couple of deer stands that were set up a few years back in the trees. The quietness allows me to not think about a damn thing except for that perfect shot. In my mind, Bucky grazes the land before coming to a stop. Standing tall, his profile view makes for a perfect magic triangle shot. This may be the trip I needed to seal the deal and retire and let Nolan take over. With over thirty years of wearing the uniform, it might just be the end.

I imagine the rest of my life with Ann, moving up here, maybe helping her with her restaurant. That wouldn't last long, I'm sure. I'm good with a knife, but I'd be more inclined to stab someone for pissing me off, and Ann would have to fire me. Maybe I wouldn't help her, but there are plenty of other projects going on up here that I could manage. Take a seat in the back for a change.

A herd of deer stampede in front of me, not even fifty yards away. I stop, turn off the engine, and watch them frolic about, the fawns chasing one another. I pull out the thermos, pour a cup, and lean back. Couldn't think of a better spot to sit and take it in. They're smaller than what I want, so I make no attempt to shoot any of them. This gives me hope that I'll see something tomorrow.

Ann will love the untouched white, fluffy snow. I'm sure she'll tell me about her childhood while we're here, as always—about all the snowmen and forts she and her older brother made every winter and the snowball fights. She hated that she never won, but now she would love nothing more than to see her brother throwing a snowball at her again. It's a good thing she didn't know me back then because her brother would have hated me. She would have never lost one fight with me by her side.

The deer finally skip out of the area, so I finish up my coffee and follow suit. Reaching my second hunting spot, I clear out the snow, spread the corn, and check the stands for a clear line of sight. The weather is damn near perfect right now—not too cold to be up in the stand—though tomorrow morning, I'm sure the temps will be in the lower twenties. I should be warm in all my layers, and if I have to field dress a deer, that'll be a good workout to help keep the warm blood flowing.

My mind was carefree all the way back, and before I knew it, I was pulling up to the cabin, where a maroon, four-wheel-drive Jeep Cherokee was parked outside.

She must have heard me pulling up. As I open the door, her slim figure leans in the doorway to a candlelit bedroom. My body tingles down below and my heart beats faster in anticipation. She's draped in a long tan coat that's open, exposing her naked body from her stomach to her crossed legs and high black heels. She drops it to the floor the second the door closes and says, "Oops!"

She stares at me with those big brown eyes and parted, hungry lips that suggest she didn't come to chat. Her long, brown hair curls perfectly around her breasts, her hard nipples standing at attention. Something deep inside me awakes and I tear off my jacket and anything I can quickly remove. I grab her hard and kiss her smiling mouth in a movement that says I'm going to consume her. Loneliness can do things to a person, and this was the only way I knew how to make it subside.

She lets out a small sound signaling she wants more. I grab her up in my arms and kick off her shoes, wrapping her legs around my waist. I push her against the wall and lightly bite the sensitive skin of her neck, the sandalwood and vanilla smell of her hair arousing me even more. She had already unbuttoned my pants. I thrust myself into her hard. She groans throwing her head back, which provokes me even more. I slam into her repeatedly until my last thrust brings me home. I could feel her tighten in waves over me. I'll have to pay her back later, so she's fully satisfied. After a few more deep breaths, I kiss her forehead and lower her to the ground, my pants in a pool around my ankles.

"Hi." She smiles, tracing my lips and chin with her finger and watching my mouth.

"Hey, yourself," I say breathlessly.

"So, how have you been, Major White?" she says, speaking like a mistress as she glides to the bathroom to clean up. The candlelight highlights the curves of her body, which provokes me as she turns the corner. I consider following her in there, but maybe I should wait a bit for round two later tonight. I'm not as young as I used to be, and as much as I want it, I may not have full cooperation for a quick turnaround.

She's asked about what I do and wants in my head. She deserves more; I just can't give it to her. I have yet to figure out why she stays with me. If I weren't so scared of the answer, I'd ask. I know she's lonely, and maybe I'm her someone else too. I don't ask her many questions. Shit. I've taken too long to answer. She's going to know that something is off. She steps back out after a very pregnant pause.

"What is it? You can tell me things, you know," she says in a weak voice. *Fuck, here we go again.* This happy reunion is shorter than usual.

"I've just had a lot on my plate these days, Ann. There are things happening that I don't want you to worry about." This might cause more tension, but I say it anyway as I put myself back together.

"You think I don't worry, regardless? You might as well just tell me, Oliver." Even though she's still naked, all the glamour from earlier has dissipated.

"We're sending troops to Texas, and we have a lot of movement happening out there. I should be there, not here!"

I feel responsible for those men, and I may have just sent every one of them to their grave and damned us all. Because of the tight security we've been keeping since we moved up north, most have never actually seen a Josco or a Mod unless they knew someone who Turned or experienced those few years firsthand. I knew that Ann had seen horrors, not because she had told me, but because when she sleeps, she sometimes talks and screams. It's all too familiar to me. I guess it's one thing that makes us a good couple. We both have demons that sneak out once in a while.

"I'm sorry. I didn't know." She sounded defeated. "I'm not naïve. I don't understand why you can't just tell me this stuff. You think I don't know that things are happening out there? You think shutting me out makes *us* better?"

She doesn't realize I can't care about *us*. Not because she isn't a wonderful woman or that I don't enjoy her. I just refuse to get more attached than I already am. I can't afford to lose another person in my life.

"Ann, you know I love you."

She only half accepts this answer with a big sigh and a matching eye roll as she retreats back into the bathroom.

"You hungry?" I ask her. Food's our neutral ground.

"I'm starving."

I get the small wood-burning grill going outside. Ann brought two pieces of chicken breast that have been marinating in a lemon pepper sauce. After slicing up some zucchini and sprinkling on some salt and pepper, I throw it all on the grill. The sizzling sound jumpstart my tastebuds.

Returning inside, I look over toward the end of the counter. *You're next.* The bottle of Mary's Moonshine asks for my attention.

I twist off the cap and pour two small glasses. I take a sip and light several candles and lanterns, setting the table while the food cooks. I offer Ann the other glass of moonshine.

"I know you have a lot on your plate, and I just want you to know I understand. I didn't come here to give you a hard time or get into any arguments. I know what you've been through. I just want you to know I'm here for you." She grabs my hand. I don't pull back and only nod in response. It does feel nice. Maybe I'm already too deep and I'm kidding myself. We stand there sipping our drinks before I return to the grill. She opens a bottle of full-bodied red wine and pours a glass with a heavy hand.

Dinner was relatively quiet with the fire doing most of the talking. After we're done, she opens up about the restaurant and that she's been toying with the idea of creating a new menu. She was an executive chef at some fancy restaurant in Fort Worth during the Turning. Apparently, that's what swanky places do on occasion, change it up.

In one big gulp, she finishes the last of her bottle.

"I know I have control issues," I say, smirking in an attempt to continue to loosen the mood. Her eyes squint just enough to lure me in.

"Sometimes I like that control." Her voice was soft, and her eyes investigate mine. She raises an eyebrow and glances at the counter, setting her wine glass down. One of her fingers lightly grazes my hand suggestively, and from under the table, her foot finds its way to my lap.

Her sexual appetite is stronger than mine, or maybe it's just her need for intimacy. She gets up from the table and I push my chair back. She prances around and grabs the front of my shirt to pull me in for a kiss. Her tongue is aggressive and the length of me rises with little protest. Still leaning over me, she unbuttons my pants and changes her focus. Fuck. Her mouth and tongue take in every bit of me. I force her back to pull her thin, black sweater over her head, exposing tight nipples, which I proceed to lick and grab. She stands up while I continue to kiss her stomach. I slide her silky lounge pants down past her hips, kissing each side. She'd forgone underwear in a premeditated—but unnecessary—effort to seduce me. I finally stand and guide her to the counter she'd been eyeing. I spread her legs wide and land face-deep between them. I lick and tease as she moans for more. With her legs shaking, she grabs hold of my hair. Her moans only grow louder as she orgasms, throwing her head back and demanding, "I need you in me now!"

I pick her up and carry her over to the fireplace, falling onto a pallet of blankets, our bodies intertwined while the fire pops and crackles. Our temperatures rise and sweat forms between our bodies as I pump into her, my back moist with perspiration. She takes control and rolls me onto my back. Small beads of sweat trickle down her neck and between her breasts. Her nails scratch down my chest, and the motion of her body sends me into complete bliss as I release into her uncontrollably.

Breathless, she rolls off in a heap. We spent the next hour just lying there, panting, sweat and all. I watch the fire go from burning like the sun to a match on its last gulp of oxygen. Ann was the first to finally get up to get dressed. I resigned and did the same and then put more wood on the fire.

I sit in the leather chair while Ann snuggles into a fleece blanket in front of the fireplace with another glass of wine and a book. She looks back, her eyebrows raised, hinting that she wasn't finished with me just yet. I can't. I'm too tired. I shake my head, sink further into my chair, and lay back to watch shadows dance across the ceiling from the sway of the fire. My mind switches to the hunt tomorrow morning, dreaming of Bucky. I shut my eyes and go through the checklist in my head to ensure I had already packed everything I would need. I really don't know how long I was out before I awoke to a pair of hands in my pants and Ann staring deep into my eyes.

CHAPTER TWELVE

(Major Oliver White—U.S. Marines)

Monday, January 20, 2048

If it hadn't been for the snow sliding off the roof and crashing outside our window just before sunrise, I'd more than likely still be sleeping right now. Odd how things like that just happen when you need them to. It also didn't help that Ann's sex drive last night was that of a twenty-one-year-old college girl, and after drinking one and a half bottles of wine, she was relentless. She had more stored-up energy than a thousand stretched-out rubber bands just waiting to be sling-shotted. I need to find out who the author is for those romance novels she reads and get every book they ever wrote.

I did my best not to disturb her. She was still fully charged because just as I was exiting the room, she called out to me, slithering one of her long, silky-smooth legs out from under the thick blanket. She wasn't ready for me to leave just yet. She begged me to stay a little longer for what would have been round four. She pulled the white sheet down, exposing one of her breasts, then slowly slid the blanket across, exposing her waistline and revealing her red lace panties. It was tempting, but if there was any hope for me to stay up late for another double feature tonight, I needed the rest. My face must have said it all as she rolled over and snuggled back under the blanket, playfully uttering, "Fine, I'll be waiting."

Ten minutes after leaving the cabin, my mind finally shifts from Ann to the hunt. With the cold wind whipping around me as I navigate the terrain out to my first clearing, I can already feel the forest air recharging my batteries. Fresh deer tracks tell me that a small herd must have galloped through last night. It gives me hope that today will be a good day of hunting, and then I can finish it off with a victory fuck.

After setting up in a fully enclosed tree stand blind, the sound of rustling branches gains my full attention. Seconds later, three does dart out of the forest, not fifty feet from where I'm positioned. They zigzag across the clearing as though they're playing tag, the two leaders trying to evade the one at the back who's attempting to tag them. It was only a few moments before they disappeared into the trees on the other side. I'll stay out here all day, even if it is just to admire the view, my place of peace.

An hour in, my stomach starts to grumble. I put the binoculars down and quietly reach down into a bag, digging for a snack, when I catch movement about three hundred yards east of my position at the far end of the clearing. After patiently sitting, watching, and listening for the slightest rustle of the brush, I finally have something. And whatever it is, it's definitely bigger than a deer. I pick my binoculars back up, forgetting about my aching stomach.

The sight of dark brown fur comes and goes as it slowly treks just beyond the tree line, giving me a tiny glimpse of what's to come. I can only hope that whatever it is continues this way. I follow as it methodically patrols its path, cautious with every step it takes, stopping every few feet to monitor its surroundings, teasing me for the longest time. Then its head peeks out.

Oh, shit! I'll take that any day!

I set my binoculars down and reach for my Winchester, never taking my eyes off him. I place the rifle gently on a support ledge of the tree stand, the barrel barely sticking out of the front opening. My heartbeat picks up as I watch the bull moose through the Leupold VX-Freedom scope. His antlers scrape and push the branches out of the way, not phased one bit. I steady my breathing to calm my nerves while I wait for him to come a little closer. He walks just inside the tree line, pacing himself and heading straight toward me. He's careful, pausing every few steps and looking around. Then he walks out of the security of the trees, his massive antlers pushing the branches aside like twigs. He takes his time, stopping to nibble on a dead willow bush before fully exposing his body to me.

A hundred and fifty yards away, he stands right where I laid the corn. He shifts his body as though he knows where I am, facing me straight on. Then, just as he lowers his massive head to the ground, something startles him from behind. His head perks straight up and one ear flickers back. His rear end shuffles to the side, turning his attention in the direction of the sound. I click off the safety, my breathing slow, my nerves calm, and my eyes focused on where I need to hit. His profile is ideal for a clean shot. I exhale while placing my finger on the trigger, it only takes four and half pounds of pressure to pull back. Steadying the rifle, I continue to focus dead on the target area just behind the front left leg, a third of the way up his body. This should puncture both lungs and, with a little luck, the heart as well. With an effective shot, the bull should be dead within sixty seconds of being struck.

I pull the trigger and the bullet explodes out of the barrel at twenty-eight-hundred feet per second. The shot echoes, and the recoil of the rifle thrusts my right shoulder back. At this range, it took less than a quarter of a second to reach its mark. It's a perfect shot. Right where I wanted it to hit. The moose jolts and takes off into the woods.

Fuck yeah. I couldn't help but smile. My heart picks up speed and I wait a few moments to calm down before climbing down from the stand.

I rip the cover off my snowmobile and start tracking the massive animal. I follow a short distance from where the first drop of blood starts, but it looks like my luck will be short-lived. I kill the engine as the dense forest refuses to let me pass. I grab my rifle and follow the blood trail roughly twenty yards from the clearing before coming across his lifeless body.

"WOW!"

I take a moment to admire its beauty and make sure he's dead. He must be at least twelve hundred pounds. The antlers alone extend a good five feet across. I had my tastebuds set on some deer jerky, but this will be just fine. Ann will be excited too; she can make some amazing dinners and probably take a good portion back to the restaurant. Patrons will be excited to see it on the menu, and if Nolan is lucky, I might give him a few pounds of meat as well. There will be plenty to go around.

Back to the snowmobile, I grab the tools I need to field dress the massive bull. I make a small clearing in the snow around the animal and lay a tarp down, with the tools all laid out in an orderly fashion. I realize I'm not going to have enough bags to put all these cut sections of meat in—wasn't expecting to shoot a mammoth moose this morning.

It takes me several hours to get it done. With all this meat, I'll have to make another trip with the sled. I take two bags, making sure to grab the best meat first, like the filets, and strap them on the back of the snowmobile. I can only take about two hundred pounds without the sled.

As I'm walking back to the moose, a strange feeling comes over me. Almost like a sense of uncertainty. *Fuck, where is it coming from? Another low blood pressure thing?* I take several deep breaths before continuing on in hopes that it might shake this feeling. This R&R is supposed to be working, but why isn't it? The feeling only gets worse the longer I walk.

With my mind on my recent medical condition, I didn't pay attention to the danger right in front of me until it was too late. Subtle movement within my peripheral causes me to freeze in panic. My mystery predators expel foggy breaths like a chimney stack. I don't want to look up, but I have no choice, and with my head tilted down, I move only my eyes. Their lips curl up with a ferocious grin. Blood-soaked foam drips from the fur around their mouths. They'd already been feeding on the moose that I shot. Normally, they wouldn't challenge me. They must be hungry and see me as an easy target alone. There's no doubt they smelled blood in the air.

FUCK, my rifle! I look toward the moose carcass and see it leaning against the tree where three wolves stand facing me. My sidearm is back at the snowmobile, but I'd be dead before I even made it ten feet. All I have is my knife. Even as sharp as it is, it won't do me any good. Not against a pack of large wolves. Their heads are low in a defensive posture and their fur stands on end. Their deep growls vibrate my insides.

I slowly reach for my knife, and every inch closer I get to it, the more aggressive they become, their instincts kicking in. My heart races. Sweat drips down my back. To my right, one of them shifts to the side, and then one to the left. This is it. They're getting ready to attack, surrounding me. Just when I thought it couldn't get any worse, the crunching sound of movement in the snow comes up from behind. *Just how big is this pack and how hard up for food are they?*

I'm a fucking idiot for leaving my guns behind. I got too comfortable. Complacent. There's no time for regret; I need to think. I won't go down without a fight. I may die, but I'm taking one or two of these fuckers with me. I turn my head slowly, just enough to see two salt-and-pepper-colored wolves behind me. I can even make out several more behind them.

Fuck. Fuck. Fuck. This is going to be painful. I just hope it goes quick when it does.

I close my eyes and say a quick prayer hoping that it's heard. I've been religiously absent for a very long time, so it feels awkward but necessary in this moment.

"Well, let's get this shit over with, shall we?" I yell at them.

Without further hesitation, I turn my body to face the two directly behind me and head straight for them. The black one lunges at my face. All I could see were his sharp white teeth chomping the air ferociously.

I wanted so badly to shove my knife into his guts, but everything happens so fast. I drop my knife the second the force of his one-hundred-and-fifty-pound body tackles me and knocks me to the ground. He's faster than I expected. The wind knocks out of me, landing square on my back with him on top. His right paw grazes my temple, though I feel no pain at the moment. Adrenaline pumps through my body like a jet engine punching its afterburners. Both of my hands grip tight around his neck. I grab his fur, trying to hold him still as he shakes back and forth violently. His power is more than I can handle. I exert every ounce of strength to keep the rapid chomping of his mouth that's not even an inch from my face from tearing into my flesh. His warm breath smells of blood and raw moose meat. With all the training the USMC put me through, getting out of this situation wasn't one of them.

I only see one option ahead of me. It'll require some sacrifice and will most certainly come with consequences, but I need that knife. It's the only way I'll have a chance to survive. I won't last long with his energy. The only problem is I can't let go of his neck without paying the price. If I take one hand off, it'll be over within seconds, my neck on the receiving end of some very sharp canines. I risk a quick look to my right, searching for the knife, but my eyes are distracted by another fight altogether. Either I'm hallucinating or everything I thought up until this point was a misdirection that we played into. Even the wolf pauses to observe my distraction.

I was wondering why the other white wolf hadn't begun gnawing at some part of my body. It's because it's in the same position that I'm in—fighting, trying to stay alive. The only difference is that a five-hundred-pound Josco stands atop it in the process of ripping off a leg. But as much as I would love to watch that right now, I have more pressing matters.

My focus draws back to my wolf and what I will have to sacrifice to get the knife that I desperately need right now. My hand? I'm right-handed, so it'll have to be my left. I can live without a few digits on my left hand. Compared to the alternative, losing a few fingers is nothing.

My left hand shoots up to grip the bottom of the beast's mouth. The wolf instinctively bites down, sinking his teeth in. The pressure of his bite from both sides crushes down, causing excruciating pain. Working past it, I grip the bottom of his jaw and guide his snout back and away from my face. His bite sinks deeper, puncturing my palm and several fingers all the way through. With my hand burning from the freshly torn skin and quivering damaged tendons, the pain intensifies, escaping my body in the form of a guttural scream.

Through gritted teeth, I will my right hand to release from his fur, and I contort my body in every possible way to get closer to the knife. Seconds feel like minutes, and with each one that passes, my strength dwindles while the wolf seems to only be getting stronger. He shifts and violently shakes his head back and forth in consecutive blows, tearing my hand apart even more, so much so that I'm scared he will take my entire hand.

My search finally yields results. I feel something, but the slippery handle only gets pushed away as the tips of my fingers graze it. The snow adds to the difficulty, and I keep pushing it farther and farther away with every failing grasp. The wolf's violent shaking and twisting increases my struggle until one of his jerks nudges me closer. I take hold, gripping the knife.

I stab the wolf in the side over and over, screaming as I do. The once-fierce growl fades into a whimpering cry just as the tension of his bite subsides. My own blood trickles in a steady stream from my hand onto my face. Looking into his vivid green eyes, the lights start to go out, and his strength diminishes as the effects of the six-inch blade take its toll. I shove it deeper, twisting it as it goes in until one final yelp signifies his resignation. My hand continues to tear deeper into his side, taking my remaining strength away. The warmth of his blood soaks down my arm. I lay with the wolf on top of me, my fortitude lacking.

With deep breaths, I muscle up enough power to push his limp body off mine. He lies beside me, whining and clawing at the snow in an attempt to grasp what little life is left in him. Genuinely sorry for our exchange, I watch as he expels his last breath. His eyelids relax, resting in their final position, half-closed.

My left hand lays useless and shredded while I struggle to lean up on my elbows to look around. Eight or so Joscos stand in a half-circle in front of me. Some of them focus on what's left of the wolves, making it look easy. Others take possession of my moose—or their moose now. I know the hierarchy of where I fit into this equation. This is unreal. I blink hard, unable to believe what I'm seeing. The deep, throaty grunts of the Joscos are in sharp contrast to the high-pitched weeping and howling of the surrounded wolves, both sounds echoing loudly. Any living creature within the area would have vacated from the horrible melodies being carried through the dense forest.

My body shakes from the effects of the adrenaline and injuries, but I have to move. I would have fared better with the wolves. The Joscos will chase me down in a matter of seconds, rip my arms off, and use them against me. My mind is devoid of any rational thought of what to do now. My left hand throbs, pounding with each heartbeat. I look in disgust at the mangled mess of what's left. Desperate for relief, I lunge my hand into the snow, stifling a painful grunt of my own.

Frozen in place and covered in blood, I watch the wrath of two beasts gouging into one another, pulling the wolves' limbs with ease from their dead, limp bodies. The ones that are still alive chomp at any Josco appendages they can get at, but their teeth are like feathers on their skin.

As fast as it started, it was over. Several wolves manage to survive, tucking their tails between their legs and running off into the brush.

The Joscos are no longer occupied, so I need to get the fuck out now. I stumble to my feet, taking a step back to regain what's left of my balance. The snow crunches, and I wince at the sound. About five feet from me, one of the Joscos kneeling over a dead wolf turns to look at me. He stands and takes a step toward me with wolf blood dripping from his mouth but quickly turns his head to another like it'd been ordered to stop. None of the others even bat an eye. The one now four feet from me squints a single eye as though it's glaring at me. The other eye is missing. The Joscos are massive, even as they sit hunched over. This pack is different; they're wearing fur-like coats, just like the one Josco that had escaped from the doctor's research facility a week ago. *What the fuck?* It's like they've evolved just enough to realize the cold weather requires additional clothing to keep warm.

The one near me takes a step back and glances down at the blood-soaked knife in my hand. I know he sees it. I'm dumbfounded by their lack of action. For me to stand here and watch all this is beyond anything I could have imagined. No one has ever lived after witnessing something like this or even being in their presence.

The others are busy, except for the one burning a hole into me with his stare. *What could it be thinking? Is he the leader?* Must be. Did he tell the others to leave me alone because he wanted me for himself? Or is it that he's letting his men taste the victory of their fight first and he'll eat what's left, like a true leader. Whatever the reason, I won't last long if I don't get out of here.

I have nothing to lose, so I take a step back and pause. They don't flinch, so I take another and keep on walking just past the Josco that snatched the other wolf that was behind me. He stays in a knelt position and watches me as I stroll on past him.

"It's all yours," I say. Wolf's guts hang from its mouth. *Why are they not attacking me? Are they that satisfied with the meal sitting in front of them?* I've never known a Josco to just stand by idly. I'd even go so far as to describe them as calm.

I continue walking backward while keeping an eye on them, darting my gaze from one to the other until I reach my snowmobile. I jump on, start it, and punch the throttle all the way. I look back once and see a trail of equipment falling from the sled. I'll have to come back for the rifle at some point, but right now, none of it matters.

The snowmobile can't go fast enough. It feels like I'm going at a snail's pace, and if it weren't for the speedometer telling me I was going forty, I wouldn't have believed it. I let out a deep breath. I don't care about the puncture holes in my hand. In fact, I couldn't care less what damage the wolf did. I just want the fuck out of here.

Back inside my cabin, I slam the door, locking the single dead bolt like it would do any good. If there was ever a time to have an anxiety attack, now would be it. I fall to the floor, unable to ground myself.

"Did you shoot something?" Ann asks from the bedroom.

Do I tell her the truth that a pack of Joscos are up here with us, not even three miles away? Or do I lie? So much for rest and relaxation. My heart pounds fiercely. My hands shake so hard I could mix paint.

She glances out from the bedroom. "Oliver, are you okay? She gives me a sideways look, studying me. "Wait, is that blood all over your face? What happened?"

"Wolves. There was a pack of wolves out there just as I was finishing up," I say, shivering.

"Oh my God!" She joins me on the floor. "Your entire body is shaking. Is that your blood?"

"Some of it."

She runs to get a rag and some basic medical supplies. Her face says it all. I know it's bad, but that look makes me think it's worse than I realized.

"I thought I was going to die," I say, closing my eyes from exhaustion.

"Your hand is mauled." She grimaces at the sight. "You're going to need to see a doctor, like now. This is not good. Oh, Oliver."

I raise my trembling left hand and notice my pinky finger is gone and half of my ring finger dangles by the thinnest stretch of skin. Can't believe it's still hanging on, but I think the quick dive into the snow subsided some of the bleeding. The section between my thumb and pointer finger has a good one-inch separation, exposing bone and muscle. The wolf's teeth sliced through it like butter.

"Yep, that's pretty bad." I close my eyes again, lean my head back, and try to breathe normally again.

She gently wraps a clean rag around my palm, trying hard not to cause more damage.

"I need to see George over in Newberry. Immediately."

***

Ann left the room while the doctor and nurse stitched me up. She can't handle watching the needle and thread going in and out of my skin. George, who had met us a few minutes before, sits quietly in the corner. He walks over as the doctor puts the finishing touches on my bandaged hand.

"You got some balls taking on a pack of wolves up here. I'm surprised you only escaped with the loss of one and a half fingers." As the doctor and nurse leave, he takes off his notorious, tan-colored cowboy hat, laying it on the edge of my bed. "I would really like to know how in the hell you survived that. And don't bullshit me."

George stands just under six feet tall and could easily fit right into one of those old Western movies from the 1950s. He studied structural engineering in college and has been up here since we started a series of underground bunker projects on most of these islands in the Great Lakes.

"Yeah, about that." I lean over to look behind him to make sure no one is around. "We need to talk. A pack of wolves wasn't the only thing I saw out there. You're not going to believe this shit, and I'm not so sure I even believe it myself, and I saw it with my own damned eyes."

"This sounds promising. What'd you see, old man?"

"Old man? No older than you, asshole. Listen, there was a pack of Joscos over at my hunting spot."

His eyes widen and he runs his hands through his thinning gray hair. "What? Way up here? In this weather? You're fucking with me, aren't you? Doc gave you the good drugs?"

"I wish. Hand is throbbing with pain." I grimace at the sight of red starting to soak through the bandage. "Anyway, they're the only reason I'm sitting here on this shitty hospital bed talking to you right now. This was supposed to be a relaxing getaway. George, you and everyone up here need to leave. There's no telling how many of them there are. This year has been…" I shake my head, recounting everything that's happened. "They just stared at me. Didn't even move a muscle or threaten to attack, and I just walked out of there."

"No shit. How many did you see?"

"Wolves or Joscos?" I let out a laugh. This is so ridiculous.

"Joscos!"

"I think I saw eight. Could've been more, could've been less. I wasn't keeping count. But one thing for sure, they were different. Clothed differently. None-aggressive. Don't say anything to Ann or anyone else about this just yet. I'll figure out how to tell her, but like I said, you all need to get the hell out of here. It's not safe."

"But what about—"

"Don't worry about the Grand Island Bunker Project. It'll be here when you get back. We just need to figure out what is going on here. You could probably leave the crew out there, as they should be safe to continue. Head over to Mackinac Island and see how things are going out there. We may need these facilities sooner than later."

"Yeah, I've been meaning to do that, but we're so close to getting this one completed. Grand Island is ninety-nine percent complete. Just finishing up a few things. Mackinac and Bois Blanc Island are close as well, maybe eighty-five percent complete. All the other ones, I would put them around fifty percent complete, but they're structurally sound."

"That's good to hear." I shuffle to the edge of the bed. "I need to use a phone to call Nolan and have him get a team put together ASAP. We need to investigate why they're up here."

"They've got an office here you can use. Can you walk?" He laughs.

I give him a look. "It's just my hand. I'm not that fucking crippled."

We both leave the room and walk down the hall to an empty office with a phone.

"How do you suppose they got up here?" George asks.

"Not sure. They could have crossed a frozen part of the river or a low spot. It still doesn't make any sense, though. The cold should be keeping them from being here in the first place. Looks like we need to up our patrols during winters."

George opens the door. "Well, here you go. Let me know if you need anything else. I'll start putting out the word for everyone to bug out until we hear otherwise from you. What should I tell them?"

"I don't know. Maybe say we're going to be running some military exercises and that it's going to be loud over the next few weeks."

"That might work for some, but for others, that won't get them to leave. People are going to start asking questions, especially with short notice like this. They're going to think something is up."

"I'm sure they will. Just think of something, anything. You know them."

George walks out, shutting the door behind him, and I call Nolan. I just hope he's there. Karen answers the phone and transfers me over.

"Hey, it's Oliver."

"You just can't get away from this place, can you? How's your R&R going? Shoot anything yet?"

"That's a story for another time. Look, we have a situation up here. I need you to put together a team and get them up here. It's going to sound like I'm off my rocker, but while I was out hunting, and yes, I did get a moose, and by this time, it's more than likely been devoured by a pack of Joscos."

"What? Are you drunk?"

"Believe me, I wish I was. I want a team up here tonight so they're ready to go first thing tomorrow morning. They'll stay at the Grand Island Bunker. They'll pretty much have the place to themselves. There are still a few work crews up here finishing some things up, but they'll be fine. Unless Joscos have figured out how to navigate the waters."

"Roger that."

"Nolan, keep this quiet. I don't want mass hysteria. Not a word to the guys until they're all up here. The second people find out, all hell will break loose. I've got George sending out a message to those still up here to get out of town. I'm going to drive Ann back home. I'll need transportation. Think you can send something up to Mackinaw County Airport later today?"

"I think I can handle that. I'll send you a message when everything is lined up."

"Thanks."

I hang up the phone just as George walks back in.

"I'm out of here later this afternoon. When will you be at Mackinac Island so I can confirm with Nolan?" I'm annoyed by my current incapacity.

"I'll leave in a few hours," George replies. "Just need to button up a few things. I have a message going out now that the military will be conducting some training exercises and that they need to vacate the area. There are only eighty-seven people up here, so we'll see how it goes."

"I appreciate it. You need anything from me?"

"Can't say that I do right now." He tips his hat to me and leaves the room.

So much for a repeat sex-a-thon. I guess it's good we had several rounds last night. Retirement sounds real fucking good right now.

CHAPTER THIRTEEN

(Petty Officer First Class Jayce Brock—Navy SEAL)

Monday, January 20, 2048

Okay, backpack check, weapons check, ammo check, helmet check.

"I think that covers it." I'm nothing if not meticulous. As part of the rapid deployment force, or RDF, I had only one hour to get my gear loaded and report to Naval Base Patterson, formerly Des Moines International Airport to meet up with the other Team members. Being in a Tier 1 team, we must be ready at a moment's notice. I'm assigned to one of the many RDFs that are strategically positioned along The River. This allows for a quick deployment from our territory to locations within ninety minutes of departure. It was noted that Captain Wilkinson would meet us and ride out with the platoon. *Must be serious.*

Already prepared for such an occasion, I got dressed and was out the door in no time with Hawkeye in tow, a two-year-old Belgian Malinois with traditional tan fur, black ears, and a black snout. He has one not-so-traditional black right paw, as if he had stepped up to his heel in black paint. He's a work in progress, but I've trained him well. He's intelligent, loyal, and as stealthy as a panther hunting for prey.

His tail wags as he darts out the front door, heading straight for the truck and tagging his front paws on the passenger-side running board. He looks back at me, tongue hanging out of the side of his mouth, beckoning me to be in as big of a hurry as he is. If he only knew. He turns in circles, waiting by his door and ready to jump in.

"Alright, alright. Not sure why you're so excited. This isn't what you think it is, bud." I open the door and he leaps into his favorite seat with ease, flinging snow all over the place.

"Hey, man, wipe your paws! You know better." I give him my best stern look but then pat his back as he stares out the window panting.

With the turn of my key, the truck roars to life and while the engine warms up, I load up both of our gear and soon we are on our way. Living just north of the base, it's a short ten-minute drive even with the snow packed roads. As my hands guide the way, my mind searches for an explanation to why we're meeting up. Is this a drill or does this have something to do with the recent events.

We pull into the parking lot, two Osprey CV-22s have their turbine engines idling and one of the pilots outside performing all the pre-checks prior to our takeoff.

"Where are we going, Hawkeye?" He tilts his head, as if he's waiting for a certain command. "Let's go see what our mission is, buddy."

I put on his tactical harness that will help keep him warm but also allows me to attach some additional gear to it: handguns, ammo, small stuff. Nothing that'll weigh him down too much. I make sure his leggings are packed just in case we get into some high snow areas. He's a bit of a wimp when it comes to snow. Not that I blame him. I wouldn't want my junk dangling in the snow, either.

After a few greetings and fist bumps, I walk up the rear ramp and stow my gear. I find a seat in the middle with Hawkeye at my feet, still excited by all the buzzing around. We seem to be missing a few others but receive word that we'll be departing within the next ten minutes. Petty Officer Second Class Brandon Foyle walks in and sits in the seat next to me.

"What the fuck is this all about?" Brandon asks, his big green eyes shifting as he takes in the cramped fuselage. "Anybody say anything?"

"Nothing. Was told to get my butt here, and here I sit," I reply, patting Hawkeye on the head.

"I hear that." Brandon stands up to stow his gear and then sits back down and gives Hawkeye a scratch behind the ears, causing his tail to wag hard as his entire hindquarters move from side to side. "You miss me, Hawkeye? You're such a good boy. Yes, you are." his voice gets higher and cutesy, as if he's speaking to a baby, which is extra ridiculous given his buff stature. "You're my best friend since you bit the CO's leg last month." Hawkeye flashes him those big, brown doe eyes, his tongue still bobbing up and down.

"Dude, don't even start. I got so much crap for that." I sigh and shake my head.

While out on physical training, our Commanding Officer, Lieutenant Derrick Heart, was running alongside us when Hawkeye decided to veer off a bit, and the CO accidentally kicked him in the back of one of his legs. In retaliation, Hawkeye turned around and nipped at his calf. He didn't puncture the skin, but it did startle the shit out of Heart. He tripped over his feet and landed face-first in the dirt. Hawkeye and I had to run an extra two miles for that little incident, which Hawkeye didn't mind, but I sure as heck did.

"Late as usual, MUPPETs!" Brandon announces to everyone, as a few Team Guys taper in. Several return the comment with a middle finger.

"Fuck you. You're the most useless, pathetic person ever trained, not me. Besides, your wife was in the middle of finishing me off when I got the call. I would have been here sooner, but she had to start all over." The newest and mouthiest FNG stows his gear as the shit-talking commences. Brandon stands up like he's about to start a fight.

The cabin erupts in laughter but comes to an abrupt halt the second Captain Wilkinson walks up the ramp to our Osprey. We stand tall and salute.

"I'm glad to see everyone is in good spirits." He looks to Lieutenant Heart, who's standing to his right, just inside the Osprey. "Everyone accounted for?"

"Yes, sir!" Heart says.

Not wasting any time, Captain Wilkinson jumps on the comms so everyone can hear him clearly, briefly advising us of our mission. We're dumbfounded. Apparently, that stray Josco last week wasn't a fluke. Now, Major White reports a whole pack of them. Who fell asleep at the wheel and let this slip by?

I gaze down at Hawkeye and give him a pet on his head. *Dang.* This will be a true test for him as he's never encountered a Josco. We've performed simulations with people donning suits that replicated Joscos, but we're about to find out just how good Hawkeye is. It took me over a year of begging to get him approved to go on ops with us, and I had to prove he could perform. I thought last month's incident with my CO was going to end it before it ever began, but here we are.

The Captain made it clear that if any mission details were to get out into the public eye, we would have some serious hell to pay. The Major wants this kept quiet until we know exactly what we're dealing with. The last thing any of us need is four million people going crazy and jeopardizing the safety of our territory.

The Major will meet us later tonight to give additional details about the mission and everything he encountered while he was out on R&R. My stomach churns. Since I was nine, I've only been in earshot of him on a few occasions, and it's been years since I've seen him. I respect the man and everything he has done, but that's as far as it goes with me. We didn't separate on the best of terms, and even though I was only a kid, it left a scar deeper than any knife ever could. Sometimes I think he forgets that I lost someone, too. A flood of vivid memories that have been buried for fifteen years come rushing back.

The Major isn't my biological father, though he and Lily raised me from one year old to when I was nine. They found me just after the Turning.

I recall the day he came home from a trip where he was scouting out land for future projects and told us about a cabin—the one we're heading to now. He was so excited. He was a different person then, but he came back talking about "true cabin living." I believe those were his exact words. It was something he had done as a child and wanted to pass along to me. He told me hunting stories at dinner and about the bond that was created between him and his father—a bond that I would never get to experience. The Major wanted more for me, but mostly I think for me to get away from the daily craziness. He didn't want that life to be all I ever saw.

Months after we acquired the cabin, Oliver took me there for my first hunting trip. The day was like any other. It was late morning; we were about to pick up and call it quits so we could start making our way home. Just as we were packing up in the hunting blind, several bucks came out of nowhere, strolling across the clearing with a few does. He nudged my shoulder, telling me to get ready. I was nervous and fumbled my rifle, but I regained my composer, grabbing it with confidence. He whispered to me, guiding me through everything, telling me to calm my breathing, focus on the target, where to aim, up to the point of me pulling the trigger. It was my first deer. To this day, it was the biggest nine-point I had ever shot. I was so excited to come home and tell Mom everything.

Once we finished field dressing the deer, we threw our stuff into the truck, and we were on the road home. I was surprised at how unorganized and untidy we had screamed out of there, in complete contrast to the Major's beliefs. The ride home was the longest ever. The anticipation was killing me. I could hardly sit still. I still remember the wide, toothy smile on the Major's face after I shot that deer, although I'm pretty sure my smile was bigger. After that, I can't remember seeing it again.

It was dark outside, but as soon as we hit the driveway, I swung open the truck door before we came to a stop. He scolded me as I ran away, but I didn't care. I pumped my arms hard and ran as fast as my little nine-year-old legs would go until the air was sucked out of my lungs by something I would never forget—the memory permanently burned into my brain. My world stopped, and I was frozen like a terrified animal waiting to get hit by the oncoming lights. Every muscle in my body felt weak, as if I had no control over it. It would be the first time I witnessed the Turning; I'd only ever heard about it from others. It was happening right in front of my eyes, and I knew it was a death sentence. It was the first thought that entered my mind when I saw her.

"Mom?" The word was so soft that I'm not sure it even came out. My stomach churned like something was trying to rip out my insides. I stood there, unable to move, while she violently shook about the hallway, like a demonized soul taking over its victim. She was lost inside our own home. Lost in her mind. Like a warrior coming home to herald the town of good news, that day was supposed to be a day of joy, where I told her about the first deer I shot.

The process must have started right before we left for the hunt. She was supposed to come with us, but since she wasn't feeling well, she decided to stay home. She didn't want to ruin our trip. What was only a few seconds felt like hours. Standing there in the hallway, the only thing I could feel was the tears falling down my face. Pictures, our family pictures, had been ripped off the wall, the glass inside the frames shattered, leaving it like sparkling confetti strewn across the floors.

The door closed behind me as the Major entered the house, but I never looked away. He didn't realize it at first, but when he did, time came back to reality for me. The next thing I knew, the Major grabbed me and carried me outside, telling me to go next door and wait for him there. Even at nine, I knew what had to be done, and I tried so hard to think about something else. No way my dad, the Major, could do it.

Sprinting through a fog of thoughts and tears, I banged and knocked on the nearest neighbor's door so hard that my hand ached. The door flew open after a few seconds of my intense banging. Mr. Thomas, an older gentleman, stood cautiously in the doorway, revolver in hand. I think they must've been asleep. I didn't say a word. I just ran past him, straight to their couch and buried my face into one of the orange floral cushions. Mrs. Thomas popped into the room, likely curious as to what was going on. All I could do was sob and yell at her. Mrs. Thomas wrapped her arms around me and made a hushing sound.

Mr. Thomas ran over to my house to see what was going on. A single gunshot rang out in the quiet night air. My entire body flinched so hard; it was like I was the one being shot. Oliver let out a pained scream of anger, a deep howl of sorrow that still wakes me in the night. In that moment, I knew she was dead, gone forever from my life. In a matter of minutes, the life I knew was over. There was nothing any one of us could do but what had to be done. It turns out he could do it.

It sent shock waves throughout the town over the next few days; there was no escaping it. There hadn't been a Turning in some time, and people were worried that it was still happening, especially to the Major's wife. We thought we were safe and that the Turning was a one-time event. We were wrong.

The Major was never the same after that day. I was just a kid, and it was like I never existed. He could barely look at me, let alone talk to me. Guess I just reminded him of what happened, so he cut me out. We grew estranged, which ultimately led me to live with one of my friend's family. He just couldn't handle it. Nolan had to take the reins while he got his head straight for almost a year. With all that Lily and the Major had been through, him being forced to take her life was tragic. That was the second time he had had to do something like that. First to my biological mother when I was a baby and then to the love of his life. We haven't spoken one word to each other since I moved out. Resentment was the only emotion I had for him for leaving me, but those days are long gone. After all, he did save me in the beginning.

The bounce of the Osprey touching down wakes me from my stupor, and I choke back the lump in my throat that always seems to pop up when I think about the past. I glance at my watch; it's just after twenty hundred hours. The twenty-four of us grab our gear and exit out the aft bay door. We join the other team that flew alongside us. None of us even knew there was a small airport on Grand Island until the Captain told us about it just a few short hours ago. He gave us another reminder of our gag order. Our lips, as always, are sealed.

As we exit, several of the Team Guys talk about how the Major is losing it. That he was in the hospital the other day and now everyone thinks he can't handle the pressure of the position anymore. Even though I have my own personal heartache for the man, it was all I could do to keep from punching them in the face. He's done a lot for us, and that earns him respect.

After gazing around the small airfield, Heart gets our attention, loading us up in one of the four troop transports that have been awaiting our arrival. The flight crew hangs back and stores the Ospreys in one of the few hangars that look brand spanking new, from what I can tell in the dark. Several other vehicles wait, as they'll be joining us once they secure the birds. They're our ride out of here in the morning.

I take a seat at the rear of the truck. Hawkeye paces back and forth, panting, jumping all over the place, on everyone's gear. I haven't ever seen him this edgy, but I guess we're all a little anxious.

"Who's controlling who?" Brandon jokes.

"I don't know what his problem is. Something's got him all riled up." I tug back on his leash and pet under his chin. "What's wrong with you, buddy?" He sits but stays focused on his surroundings like something is out there. "Calm down, boy."

We head out into the dark night on a gravel road, unsure of where we're going. The street is lit by dim lights lining one side of the road. Didn't think they would have electricity running on an island like this. Some of the guys rumble about hearing that there is some top-secret facility up here that they've been working on for over a decade. I guess we're about to find out.

"Psst." Brandon leans in close. "You really believe this shit? Joscos way up here?"

I shrug my shoulders in response, sinking a little lower on the uncomfortable bench to try and relax. Everything we've ever known about Joscos is that they stay far away during the winter months, and if this is all true, it's a game changer. I lean my head back and stare up at the canopy with hundreds of tiny, quarter-sized holes in it. Piece of crap truck.

It was a short ride to the facility. There's no security or fence to keep anyone out. Just an open field, maybe a hundred yards by a hundred yards, with nothing but trees all around. The building wasn't anything fancy: a gray metal facade with four walls and a massive sliding door. A couple dim lights mounted to the roof shine down onto the snow-covered dirt lot.

We jump out and walk around to the front of the vehicles, waiting for something to happen. One of the drivers jumps on his radio. "We're here. Open her up." The sliding doors split down the middle and separates. Hawkeye looks up to me.

"Don't look at me. I have no idea what this place is." His head tilts again like he's trying to decipher what I'm saying.

Lights slowly pour out of the building, giving the white snow a yellow hue. We start walking closer to the building. It's a good thing too because it's starting to snow.

A skinny man wearing glasses and dressed in jeans, a flannel long-sleeve shirt, and an orange vest stands waiting for us next to a massive industrial elevator that's open, ready to gulp us up. Four elevators line the back wall. They are so big you could easily fit two tanks inside one.

"What the fuck is this place?" a quiet voice says from the front of the group. Several conversations echo through the space. The question remains unanswered for the moment.

Once we're piled into the building, the sliding doors we just walked through start closing with a dense mechanical whine. We look back at the doors and then at one another, our curiosity piqued.

Large metal containers are stacked up along either side of the building walls, all the way to the thirty-foot-tall roof. Two wide staircases sit on both ends of the elevators. That must be in case a lot of people need to get down here in a hurry.

"Welcome to the Grand Island Bunker. My name is Doug, and I will be your host for the night." The man's tone is rehearsed, like he's been practicing for such an occasion. "I'm sure you have a lot of questions. This is just one of four facilities on this island, all of them connected by tunnels. If you would please enter the elevator, we'll go ahead and go down, and I'll tell you a little bit about what we have going on here."

"Go down where exactly?" Heart, our CO, asks.

"It'll be fun. I'll tell you about it on the way," Doug replies, guiding us into the elevator.

We hesitate a moment before one brave soul finally steps forward. Then, all forty-eight of us and this Doug guy enter the oversized box to take us to the depths of the unknown. Doug lowers the handle, and the protective gate lowers to keep us from falling out of the elevator. He then pushes another button, and the lift starts to lower much faster than what I would have expected or preferred. My stomach, which was already in my throat, rose a little more.

"We started building these bunkers shortly after we started construction of The River. And just so you know, we're still not complete. This is the initial one. We're close, but you guys will be our first guests."

"Bunkers for what?" someone asks.

"In short, these are our fallback bunkers. A last stand, if you will. If one day we ever get overrun, and we're no longer safe within our territory, this is where we'll come. The Major is just about to send out communications about this place. We have four on this island, and like I said earlier, tunnels connect between them and many more like it on several other islands within Lake Superior, Lake Michigan, and Lake Huron." He continues talking as we descend. "This facility can hold up to a hundred thousand souls. Some of the other ones can hold much more, but being that this was the first, we wanted to ensure this would work. It's a good thing we still had engineers left." He laughs. "Me being one of them."

He's clearly proud of his achievement. "Anyway," Doug continues. "This facility goes to a depth of two hundred feet, and yes, those stairs you saw earlier go all the way down. So, if any of y'all are up for a little workout tonight, feel free. I'll keep the blast doors open, which are about midway down."

Within a matter of moments, we reach the floor labeled living quarters. Doug jabbers on as we exit the elevator. "There are three other floors down here. One of them stores food, supplies, the armory, and a bunch of equipment—spare parts and so on. Another floor has the mechanical systems that keep this place going. You probably didn't notice when you flew in as it was dark, but there are thousands of solar panels topside that power this facility and the three other ones." Doug notices the last person to exit the lift. "Looks like we all made it. If you will follow me, I'll show you where you'll be sleeping tonight." None of us follow, as we're all thunder-struck by what we're seeing. As he walks away, he continues, "The fourth level, which is the top, is for processing newcomers, a recreation level…"

We aren't really focusing on what he's saying. I know my mind is racing, trying to process everything.

We take in the sights, mouths gaping. I'm sure Doug was fine with it since his creation is a sight to see. Floor to ceiling must be twenty feet. Gray concrete walls surround us, and concrete columns are positioned everywhere to support the underground structure, which I can only imagine is a ton of weight. It was stark, for sure, but impressive, nonetheless.

Doug waves a hand after noticing no one is looking at him. "What you are viewing is the chow hall. The rooms are off to the sides, but this is where everyone staying here will eat. The kitchen is at the very back, which you can't see since the lights aren't on. I would give you a tour of the entire facility, but that will have to wait for another day. So, if you will follow me, once again, I'll show you to your bunks."

We pick up our gear. "Come on, boy." I tug on Hawkeye's leash. "I sure hope they have a doggy restroom for you down here, or Doug here is not going to be happy with you."

"Alright, everyone, accommodations are to the left." We follow Doug into a room that can sleep up to a hundred. "There are more private quarters for families, but those aren't ready yet, so you will have to bunk in here for tonight."

"We'll be just fine, Doug," Heart confirms.

"Good deal. The Major is waiting for you in one of the conference rooms. If you all want to stow your things, I will take you there."

"Alright, men. You heard the man," Heart says. As if we'd rehearsed it a hundred times, we each throw our gear on a bed with clean sheets and follow Doug. As we enter the conference room, Doug stays outside and holds up a finger to me.

"Sir, for the dog, there is a place for him if he needs to go." He points down the long, dark hallway. "You can't miss it. Sign says 'Dog Park.' I'll make sure the lights are on. It's a small area, but just in case he needs to do his business."

"Thank you, sir." I shake his hand. "He went just after we landed. Hopefully he can hold out till morning, but good to know. I appreciate it."

I take a seat; Hawkeye lays down right beside me. I give him a chew toy, one without a squeaker. The Major and Nolan are standing up front with a projector displaying an aerial map on a large white canvas. My eyes go straight to the Major's hand wrapped in cloth with a little red around his remaining fingers. My stomach is still in knots, and I'm wondering if he will acknowledge me. Heck, I wonder if he would even recognize me.

Nolan starts off the meeting by reviewing the mission details. We'll depart at 0600 hours. The Ospreys will take us to where the Major last saw the pack. From there, we'll locate any evidence that we can use to start tracking them. A chopper will be in the area using its thermal heat technology to pick up any traces. The problem is there is so much land to cover and no idea which direction they were headed. By now, they could be across the state or hiding away somewhere. By morning, the tracks will be covered from the incoming weather, but it's good to know several choppers will be on standby for a quick response.

The Major took a back seat for most of the discussion, only chiming in on a few details that he witnessed. He even comments that he's not going crazy. Word must have got to him. It made for a good laugh, and I may have seen the Major smirk, but nothing to go announcing to the world.

We spend the next hour reviewing maps, going through the plans in case something goes wrong, asking questions and so on. The typical mission briefing stuff. At the end, Nolan and the Major say their goodbyes and wish us luck and then depart. It was now in our hands. He didn't look at me. Probably for the better, as it would suck if my face betrayed my emotion.

Most of the guys head to the chow hall to eat their MREs. I retreat back to the bunks for some quiet time while I eat mine alone. I give Hawkeye his own MRE: beef enchilada. Not my favorite, but he loves it. He won't love the pressure that'll be pushing up against his insides once that gets processed. Damn. I didn't think this through. I'm gonna have to clean that up.

Once everyone finished eating, they pile into the bunk room to shoot the breeze, take a shower, or get ready for bed. An hour after eating, Hawkeye starts doing his dance routine, which means only one thing; he needs to take a dump. Great. I disconnect his leash and we walk down to the dog park. He runs around for a bit, sniffing every corner. He keeps looking at me like he's waiting for me to give him permission. It's as if he's unsure whether he can take a crap here.

"Do your business, buddy. Go ahead. Doug says it's okay."

It took him another minute to find his perfect spot, but when he did, I could tell this was not going to be a pleasant cleanup.

"No more beef enchilada for you. Jeez, Hawkeye. If we were outside, that would be steaming. You're gonna be sleeping on the other side of the room tonight after that heaping mess."

I clean it up the best I can and toss the bag in a nearby trash bin. Doug had better empty that out first thing in the morning.

"Satisfied, are you?" I look at Hawkeye, who seems oblivious to my passive-aggressive comments. "Come on, let's go. It's bedtime."

It was good for him to let out some energy and have some fun, because come tomorrow, it's going to be all work.

CHAPTER FOURTEEN

(Petty Officer First Class Jayce Brock—Navy SEAL)

Tuesday, January 21, 2048

I can honestly say that waking up to a cold, wet nose to the face is not any better than our CO coming in and yelling at everyone, but Hawkeye is ready for the day. I wipe away Hawkeye's snot from across my cheek and glance at my watch.

I poke Hawkeye's snout as though it's a snooze button. "I had another eight minutes to go, bud. It's four-thirty-seven. Couldn't you have waited?" I give him a pat on the head and peek around the room to see if anyone else is up. A few were checking their gear, preparing for the day, while others were still dreaming, causing a menagerie of snores to echo through the air.

Hawkeye bumps me again. "Alright, I'm getting up." I pull on my pants and a pair of socks as the concrete floor is freezing. Hawkeye's doing his potty dance, so I take him down to the dog park for a quick release. We bump into Heart in the hallway.

"You keep that fucking mutt away from me." He makes a noticeable zag to the other side of the hall.

"You'll hurt his feelings, sir." I make a frowny face.

He ignores me and continues on, "Coffee and food in the chow hall at zero-five hundred." He calls back in a stern voice, "Doug and his workers were kind enough to make us breakfast this morning, so eat as much as you can. There's plenty."

"Yes, sir."

As Hawkeye does his thing, getting rid of the last of the beef enchilada from last night, I hear Heart's booming voice yelling at everyone who is still asleep to wake up and get their crap together.

"Come on, boy! Let's go see what they made." He comes running back with a tennis ball in his mouth. "Let go, Hawkeye." He clearly wants to keep playing but releases the ball obediently.

The chow hall is set up with several tables decorated with fancy metal containers and a small heating element underneath to keep the contents warm. Silverware and plates are nicely stacked on one end with condiments on the other.

"Man, what a treat. Look at this spread," Brandon says. "I'm filling my pockets!"

"Probably not a good idea since we'll be tracking down Joscos."

"Such a bubble popper, Brock." I shrug and move on.

Petty Officer Third Class Carl Hutchens is the first in line. "Damn, would you look at this!" He lifts each of the lids and peeks inside. "Eggs, bacon, sausage, pancakes, oh my." I salivate at the choices.

Doug and a few of his workers walk in from the kitchen with jugs of water and orange juice. After setting them on a separate table with plastic cups, they join us in line. I grab an extra plate and scoop several heaping spoonfuls of food for Hawkeye. I'm sure he'll down this in a matter of seconds. Everyone rushes through the line and takes a seat, scarfing everything down as fast as they can. The buttery pancakes with syrup are the best. I haven't eaten pancakes in quite a while, but the way they are made, almost like they were deep-fried, has me going back for more. Hawkeye also has seconds, as he loves eggs and bacon. Who doesn't? I hope this doesn't come back to bite us later. I'm going to need a nap after eating this.

Heart finishes up and goes through his pre-mission speech, highlighting our objectives, while the rest of us finish stuffing our faces. At 0530, we go back to the bunks, grab our gear, and do a once-over to ensure we don't miss anything. Hawkeye is geared up, and by 0545, we're all packed into the elevator heading topside. The flight crew left well before we sat down for breakfast to conduct their pre-flight inspections, so they should be ready by the time we arrive.

Snow is a possibility, so this should make for some fun hiking later. We load up in the trucks and get back to the helipad, where the Ospreys are warmed up and ready to go. Nerves have me a little jittery, but that's typical. Within minutes of boarding, the rotors rotate forward and we're on our way. It's a quick ten-minute ride from here to the Major's cabin. The idea of being back there sends an uncomfortable jerk down my spine, but I ignore it and think about the task at hand. We'll be touching down at his hunting spot clearing, near where the incident took place.

The men's faces show a bit of mixed emotions. Some live for this stuff, while others look like they would rather be elsewhere. I fall into the latter. My only hope is that this was a random fluke, a rogue pack that just got lost on their way south. But that doesn't make any sense. Josco's have a remarkable sense of direction, so there must be another reason for them to be up here. Maybe they're outcasts and have been banished from their home. But why up here? Certainly, they must know it wouldn't be safe for them here.

My mind starts picking apart scenarios. Is this something tactical? A secret covert group of Joscos? But then, why did they let the Major live? This begs the question: Are other packs secretly crossing The River elsewhere? Because if it's not a random pack, are we looking at a year-round war with these beasts? If this becomes normal, our last days might be coming to an end, like Doug mentioned, and it won't be long before they wipe us out or we're forced to live out our days underground in a bunker.

I put on Hawkeye's leggings just before the Osprey touches down. There's a foot of snow on the ground and the last thing I want is for him to get frostbite. I'd have to carry his sorry butt everywhere. He's usually fine in the cold weather, but I don't know how long we'll be out here; it could be an hour or ten days.

Our point guy gets moving the moment he steps foot off the bird. We fall in line and start our trek to where the Major's moose fell dead. Hopefully Hawkeye can pick up on their scent or at least give us an idea of where they are headed.

"Damn, maybe the Major isn't losing his mind," Brandon comments as we come upon the location.

This was a massacre—crimson stains on everything and patches of wolf fur on the ground. Not much snow has fallen in this area since, so that's good. Hardly any bones are left. Whatever was here took every piece of meat they could gather before taking off. Tracks lead away in all directions. There are so many, it's hard to tell where they were going or where they came from. Hawkeye's nose doesn't know where to start, but he's picking up something.

"Listen up!" Heart says. "Pair up into your teams and start looking for any signs that'll give us an idea of where these fuckers went. Also, check for clothing or anything that'll be useful for Hawkeye. Jayce, what's going on with him?"

"Nothing yet, sir." He's sniffing everywhere. I let him roam, hoping he finds something useful. "With so much blood between the moose and the wolves, it might be tough for him to pick up any scent in this mess. We need something with the scent of Josco on it."

Brandon and I, along with our platoon, trek northeast in the direction Hawkeye starts moving. Fragments of bones lead this way. Plus, most of the footprints appear to be going down this path where the snow has been flattened. Splats of blood here and there give us some confidence. There's not much up here; the terrain is flat and wooded, and each passing tree looks like the next. Hawkeye hops around like a fox in the deeper areas, which I find entertaining.

Brandon calls me over. "Look at this."

A clear path of solid footprints continues northeast; it's as if they were wearing shoes. The Major advised us that the Joscos were wearing clothes of sorts, including rags or hides strapped to their feet. How in the world would they have known to do that? If this is real, what sub-species of a Josco are we dealing with and what other domesticated tricks do they have up their proverbial sleeves?

It isn't long before someone finds an article of clothing lying in the snow, looking like it'd been torn off by a wolf. It's dingy and raggedy and something only a Josco would wear. I connect Hawkeye's leash and dangle the cloth in front of his nose. He takes a good sniff and starts heading northwesterly. Heart radios the chopper in the area, lets them know we might have something, and provides them with a SITREP. Lake Superior is directly north of us, maybe fifteen miles, so unless these things started swimming, they only had two options: east or west.

For three cold hours, we follow their tracks, and my toes are starting to feel the effects. Hawkeye doesn't show any signs of slowing. I'm wondering who is walking who here. *Can Joscos get frostbite?*

"There's a lot more traffic here than we were led to believe," I say to Brandon.

"You ain't lying. It's hard to tell how many of them there are. This path must be a hundred feet wide. Could be hundreds of them."

We stop to chat with Heart. He gives another SITREP, and we continue.

"You find any more of them cars you're always talking about?" Brandon asks.

"I did, actually. Two, in fact! Last month, just outside the Chicago area, I found an orange 1969 Chevrolet Camaro SS with a three-ninety-six and a green 1971 Plymouth Hemi 'Cuda convertible with a four-forty cubic inch engine. Both sitting in a massive garage that could probably hold twenty cars in one of those fancy big neighborhoods. Spent a week up there before coming across those gems. Had to make two trips since my trailer only holds one car. I need to get a bigger trailer."

"A 'Cuda? What the fuck is that?" Brandon asks.

"An awesome car is what it is," I reply, almost wanting to slap him for not knowing.

"I guess."

"You guess? Man, I read an old car magazine that said one of those sold at an auction for over six million dollars way back when."

"I like my Jeep." Brandon picks up a stick and throws it, distracting Hawkeye for a second. "It gets me to where I need to go."

"I know what you drive."

"It's a Rubicon!" He says it like he knows what it means.

"That it is, Brandon. Anyway, neither of them runs. I need to get under the hood and figure out what's wrong."

Eight years ago, I saw a red 2002 Dodge Viper RT/10 that got me hooked on muscle cars, and I haven't been able to shake the bug since. There's just something about the design and sound of that era of muscle cars that has me wanting more. Just around the corner from where I live, I have a warehouse full of about forty muscle cars, mostly American: Ford, Chevy, and Dodge. Most of them run, and the ones that don't are just a few parts shy of getting there.

***

We've trekked nearly twelve miles, almost to a town called Grand Marais, and within the last two miles, it started snowing. Not that little pea-sized stuff, either; these are large grape-sized flakes that have reduced our visibility to twenty feet.

"You alright? What is it, bud?" Hawkeye stops dead in his tracks and lets out a low, deep, rumbling growl. I throw my hand up in the air, signaling everyone to stop. I raise my rifle and peek through the scope, scanning for anything, but the heavy snowfall stifles my view. Brandon kneels right beside me, scanning his sectors.

"Dammit!" Brandon says. "I can't see a thing in this shit storm."

Hawkeye gets more aggressive. He raises his snout, showing his pearly white canines, his posture stiff and his fur at attention.

"He sees something. His eyes are locked on whatever it is," Brandon says.

Heart runs to our position and jumps on the comms, advising the pilots to get to our location ASAP, and that's when I pick up faint movement straight ahead. Bodies. A line of large bodies converge around us from our nine o'clock to our three o'clock. It's like they were waiting for us and knew we were coming.

"What do we do, Lieutenant?" a voice calls out from the back.

"Don't shoot!" Heart responds. "Stay calm."

"What do you mean, don't shoot? We're surrounded by fucking Joscos," Hutchens shouts. "And why the hell aren't they attacking?"

"I don't fucking know. Nobody breathes until I give the order. Hold your position," Heart repeats.

Hawkeye starts to whimper, cowering down like he's about to receive a beating.

"I guess this serves as official evidence that the Major's not crazy," Brandon says as he nudges my shoulder.

"Not the time, man." I don't show my full irritation. I can't, as I'm completely frozen.

We group together in a tight circle for an all-around defense, with our backs to one another. Heart and our radioman stand in the middle. We have our weapons raised and pointed at the slow-approaching threat. My twisting stomach shoots a wave of nausea up my throat. I've never seen so many before. More than the eight or nine we thought we were up against. The Major needs to learn how to count again. Our entire lives, we've been told they were afraid of the water and the cold. I think we just debunked one of those myths.

The closer they get, the more they come into focus, and it's evident that these Joscos are different—more advanced. They're wearing heavier clothing, almost like Neanderthals in the times of woolly mammoths.

I hear several prayers being sent up to the heavens, and I'm thinking I should be doing the same. I've never known a Josco to just stand by idly, waiting for an invitation to attack. Everything we've been taught was to shoot first and ask questions later.

Suddenly, they stop and just stand there as though ordered to do so. I don't hear a word being uttered, but somehow, they all knew to stop at the exact same time.

"Lieutenant, I have movement. Twelve o'clock," I advise.

Hawkeye crouches behind me and peeks around my side. I wish I had someone to hide behind.

Heart walks up behind me.

"It's a single Josco walking toward us, sir," I tell him as I continue to look through my scope. "It's definitely carrying something in its arms."

"Hold your position. Do not fire!" Heart orders.

My head pounds with a sudden, sharp pain. Not one of those headaches that slowly builds over time. No, this one threatens to make me pass out with its short burst of intensity. Hundreds of images, pictures that I can't seem to focus on, flood my vision through closed eyes. It's like someone is taking over my mind, shoving experiences I've never seen before into my memory. Glimpses of two groups of Joscos battling one another scroll through my mind.

Hawkeye lays in the snow, looking up and clawing at me with his paw as though he's asking if I'm alright. My eyes hurt and my vision blurs. The bright reflection of the snow blinds me further. My weapon falls, but my sling keeps it from falling into the snow.

"What the fuck, man? You good?" Brandon asks.

I let out a quiet grunt. The pictures in my head come to an abrupt halt and fade away as fast as they come.

"Jayce! Jayce! Are you okay?" Heart shouts.

The pain subsides just enough for me to grab my rifle, raising it back up, but with shaky arms. I stay in a knelt position, unable to speak yet.

"I'm fine. Just a headache. I'm good. I'm good." *I'm not good.* I'm freaking out.

The lonely Josco stays its course toward us, not faltering or appearing scared in any sense. It's just taking a casual walk as if it's going to the store. It gets within twenty feet before it stops. I can't make out what it's holding. It's heavily wrapped in black animal fur. It looks primitive with its head covered.

"Is that a weapon?" Heart asks as he stares through his scope.

I watch as the Josco looks down at its cargo. Its face shows only a dirty, battered, and beaten grimace. I can't tell you whether it was twenty years of age or fifty. They have the same enlarged features.

It turns back to the other Joscos behind him. Is its clan feeling the same way we do? Flashes, again, streak one after another through my mind. It feels as though it's some kind of warning.

"What do we do, Lieutenant?" Brandon asks.

"I don't know. Give me a second!"

"We may not have a second!" another soldier calls out.

We're thinking the same thing. We're dead if he gives the wrong order. We could be either way, but as it stands, they're not showing any hostility toward us.

"I don't think they're here to harm us, sir," I blurt out. "If they were, we'd already be goners."

"Yeah, well, how about you go over and see if it wants to shake your hand or see if it's carrying a white flag to surrender," Heart replies, jumping on the radio asking for guidance.

I contemplate that option. It would definitely be the dumbest thing I've ever done, but what else is there to do? This standoff is going to end in one of three ways: we're dead, we're dead but we take a bunch of Them with us, or we walk out of here unscathed. *Har har har!* The first seems most likely.

"Okay, screw it!" I lower my weapon and stand tall, handing Hawkeye's leash over to Brandon. "Take this."

"You aren't fucking serious, are you? What the hell are you doing?" Brandon takes the leash.

"I'm gonna walk over there. Clearly, they're not here to hurt us."

"I was fucking kidding," Heart says. "Put your weapon back up and hold your fucking position! That's an order!"

"Sir, the Josco's just standing there. I feel like it's inviting one of us to come over," I say with confidence.

"I gave you an order, Brock! Hold your position," he demands again.

I ignore him. I can't believe I'm disobeying my CO. I may get demoted for this and put in a deep, dark hole when this is over. Heck, the Josco might put me in one anyway, so does it really matter?

I take a step forward. Heart angrily whispers, "Get the fuck back here!" but I block him out. One step turns into two and then ten. The next thing I know, I'm standing just feet away from a Josco. I'm hesitant to lower my rifle as I still can't see what it's holding. As a good-faith gesture, I slowly swing my weapon back behind me and hold my hands up to show it that I'm no threat. I hope it understands. Its face shows only a furtive look. This better not be a trick.

Turning back to my men, I see Heart, red-faced and mouthing the words, "Get back here. That is an order!"

I've made it this far. I may as well go a little further. The Josco hasn't charged me. It hasn't done anything thus far to show me it's a threat. At six foot three inches, I'm standing even with its clutched hands. The Josco stands well over eight feet and is as wide as a grizzly bear. It could crush me with no effort at all.

I take two faltering steps closer. It smells like a wet dog in the middle of summer. Its eyes aren't the wicked, dark, soulless black we've come to know. They're normal with color and a sense of life. We both stand there eyeing each other, gauging whether or not we can trust one another. My knees quibble. I have no idea what to do. Do I say something? Do I extend my hand to shake like I do when meeting a new person for the first time? A fist bump, perhaps? Shoot, I'm lost for any reasonable actions to take.

We wait for the other to make the first move. Both sides quiet behind us, as I'm sure my team is on pins and needles waiting for whatever is to come of this historic meeting between us. My mind is blank, and as we're standing there, it tilts his head up as though it hears something. Is someone telepathically talking to it? A few seconds later, I understand why it did it. The thumping of helicopter blades cutting through the air makes me wonder if it's going to see this as a threat and change the current calm situation into a frenzy. A growly mutter slides from its twitchy mouth. I didn't get the impression the growl was for me but more like it was telling its people to stand down.

The helicopter pilot screaming holy heck into my earpiece startles me. I'm sure the Josco could hear it as well. The pilot advises us of the thousands of Joscos lighting up his monitor and asks what he should do. Heart jumps on and tells him to stand down and wait for his orders. The pilot isn't too happy about it. Heart puts the conversation to an end by telling him to shut up and back off for a second while we handle things from the ground.

My focus returns to the Josco as it rearranges what it's carrying and goes down on one knee. I react with a shuffle backward, reaching for my weapon, but I don't swing it fully around. The sound of my platoon's weapons shifts behind me. The object in its arms squirms as it kneels. Is it an animal? Perhaps some sort of peace offering? *Here you go, here's a baby wolf, let's be friends.* But it's not. It's the last thing I would have expected to see a fully grown eight-and-a-half-foot, five-hundred-pound Josco carrying.

"What the…" The Josco's eyes hint at sadness—if that was an emotion they could even feel.

All I can see is the top half of a newborn human/Josco baby's face. It's perfectly swaddled like a newborn baby. It appears to almost be like us, but something about it feels a bit more advanced. It's calm. It opens its eyes and looks at me as though it's processing me.

How is this even possible? Is this why they're not attacking? To protect their young. Are there more of them? This means there are females out there. I tilt my body slightly to the right to gaze behind it, hoping to see a female, but between the snow and their heavy clothing, there was no good view. And as fast as they showed up, the group of Joscos retreat.

The Josco then stands up, its blue eyes penetrating mine.

I turn my head to face my CO and mouth, "It's a baby." His glare tells me he's unable to understand what I'm saying.

I turn back around, and by this time, the baby-carrying Josco follows its pack, walking away from me. I'm lost for any sense of what happened and what I witnessed. It was as if it were using the baby as a white flag.

"That was really fucking stupid, Petty Officer First Class Brock," Heart says as he walks up behind me.

"Maybe, or I may have just saved all our lives, sir."

"How the fuck am I going to explain this one to Nolan and the Major, Jayce?"

"Start with the truth, sir."

"The fucking truth. No one is going to believe this shit."

I turn to face Heart. "I bet the Major will."

He only shakes his head. "What was it carrying anyway? I couldn't understand what your order-breaking mouth was lipping."

Brandon and the rest of the platoon slowly walk up to us.

"It was carrying a newborn baby."

"Excuse me?" Brandon says.

"You heard me."

We stand quiet, watching the Joscos vanish in the snow, heading northeast. Once they're gone, Heart gets on the radio with the pilot and orders them not to attack. The pilot has a few choice words, but Heart eloquently advises him of the situation and to stand down.

Surprisingly, the Major and Nolan agree with Heart, and the only order given is for the pilots to tail them and keep an eye on what they do and where they go. We don't have any civilians up this far, so the Josco group should be fine as long as they don't disturb the peace.

It's a somber flight back to HQ. No one speaks a word to me like I'm a lepper; I tend to be a loner anyway. But I know what they're thinking. I'm an idiot for breaking command. I would be thinking the same if I hadn't seen the images that still make my head ache. Heart did inform me that Nolan wants to speak ASAP when we return and that he'll be waiting for me upon arrival. Great.

Tuesday, January 21, 2048

My hands tremble from nerves, but slow, deep breaths help calm me down. Everyone's feeling the pre-departure jitters; it's a strange mixture of excitement, anxiety, and fear rolled into one. My gut's not feeling right about this one, but then again, none of them have ever given me the warm fuzzies. Each mission has its own level of unknowns and complexities, but this one soars well above the others. Anxiety should settle in a few hours once we've hit the road.

Along with our night's out, Maggie never attends the "departure parties." Of the hundreds of missions, she only went to a few back in the beginning when I was just a private. To her, it's turned into a superstition that means I *will* be seeing you again. At first, it bothered me to see everyone else's loved ones, but I grew to understand her reasoning, and with her not here, it keeps me focused on what I need to be doing. She gave me a tear-filled goodbye this morning and a tight hug that I can still feel wrapped around me.

While everyone is huddled outside the hangar saying their goodbyes, I perform one final walkthrough of the vehicles to keep my mind busy. We've inspected the vehicles more times than we can count, but it never hurts to do another one. Plus, it builds up my appetite for the homemade breakfast tacos sitting on a table just inside the hangar bay door. Sergeant Martinez's wife woke up early and made four hundred breakfast tacos for us. It's been a tradition the past four years since he joined our crew. Scrambled eggs, cheese, bacon, sausage, and salsa. Damn, I'm gonna miss real food for the next few days.

I climb in the passenger seat of the dark green M1114 Humvee with custom swing arms for each of the doors that are equipped with M240 machine guns with a quick-detach mechanism. We may not be the most aerodynamic vehicle, but we'll have plenty of firepower with us as we travel the unknown.

Once on the road, we'll be positioned within the main body of the convoy, and with our destination roughly eight hundred miles away, it's an estimated travel time of sixteen hours. We've calculated refueling time and short, unexpected detours, but if everything goes as planned, our timing shouldn't be too far off.

I glance at my watch; ten minutes until we depart at 07:00, and our ETA at Fort Hood is around 23:00. So, with the little bit of time I have left, I revisit the map while applying a copious amount of salsa onto a taco and take a large bite.

The driver's side door opens. "All set?" Corporal Brad Gillis asks as he jumps in with a hand full of tacos. He's twenty-three years old, lean, fit, and full of energy. He's been with us a few years, and he's a damn good soldier.

"Ready as I'll ever be." I look up from the map to see everyone splitting off into their respective vehicles. Jared enters shortly after and takes a seat in the back.

"You gonna get us there safe and sound?" I ask.

"That's the plan, sir."

"You good back there, Jared?" He appears sober and alive this morning.

"Sure," he says with a mouth full of taco.

"Well, sit back and relax. We have a long day ahead of us." I take another large bite. "…and enjoy these tacos while you can. It's MREs from here on out, boys." Brad starts the vehicle, and the diesel engine roars to life.

"I think you need to have a talk with Martinez," Jared says as he crumples up his wrapper, tosses it out, then closes the door. "I heard his wife made some extra special tacos just for Sean and his guys."

"No shit? I thought we were all one team," I say, a little disappointed.

"May have to do some recon when we get down there. See where the fuck they're hiding them tacos." Jared's voice is soft but stern.

"Damn right, we do."

It was good hearing the determination in his voice, we haven't heard that in a while.

"Alright, here we go, gents," Brad declares. He looks over at me. "It's not too late to back out."

"The fuck it is. Try explaining that one to the Major and Nolan." I point straight ahead.

"You could say you came down with an extreme case of the squirts," Jared says, trying to keep a straight face. Brad bursts out laughing, and I throw my balled-up wrapper at him. Maybe he is getting back to his old self.

We exit the hangar and maneuver into our predetermined spot in the convoy, with Sean taking point. He'll be responsible for setting the pace and making sure we stay on schedule to Fort Hood. As the vehicles get into position, moving into a column formation, we stroll past the families standing in the cold. Most are sobbing, but for me, it's bittersweet that I didn't have to pull away from Maggie like that. I don't even know if I could this time.

"You guys want to hear some music to get things started? I know a guy I used to work post duty with, and he gave me a CD he and his band made. Heard a few songs the other night at the bar. They're pretty good," I offer.

"They got a name?" Jared asks.

"Better Days." I read the words scribbled on the white paper sleeve.

"Play whatever you want. I'm going to sit back here and relax while I can. Sleep is going to be difficult the next few days." I glance back as Jared leans his head against the window.

"I don't really give a shit either," Brad replies as he makes a left turn to leave the airport property.

"Ladies and gentlemen," Sean announces over the radio. "I would like to welcome you onboard this nonstop shit show service from Joint Base Eppley to beautiful, sunny Fort Hood, Texas, where temperatures are a balmy fifty degrees. This is your Captain speaking, if you didn't already fucking know, and I would like to remind everyone to keep your seat backs and tray tables in their full upright positions as this is going to be one bumpy ass ride." There are smiles all around. "…and your ass better be planted securely with your seat belts fastened. Our travel time is approximately sixteen hours. If you would like a snack, please contact your nearest attendant, Lieutenant Dodson, and he would be more than happy to bring you a little sack of salty peanuts."

"Fuck you…little sack of peanuts," I reply over the airwaves. "You weren't complaining last night!"

Jared and Brad are hysterical over Sean's attempt to insult my nut sack. "Well played. I'll give him that." I could only shake my head as I stared out the window.

I jump back on the radio. "Payback's a bitch, Sean. Just remember that."

"I look forward to it!" he quips back.

We navigate through the city streets until we reach the bridge post and say our final goodbye over the comms, leaving the last of civilization. It was eerie to pass over to the other side. We haven't done that in a long while. It's like entering another world, and a few minutes later, we make our final turn to get on Highway 75 to head south. Rusted cars line either side of the highway but leave plenty of room to navigate through. Long before most of us were in this position of conducting supply runs, the crews before us spent years clearing the highways and roads that lead in and out of Omaha. They only made it four hundred miles in this direction. I guess they never thought we would be traveling past that.

A white sheet of snow blankets the ground, and the road itself still has an inch or so of snow, but we keep a steady speed. We pass through southern Omaha a short time later, and even though we're just across The River, my eyes are glued to our surroundings. Hard to believe a place that is just a few miles away is devoid of human life. Buildings along the highway are in disrepair, burned down to the foundation, all remnants from another time that was unfamiliar to most of us on this mission since we were born right at the time of the Turning or shortly after.

***

Three hours later, we arrived at our first checkpoint, Topeka, Kansas. We spot a few Mods wandering around along the way. We have strict orders not to shoot them unless they are a direct threat. The last thing we want is to draw attention to ourselves. Plus, we need to save our ammunition for the real fight if it comes down to it.

Sean makes a SITREP back to HQ advising them of our position and time, ensuring we're on schedule and that everything is going as planned. Repeater stations were set up years back so we should have good comms with HQ for the entire trip. We'll have to set up a few new ones along the way once we're past the four-hundred-mile point. While Sean talks to them, we run through the protocols to prepare the two R-11 refueler trucks. We'll create an assembly line by setting up both refuelers, each holding six thousand gallons of diesel fuel, at the front of the convoy, closely guarded by several Humvees. This way we can have four vehicles being fueled at once, one on each side of the refuelers.

As the fuel trucks get into position, we launch several drones to monitor the surrounding area. With their thermal capabilities, we can see anything coming at us from any direction and from several miles out. Should take about one hour for this stop.

Brad moves us into place just in front of the refuelers while Jared jumps on the .50 cal. Several snipers jump up top of each of the M-CIWSs so they can get a good view of the area. I grab my rifle and step out along with Brad to stretch our legs.

Over the radio, we hear, "Drones are in the sky."

With everyone at the ready, we begin fueling and go into radio silence unless there is an emergency. The only person allowed to talk is the fueling truck operator to announce the completion of a vehicle and for the next to move into place.

Halfway through the process, one of the snipers reports movement from the west about two hundred yards out. We grab our binoculars to investigate while we wait for him to confirm the threat.

"Looks like there's a small group heading this way," the sniper announces.

"Pull the drones in tighter," Sean orders the drone operator. "I want to make sure there isn't anything hiding behind those Mods as a decoy."

The drones only identify the Mods, and Sean then orders the snipers to take care of the problem. Their rifles are all equipped with suppressors, and they soon enter into a friendly competition of picking the Mods off one by one with perfect headshots.

With the Mods gone and all the vehicles fueled up and ready to go, our wheels start rolling again. As we move, getting back into formation, the drones fly back to their docking stations located on top of the cabs of their respective M-CIWSs. For the next while, there isn't any excitement other than the highway changing names to 335.

Sean makes his second announcement. "Attention everyone. Just a friendly reminder that our next stop will be just north of Oklahoma City, still located in hell. Please sit back, relax, and enjoy the lovely service entertainment we don't offer." We all get another good chuckle.

I pull out the map with our route highlighted. The highway here is congested with busted vehicles, so we must take a small detour to get to Oklahoma City. From the photos taken during the recon, it looks as though someone put up a blockade and didn't kindly remove it for us. I study the map a little more just in case, but we have no choice but to add about fifteen miles of side roads to the drive. Unfortunately, there isn't a more direct way. It is what it is.

We pass through a plethora of small towns before coming to the farthest location we had ever traveled to in the past, Wichita, Kansas. McConnell Air Force Base to be exact. We picked up two KC-135R Stratotankers years ago. They needed some work, and we spent an entire month down here to get them back into flight-ready condition. Put us in good standing with the head of the Air Force. The KCs are currently sitting at Chicago O'Hare. Not sure what we'll use them for, but it's always good to have a refueling aircraft on hand in case you need it.

After passing through Wichita, the trip remains uneventful, making me drift into a dreamless sleep. Long car rides make me tired. Jared nudges me hard in the shoulder, startling me awake just north of Oklahoma City so we can start going through our refueling protocols once again. I roll down the window. It's notably colder here as compared to Topeka. Twenty degrees colder to be exact.

We make it to our planned exit and navigate through several streets to the east of the city to make it south of Norman. We clear a few streets that are blocked with sedans and station wagons. Nothing a few of our military trucks with modified bumpers can't handle.

***

We cross over the Red River. It's hard to see with darkness blanketing the horizon but from what I can tell, it looks like it's flowing. A partially cracked sign with quite a few bullet holes greets us on the other side. Welcome to Texas! The state of the sign doesn't make me feel very welcomed, but we finally made it...well, almost. I roll down the window and stick my hand out to get a better feel for the weather. It's not as cold as I was hoping with mostly overcast skies and maybe even some rain the farther south we go.

We make one more refueling stop a few miles into Texas, giving us an opportunity to walk around, take a shit, and shoot the breeze with one another. It was a much-needed break from sitting. My watch says 18:30. We still have five more hours until we reach our destination. We're a little behind but still on track in general.

"You're not going to believe what I'm seeing. Look to your right, everyone," Sean announces as we reach the town of Gainesville.

There's an open field with hundreds of grazing cattle, as happy as can be. *What the hell?* The Joscos and Mods should have killed and eaten them by now. Sean slows the convoy, but we don't stop moving. *How is this possible?*

"Is it me, or do these cattle look well-fed and taken care of?" Brad asks.

I jump on the radio. "Somebody's definitely looking after these cattle. You might want to alert HQ about this. How did they not pick them up on the recon mission? Thermals should have, if not aerials."

"I could go for a steak right now," Jared chimes in licking his chops.

"Yeah, me too." Brad agrees.

We didn't waste much time gawking at the drive-through zoo, but Sean radioed it in. Not twenty miles later, we come across something else, but this time it brings us to a complete stop.

Sean orders one of the M-CIWS to be activated, drones in the air, and everyone to be ready. Jared climbs up to the .50 cal. We don our night vision gear and prepare for the worst.

"Listen up. We've got a vehicle dead ahead approximately a hundred yards. It's partially blocking our path which isn't the problem. I don't have this vehicle identified on any of the recon maps so it's new," Sean states, and I confirm.

Sean exits his vehicle and makes his way back to one equipped with monitors to review drone footage. "Sean, I'm heading up to you," I say grabbing my rifle.

"Roger that."

We sit huddled together in the back seat and watch the drone footage as it flies over the wreckage.

"Accident looks recent," I say.

"Damn! Look at that. Something smashed hard into the passenger side of that van," Sean says.

"Yeah, that looks like the work of a Josco," I muse.

The van is turned onto its side. It skidded about forty feet judging from the skid marks.

"Look." Sean puts a finger on the monitor. "There's a Josco. Damn thing got ripped to shreds. What the fuck would be able to do that?" he asks.

"Another Josco." I state the obvious. "Does that van look familiar to you? I've seen it before."

"That can't be the doctor's van, can it? What the hell was he doing all the way down here?"

"I think you're right, can't be a coincidence." I agree.

"If that Josco didn't survive, there's no way in hell that doctor could have. Go up a little higher." Sean tells the drone operator. "I want to see the surrounding area. Make sure there are no signatures getting picked up."

"Yes, sir."

We wait in silence watching the monitors.

"Nothing. Doesn't look like there's anything else out there," Sean says. He looks at me. "What do you think?"

"Well, whatever or whoever did this is probably long gone by now. I say we take a quick look and then push through. No more than five minutes, tops."

Sean takes a moment while the drones survey the area. I could see the few brains cells Sean has left working hard on this one.

"Okay, we'll push on past this wreckage. Make sure we're safe. Six of us will come back and check it out. Sound good?" Sean says as he glances over to me for confirmation.

"That's what I would do if I was in charge." I give Sean a wink. He shakes his head.

Sean jumps on the comms and gives everyone a rundown of the plan. We push forward to what seems like a safe distance beyond the wreckage.

The land is open around us, so it's easy to make out anything suspicious. Two men stand watch with their .50 cals while the four of us search the van. We arrive at the dead Josco first. The left leg has been severed from the body. Blood everywhere. Half the leg has been gnawed to the bone. Its jaw was ripped from its head, exposing the tongue and insides of its throat.

"Fuck me. That had to hurt," I say. "I'm surprised there's still some meat left on these bones.

"You think another Josco did this?" Sean asks.

"It definitely fits their MO. It's the only reasonable explanation I can think of. Maybe they got into a fight over who wanted to eat the doctor?" I want to laugh, but the scene is unsettling.

"Hey guys, come take a look at this." Riley chimes in. We look over to see her ransacking through the back of the van, where both doors are severely damaged.

"What is it, Riley?" Sean asks.

"Found an arm," she says, lifting it up with the tip of her rifle.

"Yeah, so?"

"Come see what's *in* the arm."

We walk over, flashlights pointed down.

"An IV stuck in its vein. Why would there be an IV?" Sean says, leaning down to grab the clear plastic cord to inspect it.

"This definitely confirms it's the doctor's van," I say.

"How the fuck do you even get close enough to stick an IV in one of these fuckers?" Riley asks.

"Good question. One that I'm not so sure I want to know the answer to right now," Sean says. "Alright, let's get the hell out of here. This is taking up too much time."

"Hey, Sean, I think I have something else," Riley says, rummaging through more of the van.

"Now what?" Sean yells out.

"I don't know. It's a metal container."

"Is it heavy?" I ask.

"Not really. Maybe forty pounds. There's some other stuff back here as well. More containers."

Sean hesitates. I know he wants to get going, but he also wants to grab everything he can. Sean calls up a few more men.

"Listen up. I want everything. We got two minutes! We'll look at it later when we get back home." Sean orders one of the box vans to come back, and we spend the next minute loading everything that might be useful. Not certain what we'll find, but I'm sure it'll be interesting. We finish and continue our journey.

A few hours later, our convoy exits Interstate 35, traveling west onto what used to be US-190, toward Fort Hood. It's nearly midnight, and we still have another twenty miles to go. We're wide awake, ready, and expectant. Jared messes with his night vision goggles. Brad's eyes are glued to the road in front of him, making sure we don't plow into the vehicle in front of us. I'm staring wide-eyed into the unknown.

"I can't believe we're here. This is fucking crazy, Scott," Brad says, staring at me through his night vision goggles.

"You keep your eyes on the road," I scold. "Let's just pray the rest goes as smoothly as the ride down here."

"I started praying the second we left. Hell, I even prayed for a snowstorm to whip through Omaha to keep us from leaving in the first place," Jared says.

It's foreign. Empty. Dead. We hit a few roadblocks along the way. The pavement is cracked and dilapidated, with weeds and grass forcing their way through the fractures.

"Should we check in with the guard?" Brad jokes as we pass through the busted gate.

"Nice one." I bump Brad's shoulder with a fist. "You're with me, so no need." He laughs.

We arrive at our location and set up a perimeter on an empty tarmac. It gives us 360 degrees of unobstructed view, which helps with the M-CIWS's line of sight.

"Everyone, you know what to do. We've practiced this a few times now, so let's do it. I want eyes in the sky, and I want to know about every movement out there. I don't care if it's an ant wiping his ass. I want to know." Sean runs through the checklist. We ensure everything is in place, set up and get the M-CIWSs ready, then strategically maneuver our vehicles into position, and so on. At first light, we start working. It takes roughly an hour to get everything set up, and once completed, Sean and I go through the next set of mission details and scope out what we can from base camp.

I order my men to get some rest. There's no way I'm going to sleep tonight, and I probably won't tomorrow, either. I stay up with four others. Two will monitor the systems, making sure the M-CIWSs don't take out an unsuspecting animal that's passing through and scare the shit out of us. Two other snipers equipped with suppressed rifles are ready to quietly take out any Mods or any other threat that might stumble into our safe zone. I keep the coffees flowing so the men's eyes stay wide open.

CHAPTER SIXTEEN

(Lieutenant Scott Dodson—U.S. Marines)

Wednesday, January 22, 2048

As the sun starts to create its orange hue along the eastern horizon, I grab half of my team to venture outside the confines of our safe haven. I leave the other half with Sean and his group, providing security as they pick apart and load up anything they see of value.

Our small convoy of three Humvees and a couple of box vans head north along an old taxiway. I'm positioned at the tail end, where I get a lovely visual of the Josco Brothers sitting in one of the vans, dangling their feet out the back. Bryan is swinging his feet like a little kid; I laugh at the unnatural sight. Damn thing is riding a little low with the two of them with their modified M134 Dillion miniguns attached to custom exoskeletons engineered to fit their oversized, muscular frames. With the help of a few engineers, they created their own personalized suit, each one capable of carrying two 750 round containers of 7.62x51mm that is belt fed to a minigun for each arm. The two of them are force multipliers. They got the Rolls Royce of weapons furnished with custom grips and triggers. Their sausage fingers are just too big for anything we small, regular folk carry. It would be like me carrying a toothpick-sized gun.

As we drive to our first location, I roll down the window to what I thought would be fresh air filling the cabin. Instead, a rotting stench causes my face to pucker, so I roll the window back up as fast as it'll go and hear several "thank yous" from the back seat. It's not as cold as I would like. Even at fifty degrees, we still stand a chance of seeing

204

Joscos. Down here, they've been known to travel in packs well into the thousands, like a herd of wildebeest migrating the African outback. I can't imagine coming across that many at one time. The most I've seen in one sitting was maybe a couple hundred, years back while on post duty. We had to call in air support, and two A-10 Warthogs swooped in and saved our asses. It was a spectacular display of their 30 mm Gatling guns plowing down the enemy. They looked like little ants pouring out of an ant hill after being poked with a stick. We stood there in awe, with our binoculars glued to our eyes, watching their limbs explode from their bodies. The vivid scene—a constant red mist filling the air—replays in my mind. The icing on the cake was when two AH-64 Apache helicopters came in and finished them off. Most satisfying ten minutes of my career. The two choppers stayed and completed the job until the last Josco's head exploded.

Driving around Fort Hood proved it was a massive base that was over 200,000 acres when it was operational. The base was only outfitted with one runway, which sits just to the west of our current position, and surprisingly still looks to be in good condition. We take a left, heading west, at the north end of a crumbling part of the runway. We could spend months here and probably never see all that this base has to offer. Hundreds of buildings line the deserted streets. It's sad to stare out the window and see everything just sitting here in decay. Years of sun, weather, and nature have eaten away at everything. Helicopters of all sorts sit toppled over.

One, in particular, catches my eye; its broken blades lay sideways, likely damaged when the pilot was trying to take off during an attack. Poor bastard didn't stand a chance. The entire right side of the fuselage is gone. We navigate past tanks that lay on their side with their tracks torn from the road wheels. The tarmac is riddled with varying-sized craters from grenades and artillery, as if a meteor shower fell directly on this place. The aerial reconnaissance photos do nothing for the real-life version. We navigate around the massive potholes, avoiding as much wreckage as possible.

We give Sean a SITREP as we pull up to the two hangars we identified before we left, just across from where we set up base camp, and in return, he advises of a good find in one of the other priority hangars on our list. A lot of Humvees are in almost-mint condition, along with many expertly stacked parts. It's like they knew we'd come eventually and had it organized for us and ready to load up.

While Sean focuses on his task, we reach our first destination and circle the building to get a good look before getting out. Mother Nature has done her part consuming every inch of the exterior. Vines have crawled all the way to the peak, and weeds as tall as me litter the ground making it almost impossible to walk up to the building. I'm ninety-three percent sure we packed some machetes. Even the nearby trees have punctured through the metal siding, but structurally it appears to be sound.

"Stop!" I order Brad, noticing something odd between the two buildings at the rear.

"What is it?" Brad asks, craning his neck around to see what I'm looking at.

"Something doesn't look quite right, but I want a closer look to be sure. Stay here, keep the engine running, and look alive," I order Brad.

I get on the comms. "Everyone stay alert."

I request the Josco Brothers and Riley to join me at the alleyway to the rear of the buildings.

"Whatcha got, boss?" Bryan's heavy footsteps crunch the gravel.

"Well, for starters, why is this area more manicured than the surrounding area?" We scan the ground, and it looks as though someone recently mowed.

"And secondly, why are there two huge-ass generators with wiring connected to both of these buildings?" Riley jumps in before I can finish.

"Exactly." I exchange a nod with her.

"Maybe someone couldn't stand the heat and wanted a little A/C! I heard it gets hot down here in the summertime," Frank says, doing a little dance.

"Why are you dancing? Don't," Jared says, shaking his head.

Frank gently caresses Jared's arm with the tip of his minigun and rolls his hips, mouthing something sexual at him.

"Stop flirting with each other!" Attempting to ignore their exchange, I walk over and pick up a five-gallon plastic can of what I assume is diesel fuel sitting next to the generator. There's maybe a gallon left inside.

"What are you thinking, boss man? Want to start it up? See what it does?" Staff Sergeant Nathan Bueche asks as he's patrolling.

"No, but I do think they were recently used. For what purpose, I have no idea, but I think we're about to find out. Let's load up and head to the front and see what's inside."

We make our way to the front of the buildings, backing in our vehicles in case things go south. With weapons in hand, we exit, leaving a man positioned at each of the .50 cals.

We never just go into a building—not anymore. Years back, we came across some structures that were booby-trapped. Several men lost limbs, so now we make damn sure there are no surprises before entering. A few men inspect the exterior perimeter while the rest of us keep watch.

"Smell is worse in the front," Brad states, waving a hand.

"Maybe we should enter through the rear." Riley suggests.

"We can make that happen sweetcakes!" Nathan winks at Riley.

"Not even in your wildest dreams." Riley gives Nathan the middle finger. "It's not bad enough that I have to deal with the man smells in the van, but now we have a warehouse full of stank." Riley plugs her nose using her pointer finger and thumb, then glares at us.

"I'm pretty sure that's the same smell from earlier when I rolled down the window. That's the smell of something that's been rotting for a while. No doubt about it. Maybe those generators were used to keep food cold, and now all that food is way past its expiration date."

"Great!" Bryan says in his deep, thundering voice, stretching out his arms with his miniguns so far that he looks like a circus freak.

"Watch yourself with those things. You might poke someone's eye out," I say jokingly as Bryan walks up from behind. "Well, it just wouldn't be right if the first thing we came across wasn't an infestation of nastiness," I respond with a smile.

"I'm ready!" Frank kisses his guns. "I'm ready for anything."

The guys return from their inspection and give me the okay to enter. I send Jared in along with seven other men to sweep the inside while the rest of us set up a perimeter and keep watch outside. Not three seconds pass before I get a call on the radio that sounds of men retching.

"Scott?" Jared chokes and coughs over the radio.

"Go ahead." There was a pause before he came back on.

"You might want to come"—there's an even longer pause—"in here and look at this. You're not going—"

"You're breaking up, man. What's going on?" I respond.

"—to believe this shit." Jared sounded as if he was dry heaving between his words.

"Shit, you guys literally just walked in there." I lean back on the hood of one of the Humvees.

"Man, just…in here," he says, coughing. "And bring…a…mask. It…reeks."

"He's such a baby," Bryan says. "It can't be that bad."

"Alright, if you can hear me, Riley and I are coming in. Don't shoot." I gesture at Riley to follow me, even though she gives me a pleading look to stay.

The smell gets more rancid with every step closer we take toward the building. Tears form in my eyes, and we haven't even walked inside. Two men run out with their hands covering their mouths and nearly knocking us down as we approach the door. A few steps closer, Riley and I would have been on the receiving end of their partially digested breakfast. They stand just outside hunched over, emptying the contents of their stomachs.

"Damn!" I wince, covering my nose and mouth with a mask and click on my flashlight as I pass through the front doors.

"Hey, thanks for the invite," Riley replied, coughing out some sarcasm and using her shirt to cover her nose and mouth.

We walk past a small office area where a few other men are covering their mouths, trying not to gag. If the smell wasn't an indication of the shit we were about to see, the swarming of the flies, gnats, and just about every other insect that had wings buzzing around here would have given it away.

"Who farted?" I point my light in Dan's face, trying to get a laugh. "Was it you?" He doesn't laugh. In fact, his eyes have so many tears I doubt he can even see.

"Sir"—he coughs—"you really don't want to go in there. May we be excused from this building?"

"Just hold tight and let me see what's going on." I bat the air with my hand, holding the flashlight and trying to keep the insects from landing on my face.

At first glance through a large glass window into the warehouse, it looks like a temporary hospital facility with white sheets held up by makeshift stands. Possibly set up after the Turning, which makes sense for the generators to be out back, but they look too well maintained for something that happened that long ago. Besides, whatever is here would be long decayed. After passing the threshold from the office to the warehouse area, it became obvious that this was no hospital. Not even close. The paper-thin mask I'm pressing hard to my face is doing nothing for the smell or the millions of flying insects. The sight only adds to the horridness of it all. The only positive is that this answers a fifteen-year-old question we've all been wanting to know.

Riley and I walk up to Jared, who's standing with his light in one hand, shining it on one of the giant makeshift beds and his other hand covering his mouth. I offer him the paper mask I was using.

"Really?" He snatches it from my grip.

"It's all we have," I say as he brings it up to his face.

My head follows his light, illuminating the horror next to us.

"Oh my God." My face winces and bile collects at the back of my throat. I swallow to will it back down.

"Nope, fucking nope." Riley shakes her head and makes a beeline out of the building, and I do nothing to stop her.

"Yeah," Jared says.

We've seen some horrible things in our line of work, and I would like to say I have a strong stomach, but this was the most disgusting, most wretched scene my eyes have ever taken in and my nostrils have ever smelled. I can't take it. I sprint out of the building, Jared in tow. The rest of the men clear the offices behind us until no one is left in the building.

"Fuck, someone get these bay doors open!" I keel over, gagging. The entire contents of my stomach come out like water from a fire hose. "Let's get some air flowing in there." My eyes and nose run so much that I don't know who I pointed at to open the doors.

"Hey, Sean, you got a copy?" I jump on the comms, coughing into the mic, and then spit out some leftover stomach chunks that were caught between my teeth. With a big sniffle, I catch my snot with the sleeve of my shirt. This is far worse than gas chamber training.

It takes him a minute to respond. "Yeah, go ahead."

"I need you to stop what you are doing and come over to our first location."

"What? You already need my help, cupcake?"

"Hell no. You just need to come. If you don't see it with your own eyes, you won't believe me." I wipe my mouth with the opposite sleeve and spit again.

"Alright, give me a few. We just found another building with a ton of parts."

"Roger that. We'll be waiting. We're in no hurry. Over." He can take all fucking day and I wouldn't care. Let that shit air the fuck out.

While we wait on Sean, we get to work prying open the large metal doors; they protest, screeching in agony with every inch they slide open. We make note of the shorter vines that have been cut away from around the doors, another sign that someone has been here more recently. After twenty minutes of using every bit of muscle strength we have, we finally get the doors open. A massive, dark cloud of bugs swarms out of the hangar as if the light of day cued them that it was time to leave. I take a step back, allowing the wall of bugs to vacate the area; the sunlight not only rid us of the bug infestation, but it also revealed the entire interior. All we can do is stand there in silence, at a safe distance. Just when we thought a Josco could be the worst thing imaginable, something like this presents itself.

We take a break, resting our bodies until we hear a vehicle fast approaching. *It's go time.* A Humvee swerves around us and pulls right up to where I am relaxing as though they are a VIP.

"Alright. Here I am. Let's see it, Scotty. What'd you make me come all the way over here for?" Sean spouts off, jumping out of his vehicle. He waves his hand in front of his face from the smell. "This ought to be good."

"Gentleman, this way to your date." I motion him to follow.

"Real funny," Sean says.

"This will make you gag. Well, maybe you're into this kind of shit, so you might like it." I slap his arm. "I would tell you to wear a mask, but it won't do you any good against the smell. Maybe the bugs won't be as bad since we opened the doors."

"Ha-ha, you're funny," he says and then takes in a deep breath. "What the fuck is this place?"

"Let's go in a little deeper, shall we." I lead the way.

Brad, Sean, and I walk up to the nearest bed, and everyone else stays back. Flies still swarm around us, as only a portion of them had vacated since opening the doors. Sean attempts to swat them away, but there are far too many of them. I pull back the nearest curtain. Sean turns his head in disgust, flinching at the sight. His nose twitches.

"Fuck me. Yep. You did it, Scott. I could have done without this. Pictures would have been just fine."

"This hangar is full of them. There's gotta be over a hundred beds in here. All laid out the same." I say.

"They all look like this, all shackled up and sliced open?" he asks, grimacing.

"From what we've been able to see, yeah. We haven't ventured too far into the building, and I'm willing to bet the hangar next to us is set up the same. We haven't even bothered to look yet. I don't plan on going in there, except maybe to sneak a peek."

"Fuck, I don't blame you." He coughs some more and takes a few steps back.

Hundreds of female Joscos lay on blood-stained beds, naked, and restrained with IVs still in their arms. It's clear the animals and insects have had their fill. They are set up in perfect rows with only a few feet of space between them, just enough to walk past to the next row. All of them are butchered and infested with maggots and every other insect that feeds on this shit. Some of the Joscos have had their feet sawed off just above the ankles and were poorly cauterized. I can only assume their feet are missing to have kept them from escaping.

"They all appear to have had C-sections?" Sean asks questionably as he looks around. "Have you seen any babies? There's a couple sonogram machines over in the corner."

"No babies. But like I said, we haven't looked around the entire facility. Not sure what to make of this other than this must have been some type of experimental breeding facility. Oddly enough, from what we can tell, they seem to have died around the same time, giving birth to whatever monster came out of them. They don't look as though they've been dead for very long, though. Maybe a month?"

"Yeah, they're still pretty fresh from the looks of it." Sean kicks a blood-stained towel out from under the bed.

The Joscos appear to have been starved. Their bodies were covered in bruises. Some had broken bones and others appeared to have self-inflicted injuries, possibly from trying to get away.

"Dude, take a look at this. We didn't see this earlier." I point to a poorly written five-digit tattoo along the hairline of its forehead. I walk over to a few of the others, each of whom has a different number.

"Who do you think did this?" Sean asks.

"How the fuck would I know? Definitely not a Josco, that's for certain. I doubt they have a steady enough hand nor the executive functioning to do shit like this." I picture a Josco wearing scrubs and holding a scalpel. *Yeah, that's a hell no.*

"No, I guess not. You think humans did this?" Sean says.

"Has to be," I reply.

"Someone like Dr. Anderson?" Sean muses.

"Could be. That guy seems fucked up enough in the head to do some shit like this." I'm starting to put the pieces together. "He took off for years at a time, right? Maybe this is where he's been hiding."

"This isn't exactly the safest place for humans to be doing experiments. I mean, we're here with sixty guys and a million rounds of ammo and tons of artillery, and I don't feel good about it," Brad chimes in.

"Unless he has a brigade of soldiers with him, I doubt he did this. Not alone, anyway."

"Well, whatever is going on here, it's all fucked up. I'll get on the radio and advise HQ about this. I really hope they don't ask us to bring one of these back with us." Sean raises an eyebrow toward me.

"You don't want her sitting next to you on the way home?" Brad asks, nudging him on the shoulder.

"Hell no." Sean shakes his body in disgust. "Like I said, I'll find out what HQ wants, and if they order us to bring one back, guess what?" Sean points to me. "You're taggin' and baggin' 'em. You fucking found them." We pause for a moment, looking at the sight, still in awe.

"The fuck I will," I reply.

"Well, see what else you can find. Maybe there are papers or something else that could be useful. This all looks scientific and shit." He waves his hand in the air.

"Yeah, I'll let you know if we find anything." Here's to hoping there are no more surprises.

"Well, have fun, kids. I'm getting the fuck out of here. You might want to keep a watchful eye." He takes a suspicious look around. "Whoever did it might still be here. Have fun, cupcake," he says with a smirk and walks off.

"Thanks." I give him the finger.

As soon as Sean clears the scene, a pissed-off Riley storms toward the bed. Her jaw clenched tight, taking deep breaths through her nose. I hadn't seen her since she fled the scene earlier, but we all deal with this stuff differently, and I wanted her to have her space.

"Riley, are you good?" I've seen her mad, but this is different.

She screams a deep, pained sound and turns her gun, using the butt like a baseball bat, and shatters the nearest sonogram machine. She continues to hit it until only a few larger pieces remain. She turns her gun back around and wipes a stream of tears from her red face.

"This is bullshit. They may have been Joscos, but they mutilated these females, and for what? I hate this. Let's do what we need to do. I'll be fine." Riley shakes it off and straightens up before getting back to her duties. I respect the shit out of her, and I didn't even think of how she might feel about this situation. She's a soldier, though, and I would never treat her any differently; she would hate that.

We searched both hangars as quick as possible and determined there was nothing more to see. Everyone was getting sick from the sights and smells. I don't want my team having to sit it out the rest of the trip, so I make the decision to get out. We take plenty of pictures and videos before moving on.

We hit up several other buildings in the area that are identified as "of interest," and luckily, there is not a single thing interesting about any of them. We keep a record of the equipment we come across, marking it on a map as we move along, so that one day, if we do decide to come back—and I pray to God that we don't—we'll know what's here.

With the sun setting, we make our way back to base camp, where Sean and his team still have some work to do. We do our part to help, while the other half of my team continues to be Sean's private security detail until they finish for the day. With the sun dipping below the horizon, we set up the perimeter and hunker down for the night.

CHAPTER SEVENTEEN

(Lieutenant Scott Dodson—U.S. Marines)

Thursday, January 23, 2048

The restless night had me sitting in the command post watching monitors with the night-watch guys—goofy SOBs if you ask me. They tell some of the lamest jokes. If I ever hear another "Why did the chicken cross the road" or "Knock, Knock" joke again, I'll shoot myself. How could somebody even know that many jokes about chickens?

It did get intense a few times when the thermals picked up wildlife roaming the area. We watched a mountain lion stalking a small herd of deer at the southern point of the airstrip. It got better when one of the guys started commentating on the event as it unfolded, even naming the lion "Mr. Prance." I damn near shit myself listening to him as he described, in great detail, how it went down. He even quieted his voice as if he was trying not to spook the animals, getting close to the monitor to add to the dramatic scene. Even though the hunt only lasted a few minutes, it was some of the best TV action I have seen in a long time. In the end, Mr. Prance got his meal, dragging it off somewhere to enjoy.

The only other excitement was when one of the drones picked up a large pack of Mods several miles to the northeast. It was very odd, as they were indecisive, as if they couldn't make up their minds about whether they wanted to continue past a certain point. I'd never seen them disjointed like that before. At first, we thought there was a barbed wire fence keeping them from moving on, but when the drone flew in closer, there was no ditch or anything else that would keep them from proceeding. I woke Sean up so he could witness it too. We sat there for almost two hours, watching them walk in circles and attempting to cross the invisible barrier. Thankfully, they continued to keep their distance. Had they come any closer, we would've had to put the place on high alert.

The morning sun peeks its annoyingly bright yellow head up from the east, making my eyes burn. The second day starts off in typical fashion with a morning briefing in which I work hard not to close my heavy eyelids from a lack of sleep. Sean doesn't envision his team taking more than five hours to complete their work. So, with any luck, we'll head back home early. They have four flatbed trailers left to load up. Everything has been pre-organized in one of the warehouses so all they need to do is get the forklifts going to load the remaining items and get them secured. As for us, we have one building to check out and can leave any time after that. Maybe if we're lucky, we can head out a bit earlier. I'd have no arguments against that. I'd love nothing more than to nap in the van.

"…and no later than 1200 hours, everyone better be back. The sooner, the better. I want all vehicles fueled up and ready to bug out because wheels start turning then." We force down our MREs while Sean rambles on. There are a few quiet cheers of excitement and smiles on everyone's faces at the prospect of getting the hell out of here.

After chow, I round up my men and we make our way to the building that some old Weapons Specialist in the Army back home suggested we explore. Major White wasn't sure how great the specialist's memory was about the location but said the place might be worth checking out. He had informed the Major about some special rail gun stored there that could shoot out needle-sized bullets faster and more accurately than a powder bullet using electromagnetics. Sounds farfetched, but who am I to argue?

I pull out the map showing the route to the building circled in yellow. The road to take us there is named Hell on Wheels Avenue. *We need to rethink our street names back home.* The building is roughly two and a half miles away from our command post, so I'm a bit nervous about being this far from the hive with no protection from the M-CIWS. The road is in much worse shape than we thought, with craters that could swallow two Humvees.

It was an agonizingly slow and treacherous drive, but we arrived at our destination unscathed. We circle the building a few times. The one-story warehouse/office building is in no better condition than any of the others on base. **Most of the windows are busted out, and the mustard-colored paint is barely visible through the thick vines that have overtaken the exterior. The scene is one dead tree away from being the set of a horror film.**

We park out front and set up shop, and just like everywhere else around here, the tall weeds and grass have taken over the parking lot, leaving the ground cracked. We go through our gear, making sure everything is in order, and attach our night vision goggles to our helmets. Our destination is three levels below ground. *Why the hell did they have to store weapons down there?*

I turn to my platoon, and ask, "You guys ready?" I watch as they gather, some still donning their head gear.

"Excuse me!" Riley shouts.

"My apologies, Riley. You know I refer to everyone as a guy. It's a northern thing."

"I'm just fucking with you." She grabs her crotch. "My set is probably bigger than most of y'alls!" she says in a southern accent with a grin bigger than the state of Texas.

"Whaaaaaaaat!" Frank blurts out in a high-pitched voice.

"That's for damn sure!" Bryan high-fives her as everyone else is hootin' and hollerin', pointing at each other, damn near to the point of pissing themselves.

"Alright, alright. Quiet down, kids. Let's get our shit together, shall we." I walk over to Riley, and we fist bump. "That's right, Riley! Way to show us guys what's up. I love it."

"Well, I'm ready," Bryan says, stroking one of his miniguns.

"Of course you are, Bryan. We all know how ready you are," Nathan chimes in.

Between him and Frank, they're carrying three thousand rounds. And aside from their superhuman strength, they can see in complete darkness. We're all a little jealous of some of their abilities but not of their looks. In my mind, I wince at those Neanderthal features.

Frank and Bryan start gently rubbing their miniguns together, giving all of us a look as though they're pleasuring themselves. I just grimace, roll my eyes, and continue working.

"You guys are going to have to find other ways of letting us know you're ready besides stroking your stuff," Jared says in a muffled tone but loud enough for them to hear. Jared's comment only adds to their enthusiastic gesturing.

We've run through it a few times, but I want to make damn sure it's embedded into their brains. Some of the men will stay topside to maintain the perimeter while the rest of us go to the depths of the unknown.

"Alright, Dorsey." I put my left hand on his shoulder and look deeply into his green eyes. "You're in charge up here. Don't let anyone give you any shit, you hear me?"

"Yes, sir." He raises his hand with a thumbs-up.

"I want radio checks every few minutes. If you don't hear from us for whatever reason, you contact McCauley. You understand?" He nods. "I'll keep you posted as we navigate through the building. It should take us about fifteen minutes to locate the vault. Just make sure everyone is in position and ready. If anyone sees anything suspicious, I don't care if it's a butterfly farting in the wind, I want to hear about it immediately, you got it?"

"Yes, sir." His confidence shows as he stands up a little taller.

I nod, staring hard at Dorsey. He joined us two years ago, right out of training. This is the first time he's ever been put in charge of anything and the first he's ever been outside the safety confines of The River. Even though it's a small task, I have confidence in him.

Dorsey and his men have strict orders not to enter the building, no matter what they see or hear. I don't want them getting lost while trying to find us. Then we'd all be scattered about, not to mention introducing the potential for friendly fire.

I'm the only one who will converse with Dorsey unless I'm unable to; then, Brad owns the comms. I'll use hand signals to communicate to my men while down below until I know we're safe. I want to go in quietly so our ears pick up anything unusual. I'm hoping the old man's directions are correct. Memories can get fuzzy after so many years.

I take point, and we get into a modified file formation and walk toward where a set of double doors once stood. Inside, I lower my night vision goggles, and my world becomes green while I maintain security of the breach. For maximum security, the next three Marines filter in, scanning their sectors. With the building deemed safe, the rest of the team piles in. As we move along, we spray paint arrows along the walls leading out just in case we get lost or separated. We are quick to locate the stairwell that leads down to sublevel three. We adjust our formation as we make our way down the stairs.

After exiting the stairwell, we walk right into a hallway that's eight feet wide and then get into a rolling T formation, which allows for flexible rotation around corners and intersections. As we enter the main hallway, the stale air hits us. The corridor is littered with debris, causing a little disruption to our progress. Dark spots blot the floor and walls, which, I can only assume, are decade old blood stains. Old military pictures and posters still hang on the walls. We scrutinize every door and room we pass, ensuring there are no surprises, sounding out a quiet "clear" that echoes down the abandoned corridors.

The room should be just around the corner, one hundred feet, or so the old man had advised. We scan our zones, moving one step at a time in a smooth motion. We've been together for many years, so we know how each other operates.

The Weapons Specialist wasn't sure of the exact room number but thought it would be close to sublevel Room 323. Unfortunately, none of the doors we're passing have any form of identification number on them. I'm starting to think we may have been told the wrong building. Shit, we could be at the wrong base for all we know.

Nothing looks anything like the Weapon's Specialist said it would, but we continue. The sublevel is a labyrinth of tunnels that connect to other buildings. We walk another two hundred feet before we finally reach what we're looking for. We didn't find Room 323, but we did find Room 317.

The door is guarded by a single unfortunate soul who is missing a few limbs. All that is left are their bones and a few torn articles of clothing. Plenty of brass is spread out all along the hallway. Not even sure this person is military, but who knows?

"Poor bastard. At least you went out fighting, brother," I mutter.

The door has a heavy-duty security pad on it. They really wanted these weapons secured, but it looks like they left it open. *Damn, this place may have already been raided.* We set up a perimeter, securing the corridor, then I order Bryan to pull the thick metal vault door open while Frank enters with both miniguns at the ready. Several minutes pass before we hear "all clear," and then one by one, we filter in except for a few who stand watch outside the room.

Large pelican containers are stacked nice and neat all along the walls and on all the shelves. We walk the entire room only to find a few half-eaten remains at the rear.

"Dorsey, you copy?" There is a little static on my end.

"Loud and clear. Go ahead, sir."

"We've located the room. Get the box van backed up as close as you can to the doors. Going to send up four men with some of these containers. There are quite a few, so I need you to pick out four of your men to help. Have Paul coordinate the teams and stagger them so the four coming up will load everything and then secure the area while the next four head down. We'll just keep rotating them. I want to get these loaded up ASAP. Just have the men follow the spray-painted arrows to us. How's everything topside? Over."

"All good up here, sir. I'll have the van ready and the men waiting by the entrance. Over."

"Roger that."

"Oh, and Dorsey, get a few of those portable lights ready and have your men bring them down. Over."

"Yes, sir."

"Alright, listen up," I say, pointing to four members of my team. "You four grab a couple of these containers and start taking them up. When you get topside, tell the guys coming down to set up a light in the stairwell, one just as you enter the corridor and one just on the other side of this room. You"—I point to the fifth member—"go with them and provide support while they carry these up and help rotate positions as needed. Got it?"

"Yes, sir. Easy-peasy."

I turn to the rest of the men. "Frank, Bryan, Riley, Nathan, stay down here and look pretty. Also, make sure nothing comes at us. Jared,"—I put my hand on his shoulder—"you and I will get these containers ready for the next group to take up. We'll line them up and down this corridor. Does everyone understand their role?"

I get nothing but glares back. "Jared, let's get to work."

Jared and I return to the room and walk up to one of the open containers that had fallen over before we arrived. There are six rifle-like weapons and six magazines inside.

"Come over here and look at this, Jared. You ever see ammo like this?" I shine my light onto it while lifting my goggles.

I pick up a magazine roughly the same size as a .50 cal one, but it's nothing like I've ever seen. I pop out one of the bullets. The tip is glass-like, and there's no casing, but where the casing would normally be, there are indentions as though something folds out of it. Weird.

"Nope. But that thing looks like it could do some damage. I like it." Jared nods his head in approval.

"Yeah, I wouldn't want to be on the receiving end of this. Whatever it is?" I hold it up in the air to get a better look. "Interesting, but I don't think this is the rail gun the guy was talking about." Each magazine looks to hold six rounds. "Should be fun to fire off a few when we get back."

We start moving the containers out of the room and into the hallway, lining them up in an orderly fashion. I provide Sean with a SITREP just as the first group makes their way down. Everything seems to be running smoothly on his end as well. I advise him that we should be finished up in an hour or so and to be ready to get the fuck out of there when we do. They're ahead of schedule, so all is looking good for an earlier departure.

Forty-five minutes in, Jared and I are sweating profusely from moving all the containers. I take a break in the hallway while Jared goes back inside the room.

"Hey, Scott? Check this out. This container isn't filled with rifles or ammo."

"I'm resting, dude," I mutter, arching my back to stretch.

After moving seventy-plus cases, I'm beat. I take a deep breath before cracking my neck and going back inside. I point my light onto the contents, walking toward him.

"What the hell are these?" Jared asks.

I lean over to pick one up. "Well, this looks like a battery pack, and this"—I take a closer look—"this looks like a scope."

"Yeah, I guess they do, don't they?" he replies.

A thought pops into my head. "Go grab me one of those rifles."

"Anything else, master?" he says in a wiseass tone.

"Just get me one, please," I bark back, drawing out the please.

The strange scope is about eight inches long and weighs two pounds. I look through it but can't see out the other end. Buttons flush with the casing line up on one side. The bottom has notches that tell me that it attaches to something, and I bet I know what. I shine my light on the raised writing.

"Q-Sight Optics. Interesting."

"Here you go." Jared hands me a rifle, and I set it on top of the pelican case.

"Thank you. I'm willing to bet these two go together."

I finagle the two, and the scope slides into place through a couple of grooves. Nothing happens at first, but then several red lights on the scope start flashing.

"Damn!" Low battery. I guess we'll have to wait until we get back home to mess with these.

"Scott, you copy?" Dorsey radios me.

"Yeah, whatcha got?"

"One box van is completely full, and the other is getting close to full. We load up anymore and the Josco Brothers are going to have to find another ride back."

"Well, I guess they're staying here then." I turn back to Frank, who's flashing me his middle finger.

"Alright, everyone listen up. Let's start wrapping things up down here. Dorsey, just keep everyone up there topside, and we'll see you here in a few. How's everything else looking up there?"

"Fine so far."

"Good to hear. We'll be right up."

I turn to Jared. "Let's start tearing down these light plants and get the hell out of here."

We exit the vault just as a string of shots echo from down the corridor from an upper level. Jared and I hold deathly still for a moment, then grab our weapons and take off in a dead sprint down the corridor with Bryan on our heels.

"Talk to me! I hear shots fired!" I yell into the mic.

We come upon Frank, who's aiming his weapon toward the stairwell. Jared, Bryan, and I follow suit.

Just as I was about to jump on the radio again, a frightened voice yelled from inside the stairwell. "We have contact! Joscos are in the building, main level. I repeat, we have contact! We're heading down." Several more shots pop off from above.

I'm not sure who was on the radio, but seconds later, a body bursts through the stairwell and into the corridor, running full steam toward us.

"Fuck, Nathan!" I lower my rifle. "Is Paul with you?"

"No, sir! Just me. They came out of nowhere." He's visibly shaken and breathing like he just ran a marathon. "Paul and I were about to reach the main level when a Josco smashed right through a door, nearly hitting him. There's more than just one. A shit load."

Nathan keels over to catch his breath.

"Frank, you watch down that—"

"What was that?" Jared interrupts, with his weapon raised and looking behind us. I turn to face in the direction of where the sound came from.

"Gunfire," Bryan whispers. "Sounds like it's coming from the opposite end of the corridor."

"Dorsey, you copy?" I jump on the radio, frantically pacing back and forth.

Nothing.

"DORSEY, YOU COPY?" Nothing but silence. "FUCK! This is not happening. Not now!"

"Sean, do you copy? We have contact. I repeat, we have Joscos."

I do a quick headcount: Frank, Bryan, Nathan, Jared, Brad, and myself. After a hasty weapons check, we're set.

"Guys, we've got to go! We stand no chance of surviving down here. Bryan, you take point and find us a new exit. There must be another way out." I throw my arm up to signal silence, and then cocked my head to the side to listen.

The sound of doors and walls being smashed, and deep grunts vibrate the air.

"Fuck! Bryan, find that exit! There's gotta be another set of stairs somewhere down here because this one is compromised."

"On it, sir!"

Their heavy footsteps echo through the corridors. They're so loud that it's hard to tell whether they're above us or right around the corner. Bryan hurries his pace, navigating the maze-like sublevel. As he leads us, I can see just how massive it is. Tunnels break off in every direction.

"Make your bullets count!" I say to my men. "Anything, Bryan?"

"Sorry, sir. I'm looking!" He kicks open several doors along the way, but they just open to other rooms.

The six of us stay close while continuing along the main corridor. The sound of a door slamming open rings out from behind. Shit. My heart races. Looks like we're going to be fighting our way out of this one.

The deafening sound of Bryan's miniguns explodes beside me on an approaching enemy. Tracer rounds light up the corridor. His bullets rip through a small pack of Joscos on the receiving end, tearing them down limb from limb. Blood and body matter explode everywhere.

We release a fury of our own to the rear, firing multiple short bursts. Joscos come at us from every direction, and as we turn a corner, we're greeted by another small pack that's sprinting at us, fighting one another to be the first.

With everything happening so fast, we failed to see another pack coming at us from another corridor. Bryan lets out a gurgling wail as he's swallowed by a sudden wave of brawn. The sheer force of their weight causes them to crash through the adjacent cinder-block wall and into an empty cavity on the other side. In an instant, I fall onto my back as warm liquid sprays onto my face. I know what it is. Please don't be Bryan's. I engage my weapon until my magazine is drained. Several more Joscos rush at us, but my fellow Marines shower them with a rain of bullets. Joscos' heads explode as I regain my stance and insert another magazine.

"Bryan!" Frank yells out in anger. He runs up from the rear, unloading his weapon down the two corridors, clearing anything that resembles life. Even in the green darkness, I can see the tears falling from his face. He drops his miniguns once he's taken out the threat from both directions. He runs toward the dark cavern, busting out more of the wall with his fists.

"If Bryan is gone, we need to keep moving, Frank!" My voice strains as I scream inside the room. "There's nothing we can do!"

I turn back as a single Josco twenty yards away runs straight for us, head down like a charging bull. I pull back slightly on the trigger as I bring the rifle up to my shoulder and aim down the scope. Bullets rip into the flesh of its torso. I adjust my weapon, trying for a head shot. The Josco shuffles from side to side, bouncing off the walls. I'm empty. I fumble for another magazine from my chest rig, unsure if I'll get it in time. The corner of my eye picks up movement, and then, out of nowhere, Jared slides across the corridor floor, his weapon aimed high. He unloads thirty rounds, hoping one is a head shot. It was as if time slowed in an instant, and all I could see was a dark, massive body flying headfirst at us.

The next thing I remember, Jared is yelling my name while pulling my arm, trying to get me out from between the cinder-block wall and the four-hundred-pound gorilla. As soon as my eyes focus, I realize I'm face to face with the Josco that had smashed right into me. I panic until I register that this Josco is dead. Jared got his head shot, as half of the Josco's face was missing, and its brain matter dripping on me. I gag as Jared and I both struggle. I finally get free and quickly regain focus. I turn and gaze inside the room. Frank's fists fly through the air, landing punches on another Josco's swollen, bloody face.

"Jared, Nathan, we need to secure this area. Frank's still in there with a Josco."

"Make it fast, Frank!" Nathan yells out, but I doubt Frank can hear any of this.

Jared covers the corridor we were headed down while Nathan and Brad watch the one that splits off to the right. I cover the corridor we came from while glancing back periodically to ensure Frank is alright.

"Frank? I hate to say this, but we really need to get going." I watch as the Josco lunges at Frank, slamming him on his back.

Shit!

I hear a few shots pop off from Nathan and Jared and then look back to Frank just as he flips the Josco over and slams it into the partially collapsed wall. Frank gets to his feet, clasping both hands together to make one giant fist. He brings his fists down with such force that the ground shakes. The Josco's head explodes like a watermelon packed with dynamite. Chunks of brain matter spray everywhere.

Frank didn't wait long before rushing over to Bryan's limp body. I yell back to Frank again, but he still can't hear me.

"Brad, cover me!" He repositions as told.

I jump inside, not realizing the second Josco was still alive. Frank pushes me aside like a rag doll, and I stumble as he delivers death-blowing punches to the squirming Josco. I jerk my head from side to side to make sure there are no other threats. It's as if a tornado touched down in here, with paper and office furniture scattered across the floor. Then I see Bryan lying motionless across a broken desk. If it weren't for his weapons and clothing, I wouldn't even know it was him. He's spread out on his back with his miniguns out to the side. Having finished the Josco, Frank rushes over and sits beside him, cradling his head in his arms.

"Frank…" I wince, saying his name with as much compassion as I can, considering the danger we are still in. "We cannot stay here, buddy. We must go, now!"

"Those bastards. Those fucking bastards killed him. I can't leave him," he cries out, unashamed of his emotions.

"We don't want to leave him here any more than you," I say calmly. "Bryan was our brother too." I choke back my own feelings and replace them with the need to survive. I flinch as several shots pop off behind me. "We stand no chance of surviving without you. We need you."

I poke my head out of the room. "Guys, I need a few seconds."

"Hurry the fuck up!" Nathan yells. "I hear a stampede rushing our way!"

I place my hand on Frank's shoulder. He brushes it away.

"Seriously! We need to go, man. Bryan wouldn't want you to sit here. He would tell you to get your shit together and do your job."

Frank bows his head and says a quiet prayer, a farewell. "…until we meet again, brother." Frank looks up at me and says, "We're coming back for him."

I nod, not wanting to tell him that might not be a possibility, but I wasn't going to argue about it.

"Alright then, let's get this shit done." I give him a hard pat on his arm to get him moving. Frank disconnects one of Bryan's ammo boxes from his suit, and I help attach it to the front of his.

We exit the room. "On me, guys. I'll take point. Nathan, you cover the rear. We're going to continue the way we were heading. There's gotta be another exit somewhere. Let's move."

We hustle down the corridor. When we meet another pack of Joscos at a T intersection, Frank takes them out with one sweeping motion of his miniguns, shredding the walls and ceiling with each hit.

We run what feels like a mile before hitting another turn. The only option is to take a right since a group of Joscos is making their way toward us from the left. Their deep, hungry growls vibrate the inner parts of my ears in an unsettling way. They slap and bang their hands against the walls as they run toward us. Sweat drips from my forehead and into my eyes. It stings, but I force myself to not lose focus.

"Look!" I yell.

"Oh, for fucks sake. Please let it be stairs!" Jared says.

A sign with a picture of stairs still hangs from the wall. I bust through the door, not caring if there is a Josco behind it and thank God there isn't.

"Three floors up. Let's go!" I prop the door open with my foot, ensuring my men make it out. I keep my weapon raised toward any threats coming from above until my men clear the hallway.

Nathan is the last to enter the stairwell. Behind us, the pack of Joscos turns the corner where we just came from. They slide into the wall, smashing into one another, but then break out into a frenzy, fighting each other for the front spot. I shoot off several rounds before letting the door shut behind me. "Fucking animals."

I hurry up the stairs right behind Nathan. As we pass the second sublevel, the door we just went through slams open. I point my weapon down and unload, still moving up the stairs, albeit at a slower pace.

"They're in the stairwell! Move it!" I yell.

I rip off two grenades and pull the pins, dropping them as I ascend to the first sublevel. "Frag out!"

I've never moved this fast up three flights of stairs while lugging eighty pounds of gear in my life. My muscles are going to be dead once the adrenaline stops pumping.

Light creeps in from above as one of my men opens the exit door to who knows what is waiting for us outside. I raise my night vision goggles and push faster, pumping my legs as hard as they allow, though I can no longer feel them. Nathan enters the main level just a few feet in front of me. The light gets brighter the closer I get. I take the last step from the stairs and see Brad holding the door open. Steps away from exiting the building, the grenades explode below me, shaking my feet.

CHAPTER EIGHTEEN

(Lieutenant Scott Dodson—U.S. Marines)

Thursday, January 23, 2048

I hurl myself out of the building and into the blinding sunlight, hoping there isn't a threat awaiting my exit. To my surprise, no gunfire echoes through the empty street. Instead, my men set up a perimeter to secure the area. Brad's foot still has the door propped open. As if he could read my mind, his hand is already gripping another grenade. We both rip one off from our chest rigs and pull the pins. He tosses his in first, and I follow suit.

"Move! Move! Move!" I yell at my men.

We haul ass out of there like we robbed the place. We scurry north toward Hell on Wheels Avenue, and the grenades explode. Behind us, black smoke pours out from around the doorframe. I sure hope nothing follows because we could use a few seconds to relax and catch our breath.

I wipe my face, thinking it was drips of sweat running down my cheeks, but my glove is covered in blood and tiny fragments of body parts. I attempt to remove as much as I can, then shake my hands to get the bits and pieces off. Some of this is Bryan's. I can't believe he's gone. The guilt and bitterness of the bet we made years back and how we joked around about it plagues my thoughts. I never thought it would come true. Not like this anyway. We've been together for years and been through some tough shit, and not having him here is going to leave a deep, empty cavity in our hearts.

"I have contact, five o'clock, up on the roofline," Frank calls out from behind me.

We turn back to see a pair of Joscos parkouring on the roof's edge. Frank engages his miniguns and violently removes the Joscos' appendages from their bodies. The two fall awkwardly to the ground, their bodies making a heavy thud.

We take cover inside a crater where the rear of an overturned, charred Bradley Fighting Vehicle sits halfway inside.

"We need to get to our vehicles. How is everybody? Ammo good?" I ask, looking at what's left of my team: Nathan, Brad, Jared, and Frank.

We look each other over for injuries. The only pain that shows is for those that are no longer with us. There will be a time for mourning, but it can't be right now.

"I've got three mags." Nathan counts his out, breathing heavily.

"Same here." Jared looks over his shoulder, shaking like he's been standing outside naked in the middle of winter.

"I've got two," I announce.

Brad gives a thumbs-up, but Frank leans against the vehicle in silence. I know he's taking a quick moment to grieve the loss of Bryan. I let him have his time, but we need to adjust. We're in survival, evasion, resistance, and escape mode. Priority one is to get back to base camp if we want to make it out of here alive.

I peek up and out of the crater to get a bearing on our position. *Fuck!* We're two buildings over on the complete opposite side from where we originally entered.

"Nathan, what the fuck happened when you and Paul were headed back up?" I ask.

"We had just entered the main level when a Josco came out of nowhere. Paul must have seen it or heard something because he pushed me back." He stops to catch his breath. "I tumbled down the stairs. Last thing I saw was Paul booking it out of the building with a Josco hot on his trail. I heard more coming at us, but I didn't know what to do. I had no choice but to head back down the stairs. Paul saved my life because I would have been on the receiving end of that door had he not pushed me out of the way. Remind me to thank his ass when we see him."

We sit in silence, but Frank's eyes tell me that he's probably experiencing the same bad feeling as I am that Paul is no longer with us.

I jump on the comms. "Dorsey, McCauley, does anybody copy?" My hands shake, making it difficult to hold down the radio button to talk. No one answers.

"Where the fuck is everybody?" Jared asks, pacing back and forth while scanning the rooftops. "How did no one see them coming? It's not like they are tiny ants."

"I don't know," I reply. "But why in the hell are the radios not working. I'm getting nothing but static." Frustration sinks in.

"We're sitting ducks," Nathan adds, scanning his sector.

"You're damn right!" Brad says.

"Let's keep heading north, just up this road"—I point in the direction—"and then turn east. This will get us to Hell on Wheels Avenue and should put us on the path to where we need to be. We'll get our vehicles and meet up with Sean."

"If they're still there." Brad's negative tone seems to hit a nerve with Frank.

"Be positive, fucker," Frank blurts out.

Brad puts his hands up like doesn't want any trouble.

I take point in a five-man formation. We make our way north and then turn east, and as we turn the corner, the body of a Marine comes into focus, lying motionless on the ground. We pick up the pace.

"Oh fuck, man. It's Dorsey," Nathan announces, his hands on his helmet.

Two Joscos with gaping holes in their heads lay beside him, blood is everywhere.

"Look, there's someone else." Brad points to another teammate so mauled that we couldn't tell who it was.

"What are they doing way the fuck over here?" Jared asks. "Can't be good if they ran in this direction."

A line of bodies leads us back to where we had originally entered the building. Most are Joscos, but it appears half of the Marines we come across are the men who were topside. We stop at each of our fallen brothers—their limbs ripped from their bodies—a painful reminder of who we're dealing with.

"Fuck!" What glimmer of hope my team has disappeared with each friend we pass. All I want to do now is scream as loud as I can. There's nothing any of us can do for them, and I hate the fact that we must leave their bodies here only to be a feast for the monsters. I remove their dog tags and say a little prayer over each of them before moving on.

We turn onto Hell on Wheels Avenue and the distinct sound of the M-CIWS screams in the distance. The echoes bounce between the buildings like a game of ping-pong. The chance of meeting up with anyone else is looking grimmer by the second and confirms that Sean and his men are in the same boat as us. *Bet that's why no one is answering the radios.*

The sight of our arrival point deflated me past the brink—a feeling that I didn't know existed. That sinking feeling would be paradise to what I feel now. Not only is half my team gone, but what's left of our fleet sits on their sides, their contents scattered about the parking lot and wheels ripped off, securing the fact that we're walking the rest of the way. I did have a very brief sigh of relief seeing that both box vans were gone, along with one of the Humvees. I'm proud my men listened to my orders for once.

"Shit!" Nathan yells.

"We're not getting out of here anytime soon," Frank replies in an oddly calm voice.

We huddle along the north wall of a nearby building and put together a plan of action to get back to our command post. Our first order of business is to stock up with what we can carry and then start making our way back. The sound of gunfire and explosions continues in the distance, but it's fading. The M-CIWSs are pumping out the last of their rounds. I just hope whoever is left can make it out. Shit, I hope *we* make it out.

Rummaging through the mangled Humvees, we gather whatever supplies we can, filling our pouches with magazines, stuffing them anywhere space is available. We won't survive if we can't defend ourselves. Food is an afterthought, but I did manage to stuff a couple of MREs on my person. If it came down to it, we could survive off the land.

"Sean, you there?" I try again, but nothing.

I can't stand being without communications, and this is really fucking with my mind. Base camp is two and a half miles away, and we have no other choice but to start trekking in that treacherous direction.

"You guys ready?" I say watching my men stand solemnly.

Shallow nods from each of them. Sweat drips from their foreheads down to their chins like condensation on a cold bottle of beer in the hot sun. All of us but Frank are still taking heavy breaths. We discuss what we think is our safest travel route back to base camp and move out.

I lead my small team, navigating from building to building and ducking behind anything we come across to avoid detection. My only worry is Frank. With his bulk, he stands out like a sore thumb. He's not flexible, either. Crouching isn't his strong suit.

The echo of gunfire ceases. The only sound that remains is the crunching of dead grass beneath our feet. My hope right now is that there's a vehicle back at base camp we can use. I don't care what shape it's in so long as it drives.

A mile into our hike, my wife and kiddo steal my focus, and the last image I have of them right before I departed. Maggie was standing at the front door in tight jeans and a black long-sleeved shirt holding Abigail in a poofy, winter outfit. It could be the dead of summer and she would still want to wear that light blue panda onesie. I would give anything to be holding the two of them right now. I'd never let go.

A Rolodex of memories flashes through my mind but stops on the day we met. I was nineteen, and she was eighteen. It was my very first mission, and I can't believe I'm thinking this, but I should be thanking Dr. Anderson. Otherwise, Maggie and my paths wouldn't have crossed. He was operating an unbeknownst to us research facility up north when several Joscos had escaped his custody. We were called upon to hunt them down and kill them. We spent several days tracking them until we finally caught up just south of Milwaukee, where Maggie lived at the time. They weren't making it hard to track them as they left a trail of dead bodies everywhere for us to follow.

There weren't many families living in the area then, and the ones that did were all huddled relatively close together in a neighborhood. We had an idea of where the Joscos might be headed, so we hunkered down in one of the houses. Being close, we heard a wave of gunshots and headed in that direction. Neighbors pointed us to the house where Maggie and her family were held up in their basement.

To disorient them, we lobbed flash bang after flash bang into the basement. We were unsure of the condition of the occupants, but we had no other choice if we wanted to end the Josco's destructive tour. We stormed in and witnessed the Joscos surrounding Maggie's parents like a pack of hungry lions feasting on their prey. They looked like zombies. It was a short battle, and for my first mission, it couldn't have been a better one to pop my cherry. No Marines lost their lives that day.

Once we knew it was safe to proceed, we came upon her father first who was contorted in a way Houdini would have been impressed with. Her mother wasn't in any better shape, with her arms ripped clean off. Both of their chests were ripped open, with their entrails strung out on the floor. We didn't find Maggie for a little while as she was hidden in a closet, unconscious under a mountain of blankets and clothes. I would have passed right over her had I not seen her little fingers barely sticking out from under a blanket.

She didn't remember anything until she finally came to a few days later. We could only assume she was the first to be attacked and knocked out before her parents put her there to keep her safe. It was the only logical explanation because her condition wouldn't have allowed her to hide in a closet the way she was.

We placed her into our helicopter and flew her back to the base hospital. She had a severe concussion, a broken arm, and damage to some of her internal organs. It was probably a good thing she was out cold. Knowing her now, I know she wouldn't have been able to live after seeing all that carnage. I never told her the horrors of that day, and I never will.

For whatever reason, I couldn't leave her to wake up with no one by her side and then for her to find out her parents were dead. Something compelled me to stay. I noticed the cross around her neck, and before that day, I had never really thought about God; but something came over me in that moment.

She was out for three days, and in a world of ugliness, she was the prettiest thing I had ever seen. Fair, porcelain skin with blonde hair. Her artic blue eyes set me over the edge. It took months for her to recover from her injuries, and each day I went to see her, even if just to say hello.

It took time to get to know her. She didn't talk much, and I rarely got an acknowledgement in return. She had closed off the world, and other than a few friends back home, her parents meant the world to her. With them gone, she felt that she had no reason to live, and in the messed-up world we lived in, who would want to continue?

I noticed she stopped wearing the cross, and her attitude changed significantly. She was becoming even more distant. I sensed that her depression had too big of a hold on her, and I was worried she was preparing to do something horrible. I never give up on her. I stayed with her until something clicked and she finally said hello back, her tone livelier than before.

A small explosion from base camp brings my mind back to the present. I need to stay present. My men need me to lead and find a way out of this mess. We make it to the building with all the dead female Joscos. I peer around the corner. It's all I can do to keep from punching the metal wall. *Are we ever going to catch a fucking break?*

"Well guys, I have some good news and some bad news. Which do you want to hear first?" I ask.

"Good news. I could go for that right about now," Brad replies.

"Okay, well, there are a couple of vehicles left at base camp we could use."

"Yeah, so then what's the bad news?" Jared asks.

"Take a look for yourself." I lean back and fall to the ground, landing on my ass.

Jared stands up and peeks over me. "Yeah, that's what I thought."

Two vehicles sit in the open. The only problem is there are maybe a thousand Joscos swarming the area. On a positive note, if there ever was one, thousands more lay dead on the ground in one giant heap of crimson.

"I would have loved to watch those M-CIWSs taking out all of them Joscos," Frank says.

"There's no way in hell we would survive that." Jared slides down beside me and lowers his head. "Damn it, man."

"We ain't dead just yet, guys." I remind them that we still have a chance, even as slim as it may seem.

I pull out a map to start navigating a way around. We need to get to Waco per our rendezvous. We have three days to get there for an extraction. "I hope you guys are up for a hike," I tell them. Their faces read the complete opposite.

"Hey!" I snap my fingers to get their attention. "We're still alive, and that's more than I can say for our brothers back there. Keep your fucking heads up, and push through this. Any one of them would love to still be here right now. Let's focus."

"What if we create some sort of diversion?" Frank jumps in with what sounds like a promising idea.

"A diversion?" I respond. "What do you have in mind? Right now, I don't even think a meat popsicle the size of Texas, would distract them away from our base camp." I take another look. They're like bees whose hive has been disturbed.

"Fuck. I don't know. I was just hoping one of you would have an idea. I really don't want to walk to Waco." Frank complains.

"Of all people, you're the one that doesn't want to walk?" I roll my eyes and get back to the map. "Sorry, Frank. I shouldn't have said that. That wasn't nice."

"Happy birthday to me..." Nathan quietly sings. "...Happy birthday to me. Happy birthday, dear Nathan, happy birthday to me." The four of us look at him like he's lost his damned mind.

"Um, are you good, bro?" Brad asks.

"Today's your birthday?" Jared asks.

"Tomorrow, actually," Nathan replies. "I was really looking forward to being home. I have a suspicion the wife is planning something big."

"Why the fuck are you singing it now?" Frank jumps in.

"In case I don't survive tomorrow." Nathan lets out a small laugh.

"That actually makes sense." Jared grins in agreement.

"Everyone shut up and listen." I point to our rendezvous spot on the map. "A straight shot is a little over forty-three miles from here, but we'll need to get around this lake." I trace the route with my finger. "We'll head north for roughly four miles until we reach this creek, maybe cross it if possible. We'll follow it east for a few miles and then change course to a northeasterly heading. There's no way we're going to be able to make it to Waco by sundown, but we should be able to make it to"—my finger finds its target—"McGregor, right here. It's twenty-seven miles away; and if we head out now and keep a steady pace, we should be there sometime before midnight. We'll camp there for the night and then go the rest of the way in the morning. We only have ten MREs between the five of us, so make sure you conserve, or you'll be eating bugs."

"Food." Frank rubs his belly. "I'm hungry."

"Sorry, buddy. You're gonna have to wait. Maybe we'll get lucky and find something on the way."

"I knew I should have grabbed more food," Frank says.

Just as we are moving out, the sound of fast-paced footfalls races up from behind us. We didn't even have time to react or raise our weapons, and in that split second, the tall, thick vegetation that was concealing our location split like the parting of the sea. I damn near shit myself, but when Riley's slim face appears, a sigh of tremendous relief washes over me. Frank seemed unfazed, but the other four of us almost keeled over.

"Woman! You almost got yourself killed," Nathan says, falling to his knees and grabbing his chest, panting.

We let out a collective breath.

"Where the hell were you?" I ask, very curious as to how she was still alive and appeared to be well.

"Paul came running out of the building screaming 'contact.' We turned around just as he got pummeled by several Joscos." She stops to take a few deep breaths.

All but Riley turned and looked to Nathan, who looked as though his firstborn was ripped from his arms.

She continued. "Paul didn't make it five feet from the building. Then, hell broke loose. Joscos kept pouring out of the building. We did everything we could to hold them off. They just kept coming. Didn't have time to react other than fire our weapons. We got scattered, and everyone took off running in different directions." She pauses for more breaths. "I'm not sure who made it out. I took off to the north, back to base camp, and as I looked back, both the box vans were burning tires out of there." She starts to cry and Frank grabs ahold of her tightly. "I was headed this way when I saw a pack of them up ahead and I just took cover in a building." She buries her head in Frank's stomach.

"You did good," I tell her.

"I was looking out a second-story window, and I just happened to see some movement in my peripheral and saw you guys cross. I was so scared."

"Glad to know just how conspicuous we were," Brad adds.

I slap him, letting him know this isn't the time.

"Well, we're glad you made it, but we need to hurry on out of here." I do my best to console her. "We have some ground to cover. It gets dark around seventeen-thirty." It's just past 1100 hours. "We have six hours of daylight. Let's not waste any more time."

Thursday, January 23, 2048

One by one, our camouflaged bodies become invisible as we blend in with Mother Nature's surrounding flora. Stealth is one of our greatest skills, making us who we are. Now we must put into action what's been beaten into us all these years.

Disbelief washes over me as I process everything that transpired in the last hour. I spare one last glimpse of base camp. I send up a short prayer for those that didn't make it and one for our journey ahead before letting the environment devour me whole.

As it stands, our main priority is to stay alive. We have three days to get to our exfil in Waco, and it will be no easy task. If this morning were any indication of what lies ahead, we're going to be in a world of hurt. Waco isn't far, but it's not close either. We know the odds of our current situation and our state of mind, but if we adapt and improvise, we will survive.

Our initial trek took us through a forest for several rocky miles. That did a number on our ankles—I'm going to have to wear an ankle brace for the rest of my life. The forest opens to a massive field that was once a gun range. The exposure will leave us vulnerable, only providing partial cover to our waists for a mile until we reach the other side. *No way we're leopard crawling that entire distance.* We take a knee, staying hidden within the forest's boundary as we monitor the area with our binoculars. It appears quiet, but who knows what prowls on the downside of the hill and small valley. We could walk along the edge of the forest, but that'll add time to our already precious schedule. We whisper amongst ourselves until we agree it's safe enough to walk through the field.

The next hour is quiet—odd, considering these guys can't go two seconds without cracking a joke. By now, someone in the group would have been designated as the target to poke fun at. It's almost unsettling since "quiet" isn't in their vocabulary or exercised as part of their lifestyle. I'll take whatever serenity I can because at any moment one of them could go off the rails until someone ends up getting punched in the face.

Oddly enough, we reach the ravine with no bloody noses or tears shed. We cross a dry creek where live oak trees line both sides, and four miles later, the pain starts kicking in, my adrenaline long gone. The eighty-pound rucksack is painstakingly pulling me to the ground, targeting my knees first as dull aches, but then pain trickles up my back. I'm going to have so many back issues later in life if I live through the next three days.

The pain appears to have hit everyone at once because our walk has turned into staggering wobbles. Even though we're on the brink of collapsing, we keep a steady pace toward McGregor in the blazing sun.

Halfway there, we come across a farmer's wasteland of dead corn and weeds, mostly weeds, though. Some stalks reach heights taller than Frank, so we designate him as our lookout. It's a good thing Joscos don't have snipers, or he'd be a goner.

"For fuck's sake, will these weeds ever end? If I get whacked in the face by one more..." Jared was clearly losing the battle and his wits.

"Shit, that's the last thing I care about. It's the damn ticks you need to be worried about. You can get Lyme disease from those little fuckers," Brad chimes in with his bit of knowledge.

"Great, thanks for that." Jared sighs heavily. "If I get any on my ass, Brad, you're pulling them off."

"The fuck I will!" Brad replies.

I grimace, picturing Brad with a pair of tweezers nose-deep in Jared's ass. *Gross.*

"You two need to stop being little babies about some weeds and ticks." Frank is obviously irritated. "We just lost a bunch of brothers and you two are crying over dumb stuff."

Frank's words hit me hard.

"Guys," Frank whispers. "There's a clearing up ahead. Looks like a path, maybe fifty yards."

As we kneel into position, my knees pop and crack. I'm not going to be sneaking up on anyone soon. Five pairs of eyes stare at me.

"Damn, I'm getting old. It's going to suck to stand back up." I change the focus from my dilapidated body to the path. "Looks like there's been recent traffic." I keep a low voice, pushing a patch of weeds to the side.

"This doesn't look good," Frank says. "I can smell them."

"Yeah, bet you can with that honker," Nathan adds. "Those aren't size ten shoe prints, either."

"This could be one of the thousand travel routes they take," Jared whispers. "We can only hope they haven't used this one in a while."

"Well, from the smell of it, and I'm only taking the big guy's word, it sounds like they've been here recently. What's our play?" Riley asks.

Fear contorts their faces as they wait for me to provide them with guidance. My stomach churns at the thought of coming across any more Joscos right now.

"Let's keep moving. Jared, you got point for now. We'll stay close to the field in case we need to jump in for cover. Frank, you just keep looking out for us since you have a better point of view."

"Easy enough." Frank jokingly stands on his tippy toes.

"Let's move out," I order.

We continue northeast and walk past some rusty farm equipment that's been sitting undisturbed for decades, covered in years of dust and filth. Vines and weeds have wrapped themselves over the top as if the earth is trying to claim it. It's hard to read the faded yellow words "John Deere" written across the top front of the hood cowling.

All I can think about is the joy of some father on a cold morning with a cup of hot coffee and his son, with matching hot chocolate, sitting on his lap teaching him the trade. What am I going to teach Abigail? War? How to survive or flee from a Josco? Shoot a rifle? That one, for certain! Good things to be skilled at, but that's all she'll ever know.

I wonder if I'd have been a farmer had the Joscos not come into existence? By now, I would be finishing up a hard day's work, walk into the house to a warm cooked meal, the kids running around terrorizing each other, and maybe a dog wagging its tail, excited to see me. Guess that's the kind of life the Major is fighting so hard for.

I'm distracted by Jared's fist flying into the air, signaling that he has visual on movement ahead. We duck and run for cover back into the cornfield. He points out Joscos walking straight for us, a hundred yards out on the gravel path. How in the fuck did Frank not see them? I side-eye him, and he shrugs his shoulders. Guess he's as distracted as I was just moments ago, daydreaming of a different life.

Two groups make their way toward us; one small group leads the way, followed by a larger one. Damn. My head spins. Do we engage or let them keep walking and pray to God they don't smell us once they pass? There's a slight wind coming from the north, so they haven't picked up our scent. Yet. They'll be downwind soon, and it won't take them long to smell us. Wouldn't be much of a fight either, as we're tired, hungry, and thirsty, and our bodies have damn near given up. If we attack now, we'll have the element of surprise and quite possibly take them out without getting anyone hurt or killed. My biggest concern is the spacing between the two groups, maybe twenty-five yards. This makes it more complicated. Do we take out one group at a time or split up and go for them simultaneously? I'm thinking simultaneously.

"This is what we'll do," I whisper as softly as I can. "We'll wait for the first group to pass, positioning us right in the middle." I point to Nathan, Riley, and Frank. "You three take out the first group, but once you've eliminated them, you turn and assist Jared, Brad and me on the trailing group."

Another concern is whether there are any stragglers behind the second, much larger group. And if so, how many? Unfortunately, none of us got a good look. Chances are we wouldn't survive a third wave— we would be a midafternoon snack. *I really hope this isn't the case.*

We check our weapons; even the soft click of switching the safety off could trigger them into a frenzy. I peek out from the weeds, focus on the second group, and count them out in my head. For fuck's sake. There are nine in the trailing group, thirteen in total. We're way outnumbered, but at least I'm not seeing any stragglers.

I unstrap my last grenade. Frank and Jared grab one as well. I'm optimistic each of our grenades will inflict some carnage or at least put them in a state of shock, buying us some time to take them out.

Jared's hands shake so badly that his rifle rattles against a magazine in his vest pouch. His eyes meet mine. He's scared. We're all scared. I give him a nod of assurance and gently push his weapon away from his vest.

Their heavy footsteps crunching the gravel are like nails on a chalkboard. I assumed they would be grunting and yelling all the time, but they almost seem normal. Human. Out on a lovely nature walk in the middle of a cornfield.

We stay deathly still while the first group passes. The wind picks up and the weeds rustle helping to conceal the sound our bodies make as we crawl closer to the trail. I slide the pin out of the grenade. Frank and Jared follow suit. I grip the safety lever so tightly my knuckles turn white. Then count down from five with my fingers, so we all know when to throw.

Five.

Four.

Three. We release the safety levers and soft clinks ring out.

Two.

One.

The three of us stand tall, and no sooner than I pop my head up above the weeds, my eyes meet with one of the Joscos in the second group. *Fuck me.* It was like he knew I was right here the whole time, waiting for my head to rise like a whack-a-mole. I toss the grenade and then duck back down.

"One of them saw me!" I announce to the group.

They study me with wide eyes.

"Get ready!" I grip my rifle, and we get to one knee for a quick exit. The seconds tick by slower than honey dripping out of a glass jar. *Hurry up and go boom!* I push aside some weeds to watch a Josco nonchalantly look at the grenade as if it were the most harmless thing it had ever seen. Several others slow their pace, one curious enough to lean in to get a closer look.

Either Frank's or Jared's explodes first, and we spring into action faster than the blink of an eye. Corn stalks slap me in the face, making tiny scratches across my cheeks as if they were a warning— telling me to stay put. My grenade goes off next, and then a third explodes. I burst out of the field, witnessing three Joscos fall to the ground. Finding my first target, I point north and engage my weapon with a relentless appetite for carnage, emptying my magazine. Brad engages to my left and sweeps from left to right, puncturing multiple bodies, while Jared engages to my right with the same sweeping motion. A mist of red fills the air as limbs separate from the Joscos' bodies. Frank must be directly behind me; my inner ears vibrate with every round being expelled from his miniguns.

We eliminate half of group two. Two Joscos covered in blood and guts hold their hands to their heads, looking dazed and confused.

"Changing mag!" I call out while Brad and Jared drop one of the disoriented ones with solid head shots.

"Seven down, two to go!" I yell out as the last two darts off into the field, but not before I pop off a few rounds of the new magazine.

"Group one down," Frank shouts from behind.

"That was a loud gunfight!" Brad holds tight to his weapon, aiming down the sights. Frank and the others turn to join us, and we move toward where group two is positioned. "I sure hope there are no more back there."

"We ain't done yet, guys," I tell them. "Two ran east into the field. Looks like we're going back in."

"I've got movement," Jared calls out, eyeing a Josco flailing about on the ground like a fish out of water. Brad and Jared both put bullets in its head.

"Nathan, Riley, Brad, you secure this position. Frank, Jared, on me," I order.

"Wait, we're going in there after them?" Jared asks. "I thought you were kidding."

"You're damn right we're going in after them. I don't want those pieces of shit hunting our asses all the way to Waco. Now let's get this over with."

"Fuck me," he mumbles.

"Anything comes running out, and it's not us, kill it," I order.

The two Joscos left a perfect trail for us to follow. Frank, Jared, and I move as one, so close I can feel Frank on my heels. Twenty steps in, we come to a small clearing where a Josco lies face down in a pool of his own blood, with an exit hole the size of a small watermelon in its back.

"I knew I hit one of those SOBs," I say.

The Josco twitches hard, startling Jared, who puts a few rounds in the back of its head.

"Let's go. One more." We move with urgency, following the broken weed stems.

"Two o'clock!" Frank yells.

We spot a Josco running back toward the path. Frank lays a blanket of minigun action in its direction, cutting through the cornfield with ease. More red mist fills the air, followed by a thump. We rush over to our fallen victim. The ugly bastard is damn near cut in half at the waist but still alive.

"Oh, fuck me." Jared looks disgusted.

I share in his reaction, as I'm sure my face was a mirror image. The damn thing is reaching, grasping at us, almost as though it were asking for mercy.

"Damn, Frank. Nice shootin'." It's hard to not feel a little bad for the Josco as it didn't ask for this life.

Frank stays focused on the surrounding area to make sure there's no more movement just in case we missed one or there's another group heading our way.

I raise my M4 and put a single shot in the Josco's forehead. "Time of death"—I look at my watch—"Fuck-30. Job well done. Let's get back. Make sure the others are alright."

"We're coming out!" I announce.

The other three stand in a tight circle, with their backs to one another, next to the bloody massacre.

"Take a knee, everyone. You've all earned a few minutes of rest." We plop our butts on the ground, but as soon as Brad's rear touches dirt, he stands right back up with a peculiar look on his face and walks toward one of the dead Joscos.

"Hey, Scott. Come over here and take a look at this." Brad tries rolling one of the Joscos over onto its stomach.

"Really? My legs are beat, man. Can it wait?"

"I think this thing is wearing a backpack," he replies.

"What?" I throw off my rucksack and stumble my way over.

"Why the hell would a Josco be wearing a backpack, dude?" Brad asks.

"No idea, but I'm definitely curious to see what the hell is in there." Nathan says.

I grab the bloody Josco's shoulders and pull while Nathan and Brad pushes from the other side.

"Put some muscle into it." Brad cries out, feet slipping on the gravel.

We get the thing turned over and Brad pulls out a knife to cut the straps. He peals the backpack away from the bloody carcass. Frank and Jared mosey over after hearing our struggles, leaving Riley by herself. "You good, Riley?" She gives a thumbs up, her head leaning back on her rucksack.

"I'm going to regret this." Brad looks up with a grimace while using his knife to lift the flap of the backpack, "The smell of rot is emanating from it."

Brad pulls out a blood-soaked cloth that appears to be rather heavy. He tries to hand it off to Nathan, "Don't unravel that."

Nathan steps back. "Excuse me? Fucking toss it off to the side, dude."

"Looks like mommy packed a lunch," Frank says.

"Oh, that's foul, man." Brad tosses the makeshift sack, "I think I'm going to throw up." No sooner did he get those words out, he starts dry heaving. Followed by a thick, throaty cough.

"Dude, my nostrils are stained with that smell. I'm going to be smelling this shit for hours now."

We enjoy the much-needed laugh. Brad rolls his eyes and paces a few steps until he's finished.

"You done crying, Brady boy?" Frank shakes his head.

"I'm never eating another piece of meat again."

Nathan takes over pulling a rectangular-shaped object from the bag. It's black and made of metal.

"Perhaps military?" Nathan suggests as he hands it to me then wipes his hands on the grass.

"This looks very similar to the metal containers we found in Dr. Anderson's van." I say. "Interesting."

We pass it around doing our best to avoid the slime smeared on it. There are no visible markings on any of its sides other than some scratches, but there are some seams on one of the elongated sides.

"What do you think is inside?" Frank palms it with one hand, shaking it, then passes it to Brad.

"I have no idea, but don't shake it, you big moron. Could be a bomb inside," Brad scolds.

"A bomb? Joscos are making bombs now? Really?" Frank retorts.

Everyone agrees that we don't want to leave it as it seems important, but no one wants to carry it. After a few minutes of disagreement, we agree to take turns. We join Riley and take a twenty-minute rest before getting back to the hike toward McGregor.

CHAPTER TWENTY
(Lieutenant Scott Dodson—U.S. Marines)

Thursday, January 23, 2048

Several miles outside the city of McGregor, we stumble upon a facility that appears it may have been tenanted by a business that dealt with rockets. Missile-like components are strewn across the land, possibly caused from high winds or a tornado passing through. Our walk brings us to a massive building, where I read "SpaceX Rocket Development" on a sign still hanging on the exterior. *Cool.*

"I bet this place had some cool jobs." I raise my night vision goggles, and with clear skies, the moonlight illuminates several tall structures in front of us.

"Yeah, I bet it was also loud as hell. Bet the neighbors loved them," Brad says.

Sidetracking north toward the tall structures, we come across a massive crater almost the size of a football field with a depth of fifty feet.

"That must've been some blast," Frank says as he walks up the incline of the exterior rim.

"I'm pretty sure anyone who witnessed that was turned to ashes in a blink of an eye," Riley adds as she steps forward into the basin.

"Be careful down there. I don't want you twisting an ankle," I say.

"Sure, Dad," she replies.

"No respect these days."

After musing about what could have happened there, we spread out in search of a decent structure to take a break. We settle on a half-desecrated building, missing its south-facing wall.

"My knees are beat," Riley says. "How about we just stay right here tonight?"

"Don't get too comfortable. This is a short rest. As much as I would love to stay here, I'd like to be somewhere safer." I pull out my map, computing the distance in my head. "We're just under four miles away. Maybe forty-five minutes at our current pace." I look up to see if anyone is listening, but I'm pretty sure I've lost them for the time being.

The grumbling of someone's stomach causes a chain reaction for the rest of us.

"I know we're all starving, but when we get there, we'll eat. We'll each bust open an MRE and eat like there's no tomorrow. Maybe we'll get lucky and find a steak house in Waco," I tease.

"Don't joke about food. Not now, man." Jared licks his lips and closes his eyes. I'm sure he's dreaming of a nice juicy ribeye smothered in a peppercorn sauce like I am.

I fold the map and tuck it away, then gaze up through a hole in the roof at twinkling stars. If we make it back, this'll be some story to tell the guys. HQ must know something's wrong by now, and I'm most certain word has spread to our families. Maggie will kill me if the Joscos don't get to me first.

"You better not light that!" Nathan snaps at Brad as he places a cigarette to his lips.

"Calm down, sweetheart. I'm not going to light it. You think I'm stupid?"

"Don't answer that." I snap my finger and point at Nathan. I don't need them ruining my mini vacation with a dumbass argument.

"How long has it been?" Jared asks Brad as he passes it under his nose to smell the tobacco.

"The day we left. I was thinking about quitting. I didn't even pack any but came across some yesterday in that building full of dead Josco bitches," Brad says.

"Watch your fucking mouth," Riley scolds Brad for the umpteenth time.

"Whatever." Brad throws the cigarette across the room at Riley, and she bats it away.

"I'm surprised you lasted this long," Nathan chimes in. "Not the smoking a cigarette part but being able to keep up with all the running and walking we've had to do."

Fuck. And here we go. I close my eyes and let them have their little quarrel. Maybe they'll get it out of their systems.

Brad sits up, pointing his finger in Nathan's face. "I can outrun you any day of the week, pencil dick! I'm faster than you with that gut you're growing. How far along are you now, seven, eight months?"

We stare at Nathan's round gut. Frank and Jared break out in laughter. We're clearly at the slap-happy portion of the journey.

"Pencil dick? I'll take off my pants right now. What the fuck are you laughing at, you gorilla-looking mother fucker?" Nathan throws a pebble at Frank. "And you," he adds, pointing at Jared. "You fucking drunk!"

"Hey, hey, hey! Don't start with this shit now, and for fuck's sake, please keep your pants on. We're irritable and want to get home too. Keep it together." I pause and contemplate my next words. *Fuck it.* I stand up. "Since you assholes seem to have so much energy all of a sudden, let's move out."

"Fuck," Jared swats at the dirt, grabs his bag, and stands in one quick, angry motion.

"You just had to open your big mouth, didn't you, Nathan?" Brad comments.

"Ah! You people suck!" Riley gives Brad and Nathan two middle fingers.

"Whoever speaks next is going to wish they hadn't!" I wait to see who would be the dumb fuck that spoke next. I'm quite surprised that not one word is uttered. "See, look how nice that is. Now let's move."

***

Forty minutes in, Frank is the first to speak. "Good God. What the hell is that smell?"

"Maybe you should close your mouth," Jared snarls.

"I smell it too. I don't know what it is but let's keep moving. Maybe it'll pass." I'm so tired of smelling nasty shit, especially since this trip keeps leading to something terrible every time. "Maybe it's just an old landfill."

It's almost the same rancid aroma from the hangar with the dead Joscos. We may have to rethink our location if this stench continues to linger. It's a putrid mixture of decaying corpses and a shit-processing plant. We gasp for clean air, trying our hardest to muffle the sound of our coughs for the next mile.

We push through, and the funk lightens a bit as we reach what's remaining of a baseball field near a school at the southern point of the town. The temperature has been steadily getting colder since late afternoon, but there'll be no campfire tonight.

"You guys see a good place to spend the night?" I ask.

"There's gotta be a hotel around here somewhere," Nathan whispers.

"Remember, we haven't had the best of luck with hotels in the past," Brad adds.

"Okay, fine. No hotels. Who wants to sleep in a bed anyway?" Riley was clearly hoping for at least one-star accommodation.

"You wouldn't if you were on the last mission with a hotel!" Brad replies.

"Well, wherever we end up staying, we sure as hell can't find it sitting here now, can we?" Nathan adds.

We push farther into McGregor and cautiously make our way through the small town, walking through the middle of a residential street.

A few blocks into town, Frank whispers, "Stop!", then signals he hears something.

We kneel and turn around. None of the rest of us hear anything, so I order Frank to take point and we follow him.

We damn near walk across the entire town before we hear what Frank had. We can't tell exactly which building it's coming from, but we know we're getting closer because the sound gets louder with each step. It's like someone is injured, alternating between crying and moaning in pain. Is this a trap? Joscos have been known to do things like this, attracting people and then capturing them, but I don't think a Josco could even make a sound this high-pitched.

We come to a four-way intersection, and Frank points to a building northeast of us. We scurry over and line up with our backs against the exterior wall. Brad points up, and we read the words "Law Enforcement Center" on the front of the one-story building. I enter first, followed by Riley, Jared, then Nathan. Brad and Frank make their way to the rear.

After a few more grunts, we're positive the sound is coming from inside. I tiptoe past the front office, weapon raised at the ready. Navigating the debris from the partially collapsed roof, I keep an eye on my peripheral for anything stalking in the dark. As I enter the jail portion of the building, the pop of broken glass from beneath someone's feet behind me rings out, making me pause. *Are you kidding me? Is this amateur hour?* I stop and hold my position, scanning the area in case we've been outed. The moaning stops. Clearly, whoever is in there heard.

Looking past the door frame into the cell area, I catch a flickering movement as a faint glow emanates from the back. We're not alone. Chains rattle and scrape on something. I signal Nathan and Jared to watch our backs. Riley stays close to my six as we walk to the back of the building. We take one step at a time, making sure not to step on anything else that'll give us away.

Inside the cell block, bed sheets hang from the ceiling, hiding the last cell in the row. Who in the hell would be locked up in here? I signal Riley to take a position in one of the neighboring cells.

The painful, agitated racket grows louder as we get into position, the chains frantically scraping and slapping against the wall. With

Riley in position and me standing next to the sheet just outside the cell, I prepare to rip down the stained cloth. Whoever is behind the curtain casts shadows onto the sheet. The clinking intensifies. I count backward with my left hand.

Three.

Two.

One. I tear down the sheet with a single jerk. Several candles flicker as the it flutters to the ground.

What. The. Fuck. I jump back and stand in disbelief as it fights to move away from us without success, shaking and breathing heavily like a dog.

"Is that what I think it is?" Riley inches closer with her weapon aimed right at it.

"Keep it down," I whisper. "And yes, it is." I stare at her for several moments. "That is either one knocked-up Josco or it's severely bloated."

"Fuck yeah. Joscos be gettin' freaky up in here." Jared leans over my shoulder, scaring the shit out of me.

"I told you to stay back there!" I whisper as loud as I can.

The female Josco is covered in bruises and filth, with a chunk of hair missing from the side of her head and her ragged clothes barely hanging on. The wire, mattress-less frame she's resting on must be painful. Shackles wrap her wrists and ankles with additional straps used around her torso to tie her to the bed. She's as rough-looking as they come and skinny for a Josco. Her feet extend another two feet beyond the bed frame. Even I feel a sliver of sympathy for her.

"Hey, what are y'all talking about in here?" Frank asks, entering from the back door.

"Dude, come look at this shit." Jared encourages Frank inside.

"It's a female Josco," Frank blurts out. "A locked up, pregnant female Josco."

"Seriously? Can we please be quiet? Jeez! You're not even supposed to be in here! You should be out back watching for anything suspicious," I scold everyone.

Brad pushes his way in.

"Hey, Frank, we finally found you a girlfriend," Jared says. "And look, she's already tied up so she can't run away from you."

"We're going to have to do some retraining when we get back. A lot of running. For fuck's sake, can anyone keep it quiet?"

A few of them mouth "Sorry."

Frank glares at Jared. "I hope you don't plan on sleeping tonight. You better watch yourself. We might be fine dining on your dead corpse over candlelight for our first date."

Jared's disgusted look turns into a smile. "Yeah, and I bet you'd like that. I bet you'd start with my cock," he says, grabbing his crotch.

"Okay. That was funny," I say, nudging Frank with an elbow. Sometimes these funny assholes just catch me off guard.

Frank turns to me and whispers, "I know."

"So, what the hell are we going to do with her?" Brad asks.

"I know what Frank would like to do to her." Jared shifts his hips in a sexual manner at Frank.

Frank rolls his eyes in return.

"Enough, Jared," I say. "Can we be serious for five fucking seconds?"

Frank pulls on the cell door, and it opens with a loud screech, causing the Josco to become irate and scream like a damned banshee.

"Shut the door, dammit!" Riley yells, stepping back.

"Well, I was going to ask if the door was locked, but I guess that answers that question," I say.

"I vote to put a bullet in her head and call it a night," Nathan suggests, leaning on the cell across the hall, readying his weapon.

"I second that," Brad says, preparing his rifle.

"I agree," Jared concurs. "What else would we do with her? Is there any other option?"

"Really, guys!" Riley jumps in. "Do you know how rare this must be? Besides, she's clearly been tortured and starved. I feel bad for her, and even though it would be a mercy, I really don't think we should shoot her."

"Rare? She's not a Babe Ruth trading card, for cryin' out loud," Brad says, like there's no other option.

"We're not going to kill her," I firmly say.

"What do you mean? We don't even know what kind of demon baby she's carrying. What, you want to take her home and become besties and play Uno or something? I ain't fucking lugging her ass around." Brad paces. "This is fucking stupid."

"You'll do what the fuck I order you to do." I make it very clear who is in charge. "Look, there's nothing more I would like than to put one between her eyes and call it a day, but the Major needs to see this, alive."

"Alive? We're already up a creek without a paddle, and now you want to add a Josco to the mix?" Jared adds.

"Yes, alive. Look, we could learn a lot from her," I tell them. "Have any of you ever seen a live female Josco? It's been fifteen years! And for this one to be pregnant. The Major would be grilling us filet mignons for the rest of our lives if we brought him one of these."

"Alive though? Let's just take the dead body back to him." Nathan tries to compromise.

"We kill her, then whatever's inside of her dies too. We're taking her with us. And that's final." I speak firmly. At least Riley gives me an approving nod.

"Frank, you have anything to say about this? You're quiet all of a sudden," Jared spits.

"He is the boss. We do what he says." Frank kept it short and simple, supporting me, which I appreciate.

"Coward." Jared starts walking away.

"Look, I know how it sounds, but you're being a stubborn asshole at the moment," I sneer.

"You're fucking crazy, Scott." Jared storms to the front of the building with Brad in tow.

"Look, we just have to haul her ass to our extraction point in less than two days and we're done. It's not that big of a task. Shit, look at her. She might not even make it the next two days."

"That's a day and a half of lugging this bitch around," Nathan adds.

"Again, hey!" Riley backhands Nathan.

"Sorry," Nathan says. "The thing looks like she's ready to pop now, and I don't want that thing squirting pregnant juice all over me. She pops, then who the fuck is going to handle that?" We all eye Riley.

"The fuck you looking at me for?" Riley says, shaking her head.

"Look, we'll deal with that if it happens." I say.

"Seriously, that's disgusting, man," Frank says, looking at Nathan. "Making my stomach churn with that visual."

"She's going to be a pain in the ass. Do we have anything to knock her out with?" Riley asks, looking around.

"Yeah, the butt end of my gun should do the trick," Jared says from afar.

"We're not going to do anything right now," I tell the group. "We'll come back for her in the morning. Seems to be properly secured, and I'm pretty sure she didn't do this to herself. Let's go find a place to rest before her caretakers decide to check in. I'm fucking starving."

"Sounds good." Frank agrees.

"In all seriousness," Nathan muses, "you think she likes missionary or doggie style?"

"Fucking stop or I'll throw you in with here." An annoyed Riley leads the charge out of the room with that comment.

We exit the police station out the back and find a campsite around the corner. The lot is surprisingly full of campers and one-time-luxurious RVs. We each grab our own accommodations after scarfing down a half-serving of MRE, which doesn't even begin to fill the empty void. I volunteer to take the first shift, and we alternate throughout the rest of the night. I make it clear that if anything happens to the female Josco while I'm asleep, there will be hell to pay.

***

The following morning, Nathan and Brad join me to check on the Josco. We stop just shy of entering the building after hearing voices coming from inside—human voices. We kneel and creep in. I try to peek around the corner, but I can't see anything with the debris and fallen roof in the way. They speak loudly, as clear as day, but sound like two rambling idiots. I have Brad fetch the rest of the team and have them cover the rear of the building.

Nathan and I wait in silence for Brad to return before we go inside. I want that Josco, and I'll do whatever it takes to get it. The bigger concern now is who are these people? And what the hell are they doing here with a pregnant, female Josco? Are these the people that were breeding them back in Fort Hood? *Can't be. They sound like idiots.*

Brad returns a few minutes later, and the three of us creep through the front door with weapons ready. This time avoiding the broken glass. We assume gunfire will attract their friends, so I order my men not to fire unless absolutely necessary.

We inch closer, and the sound of a metal pipe banging on the cell bars makes me flinch each time. *I fucking hate that sound.* We pass through the office and into the lockdown area, two scrawny men appear. They're taunting the Josco, getting her all riled up, standing inside the neighboring cell. One's throwing food and spitting at her while the other is banging the metal pipe on the bars like a bored kid. I want to take that pipe and smack him upside the head with it.

With the men distracted, this should be easy. I signal orders to Nathan and Brad. Brad stays back and watches our six while Nathan swings around me and takes his position within a cell off to my right. As I walk, I notice they left their shotguns leaning up against a wall more than ten feet away. *Amateurs.* I get within five feet of the one holding the pipe and let out a little whistle.

They stand like statues before turning their heads, the one with the metal pipe stares face to face with the barrel of my rifle. They turn a pale shade of white but look at us like we're the ghosts. Guess they weren't expecting company. They drop everything in their hands, and the pipe clinks on the floor.

"Who the fuck are you?" I demand.

They just turn to each other, stunned.

"Do either of you understand English"—Nathan draws out each word—"because right now would be a good time to find your voices."

The one to the right, who was throwing food, nods yes very slowly and swallows deeply, making his Adam's apple bulge.

"You guys live around here?" I ask. The same guy again nods yes, excruciating pace.

These guys look terrible. They obviously haven't showered in some time based on their matted, greasy hair. They look to be in their mid to late thirties. No way they are here living on their own. They must have friends somewhere nearby. We just need to get them talking.

"We're not here to hurt you. I know you two can talk. We heard you just a few minutes ago. I just need some information," I calmly say to them, but they only stand there, eyes wide.

Second after agonizing second of nothingness goes by. Where the hell are those three ass clowns of mine who are supposed to be covering the rear? This is going nowhere fast with these stupid fucks. The one to the left lowers his arms, looking over toward Nathan's and Brad's weapons.

"Don't be stupid." I look to the other one. "You can lower your arms as well." By giving them some freedom, I'm hoping we can start a dialogue. "Do either of you have a name."

"Fr-Fr-Frank," the one to the left stutters. Nathan lets out a small snort. I'm praying he doesn't start cracking jokes.

"Good. My name is Scott," I offer back.

The new Frank smirks.

"Something funny, Frank?" I ask.

"Ya shouldn't be hur," he says in a pitchy, shaky voice.

"And why is that?"

"They gonna get ya." He tilts his head down and then looks up with the wildest, craziest smile I've ever seen.

"Dude, you're fucking creepy," Nathan adds.

"Who's gonna get us?" A chill runs up my spine from the feeling of being watched.

We dubbed the new Frank; Frank Jr. Him and his friend look at each other and laugh.

"Okay, yup, I'm done. Can we get the hell out of here, Scott?" Nathan asks.

"Very soon."

I request for the two of them to slowly walk out of their cell. And just as Frank Jr. starts moving, the Josco erupts in a violent rage of flailing arms, beating her chains against the wall. I damn near jump out of my skin. My finger is the closest it can be to emptying my magazine into all three of them.

And just as my fear subsides, my Frank jumps in and hits Frank Jr. in the back of his head with the side of his minigun but doesn't knock him out. The other guy lunges for Nathan, and he maneuvers to the side putting him on his stomach. Frank and Jared tie up Nameless while we do the same to Frank Jr.

"Now, why did you have to go and do that?" Jared asks.

"Yur all dead men," Nameless spits out. "I'ma eat you. All ya!" He looks up at my Frank before continuing, his eyes as wide as a full moon, "Lots of meat fur me ta eat. Lots of meat fur me ta eat." The two start chanting the same line.

"He's missing a few brain cells," Nathan says.

"And teeth," Frank adds.

"Oh jeez, we have cannibals here," Riley adds, gagging.

"Well, that went fucking great," Brad says.

"Here." My Frank hands me a gun. "He was reaching for it in the back of his pants."

"Good eye, Frank. Thanks." I set the gun back where the other weapons sit.

"My people are comin'." Nameless licks his lips, what few nasty teeth he has are covered in brown patches. "Serpent's Head gonna to kill ya."

"The Serpent's Head?" Jared looks at me. "Who the fuck are these people?"

We hog-tie them and place them into one of the cells, then tie it closed. They keep yelling, so we gag them for good measure.

"Need to be quick about this. I really don't want to be here if or when their friends show up."

"There's a truck out back. I think it's theirs. It wasn't there last night," Brad says.

"Really? Fucking sweet. This could be a big break for us," Nathan adds, running out the back door to look.

"Well, don't get too excited," Brad says.

I look to Jared and ask, "Weren't you on watch this morning?" I want to smack him. I shake my head. "What do you mean don't get too excited?" I add, looking back to Brad.

The truck is not pretty and looks like it might not even make it down the road. Rusted to shit, the back driver's side tire is low and barely has any tread left. The bed sits lower than the front, making me wonder if the shocks will hold up when Frank jumps in. At least it's a four-door.

"Oh look, they even have a lovely drawing of their gang painted on the driver's side door. I'm pretty certain they spelled 'serpent' wrong. Not ser-pants." Jared laughs. "But I am very surprised at the quality of their art, actually."

It's an image of a snake head straight on with its mouth open, showing its fangs. Its body is curled up behind it, out of focus, with five solid black stars evenly spaced out around the outside with their name below.

"Yeah, you ain't lying. Somebody sure knows how to draw," Brad says.

"Okay, let's grab the Josco and get the fuck out of here," Nathan says hastily.

We head back inside the building and enter the Joscos cell. She starts freaking out in a panic. She must be in a lot of pain. Sleeping on metal wires can't be too comfortable.

"How are we going to do this?" Riley asks, looking puzzled.

I give Frank a nod.

"Finally," he replies, then smiles.

Frank rips Jared's weapon from his grip and knocks her out with the butt end of the rifle. He hands it back to Jared, with the Josco's blood on it.

"Gee, thanks." Jared dangles his rifle at arm's length, and we get a good laugh.

We find the keys to the locks sitting on the windowsill of the cell and unchain her, then peel her from the bedframe. The sound of her flesh ripping off the wire mesh makes me cringe. Perfect little red squares are embedded into her skin. Raw, bloody lines run the length of her, with small trickles of blood coming from the fresh wounds. We tie her tightly with rope and carry her limp body through the rear of the building, throwing her in the bed of the truck. Thank God the females are a lot smaller than the males or there is no way we could have handled her.

"You really think these are going to hold her?"

"We don't have any other choice," I point out.

"Yeah, we do. I can slit her throat right here and now, and we can be done with her," Jared adds, patting his right calf where his knife sits.

"Jared, don't get started with me right now. We're keeping her alive."

"Fine. Shotgun!" Jared runs around to the passenger side of the truck but grimaces after he sees the nasty grime on the seat. "What the fuck! Did these guys shit on everything?"

Nathan leans under the steering wheel and connects two wires to start the engine, and it rumbles to life. It doesn't sound great and we'll be lucky if this piece of shit makes it ten feet. The gauges are broken, so there's no telling how much fuel is in this thing. I'm optimistic. I jump into the bed of the truck and pull out my map. I give Nathan directions to the main highway while Brad and Riley get into the back seat. Frank jumps in the bed of the truck with the Josco and me.

I take in an unsettling breath as we pull out onto a road, the truck squeaks and whines with every movement. Maybe I can start to relax. Brad reaches through the back window, which is busted out, and taps my shoulder, pointing to a tattoo on her forehead.

"Same as the ones from the hangar," he says.

None of us even noticed it with the darkness of last night, the dirt on her face, and our inability to get close to her.

"I wonder how she got here?" I say more to myself than to the group, trying to fit the pieces together.

Things are not adding up: Dr. Anderson was heading down in this direction, the nicely kept cow farm we saw, this pregnant female Josco, and somehow an unlikely human colony somewhere close.

"I'm glad I decided not to kill her," I say, looking at Frank, who just nods.

Brad looks back and says, "The only good Josco is a dead one."

I wave him off and he turns back to the front.

The thought of some crazy loon out there breeding these things is beyond comprehension. There's no way those two hillbillies had anything to do with this. This is far past their intellectual capabilities.

I watch Frank as he stares at our guest. I can see it in his eyes. He feels sorry for the thing. He could have been one of them. Not a female Josco, but one of Them. Whatever process that took place when he was born was different. He probably wouldn't have lived very long after his birth if that was the case. I wonder if this Josco's baby will be like Frank?

I remove my helmet, lean back, and let the wind race across my bald head as I think about the other team. Sean is my best friend, even if he is an epic pain in my ass. I hope they made it out and we see them back home.

CHAPTER TWENTY-ONE

(Lieutenant Scott Dodson—U.S. Marines)

Friday, January 24, 2048

My mood shifts instantly. The last thing any of us want to hear is the stammering engine. Is it the fuel running out, or is the engine in this shitty vehicle just shot?

"You've got to be kidding me!" I beat the side of the patinaed truck bed with my fist. Soon after, the engine starts to vibrate violently. Then it dies with one last sputter. We coasted for twenty yards until Nathan slammed on the brakes in an attempt to be humorous. We all slide forward a bit anticipating the stop, but Brad's forehead slams on the back headrest of the front passenger seat.

"Fucker." Brad rubs his forehead, then punches the headrest.

Nathan looks back with a sly smirk and a wink.

"Piece-of-shit truck," Brad says as he exits the vehicle, slamming the door shut. The glass inside shatters and he proceeds to kick it a few times.

"I want to beat this truck up as much as everyone else, but you're making a shit ton of noise," I tell him. "Stop it."

The thirty-minute drive barely got us into the city limits of Waco. I guess we should be thankful we made it this far—it did save us a few hours of walking. The airport is still another fifteen miles northwest of our current position.

I shield my eyes from the sun as I check out our surroundings. Waste is piled up several feet high, no matter where I look. Tires, trash, even clothing litter the highway; it's the only thing my eyes can focus on. There was life after the Turning to some extent. The devastated landscape distracts me, as I attempt to pinpoint a landmark. Some of the refuse is not as decomposed as the other piles. *Interesting*.

"What a fucking dump," Brad mutters.

"Well, it beats walking the entire way," Nathan adds, trying to make the situation better.

"True that," Riley adds, snapping her fingers, then pointing at him.

"Now what the fuck are we going to do?" Frank asks as though he's confused.

"What we've been doing, walk," I say with a hint of annoyance. "This is what we've trained for." Frank clearly doesn't want to walk another foot if he can help it. None of us do, but it is what it is.

Brad opens the hood to see if there's anything he can do to get it going again. He knows his way around an engine, but the way it vibrated tells me it's beyond repairable.

"I bet it's out of gas." Jared leans against the truck, resigned.

"Why don't you go sniff the gas tank and let us know how much fuel is not in the tank," Brad snaps back.

Frank smirks but doesn't join the argument this time.

"This truck is done for. It was nice to have the wind in our hair. Well, for some of us, anyway. Sorry, Scott. Let's just go." Riley grimaces at me, then punches me in the arm.

"Riley's right, mostly." I give her a side-eye.

"We made up some good time," I say. "We'll get to our location, sit back, and relax until the cavalry shows up tomorrow. Grab your shit and let's go."

"Speaking of cavalry." Jared walks to the rear of the truck. "You guys hear that?"

"Oh shit," Brad yells. "Shit, Shit, Shit!"

The sound of untuned engines fast approaching from the southwest makes my pulse quicken.

"Is that gunfire?" Frank asks, tilting his head toward the sound of an automatic ringing in the distance.

"It sure is," Nathan replies.

"Who the fuck are these people?" Brad's question felt more like a statement. "They're going to attract every Josco in Texas with all that noise!"

"We need to get off the highway now! Frank, help me with the Josco. Let's head over to that building." I point at a shit-colored three-story stucco structure approximately two hundred yards to the northeast. It's the closest building to our position. I grab the female Josco's nasty blackened feet while Frank takes ahold of her arms, and within seconds we're hauling ass down an embankment dodging piles of trash.

We forego our normal breaching procedures and rush into what turns out to be an abandoned hotel just off the access road. We scurry to the third level to get a better viewpoint. The building's small, but it provides the best overlook of the highway. No sooner did we settle in than a train of vehicles rumble our way.

"Serpent's Head?" Riley asks, shrugging her shoulders.

The convoy pulls up fast and circles the broken-down truck several times before stopping. Armed men pour out of six vehicles, running up to it, guns raised like a bunch of amateurs.

"This doesn't look good, guys." Jared peeks out just above the windowsill. "I see four trucks and two SUVs with all sorts of fucking tactical," he advises.

"Damn, that's a lot of tactical," Nathan adds.

We each pick a window to look out of and watch. I spot several men with rocket-propelled grenades slung around their shoulders. Great. They are loaded to the brim with every type of assault rifle I can think of, looking like the hillbilly version of us. Two of them point their weapons in our general direction and empty their magazines. Bullets penetrate the walls around us. We hit the ground at lightning speed.

"What the fuck?" Nathan whispers as we hug the carpet.

"Anyone hit?" I ask.

"I'm good," Nathan says. Everyone else nods.

They reload and fire their weapons at a building on the other side of the highway.

"What the hell did we just get ourselves into?" Riley asks with wide, concerned eyes.

"How many do you see, Jared?" I poke his back.

"Why don't you fucking take a look, Lieutenant."

"Just do it," I order him. "You have the better window."

"Fuck! Fine." He slowly raises his head after removing his helmet. "Uh, let's see, five…ten…eighteen…twenty-three…twenty-nine…thirty-six. I count thirty-six ready to shoot and eat us enemy combatants."

"Yeah, I counted the same," Nathan confirms from across the room. "All fucking armed to the teeth."

"This day just got a hell of a lot better," Brad mutters. "We should have just left this bitch where we found her."

"Next time you say that I'm slapping you in your fucking pussy!" Riley holds up a hand.

I can see Brad didn't quite know how to respond to that comment, and quite frankly, neither did I, so I nod at her and move on.

"Hmm?" I let out.

"What?" Brad asks, turning his head.

"In all my years, I've never fought an enemy that could actually shoot back. This should be interesting," I say. Looking at our body armor system, I'm thinking we should have packed a little more protection.

"What an astute observation, Scott. What the fuck are we gonna do?" Jared quips.

"Yeah, these guys don't look like they came to play," Frank notes, continuing to observe.

I pull out my binoculars. A large, burly man wearing dirty, ripped jeans and a black leather vest walks to the side of the highway and peers in our direction. His face is covered in tattoos. The most notable one being a snake curled around one temple and down his cheek. Several other men join him, looking just as rough. Some have beards and some shaved heads. Most are well-built but some are as scrawny as Frank Jr. and Nameless, the anorexics.

The beer-bellied man scans the area but seems to focus in our general direction. There's a trail in the tall grass from where we ran down the side of the highway. I'm sure my men see it as well, but I keep my mouth shut. Snake Face crosses his arms and then turns back to the southwest as another beat-to-shit truck driving sporadically swings around the convoy. The two occupants exit the truck, flailing their arms in the air, but Snake Face only shakes his head in what looks like annoyance.

"Well, well, well. Would you look at that," Brad says.

Frank Jr. and Nameless rush up to the truck we borrowed from them. They peek inside, probably hoping to see at least one of our dead bodies riddled with bullet holes. Snake Face approaches them and starts yelling at the pair, pointing at them like a parent scolding their children. They get into a physical altercation that's almost comical to watch. I can't hear them, but I imagine in my head what they're saying to one another in their lazy-tongued accents.

"What's our plan?" Nathan looks at me and the others follow suit.

I pull out a map of Waco. "Give me a second."

"How about I just stick my head out the window with my friends here"—Frank rubs the barrel of the miniguns—"and take them out."

"You really like those miniguns, don't you?" Brad smirks.

"No! Don't do anything," I say. "They're two hundred yards away, and we have no idea what they're capable of or how many others there are. I also don't want to give away our position. We need to be smart about this. They may be some crooked-looking backwoods hillbillies, but they know this area and we don't. So please, don't do anything stupid."

We continue monitoring them while I think of a plan. *Think, Scott, think.* Survival is priority one. We need to get as far away from the hooligans as possible and without being detected.

"Alright, this is what we're going to do. First, we need to tie that thing up as best we can. We're still taking her with us." I look at Brad, who rolls his eyes. "We're going to leave her here for now and hope that she doesn't wake up, chew through the ropes, and bail on us. She's weak, so I don't think that'll be an issue. She has a gag in her mouth, so she won't be making any noise either."

"Scott, you just might be a father by the time this is all over with," Nathan says, staring at her round belly. "Shall I say congratulations now, or maybe wait?"

"Nathan, shut up. Since you have this newfound love affair with her, go ahead and tie her up good and tight," I tell him. "I don't want her moving an inch."

"Oh, I bet he's good at tying them up. It's the only way he can get a girl to stay the night." Frank is finally able to make a joke before anyone else.

Riley high-fives Frank.

"Um, Lieutenant," Brad says.

"What now?"

"They're back in their vehicles and splitting up."

We scurry back to the window to watch. Three trucks and one SUV head north along the highway. The other two pull off to the south side of the highway and exit right in front of us.

"Fuck me!" I throw my head back in defeat.

After Nathan ties up the Josco with more knots than Frank Jr. can count, I run through the plan with everyone focused.

"What are our rules of engagement?" Nathan asks.

"Shoot to kill. If we get caught, judging by what Frank Jr. and Nameless said earlier, we'll be on tonight's menu, and then there would be no chance in hell of HQ ever rescuing us or knowing where we're at or what happened. I have a sneaking suspicion that these people don't want us getting out of here alive." I wipe sweat away from my forehead.

"How about we just give them Frank. They seem to just want his meaty body." Brad could hardly hold a serious face while saying it. Frank throws a punch, hitting Brad square in the bicep.

"Fucker, that hurt." Brad rubs his arm, glaring back at Frank.

"How did I get stuck with you little misfits, like a bunch of kindergarteners? Can you fuckers focus for one second?" I demand their attention. "Inventory, now!"

We check our weapons and gear, and then I double-check the Josco, making sure she's well hidden by some busted furniture. I place the confiscated metal container from the cornfield Joscos in the corner and cover it with trash and carpet. I order my team to clear out while I conduct one final inspection to make sure nothing is out of place, ensuring we covered our tracks. Then we exit out the east side of the building, away from the highway.

The tall, thick grass and debris help conceal us. We need to take advantage while they're in smaller numbers. Who knows how many of them there are and how many of their friends they notified? When the time comes, we need to strike fast and hard before they regroup.

We keep off to the side of a main road in search of a street that will work perfectly for what our plan requires. If a vehicle comes down it while we're positioned high up in buildings on either side, we could pick them off easily while staying covert.

It doesn't take long to find the ideal setup a few hundred yards from the hotel. I order Brad, Nathan, and Jared to space out among three buildings on the north side of the street. Frank, Riley, and I take the south. As soon as we get set up, we observe two vehicles driving on an adjacent road. They stop to chat, sitting roughly one hundred yards to the west of our location.

"Come on, you idiots. Turn down this street." I watch through my scope.

The longest five minutes on the planet tick away at a snail's pace until the SUV finally turns onto our street. The other truck stays put.

"Get moving truck!" I mutter. "Don't need you sticking around for this."

I'm not sure if these guys are decent trackers or if they just got lucky, but the desert-colored SUV with large mud tires creeps up our street, heading right for us. The truck's tires squeal, and they drive onto the street that parallels ours.

Frank's objective is to take out the engine and then move on to the occupants. His beloved miniguns should do the trick. The rest of us will pick off any leftovers.

Fifty yards out, I check my weapon, making sure I'm good, then I peek through my scope.

"I count six occupants," I whisper into my mic. "Armed with what looks like AKs and AR-15s."

Up front, the driver and his passenger scan their side of the street with their rifles pointed out the windows. Two sit in the middle, where both windows are rolled down with occupants hanging out of each, and then two more hang out the back, seated on the window frame. One tap of the brakes or gas pedal and those two will be goners.

Out of the corner of my eye, I see Frank move into position, with the tips of his miniguns sticking out a foot from the busted window.

They have no idea what's about to happen to them, and it's going to hit them hard.

The SUV passes directly in front of us. My fingertips tingle and my heartbeat thrums in my ears. I give Frank the hand signal. He unleashes his weapons in a fury of fifty rounds per second, hot lead pelting the hood and front fender. It catches ablaze in a glorious repercussion. The passenger side of the SUV becomes riddled with a ribbon of bullet holes. Both the driver and co-pilot are taken out in an instant, followed by the guy hanging out the back seat of passenger window falling to the ground in a heap. The two hanging out the rear window have no other choice but to bail, abandoning their post and running to the opposite side of the vehicle. Two of my guys from across the street take them out with perfect shots to their chests, forcing their bodies to fly backward with their feet in the air. *Nice.*

The flaming vehicle swerves right and hits the curb, coming to a stop.

"That's one group down," I say, giving Frank a thumbs-up.

Our location is now compromised, so we regroup at the southwest corner of the street. The other truck's tires squeal as it makes a beeline back toward our street.

"Good job! Now we need to figure out how to take out the other truck before all their other friends show up." I shift uncomfortably in my position, unsure how we should proceed.

"Let's just do that now. Catch 'em off guard as they turn the corner. Meet them head-on," Brad suggests.

"That might work. They wouldn't expect to see us out in the open like that. Everyone good with that?" I look around.

They nod in unison, looking confident, so we jog south in formation. Our plan is simple. We split the road, with Frank, Riley, and I on one side and Nathan, Brad, and Jared on the other. We'll use the cars as cover until the right moment when we pop out like jack-in-the-boxes to greet them.

The four-door truck comes screaming around a turn, fishtailing and nearly losing control. The passenger-side occupant blindly fires his weapon in our direction. The bullets ping around me in a shower of lead. With no fear, Frank steps into the middle of the road from behind a bus and lights up the truck as they come racing toward us. The truck's .50 cal operator then opens fire, and we dive to the sides, ducking behind shells of cars that offer little protection.

Frank repositions himself and lets loose, disabling the truck's engine and making minced meat of the front two occupants. The truck coasts along the street toward us at blistering speed. The .50 cal operator is now on the ride of his life, but he's shielded by thick armor. Frank's bullets ping off the armor plating. I shoot three round bursts to keep the operator behind the armor so he can't get a good visual of our position. We need to keep him off that .50 cal.

Another person emerges from the rear driver's side window and fires his weapon at me. The truck continues to plow toward us, now only twenty feet away. I duck for cover. Riley scuddles forward beside a parked vehicle with no wheels and bursts out of the back end, taking aim with her M4. Several rounds hit around the truck's doorframe. She refocuses, she hits him square in the chest and once more on the side of his head for good measure. A red streak smears over the side of the truck and across the black armor in the bed, sure to cover the man tucked away behind it.

Another occupant extends his arms from the rear passenger side window; only this time, he's lobbing what looks like grenades over toward Nathan, Brad, and Frank.

"Grenade!" Nathan's voice screams, and they dive for cover in between two charred vehicles on their side of the street.

It was a good thing this person didn't know exactly where my guys were standing because the grenade explodes nowhere near their location. The truck sideswipes vehicles lined up on the opposite side of the road, slowing to a crawl.

Jared comes up from behind a truck bed in front of me and unloads his weapon, pelting the front windshield and then walking up to the truck as the vehicle rolls directly in front of us. He extends his weapon inside the back window, over the dead guy hanging halfway out, shooting the final hostile within the cab.

Simultaneously, the man in the bed of the truck grabs an automatic rifle and shoots aimlessly in front of the truck and to the side. He spots me on the ground, completely missing Jared right next to the truck. Riley comes up from behind a Volkswagen Beetle putting several rounds in his side. The truck finally comes to a stop after running into a parked silver sedan. We circle the vehicle to ensure there are no more threats.

"Damn good shootin', Riley!" I yell out, hyped up from the exchange.

"How about we try not to take out the vehicle next time so we can get the fuck out of here," Brad says desperately.

"Yeah, that's probably a good idea," Nathan responds.

I point to Brad. "Good thinking. Alright, Frank, no shooting engines. In fact, you don't shoot at all unless you absolutely have to. We'll get the next one." More tires squeal in the distance.

"Come check this out," Brad says as he rummages through the bed of the truck, finding several black pelican cases.

"What goodies do we have in here?" Riley says, rubbing her hands together.

"Well, what are you waiting for? Open them up. We ain't got much time," I order Brad.

Nathan unlocks one of the crates and opens it. "Oh, baby yes," he says as he raises a six-round 40 mm grenade launcher.

"Sweet, and there are two more crates."

CHAPTER TWENTY-TWO

(Lieutenant Scott Dodson—U.S. Marines)

Friday, January 24, 2048

We grab a couple of grenade launchers when a muffled voice calls out from inside the truck cab. It would be virtually impossible for anyone to survive the punishment we just dealt.

"Is that a radio?" Riley asks. *That makes more sense.*

"Sure sounds like it! Sweet!" Nathan scrambles to the cab.

He rips the door open, rummaging through the vehicle, tossing out trash, and pulling out bullet-riddled bodies. The sound gets louder with every handful of garbage that gets thrown out.

"Got it! Oh, man. YUCK!" Nathan holds up one blood-soaked, hand-held radio. "Fucking gross." He shakes the radio with a flick of his wrist.

"Here. Use this." I toss Nathan an oil-stained rag from the bed of the truck, and he starts wiping it off the best he can.

"Les get dem son's a bitches!" a voice yells over the radio.

"Fucking great." Riley mumbles.

Chatter erupts over the airwaves, and it appears they are communicating our location to others based on the gunfire they heard moments ago. Not sure how many, but reinforcements are on the way and will be here in moments. *Damn.*

They keep calling for guys named Art and Red. I peek in the cab and can only assume since they aren't responding, Art and Red are part of the recently deceased. Nathan tosses me the radio, and I place it in a pouch in my vest. Now we'll know their movements and hopefully stay one step ahead of them.

"Y'all sees that meaty fella yet?" The sound of two idiots scuffling over the radio causes some static, which is followed by incoherent speech.

We turn to Frank. "I think they're talking about you." Jared nudges him. "Sounds like our buddies, Frank Jr. and Nameless."

"I'm gonna sheesh co-bob that big fooker," the same voice calls out over the radio.

"Did he just say shish kabab? Sorry, man. Looks like you're going to be feeding a village later tonight." Nathan smirks.

"Thems tuk ma Josco bitch!" another voice calls out.

The two voices go back and forth, taking up the airwaves.

The deep raspy voice of a man comes over the comms, perhaps Snake Face, the likely leader of the Serpent's Head cult, saying, "Get off the radio, you fucking fools! No one sleeps until we bring them back dead or alive. And find that Josco! I want her back with a pulse." The man continues to ramble on.

On a positive note, they think there are only four of us. I guess Frank Jr. and Nameless actually don't know how to count that well. I'm still a bit confused as to how these people have survived through the years. How are they living this far south and, by most accounts, thriving? Makes absolutely no sense to me. Maybe they have been keeping this female Josco alive as a bargaining chip.

"We need to go. Now!"

We form into a staggered formation and head north through a subdivision. Our extraction point is within grasp to the northwest, close enough that I can feel it calling me home. Now, the goal is to make it undetected from here on out, but with the female Josco in tow, it's going to be even more complicated. We need the cover of night, where we do our best work, but we're nowhere close to that time. We still have five hours of daylight.

With two of their vehicles out of commission and eleven of their men dead, my gut tells me we haven't even leveled the playing field, but my hope is that we've at least scared them into thinking we're a force not to be reckoned with.

Tires squeal on the streets around us. The radio chatter doesn't specify our exact location, but it's obvious they know our general whereabouts. We navigate through backyards, staying off the main roads, using buildings and mounds of debris to stay hidden. We wind our way back to Highway 84, but farther north of where our commandeered truck broke down. We take a quick breather and scout the area.

"What about the Josco?" Brad asks as though he's actually concerned about her.

"Now, all of a sudden, you care," I respond.

"Hell no. Just hoping you gave up on her with everything that's happening," Brad replies.

"Oh, I'm coming back for her later tonight. With or without your guys' help."

"Since we have one of their radios, how about we use it and make it sound like we're heading in another direction, east, maybe?" Riley offers. "I mean, how hard could it be to sound like one of them?"

"Fuck all of you," Nathan says, shaking his head after we point to him.

"That could work. Here, Nathan." I hand him the radio. "You sound more hillbilly than any of us. Add a little southern charm while you're at it."

Brad taps my shoulder and points west. I gaze over, then put a finger to my mouth, signaling everyone to be quiet.

We get down low on the ground behind a pile of rotting wood mixed with an array of old plumbing materials. Frank takes a knee. A group of twenty or so men on foot, armed with a variety of rifles and spaced out with thirty feet between them, are walking directly toward us, one hundred yards away. If they continue walking in this direction, they're going to come right up on us. As we're assessing our current situation, the sound of vehicles approach from the east. *We're fucked.* The north is too open, leaving us vulnerable, and I really don't want to head back south. The best option is to continue west and take our chances with the group heading our way.

"We need to cross here and now. You guys see that tree line just beyond the highway?" I point in the direction of a cluster of tall pines.

"Yes, sir."

"That's where we need to be. Frank, since you're the fastest, you and I will hold this position and provide cover fire until they get across and are safe. You four book it when I give the signal. When you guys get in position, you'll provide cover fire for Frank and me when we cross. We'll regroup and try to lose them in the forest, heading toward our extraction point. There's a lake due west of here. If, for whatever reason, we split up, we meet at the airport north of the lake. Understood?"

"Yes, sir."

"Might be your lucky day, Brad. We might just have to forego the Josco." I concede, a little perturbed by the elation on his face.

"Frank, you and I are up. Let's do this." He nods, ready to deal out some punishment.

The group ahead of us is disorganized and lazy in their approach, with their weapons pointed down, now fifty yards from us. Brad readies one of the grenade launchers we seized earlier while I ready the other one, making sure the spring is charged so it will rotate to the next grenade. I close the back plate, and it's ready to fire.

"Go time, Frank!"

Frank stands up and out of the rubbish, unloading short bursts to conserve his ammo. He sweeps his miniguns back and forth. He takes out several men before they know what hit them. The rest scatter like cockroaches, ducking, hiding behind whatever is near them. Riley, Nathan, Jared, and Brad take off in a dead sprint. It's one hundred yards to the tree line. Between the weight they're carrying, their current physical condition, and training, they should make it in twenty seconds.

Frank takes a breather. I peek out, aim, and shoot several short but precise bursts, hitting two that thought they were well hidden behind a rusted SUV. Their bodies fall back, their heads disappearing below. I switch to the grenade launcher as bullets whiz past my head. Several men run behind a pile of propane tanks, maybe forty yards away. We're about to see if these things are empty. I move into a better position, ducking behind a slight uprise in the ground, and aim the heavy launcher before pulling the trigger.

A thud sounds out, and away the first one goes, hitting just short of the tanks but spraying the men behind it with a wave of dirt. I make a slight angle-up adjustment and pull again.

This time, it's a direct hit, sending metal chunks into the air thirty feet, the shrapnel spread far and wide. *They're toast.* Then I launch the remaining four grenades where I last saw people running. Four consecutive explosions ring out, one after another.

Brad launches all six of his grenades with only a few seconds spacing each one, creating a continuous wall of dirt and debris flying through the air. Other than the crackling of fire and the ringing in my ears from the explosions, I see no heads and hear no gunfire.

Frank waves his arm to get my attention, pointing to our men and letting me know they made it across.

"We're good," Frank yells out.

We run toward the highway while the others provide cover fire for us. We make it halfway when Frank notices a hostile group emerging fast on our men from deep inside the trees. They must have been tucked away within the forest, out of sight. We didn't have a chance in hell to respond. Within seconds, Nathan, Brad, Jared, and Riley are surrounded by a hundred enemy soldiers.

Frank and I take shelter and watch as Nathan spins around to fire a shot, but he's too late. He didn't even get his rifle shouldered before getting hit and going down. Jared and Brad fire several shots before they're overcome and tackled by the group.

There's nothing Frank or I can do for them. As a soldier, we've always lived by the motto "No man left behind." Frank and I could rush toward them in a blaze of glory and help, but even with all our training, we just don't have the numbers to take them on. We'll have to find another way.

"We're going to have to come back for them, Frank!" It was painful to say, but we had no other choice.

We redirect to the northeast, charging ahead as fast as we can along the south side of the highway, looking like two convicts who just escaped prison. We don't look back and as we sprint away, a .50 cal opens fire from a vehicle behind us, the rounds pelting the ground around us and whizzing past our heads. We keep hustling for at least a mile and a half until we feel it's safe.

We come to a neighborhood and do our best to hide our tracks by staying off the grass and sticking to the sidewalks and streets.

"That house," I say, panting and pointing. "Right there." The fence on the right side of the house at the end of the cul-de-sac is knocked down, so we carefully maneuver to the back door. It's unlocked and Frank enters first. I shut the door, falling to the floor in a heavy heap and gasping. My mind is fuzzy, and I'm dizzier than I have ever felt. The looming feeling of nausea threatens my ability to stay conscious, but I fight the urge to pass out by taking deep breaths through my nose. I'm jealous that Frank looks like he could run a marathon, not even breaking a sweat. His eyes stay glued to the backyard, watching for movement.

"You stay here. I'll cover the front." I struggle to stand up but muscle my way through the pain, using the wall to steady my stance.

"You got it!" Frank's eyes remain focused outside.

I reach deep inside for what little energy I have left and walk shakily to the front, continuing to use the walls for support. I do my best to avoid the broken pictures hanging on the walls, but I can't help but notice that it seems as though someone took a hammer to them. Broken glass is scattered on the tile floor. It was like some teenager came in and vandalized everything in sight.

I pass through the living room and then on to the dining room, where I find a decent spot on the floor. The bay window offers a perfect view of the street, a hundred yards down. I get on my knees and prop my rifle on the bay seat. If anyone walks or drives up the street, I'll know it.

It took nearly an hour for my breathing and my heart rate to slow and my mind to calm. But regret sinks in. We should have stayed and fought. My mind replays the scenario, and guilt dictates all the things I should have done. Nathan had the radio, so we have no idea what's going on with the others. I can only hope that he is okay and his wound isn't life-threatening.

***

Another hour ticks by, and I haven't heard or seen anything that would cause trouble. I get up, remove my rucksack, and stretch.

"Anything?" I ask Frank as we glance out one of the kitchen windows that has a clear shot of the next street over.

"Nothing."

"Same."

It feels good to take a deep, satisfying breath and expand my lungs without the restraints of the rucksack straps. "Nathan went down. It's the only thing I can think about." My fists and chest tighten.

"Me too. It didn't look good, Scott. They must've been hiding back there waiting for us. They had to have known our exact location."

I slide down the cabinets and lean against them, broken plates and silverware scattered on the floor beneath my feet with no idea what to do now. I'm lost.

"They had to have taken them somewhere close, right?" I ponder the possibilities of where that could be.

"Well, we can't take on the entire group. We'll have to wait until tomorrow when our guys get here." Frank relaxes from his post and walks closer to me.

"I know, but even if we make it to our extraction, it'll be a good two days before we're back for a rescue mission, if the Major even allows it."

"You know we can't go beating ourselves up about this. We're not going to leave them behind. We'll get back home, load up and come down here with a shit load of soldiers, find them, and then blow this town to smithereens!"

Frank's positive tone gives me a little hope, but of course, I'm beating myself up over this. My decisions led us here.

"You didn't have many choices, and I would've made the same calls. Regarding the Major, he has no choice but to send more soldiers back," Frank says, standing tall. "I lost my brother yesterday. I'll do it myself if I have to, and I'll die doing it if it comes to that."

"Ooh-rah." I felt it was the only worthwhile response.

"You're damn right, ooh-rah. So, what do we do now?" Frank asks.

"I really have no idea. Maybe we wait until nightfall and use the darkness to our advantage. Get the Josco." I shrug my shoulders. "And make our way to the airport. We'll look for signs of our team along the way. Maybe we'll catch a break and see where these guys are hiding."

"Then that's what we'll do."

It's 1530 hours, and we still have a couple of hours until nightfall. I walk around the house to clear my head while Frank stays put. I look at what's left of the family pictures hanging on the wall. Nice family, from what I can tell. Wonder if any of them are still alive? It's a good-sized house with a second story. I walk up the stained carpeted stairs, which creak with every step. The stairs lead up to an open room where a pool table sits in the middle with its cover still nicely placed on top. A custom-made walnut bar is tucked away in the corner with a variety of beer signs hanging on the wall behind it. I hightail it over and swing open the cabinet doors, looking for anything to wet my lips.

"Damn, nothing," I whisper to myself.

I lightly tug the dingy white string to open the blinds, just enough to let some light in. My eyes are drawn to the scarlet flag with the gray and gold emblem of the Corps on the far wall. It makes my heart beat a little harder and makes me stand a little taller. It's perfectly centered on the wall, surrounded by military photos, awards, and plaques. Above the flag, a two-part shadow box sits, with an expertly folded American flag atop and ribbons, medals, and patches below it.

Frank's heavy footsteps distract me for a moment until his head pops up above the steps.

"Check this out. A Marine lived here." I walk over to the wall, meeting Frank as though it was timed. "Staff Sergeant Curtis A. Booker," I read from one of the many plaques. "Twenty years devoted to being a Devil Dog." We both stand quiet, admiring the things this man accomplished as a Marine. "Think we'll ever get an award like this?" I ask more as a joke.

"Probably not in our lifetime," Frank says.

We stand in silence, reading articles about everything this man achieved as a Marine. He reached the rank of Colonel and did eight tours between Iraq and Afghanistan. The group photo of him in Iraq with his brothers and a palace in the background reminds me of all the photos we have plastered in our Ops room. It may have been a different war, a different time, but they're no different than us.

***

At nightfall, we share our last MRE together in a dark closet, with our flashlights casting shadows around us. If tonight's our last, at least we won't go out starving. It's a quiet dinner, the only sound being the crunching of crackers smothered in peanut butter and strawberry preserve. We consume every crumb, then lick every finger twice to make sure nothing is left behind. We take a moment to plan out our route to pick up our plus one back at the hotel. It may come back to bite me in the ass, but we need to bring her back with us, and at this point, it's the only thing I can control.

Ready with our plan of action, there's nothing left but for us to bump fists and for me to don my night vision goggles. We exit out the back door to a quiet, moonlit night. The silence is uncomfortable. Are they out there somewhere waiting for us, or have they gone in for the night? The noises earlier had to have drawn the attention of some very curious Joscos.

I take point as we navigate the streets back to the hotel, stopping periodically to listen and make sure we're not being followed or that there are no threats in the area. Aside from a few birds chirping, I hear nothing. I'm wondering if maybe the Serpent's Head knows something we don't, and they're hidden away at night because that's when the freaks come out, though I don't know how it could get much weirder.

It takes two hours, but we make it back to the hotel. We painstakingly check every room on every floor up to the third level for any threats. When we enter the third floor, we hear her muffled moans. *Someone's awake.*

We searched all the rooms and even looked outside a few of them at the surrounding buildings to make sure they were not occupied with snipers and soldiers waiting to ambush us. Frank and I give each other a nod, confirming we both agree it's as safe as it's going to get, so we move on to the room she's located in.

We keep her gagged, but she's clearly hurting. Starving, I'm sure. She looks horrible. Her eyes have the glazed look of death. The last glimmer is fading fast, and I can't believe I feel any sort of sorrow for her, but somehow seeing her makes my heart ache. I would be very surprised if she lasted through the night, but these things are fighters. We see them as if they're the enemy, but she isn't. What she became was the enemy, but that wasn't her fault. She used to be someone's daughter, maybe a wife, and could quite possibly be a mother before too long.

Frank and I create a makeshift stretcher with several sheets, some rope, and two metal bed frame rails. But before we start making our way down, Frank hears something fall from one of the levels below. Was she being used as bait, knowing we would come back for her? Maybe it's just someone making their rounds?

We carefully and quietly set the stretcher down in the hallway. I signal for Frank to position himself at the end of the hall, and I'll set up in the room just off the stairwell so I'll have a perfect view of whoever comes up. There's only one set of stairs in the building, so we shouldn't have any surprises behind us. I duck behind some furniture, my weapon pointed right at the stairs. Shallow footsteps approach. My heart speeds up. The creaking stops, so they're more than likely pausing between the second and third levels. They continue, but slower. Through my night vision goggles, I can barely make out the shoulder of a person close to the stairwell wall. They stop just shy of stepping foot on the third floor. If only they would move over just a foot so I could see them. I hope it's just the one.

Whomever it is, stays deathly still with one weapon clearly visible and raised at the ready. The Josco's moans are loud enough to be heard by our late-night guest. They take that final step onto the floor, and the last thing I hear is Frank's voice calling out breaking the silence.

CHAPTER TWENTY-THREE
(Major Oliver White—U.S. Marines)

Friday, January 24, 2048

A heavy-handed knock echoes through my apartment, reverberating in my dream as a shot from the gun I have pointed at Lily's black eyes. Warm tears run down my cheeks as I shoot her for the thousandth time.

"Oliver, open up!" a deep voice calls out.

My body refuses to react until her limp body falls to the ground, morphing into an angry wolf drooling with foamy blood. As it lunges forward, I'm awake and suddenly aware that someone is at my front door. I rub my mangled, throbbing hand, the memory of the teeth piercing my skin renewed.

"Oliver," the deep voice repeated over and over, followed by the hard pounding getting louder. "Open up! We made contact with Sean." It's an irritated Nolan, unmistakable.

"Yeah…" My voice comes out as nothing but an inaudible grunt, so I clear my throat and try again.

"Yeah, I'm up." The emotions I'm trying to stuff back down cause my voice to crack.

The red clock numbers—23:56—shine brightly in the dark room. *Can't believe I was able to fall asleep.*

I struggle to stand while grabbing a pair of black sweatpants lying at the foot of the bed, then stumble toward the door, still shaking off my nightmare.

"Let me put some pants on."

"Yes, please," Nolan says, emphasizing the please.

In a lazy shuffle, I tug my pants upward, gravity forces me to the floor, hard. Pissed at my lack of coordination, I rub my aching right hip, then unlock the dead bolt and open the door. Nolan rushes past me and flicks on the light.

"For fuck's sake, Oliver, you look like shit." Nolan takes in my disheveled appearance. "Get whatever you need together. We got word from Sean and his team. They just crossed into Kansas."

"What do we know?" I blink hard, wiping my eyes with my knuckles and stretching, trying to encourage my body to wake up more.

"Well, it's not all bad news, Oliver, but we did lose men down there," Nolan says crossing his arms.

I take a seat on the corner of the couch to process that information. We hadn't heard from either team since just before 1100 hours. I've been thinking of worst-case scenarios ever since, but I was hopeful it was just the radio comms acting up, but it now appears that wasn't the case.

"QRF is on the way. They'll be at Fort Hood in a couple hours."

Soon after we lost comms, we alerted the Quick Reaction Force standing by to be ready at a moment's notice. Normally we would take the time to think about such a mission, but it was me who sent these men down there. If there is any chance that one man is still alive, I'll take it. I'm glad Nolan didn't wait for my permission.

"Good! And send any assistance Sean needs. Do we know if they have any wounded? What's going on there?"

"A few men, yes. I've already sent choppers to their location. Should be there soon."

"You seem to be on top of it." I let out a small sigh of relief, knowing that we do have survivors. "Did Sean provide a SITREP?"

"Only that it happened so fast and that they barely made it out alive. He said thousands of Joscos came out of nowhere and chased them until they hit Waco, and then they just backed off. Comms didn't come back online until they crossed into Kansas. Very strange. He said it was like their signal was being jammed."

"Strange indeed. And Scott?"

His slow response told me everything I needed to know.

"We don't know. A few of his men made it back to base camp but judging by their report, it's not looking good. And by their account, both teams were attacked simultaneously. Like it was planned."

"Dammit! Let's go then, but I'm going to need some coffee and a clean shirt."

"Coffee is in the jeep, and yes, put on a shirt for cryin' out loud. No one wants to see that white, flabby chest."

I puff out my chest and glare at him before strutting back to my bedroom to get ready. "Give me two minutes."

"You look like a peacock." Nolan laughs a deep chuckle at his own joke.

I reemerge in short time wearing my daily uniform, and being of few words this late at night, I go out the door and motion him to come on as he rolls his eyes, slamming the door shut.

In the jeep, I reach for the coffee, thankful that he had the foresight to bring me some. Nolan starts to speak, but I hold up a finger for him to wait a moment. He purses his lips and sighs, tapping his fingers on the steering wheel as I gulp down a few more sips of joe. I let the warmth make it all the way down my throat before I bring my finger down.

"Okay, you may speak," I confirm, more refreshed and ready to hear him.

"I don't like you this late at night, you know that?" Nolan gives me a side-eye and starts the vehicle. "As I was saying, we don't really know much yet, but once Sean is back at HQ, we'll get him in and get a rundown. We're still hopeful we'll see some of our team at the extraction point in two days."

"We can only hope," I whisper, staring out the side window. "Step on it. We need to be ready for their arrival."

At HQ, everyone is scrambling to get ready for Sean and his team. Hundreds of people work tirelessly. It's no surprise to see family members giving a helping hand. I know what they're going through right now. Wondering if you're going to see your loved one again can eat away at you. Keeping busy is the only solution.

Nolan and I make sure the hospital is ready for worst-case scenarios of our injured with missing limbs or severe head trauma, not that different from wars past. With the medevac arriving soon, I help by preparing the operating rooms based on the injuries we've been advised about. Stretchers and other medical equipment are positioned for their arrival so we can get them back and prepped for surgery as fast as possible.

"First chopper is inbound!"

People scramble to their posts while I run outside. One by one, helicopters land with medical teams standing by ready to care for the wounded. I help the doctors and nurses offload those with missing limbs. The scene gives me flashbacks of the days in Iraq and Afghanistan. Wars have left so many soldiers in a crippling state, both physically and mentally. This is just another reminder of the effects war has on the people we love.

An hour later, Sean and his team stroll in, and again, we focus on those with injuries first. Even though his team is beat and tired, they help until every last team member is properly taken care of.

At Sean's first chance, he heads straight for me. "Anything from the QRF?"

"Nothing yet. They should be there shortly. We've been in constant communication with them, but they've been cutting in and out ever since they crossed into Oklahoma. You have any idea what that is about?" I ask.

"No, sir. We set up the repeaters, and they were working perfectly fine up until the attack," Sean says, placing his hands on his hips.

"You think someone could be jamming the signal?" The question sounded dumb.

"Joscos are many things, sir, but jamming our radios doesn't seem like something they would be capable of," Sean replies.

"No, but something is interfering with our comms, and the fact that they went out just before the attack is not a coincidence. Something isn't right and we're going to find out what it is." I look down at my watch. "Let's go debrief quickly. We have an hour before the QRF arrives on location, and I want to know everything."

I radio Nolan to request that he meet Sean and me in the Ops room for a debrief along with the other officers. We pile in, Sean at the head of the table. Sean details everything regarding the attack from his position. The intermittent firing of one of the M-CWISs and the desecration of a building to the south got everyone's attention. Sean's team dropped everything and headed to base camp. Then, a second M-CWIS started firing at another building east of the one already under fire. Sean tried contacting Scott multiple times, but there was no answer. He couldn't even talk to his own men standing right next to him via radio.

Sean's team made it back to base camp within two minutes of the first shot being fired, and then all M-CWISs were focused on a target. He described it as a swarm of bees coming at them from everywhere until they were surrounded. The M-CWISs were able to hold them off as they readied their vehicles for departure, but they knew eventually the bullets would run out. Within a minute, all the drivable vehicles were able to escape along with two M-CWISs. They lost several vehicles that were overcome as they headed out, but when they reached Waco, they backed off, assuming the Joscos had grown tired of the pursuit.

Sean could only provide certain accounts of some of Scott's team when several members had barreled into their fleeing convoy with the enemy hot on their ass. They had the same experience; their radios went dead right as they were attacked. They witnessed several of their men succumb to their fate when they were overrun by Joscos. They also mentioned Scott and half of his team were either providing cover or inside the building at the time of the attack.

Friday, January 24, 2048

"Riley!"

Wait. What? Did Frank just say Riley? There is no way it could be her. The dark figure turns to face Frank's position and backs up a little to stand in front of the open door. *Oh, thank you, Jesus!*

She hightails it to Frank, and I scurry out of the room, scanning the stairwell to make sure no one was following her. Feeling it's safe, I step back in the hallway, Riley has a tight grip on Frank's massive frame.

"Riley?" I was excited but shocked to see her. "How?" I'm lost for words. She gives me a great big bear hug. She doesn't say anything and just keeps a tight grip around my shoulders. We stand there for a few moments before she backs away. Tears leave little streams down her dirty cheeks, and more threaten to fall from her bloodshot eyes.

"They got 'em. All three of them. Nathan, Brad, and Jared."

"Did you see where they took them?"

"I followed them as far as I could. Nathan looked bad. He was covered in blood." She stopped to take a deep, shuddered breath. "I think he was hit in the abdomen. I was able to hide in a pile of trash just inside that line of trees. I have no idea how they didn't see me."

I wrap my arms back around her. "You're safe now. But we can't stay here."

"I haven't seen anyone in the past hour, but I know they're still out there. I heard their vehicles, though they've pushed more southwesterly, I think."

"Good. We're heading north for a bit, and then we'll cut west to get on the path to the airport. How far were you able to track them?"

"You have your map?" she asks.

"You bet I do." We gather in one of the hotel bathrooms so I can use my flashlight to illuminate the map. "This is us here." I point. "And this is where we were when we got split up."

"Right here. This was as far as I went." She points to a neighborhood southeast of our current location. "There were just too many of them for me to continue. There are more of them than I thought. Hundreds. Maybe thousands."

"Damn. That many?" Frank asks.

"They have all sorts of weapons and different types of armored vehicles. You name it and they were pretty much driving it around. Tanks even." She adds, "Like they raided a military base."

"Fort Hood, perhaps?" Frank smirks.

"Damn good job, Riley. This is good information. This will give us a starting point for when we return to get our men back."

"Yes, sir!" She wipes away a few more escaped tears, finally taking slow, deep breaths.

"Were you able to get some chow in you?" Frank asks.

She shakes her head. "Haven't even thought about it."

"You still have your MRE?" Frank asks, a little as if he's about to rob her of it.

"Yeah," she says.

"Frank, we had ours already," I say, tilting my head in warning.

"I know. I'm just so hungry." Frank sighs, and his whole body shrugs in disappointment.

"Well, you're gonna have to hold on to it for a bit. You good to go?" Even with the darkness, I lean to search deep into Riley's eyes.

"Yes, sir! I'm ready to get the fuck out of here."

"Alright, you got point while Frank and I carry her. What's your ammo like?"

"I'm good. Four mags."

"Alright, let's do this."

Frank and I confirm the jerry-rigged stretcher will support the female Josco, at least for the time being. Riley grabs the container, and we maneuver down the stairs and slip into the darkness toward the Waco Regional Airport.

***

It took the entire night, with lots of breaks, but we made it to the airport just before daybreak. Our instructions were to meet in the terminal, just under the skylights at the southern part of the building. We tread lightly through the front door, then up to the second level. The doors are still barricaded with benches and airport furniture.

Upon reaching our predetermined location, a hunched-over figure about fifty yards ahead leans against a wall. The light barely penetrates through the mildewed skylights. Riley signals Frank and me to stop. We lower the stretcher, keeping our eyes on the slumped stranger. The Josco grunts, but our mystery guest doesn't budge even an inch. We slowly approach the figure with our weapons raised, leaving a wide birth as we work our way in front of them. Maybe it's one of ours. Who else would be here?

I walk up to him, literally inches from his face. "Gregg Cooke! Is that you?" I'm shocked to see another team member at the extraction point. His droopy eyes were barely open, and he looked drugged. I think he's dreaming.

"Huh?" He wipes his eyes.

"It's Scott Dodson. Hello. Wakey, wakey." I say.

"Frank and Riley are her too." Frank says poking Gregg's shoulder with one of his miniguns.

Gregg opens his eyes and nearly jumps out of his boots, with his side arm drawn in our direction.

"Whoa! Whoa! Whoa!" I throw up my hands in an act of submission. "Friendlies here." He looks exhausted and not in his right mind.

"I-I thought I was the only one that made it out, sir." He stands and throws his arms around me, sobbing.

"I was on the back side of the building when the Joscos attacked. I tried to radio you and everyone else, but I just got static. I hunkered down in a nearby building, hoping a Josco didn't see me. What the hell happened out there?"

"Long story, but the short version is that shit got really bad, really quick. In the end, Brad, Nathan, and Jared were taken hostage by a group of humans who call themselves the Serpent's Head, just south of here."

A grunt comes from behind us. "The fuck was that? You get followed?" Gregg's voice is panicked. He raises his weapon toward the hall we just came through.

"Get on your feet, soldier. Follow me, and I'll show you." I turn around and emphasize with my hands. "Just don't shoot it. You shoot it and I'll shoot you." He lowers his gun as we walk over to her. Frank and Riley remove the bed sheet covering her body.

"Oh shit! What the hell is that?" Gregg asks.

"It's a little something we picked up along the way."

"I thought…wait, didn't we see all those pregnant Joscos back in Fort Hood? Weren't they all dead? How did you come across a live one?"

"Back in McGregor."

"Really? I walked right past that place yesterday. Stayed just outside it. I stayed away from all the cities."

"That's what we should have done," Frank chimes in.

"Anyway, I'll tell you all about it on the helicopter ride if we ever get out of here. Whoever lives around here may still be looking for us. Plus, I'm tired. I want to get some shuteye while we wait."

After ordering Gregg to keep an eye out for us, I walk over to the exterior wall and plop down on the ground. Sleep overcame my worn-out body and mind so quickly that I don't even remember closing my eyes. I'm sure Frank and Riley do the same. As for Gregg, he may have stayed awake staring at the pregnant Josco. I don't know, and I don't care.

***

The sound of Gregg chomping on crackers wakes me.

I wipe my eyes. "Please tell me you have another one of those?" I ask with a painful, growling stomach.

"Umm…we did. Frank is feeding her the last one right now. I told him not to, but he didn't listen."

"What the fuck are you doing? You know I'm fucking starving!"

The conversation woke Riley. "What the hell, guys?"

"These assholes just gave *her* our last MRE."

"I thought you wanted to keep it alive. I was just helping you out, sir." Frank quipped.

"Awe. I see. You guys are fucking with me." I shake my head.

"Payback's a bitch," Frank adds.

"Looks like you two are becoming quite the friends," I say.

It's fascinating to stand here and watch Frank handfeed this malnourished Josco. The thing looks like what you would have seen in one of those old timey save the animal commercials where the animal was abandoned on the side of the road and the people try to bring it back to life. Her bites were surprisingly gentle, unlike the Hungry Hungry Hippos game that I have pictured in my head. Her head rolls over and her eyes find mine, and it was almost as if they were speaking to me—saying thank you. There's a calmness in them that hasn't been there since we found her. Maybe it's the fact that she is in better hands now than where she was in McGregor. Looking at her now, her eyes don't have that dark kill look to them.

"You wanted her alive!" Frank says softly as he reaches in to give her another bite.

"We're just playin'. Here you go." Gregg throws me an MRE. "I have a few more as well, if you're really hungry."

"Hell yeah, I'm hungry." I read the package. "Chili and macaroni! This is a good one!" Honesty, it could have been puke-flavored bark, for all I care. I tore into it, eating everything and licking any wrapper with sauce left on it. I almost asked for another one, but we may need these later in case, God forbid, something happens with our extraction. The idea makes me queasy, but I choke it back and restore my hope of getting the fuck out of here.

Gregg informs us that we have twenty minutes until our ride is supposed to be here. We do an ammo check. A quick patrol of the surrounding area confirms the landing zone is clear and nothing's around to compromise our extract. Gregg was smart enough to remember the smoke, which will inform the pilots of our location. Yellow smoke would advise them to land under caution, and red tells them the zone is hot. But he only has green, signifying it's safe, so green it is.

With everything clear, we wait patiently. Gregg kneels beside me, gripping the smoke canister, ready to throw it the second we hear those blades of freedom thumping in the air.

"Where the hell are they? It's fifteen minutes past," Frank says.

"Let's give them a few more minutes. They'll be here." I say.

"I certainly hope so. It's a loooong walk back home," Riley adds.

"Shush!" Frank yells, waving his hand in the air. "I hear something."

We sit very still, careful not to ruffle our clothing. It pains me not to ask if he heard a chopper or a vehicle.

Twenty seconds later, Frank points north at the partly overcast sky, and in one swift motion, we all turn. A tiny brown speck drops below the cloud cover, and the beautiful thumping of the blades slicing the cool air is like the sound of angels singing the most beautiful melody I have ever heard. Two more specks drop, and soon, three Blackhawk helicopters in a wedge formation come into perfect view.

Gregg wastes no time and runs out in the middle of the tarmac and tosses the canister. Green smoke pours straight out and up into the sky.

"Yes!" I throw up a tight fist in the air. "Fuck, yeah!" I've never been more relieved in my entire life. All I can think about is getting home and holding Abigail and Maggie tightly. I can feel it now, and I may never let them go. I can only imagine what it's been like for her the last few days. She'll probably have mixed emotions of wanting to punch me for making her worry and hug me because she loves me.

The past few days have given me plenty of time to think about our future, and if there is going to be one, I must make a decision. It's not going to be an easy one to say the least. I've fought alongside some of the most selfless, toughest soldiers ever to wear the uniform that wouldn't hesitate to put themselves in harm's way to save another fellow brother. Walking away from the guys is going to be the toughest choice I'll have to make, but I need to be there for Abigail and Maggie.

One bird lands north of our position, while the other two circle above, providing cover. Frank and I grab the makeshift stretcher and the four of us hoof it fifty yards out onto the tarmac.

"I can't wait to see the looks on their faces when they see what's under the sheet," I yell out. Riley returns a bit of a smile.

The medic rushes out of the chopper toward me, and he takes over one grip of the makeshift stretcher.

"What the hell?" His face grimaces as he feels its weight.

We plop the head of the stretcher down on the floor of the helo first, and then Frank slides the rest of it into the chopper. Riley jumps in, then Gregg. Another chopper lands for Frank to get into; otherwise, we might exceed the weight limit of this one. I sure as hell hope we aren't leaving anyone behind. We'll be back for sure. Satisfied, I nod, turn, and jump in.

The medic reaches for the sheet, ready to evaluate the injuries. "You might not want to do that!" I yell at him over the noise of the choppers.

"Was he KIA?" he asks.

I shook my head no.

"Is he okay? Shouldn't we treat him?" the medic asks. "Why is he covered?"

I signal for the pilot to take off and they don't hesitate.

"It's not a 'he.'" Riley and I give each other big ol' grins. The medic returns a confused look, then reaches down and pulls the sheet back.

His screams cause one of the pilots to jerk the chopper as though they were getting ready to shake an enemy fighter.

"It's a fucking Josco!" the medic yells.

"Where?" one of the pilots asks. They scour the ground, searching for one.

"In the fucking chopper! They brought a live Josco in the helicopter."

The pilots order us to throw it out, and the medic slides open the door. I lean over and grab a handful of his camo fatigue.

"You toss that body, you're following it!" I wasn't playing around. I don a headset. "She's going with us."

"She?" The co-pilot asks, looking back, curious as hell.

The medic lifts the sheet again, only slower this time. "Not only is it a female Josco, but she's pregnant."

CHAPTER TWENTY-FIVE
(Major Oliver White—U.S. Marines)

Saturday, January 25, 2048

After McCauley's debrief, I had convinced myself that the chance of any survivors at the extraction point would be damn near impossible, but we've piled ourselves into the command post, sitting on pins and needles waiting to hear back from the helicopter pilot advising of any news. Holding out another three days after the events unfolded in Fort Hood would be nothing short of a miracle.

"ETA five minutes." The pilot's broken voice broadcasts over the speakers. I grab another cup of coffee and pace.

Of the sixty men we sent down there, thirty-one are either unaccounted for or confirmed KIA, twenty-three from Scott's team alone. The number of Joscos they encountered frightens me. It's disheartening to know that we're no closer to winning this war than we were twenty-five years ago. It wasn't the Joscos standard approach to attacking our soldiers either, as McCauley made it known that they appeared more organized than their typical "come in and start pounding bodies" tactic. Their attack was well thought out. If it wasn't for the M-CWISs, none of them would have survived. They followed McCauley's team from Fort Hood all the way to Highway 35, leaving a trail of Josco bodies in their wake. And what was even more interesting is that before the siege started, all radio communications went silent. If that wasn't a coordinated attack, then I don't know what is.

I turn sharply to the sound of static from the speakers and rush over to stand beside Nolan. The voice on the other end is muffled with an overlay of white noise. Our radioman responds asking for a repeat, but incoherent murmurs fill the airways.

"What the hell is causing this interference?" I yell out.

"Someone has to be blocking our signal." Nolan replies. No sooner did he say that the radio came to life.

"We have green smoke!" The pilots voice erupts over the speakers.

My head perks up and eyes widen. Cheers and laughter fill the room. The excitement in the pilot's voice was contagious as they communicate a play-by-play commentary while circling the area. They confirm four of our soldiers are on the ground, plus one who is on a stretcher. I'm disappointed we only have five, but it was great news to hear we had survivors in addition to the two soldiers our QRF found hiding on a rooftop in Fort Hood. I take a deep breath of relief, but it's stopped by a lump in my throat that I force down, the emotion trying to get the better of me.

One by one, the soldiers climb into the helicopters, the pilot naming off each one as they board. The fifth is a shocker.

"Um, sir…" there's trepidation in the pilot's voice. "Our fifth on-signer, well it's not one of ours, sir…it's a female Josco."

Nolan and I turn to each other with a look of utter disbelief wondering if we heard correctly.

I grab the mic. "Repeat your last."

"Um, yes, sir. I repeat. We have a live female Josco onboard. And not only is she breathing, but she appears to be, extremely pregnant."

My thoughts are apoplectic, and I can't seem to articulate anything. With this information, the recent activities of the rogue northern group and the debriefing we had with Lieutenant Heart and his team, mentioning one of them was carrying a baby Josco, signifies that we've been living in a bubble for far too long. What the hell is happening out there?

Not only am I impressed that these soldiers survived but somehow on their way to the extraction point managed to pick up a pregnant Josco.

We jump into action to prepare for her arrival the best we know how. I get one of my men to work with the doctors to set up a section of the hospital wing that's reinforced for a worst-case scenario. It won't be pretty, but we never thought we'd ever be setting up a med room for this situation. We'll just have to deal with her when she arrives and adjust as needed. The medic onboard informs us that she's barely holding on and likely won't survive more than a day or so without severe intervention, but I'm not going to take any chances as to her strength. Female Joscos having the ability to produce offspring changes everything.

I'm sure the hospital staff will be just as curious as we are to see what a baby Josco looks like, how it will act, and how fast it will grow. One question leads to another. What if the female doesn't make it but the child does? What the hell are we going to do with the thing once it's born? We don't exactly have a foster care system set up for baby Joscos. Who would take on that responsibility? Hell, what do we do if she lives? Release mom and baby back into the wild like a damned National Geographic documentary? At this point, I have way more questions than answers.

"Sir," Lieutenant Dodson's voice comes over the coms.

"It's great to hear your voice, Lieutenant," I reply.

"Same, sir," Scott says. "We have a serious situation. A bad one. Nathan, Brad, and Jared were taken hostage yesterday by some rogue, hostile group who calls themselves the Serpent's Head. We need to get them back, sir. Nathan was shot and I'm not sure how bad it is."

"What do you mean there's a group of hostiles down there? You mean a group of Joscos?"

"No, sir! There is a group of humans living somewhere down here, near Waco. They attacked us and they are the ones that took our men, sir. We need to get them back ASAP. I don't think they'll be alive for much longer judging from our experience with them."

I mouth "What the fuck" at Nolan. The impossibilities that keep presenting themselves are staggering. It can't be possible for a group of humans to be living down there. How have they survived for this long? How did none of our recon reveal any of this? *Our recon was shit on this mission.*

Nolan and I stay on the comms with Scott and Riley, who provide us with valuable intel regarding the human group. According to Scott, they are armed to the teeth with weapons and vehicles. Not everyone is particularly well-trained, but their numbers allow them to be a force. We need to act fast and with strength, this group can't be underestimated.

Nolan and I scurry to put a rescue mission together and send what's left of our drone fleet down there for another reconnaissance mission to collect as much data as we can, this time to look for different intel. I want to know everything, and we clearly didn't know enough the first time.

"Who are we going to send down there?" Nolan starts going through the list of soldiers capable of doing such a mission.

The new enemy isn't a bunch of wild beasts like we've been fighting. They have weapons and sound minds, and with their numbers, we have no idea what they're capable of. Are they a disorganized group that just happened upon each other to form a team or a well-established military outfit? Militia? From what Scott and Riley were able to provide, it sounds like a little bit of both.

"I'm leading this mission!" Nolan announces ceremoniously.

"You sure that's a good idea?" I ask, though I trust him more than anyone.

"Probably not, but I'm going. Like you, I want to know what this group is all about and I need to see it for myself. Besides, I'm one of the only people qualified for this fight." He crosses his arms as if expecting me to counter his offer with an argument.

I could argue a compelling enough case for him not to go seeing as he's my replacement, but I'd lose and he's right.

"It must be an all-volunteer mission. As much as I want to get our men back, I want to make sure we don't lose any more in the rescue attempt."

"We won't. I'll make damn sure of it." His voice exuded confidence. I know he can't guarantee that, no matter what resources I give him, but the passion will help the team's motivation.

We sent out requests asking for soldiers. If this is going to happen, it must be tonight. Lieutenant McCauley is the first to volunteer to go back out there. This is personal for him. I'm not surprised by the overwhelming response we receive.

Warriors line up outside within minutes of making the announcement. Once we have everyone we need, we pile into the mission room and start going through everything. Nolan takes charge of the mission, with only a few hours before they head out.

I step out for a few minutes; I need to clear my mind. My office is the perfect place to do that. With all the news, I need to start putting pieces together. I close my eyes, tilt my head back, and lean further in my chair.

"Major White, you have a visitor. It's Lieutenant McCauley," Karen beckons the second I relax.

"Not right now. I don't want to be bothered." For fuck's sake. I need a minute.

"I'll let him know, sir."

"Sir, Lieutenant McCauley says it's urgent. He really would like to speak with you right now. It's about the Fort Hood mission."

"Nolan is in charge. He can address him." What the fuck part of I do not want to be bothered do they not understand?

"Tell him I will—" My door swings wide open, ricocheting off the wall behind it with a bang.

"Sir, sorry, but I really need to speak with you! You need to see this!" McCauley barges through the door, holding a container. Karen follows on his heels in a panic, trying to stop him.

"Do you need a lesson in following orders, Lieutenant?"

"But sir, this involves you directly, or I wouldn't have come."

I let out a deep sigh. "What is it, McCauley? And this better be good." Karen drudges back to her desk, looking defeated and mumbling under her breath.

"It is, sir! Again, I'm sorry for the interruption."

"Get on with it." I massage my temples.

"We found this when searching through the doctor's van." Sean sets the metal container on my desk. "We were finally able to get it opened with the use of these magnets…" Sean slides the two magnets across what I presume is the top of the container. "Right after you left, one of the guys popped into the mission room to show me. I figured you really needed to know what's inside." Sean hesitates.

"You okay, Lieutenant?" His twisted red face shows concern.

"Yes, sorry. Um, the container is full of files of different people who lived here. I wasn't sure what to make of it all until he showed me one of the names." He pauses again, which irritates me.

"Okay, so what name is so fucking important you had to come bother me?"

"Um." He stares at the file in his hand before holding it out for me to grab. "Um. Your wife, sir. The name on this file says Lily White."

I stand up fast, and swipe the folder from McCauley's grip, not wasting any time opening it. Her first and last names are handwritten in bold black letters. Even a picture of her is paper clipped to the folder, but it wasn't one of those driver's license photos. It was a photo from a distance as if he had been stalking her.

"Sir," McCauley says quietly.

"Leave."

"But, sir."

"I said leave, now." I'm unsure of my emotions, and I don't want to be seen like this.

"Yes, sir." His face was full of pity as he backed away.

I fucking hate that look.

Memories that have been stowed away deep inside rise to the surface like a submarine in an emergency main ballast tank blow. Why would Dr. Anderson have a file on my wife and a file on so many others? At first, I thought maybe Lily went to see him for some medical reason. After all, he is a doctor. But then, as I read through several other files, familiar names start jogging my memory, horrible memories. The only reason I know them is because they're the names of citizens that Turned, just like Lily.

"Karen, please get me a list of all the citizens who have Turned in the past fifteen years. I need it ASAP."

"Yes, sir," she says with distress in her voice.

I take a deep breath and release it slowly as I open Lily's file and read. The doctor just about had her entire medical history recorded, and the more I read, the more it becomes clear, even though I can't understand most of the medical jargon. I skim through the pages. There's a date on the last page, along with some other notes. November 23, 2033. That was the day Lily Turned. I skip all the way down and can't believe what I'm reading. Log after log of detailed notes.

November 3, 2033: Injected with AIV-359-C

What the fuck is AIV-359-C? This isn't the original naming convention for the AIV shot. Nor did Lily have an auto-immune disease.

November 9, 2033: Effects of the drug have started. Erratic behavior, elevated heart rate. Effect response initiated faster than previous drugs as tested on other subjects.

I remember her saying she wasn't feeling well and that she was going to see a doctor, but I had no idea she was seeing Dr. Anderson. And then, the last log makes my chest tighten.

November 23, 2033: DNA restructuring and cell reprogramming initiated.

Transformation — Was in Progress. SPECIAL NOTE: Subject terminated by spouse shortly after transformation started. Transformation was not fully completed.

My wife was a fucking test subject to this piece of shit. There's not a word to describe how I feel. My wife would still be alive today if it weren't for him. I slam the file on the desk just as Karen walks in.

"Here you go, Major. Anything else?" she asks timidly.

"No!" I spit out, having no capacity for chitchat.

I go down the list Karen provided, pulling corresponding files from the container as I read their names: Melanie Gresko, who was one of the first to Turn after we established this territory. Amber Brighten, who was Bryan's mother; he was Josco Brother number one. She passed away while giving birth to him, and the same with Sharon Kelly who is Frank's mother. The list goes on. Twenty-four of the thirty-two names on the list have a file. All females. The other eight don't appear to be a part of our society and I have no idea who they are.

I open one of the male's folders to a person's name that isn't on our list: Adam Trevor. That name sounds familiar. "Where have I heard the name Adam before?" It hits me; it's the Josco named Adam T. from when we visited the doctor last week. *Coincidence*?

I open his file, and a picture stares back at me, but there's no way to tell if they are the same person. The photo shows a sickly person lying in a hospital bed, his eyes barely open. His file dates back to 2013. It lists his date of birth, weight, blood type, standard medical history notes, and also mentions that he was a test subject for the medical drug AIV-288-A that was being tested. He was diagnosed with stage IV lung cancer on August 24, 2012.

Is this patient zero? The first Josco? But he was treated several years before the Turning. Nolan comes in, startling me.

"Fuck, does anyone knock anymore?" I glance at the door. "Don't you have somewhere you need to be, like getting this mission ready?"

"Team's fine. I gave everyone a five-minute break. McCauley just informed me about some container full of folders, with one belonging to your wife. What the hell is going on? You okay?"

"No, I'm not okay, actually." I toss him Lily's file.

"What is this?"

"Fucking read it." I wasn't in the mood for politeness.

He looks at the front cover and shakes his head. "This can't be good."

"It isn't. The last two pages are the more bothersome ones if you want to skip ahead."

I watch his facial expressions go through the changes as he reads. Disbelief. Shock. Anger. He takes a seat after a minute, placing a hand over his mouth. "I am so sorry, Oliver. That's fucked up!"

"Here." I push the container full of files closer to him. "Sean found this in Dr. Anderson's van. Most are just like Lily's." I point to her file, which is still in Nolan's hand. "They're all female except for these other ones. I have no idea who they are. They didn't live here, from what I can tell."

"So, he was experimenting on our people. Women? Turning them under the rouse of a helpful drug?" He thumbs through the files in the container as he continues. "Why would he do this?" He pauses. "So, when he left, he burned whatever he didn't need." He pauses again, putting the pieces together. "And all these files are females? Interesting."

"Yeah, and why suddenly are we getting reports of baby Joscos out there? First with the rogue group that is currently up in Canada, second with the hangar full of dead female Joscos that received C-sections, and third, the pregnant Josco headed our way. I don't think he was doing any research to help us. We provided him with citizens to perform these experiments to further whatever the hell he was doing. I think he was trying to figure out a way to reproduce these fuckers, and he used our people, my fucking wife to do it! I'm beginning to think the Josco that had escaped last week was from the northern group. Maybe this new breed is capable of reproducing?"

My jaw hurts from clenching it so hard.

"A week before Lily Turned, she was irrational. Just irritated and angry all the time. For the life of me, I couldn't figure out where that hatred was coming from. That's why I took Jayce away that weekend on the hunting trip. The bastard did this to my wife!"

My empty coffee cup makes for the perfect projectile. All my rage is taken out on the small ceramic receptacle as it smashes into the wall and crumbles to the ground in one swift movement. I take a few deep breaths to prevent me from clearing the entire desk. Nolan is smart enough not to say anything or give me any pitiful looks as he lets me have my tantrum.

"What is it now?" I yell eyeing another figure at my door.

"Sorry to bother you, sir. We were able to open the rest of those containers. Here you go."

Nolan helps Sean set them on my desk and as soon as he lets go, he hightails it out. Then Nolan starts filtering through as I stand there, my face likely as red as a tomato as the heat rolls off it in waves. I could tell by Nolan's reactions that he was reading something interesting.

"You come across something else?" *I'm not sure I want to know.*

"Oliver"—Nolan's eyes move rapidly back and forth on the page—"I think you might be correct when you said there's another group of Joscos."

"Really?"

"Listen to this. 'Upon further research, we tracked a distinct group of Joscos into the Northern Region. They don't exhibit the same aggressive behavior patterns. They appear to be more docile until they're threatened, and then they become just as aggressive. They show the same pack mentality but appear smarter, teaching themselves how to adapt and dress. Continued study required. Cause of variation: unknown.'"

Nolan looks up from reading. "These are Dr. Anderson's handwritten notes. And this entry is dated January 3, 2048. There's more." Nolan turns a page. "Adam and the others were able to subdue and capture one of these variations while out on patrol."

"Adam?" I interject. "Patrol? What the fuck is going on here? Are we talking about the same Adam, as in the Josco, Anderson had at the facility?"

"I don't know, but it sounds like Dr. Anderson was working WITH the Joscos," Nolan says. "This is from January 8."

"That's the day our patrol gunned down the Josco."

Nolan continues, "The new breed showed no submissive behavior toward Adam like the others. In fact, he was very aggressive toward Adam and the other three. He didn't eat any of the food that was provided. He only paced back and forth up until the moment he broke out. Holy shit, listen to this: 'Adam pursued the new breed through the forest until a patrol spotted him, then returned.'"

"That makes no sense. The Josco returned? How would Dr. Anderson know that Adam saw a patrol? That would mean the doctor can communicate with the Joscos."

CHAPTER TWENTY-SIX

(Major Oliver White—U.S. Marines)

Saturday, January 25, 2048

Nolan exits my office and I'm left to sift through the packed containers Dodson and McCauley uncovered from the doctor's van. It's eye-opening to say the least. Four containers full of data, including external hard drives and DVDs; it will be interesting to find out what's on them.

As I'm getting everything organized, I notice a large map of North America folded and wedged under the lid of one of the containers. I unfold it and take it over to my desk to investigate further. The yellow lines highlighting multiple routes grabs my attention. Routes stretch across the US and into Mexico, with areas circled and notes scribbled all over it. The research facility is highlighted and appears to be a waypoint between what he was doing down south and a facility up in Ann Arbor, Michigan, where Josco Genetics was once headquartered.

I jot down notes on my dry-erase board on the far wall. We'll be visiting Ann Arbor in the not-so-distant future and maybe these other locations that aren't far away. I trace several other routes, noting that the hangar down at Fort Hood, where Scott found the female Joscos, is circled. An arrow next to southern Florida points to a note that reads "manufacturing facility." Waco is also circled but there are no notes. Is he working with this outfit or just aware of their presence? I shake my head in disbelief and roll my head to stretch my neck, affording me a minute of thought.

So much data to sift through. I switch back to the folders since the map isn't satiating my need to know what the fuck is going on. It's like reading a page-turning thriller. I can't stop reading. But because this is my life and not a work of fiction, the more I read, the angrier I become. Obviously, he's conducting all the fucked-up experiments to keep these Joscos alive and well, not to eliminate them. His research was never about helping us survive; it was only about further advancing the Joscos.

My head pounds. All this information is too much, and I have a limited time to process it. My phone rings. A distraction. It's word that the three choppers are inbound, with an ETA of 18:37. I glance at the clock; it's 18:22. I've been here for three hours, and I still have two other containers to go through. Can't wait to find out what's in there, but for now I need to shift gears and put on my game face. I shove my emotions down deep for now.

The building is quiet as I leave and jump in a nearby Humvee parked just outside. I drive over to hangar four, where a large group of people are already huddled together in the cold, waiting for Scott and his team's arrival. Doctors are standing by with a stretcher for the Josco, as well as McCauley and a herd of other Marines. Damn near a couple hundred people.

I park and walk up to Nolan, who is standing there with several other officers. "Gentleman," I say, adjusting my beanie to cover my ears more.

"Oliver," Nolan says as I extend my hand to shake his and the others.

"After you left, I found a map with this Waco location circled and a highlighted line that extends west almost to San Angelo and east toward Louisiana."

"Really?" Nolan looked intrigued.

"I'm not clear as to why, but several other locations are circled along that highlighted route. There's a lot of information to sift through in these containers, but you need to be very careful. Doc might have something to do with the Serpent's Head."

"Good to know," Nolan says. "I'll come by and look at the map so I can pass it along to the Team. This is good intel."

We discuss a few other options regarding the mission, like additional air support with the other officers. Nolan briefs me on the mission details and sounds like he's considered every conceivable option for anything they may encounter.

"Where are these choppers at? We still have a few things to button up before we head out," Nolan says. "And knowing Frank and Scott, once they hear about this mission, I'm sure they're gonna want to go as well." Nolan crosses his arms. I can tell he's getting anxious; it's been a while since he's been on a mission like this.

Across the crowd, Scott's wife stands holding their daughter, looking impatient and worried. "Not if she has something to say about it." I point over in her direction.

"Yeah, that's a tough one." Nolan says.

The thumping of the helicopter's blades grows louder, and soon after, we see the navigation lights flashing in the distance. I glance over to the family members who are hugging each other with tears of relief pouring down their faces. Guilt sets in as I think about those who don't have someone coming home. The families rush out before the doors slide open. Nolan and I wait to let them have their moment together while we watch the doctors roll a stretcher over to the helicopter to unload the Josco. Startled screams echo throughout the tarmac.

"Should we have said something?" Nolan smirks.

Frank's mighty stature appears from another chopper and makes a beeline to us. His face focused.

"When do we leave, sir, to get our brothers?" his determined eyes stare into mine demanding an answer.

"Tonight," Nolan says.

Frank snaps his head toward him.

"I'm going, sir," Frank says as he steps in front of Nolan.

"Are you sure you're up to it?" Nolan asks. "You don't need some rest?"

"I slept on the way here, sir. I'm ready." Frank says.

"Good to hear. Get a shower because you ain't riding all the way down there with me smelling like that. Fill your stomach and be in the Operations room in one hour. We leave in two hours."

"Yes, sir!" Frank nonchalantly sniffs his underarm as he walks away.

Our attention shifts to the doctors and nurses attempting to transfer the Josco from the helicopter to their undersized stretcher. The nearby families retreat to a safer area while the outmatched hospital staff attempts to care for her, unsure of where to grab her.

"This thing shouldn't be too much trouble, right? I mean, it's barely alive, and the medic gave her enough drugs to knock out a horse," I say. Ironically, she starts fervently punching and kicking the air, loosening one of her arm straps.

"Damn, look at her go. There's still some fight in her," Nolan says.

A few Marines step in to help hold her down long enough to get her lifted and tied onto the awaiting stretcher. The hospital staff then carts her off to a nearby ambulance. I can't help but stare like everyone else. Murmurs surround us with questions about why we would even bother to bring the Josco back. But questions need to be answered, especially after our recent discoveries about Dr. Anderson's research.

"Let's go talk with Scott," I say. "We need to get moving."

"Yes, we do," Nolan confirms.

We keep our distance as not to intrude on any of their discussions. Scott, Riley, and Gregg each step away from their loved ones and move toward us.

"Welcome back!" I say, looking at their rough condition. They're exhausted with tired eyes, blood and dirt smeared all over them and their fatigues. They salute, and Nolan and I both return the gesture. We don't get the same welcome from their families, though. If their eyes could stab us, we'd be in pain right now.

"Good to be back, sir," Riley says, shivering from the cold.

Nolan gets straight to the point. "I understand if each of you says no, and I wouldn't expect any other answer, but we're heading out tonight to get Nathan, Brad, and Jared back. You don't have to answer right now, but if you decide you want to go with us, be ready. If you choose to, I'll brief you on the way up. I will be leading the rescue mission personally."

Scott sets his rucksack down and turns to look at his wife and kid. She clearly heard what Nolan said, as she shakes her head with a stern "no," and her eyes plead with him, tears starting to well up.

"As much as I would like to fuck them up right now, I need to be here," he says. "Abigail and Maggie were the only thing I could think about while down there." Scott's voice is tired, but you can hear in his tone that he wants vengeance. Relief washes over his wife's face. "I know you guys will bring them back."

"Lieutenant, get some rest. You've earned it!" I salute Scott, and he returns the gesture.

Scott picks up his rucksack, eyeing Nolan. "Want some of the action too, I see?"

"You're damn right! We're not only going to get our men back, but the biggest can of whoop-ass is going to be dropped on anyone who fucks with our brothers and sisters." Nolan and Scott fist bump and exchange ooh-rahs.

"Well, I wish I could join, but happy hunting, guys," Scott says as he limps away to his family.

Nolan turns to Gregg and Riley. "Be in the Operations room within the hour because wheels are up at twenty-one hundred."

Riley apologizes, advising that she can't go back right now. She's tapped out and it shows. Gregg says he'll be there. He may be tired, but nothing motivates a person like revenge.

Back in the Operations room, I shadow Nolan as he finalizes everything for the mission. He rallies the soldiers, the pilots, and everyone supporting this mission ensuring everything is coordinated down to the second. A squadron left to recon the area the second we said the mission was a go. We should be hearing back from them any minute. There are a lot of moving parts, and the one thing our military is good at is getting a plan together in short order.

It's roughly 675 miles from Omaha to Waco, and with a C-130's cruising speed, they should be at their destination two hours from departure, arriving sometime around 2300 hours. Nolan didn't leave out any resource we have available: air or land. Whoever these people are, they're going to wish they never fucked with us.

***

With everyone loading up at the rear of the aircraft, I extend my hand to Nolan. "Go get 'em!"

We salute and shake hands. "Yes, sir!"

"See you around mid-morning tomorrow," says Nolan, exuding confidence.

I stand by and watch as the last soldier steps onboard before leaving to go to my place of refuge at the southern outpost. I follow the flickering lights until they are gone, feeling helpless yet again.

CHAPTER TWENTY-SEVEN

(Captain Nolan Wilkinson—U.S. Navy)

Saturday, January 25, 2048

Humans. This is the fight I know, the one I'm good at. We haven't confronted people, not for a long time anyway. Not since before the Turning. We've had skirmishes here and there with outsiders, but not anything like what we're about to encounter. And even though this group may seem like a bunch of backwoods country folk, they do appear to be well-armed, somewhat trained, and organized. Anyone who has lived this far south in Josco territory can't be taken lightly.

Shortly after takeoff, we received word from the recon squadron that nothing came up, just like the first time. How is that possible? Either we're searching for ghosts or they have a damn good hiding place that's undetectable by our technology. Once on the ground, we'll know for certain if they're in the area. In addition to the intel we received from Scott's team, there should be signs of movement that we can use to track them down.

Twenty minutes out, our Jumpmaster walks the cabin, inspecting each of us to make sure we're fit. With an hour left before we jump, the C-130's pilots set the plane's cabin pressure to ten thousand feet, and we started taking oxygen. Anyone showing signs of decompression sickness will sit this out. When descending, any nitrogen in the blood could result in bubbles that could cause severe damage or possibly death.

The Jumpmaster gives me a thumbs-up, and with ten minutes out, he gets the signal to open the rear bay door. The interior lights go out. Heads perk up and ass cheeks pucker. We'll free-fall from an altitude of twenty-thousand feet for a High-Altitude Low Opening (HALO) jump. We're not too worried about radar, but a low opening of our chutes will reduce the amount of time our parachutes are visible if the Serpent's Head group is out watching for our arrival. And if all goes well, two minutes after opening, our feet will be on the ground, landing roughly twenty klicks north of where Riley advised us of their possible location. With little intel on this group, there'll be no room for error. But with any enemy, and after the past few days, I can only assume they will be expecting our visit in some form or fashion. But they're not going to know what hit them once we find 'em.

The level of determination on my soldiers' calm, unshaven faces is palpable. The only sign of nerves is the subtle shake of a leg bobbing up and down. Some finish writing their letters and tuck them in a pocket, while others sleep or perhaps question their judgement for volunteering on this mission. I don't blame them; we've all questioned a mission at one point in our career, but we do have an objective, and we will complete it.

I lower my night vision goggles, and one by one, my team follows suit. A minute later, the Jumpmaster signals us to stand. We disconnect from our oxygen and switch to our bailout bottle, then inspect each other's gear to ensure everything is in good order. Every one of us is important to the success of this mission. We're only as strong as our weakest link.

With everything in good order, the flight crew releases a crate holding Frank's miniguns and some other gear. We're given the green light to go, and the Jumpmaster then points to the two rows of thirty and signals them to start making their way back. Then, one by one, team members disappear over the ledge into the night horizon. I live for this shit. Being the last one out, I take a deep breath and hurl myself into the cold.

A peaceful calm cascades over me as the rush of cold air circles my body. I speed toward the green-hued surface, with each of my team members lined up in a perfect row below me. Muscle memory takes over, and my arms, hands, and legs work together to keep my body forward in a controlled free fall. I briefly close my eyes to remember a time when the world was full of laughter, like when I was sitting on the beach around a warm campfire, telling stories of past missions with my brothers. I can still see their shadowed faces.

My teammates' flashing strobes line up perfectly. I check my altitude indicator, passing through fifteen thousand feet. I tested our comms; all appear to be working. I make a small course adjustment to stay aligned and then check my altitude indicator again.

One by one, parachutes pop open like air bubbles forming underwater, each one perfectly spaced. I glance at my indicator and watch as I pass through two thousand feet, then pull my cord. My body jerks, forcing my focus to the horizon, the moon casting a shallow light against the background of clouds. Below, there's still a damned near perfect row of green rectangles from my team's parachutes. I spend the rest of my journey back to earth staring at a full moon, enjoying the view, and occasionally looking down to ensure I don't get off course. I won't be seeing a view like this again anytime soon, so I take in every moment I can, letting the air flow over me in a refreshing bath of cool air.

I pull down the parachute cords and float until my feet gently touch the ground. Stuck my landing, a perfect ten. I disconnect my harness, wrap up the parachute, and then toss it out of the way behind some trees. My team quickly and quietly secures the area around the crate while several other team members open it. Frank doesn't waste any time putting on his rig while the rest grab everything we need. I do a head count, making sure everyone is accounted for, then make my call.

"Whiplash Main, Whiplash Main, this is Whiplash Actual. Over," I whisper into my mic.

I wait a few seconds before repeating.

"Whiplash Main, Whiplash Main, this is Whiplash Actual. Over."

"This is Whiplash Main. Go ahead Whiplash Actual. Over."

"Boots are on the ground. Over."

"Roger Actual. Good visual on strobes. Over."

"Copy that, Main." This will allow easy identification and tracking of our movement from the E-3 Sentry, an airborne warning and control system known as AWACS. Our eyes in the sky that'll monitor the area for hostiles and keep us informed as to what they see.

"Whiplash Main, this is Whiplash Actual. We are heading out to primary target."

"Roger that, Actual. We have a clear visual of your location. Cleared to primary target. Over."

"Roger that. Moving out," I reply.

We do one final check of our weapons, and once everyone is in place and good to go, I take point, and we head out.

In all my years and in all my travels, I've never stepped foot in Texas until now. I've always wanted to come here and try the BBQ. Heard it was the best. Before the Turning, it was a goal of mine to one day travel the state in search of the best BBQ Texas offered, but that goal got squashed. We were lucky enough in that several survivors living in our territory were from Texas, and they were able to fulfill that bucket list item, as well as teach me the ways of smoking meat. Damn, this meat thought is making me hungry. I'll stow this thought away for when we're heading back. It'll give me something to look forward to.

I set a three-and-a-half mile-per-hour pace to our first checkpoint, which is exactly one mile away from our landing zone. It's a bridge on Herring Avenue that crosses the Brazos River, which I'm hoping isn't in too bad a shape so that we can cross. We need to hit every checkpoint on time. I want to make sure this mission is completed before sunrise.

The bridge is barely hanging on. Chunks of concrete are missing, leaving large gaping holes along it as though artillery hit it directly. The guardrails on both sides are completely gone, and rusted cars dangle off the edges. The south side of the bridge appears to have been a dumping ground for vehicles, with stacks of cars in the water almost level with the bridge itself.

"Careful, everyone. Watch your step," I warn my platoon.

We tread lightly in a single-file line, navigating around the holes. I stop on the other side and wait for every member to cross. It took us just under eighteen minutes to get here, which is a little slower than I wanted, but I'm not going to start yelling or making them do pushups.

With eleven miles to go and a short rest period halfway there, we should make it to our primary target location around 0300 hours. We can then start looking for signs of where they might be hiding.

Waco is exactly as I pictured it, just like every other city or town I've been to since the Turning: buildings consumed by fire and explosion, riddled with bullets, cars overturned, and overgrown vegetation. Shit, there's even evidence of what could have been a tornado with toppled trees blocking streets and laying on roofs. Everything was left to rot in the elements, just like everywhere else.

We passed a few fast-food restaurants I remember eating at as a kid. Most of these soldiers will have never heard of them or know about the mouthwatering flavors. My hope is that their kids will have a better future than what they're living right now.

We make our way with ease to the second checkpoint, having traveled another two and a half miles to a cove on the east side of Lake Waco. The overgrowth helps conceal us, but anyone with a keen ear would hear the crunching of the tall, dead grass beneath our feet. We try to stick to the roads, but sometimes that just doesn't work with debris piled up everywhere.

The entire scene makes me recall when the Major saved my ass. My mind flutters back and forth between that time and now while listening and looking for any signs of a threat. I'll never forget scavenging on nights like this when we were running the empty streets. Only then, I didn't have the resources I have now. That last day was a bloodbath, at least for what was left of my group. There were a few SEALs with me and some other military personnel, maybe half still alive today, but most of that group were just everyday citizens with little to no training or survival skills. We lost a lot of good people that day. Families were torn apart, literally. Images of their faces have been permanently burned into the back of my eyes, and their screams still ring in my nightmares.

A tap on my shoulder gets my immediate attention. With my mind elsewhere, I didn't realize I had overshot our halfway point.

"Alright, let's make this quick. Take thirty," I whisper into the mic.

Frank approaches from the rear and takes a seat next to me while the others gather in their own small groups but stay close. I don't want to say they're overly cautious, but they're never going to finish their food if they don't stop looking around. On the other hand, Frank eats like he doesn't have a care in the world. I guess a few days in the wilderness will change a man.

We sit in silence with our own thoughts. I open a beef ravioli MRE and start digging in, hoping the sound of chewing and smell from our food doesn't attract any unwanted guests. I finish and lean back, staring at the stars while listening to the chirp of bats flying above our heads. If our lives were only that simple. Free to live as we want. How easy it would be to just get up and fly away.

I do a swift headcount, and then we're back at the grind. To stay far enough away from the primary target location, we hug the lake all the way to the southern tip of it and then follow a river that extends west before curving north. We circle around it until we find a church, where we'll set up, just east of the search area.

We sweep the perimeter of the church to make sure there's nothing inside. It's safe to enter, so we secure the area and get overwatch into their position. Snipers will have a perfect 360-degree view from the roof. There's an airport to the west of us in case we need an exfiltrate.

While everyone gets into position, I pull out a map and go through it once again. We know they came from the south along Highway 84, but how far off the highway are they or how far south are they? Their response time was relatively quick, but from where?

"Whiplash, Main. This is Actual. Over."

"Go ahead, Actual."

"We've secured the church just south of our primary target. You see anything?"

"Negative, Actual. Nothing is showing up on any of our systems. Over."

I was really hoping to have something, but it's looking like we have no other choice but to do this the old-fashioned way—get out and walk it.

CHAPTER TWENTY-EIGHT

(Captain Nolan Wilkinson—U.S. Navy)

Sunday, January 26, 2048

It's 0400 hours, and we've been stalking the moonlit suburban neighborhood for almost an hour now. We're nowhere closer to finding them than we are to finding a good steak house. It's clear they use these roads to travel along as there are two distinct tire paths that have worn away the decaying foliage underneath. I'm beginning to think this area is just a travel route they take to get from point A to point B. Riley only made it this far when following them, so they could have traveled even farther out.

We need to rethink our situation. I signal everybody to bring it in and take a knee, securing the area on a street named Twin Rivers Circle, where the neighborhood club stands partially erect. A pond sits to our south and a fairway of an old golf course to our north.

"Whiplash Main, this is Whiplash Actual. Over."

"Go ahead, Actual."

"We need to extend our search area. We're not seeing anything other than a heavily traveled neighborhood. Doesn't appear to be anybody home. Over."

"Roger that, Actual. We'll extend our search area by twenty miles. Over."

"Copy that, Main." I take a deep breath and exhale loudly.

I turn and walk to Frank, then kneel beside him. "We haven't heard a peep or seen one flicker of movement since arriving. How's that possible?"

"I don't understand it, sir." He shifts his body and his miniguns clink and scrape the concrete. "We should have seen something. With the number of people Riley observed crawling all over this place, I would have bet we'd have seen something by now. I can't tell if it's too late, or too early, depending on how you want to look at it, but I would expect someone to be out and about. You would think they'd be expecting us and have men everywhere."

"Exactly," I interject.

Frank continues, "They've been driving all over this place. That part's clear."

Silence takes over for a moment before Frank speaks again. "They can't be far. We passed right by this neighborhood, and they were on us within minutes of that truck breaking down. This is the only neighborhood we passed by that makes logical sense."

"If they were here, we'd see something." I take another look at the street and houses.

Chief Petty Officer Raney walks up and kneels alongside us. "You guys notice anything odd about this neighborhood?"

My brain kicks in, and then something I should have noticed much sooner comes to light.

"It's empty," Frank says before the words come out of my mouth.

"Bingo," Raney says.

There's not one vehicle parked on the streets or in the driveways of any of the houses.

"There's definitely something not right about this. Every neighborhood we've ever seen has vehicles parked in the streets or driveways, rusting away, sitting on blocks either flat as the D-squad tits at a strip joint or their wheels and tires missing," Raney says.

Frank raises his hand, and Raney and I look at him, confused.

"Are you really raising your hand to ask a question?"

"I was just curious. What strip club you visiting?" Frank looks at Raney, sounding more sincere than joking.

We shake our heads. "Get your head in the game." I slap Frank's leg. "The head on your shoulders, not the other one."

"Yes, sir." I sense a bit of embarrassment from him.

"I'm just fucking with you but stay focused." I try to lighten his mood. I guess he was serious.

I do run a tight ship, and there's a time for cracking jokes and a time for seriousness. I know Frank is the oddball, being an implant with a bunch of SEALs, but he and Bryan were notorious jokesters. He's a damn good soldier. When the shit gets rough, he's one tough son-of-a-bitch you want on your team.

Raney pulls out his map. "There's only one other possible place they could be. There's another neighborhood Frank and his team passed two klicks from here on the south side on Highway 84, south of the airport."

Before I have a chance to respond to Raney's comment, chatter comes over the comms. "Whiplash Actual, this is Main. Over."

"Hold that thought, Raney," I say. "Go ahead, Main."

"That's a negative on any visual. We've scoured the area, and we're not picking up a single movement."

"Roger that, Main." I feel beaten, defeated that this group is outsmarting us. Raney waves his hand to get my attention, then points to the map.

"Main, you copy? Over," I ask.

"Go ahead, Actual."

"There's a neighborhood just south of the airport, west of our current position. Can you check that place out? Over."

"Copy that. Stand by."

I look to Raney. "Let's trek back to the highway and take it to that other neighborhood. Right now, this is our only option."

"Roger that, sir."

We may have underestimated these people. They could be tucked away right now, looking at us from any of the hundreds of buildings in the area. We don't have the time or the manpower to search every building, which is frustrating because, in any other scenario, we'd have more intel to go by.

We circle around Twin Rivers Circle, then take a left on Twin Rivers Boulevard, spitting us out on Highway 84. We hang a right and stay close to the outer road parallel to the highway and make our way west.

A few seconds into our walk along the feeder road, I hear a voice call out from Petty Officer Third Class Burris's, "Did you guys see that?"

I signal everyone to stop, and we regroup into a secure formation.

"See what?" I look back toward Burris's location. He's pointing his rifle toward the neighborhood we just walked out of.

I hustle back to his location. "What did you see?" I ask.

"I saw a light turn off from that house." He points to it. "It was only for a second and then it turned off. But I definitely saw something, sir."

I raise my rifle and look through the scope. I'm not seeing a thing. The road we're on sits lower than the neighborhood, and with the cinder-block fencing partially gone, we have a perfect view of the backyard and the rear of the house.

"Did anyone else see a light come from that house?" The men nearby shake their heads no in unison.

"I know what I saw, sir." Burris's voice is confident. "I saw a damn light come on from that southwest window and then turn right back off."

"And you're sure it wasn't the glare from the moon?" I confirm.

"Yes, I'm positive, sir."

I call upon Raney, who meets us at our position. "I need you to get some guys and check out that house and have them report back."

Raney gathers four guys, Martinez, Kyle, Hall, and Mock, and gives them their marching orders.

We secure the area; overwatch finds a small stone structure at the entrance of the neighborhood and climbs on the roof. They have a perfect view of the backyard fifty yards away, an easy shot if it's needed. We position men up and down the road while Raney and a few soldiers run off to the front of the house. I stay with Burris and a few others directly south of the house about one hundred feet away, and we watch the four guys march discreetly toward the rear of the house.

Mock leads them to the back of the house and they kneel, two on either side of the window where Burris saw the light come from.

"The blinds are closed. I can't see anything," Mock whispers softly into his mic. He then moves to the back door and checks it.

"Back door is locked, moving to the front of the house." Martinez falls in behind Mock while Hall and Kyle stay put, securing the rear.

I'm skeptical. If he had seen a light, it most likely would have been a flashlight because I can't imagine any electricity going to these houses. We have nothing else to go on, so there's no harm in pursuing it.

A minute passes before Mock's barely audible voice is heard again. "Front door is unlocked. We're going in."

Once inside, they sweep the house as they navigate the inside to the back to unlock it. It's an unnerving fifty-seven seconds before we hear back.

"Unlocking the rear," Mock says, and we see the back door slowly swing open and watch Kyle and Hall enter.

I watch intently from our position. Occasionally, I see one of their strobes flashing through a window. They keep radio silence just in case someone is inside. I started to think that if someone had been there, maybe they exited the front of the house and were no longer occupying the space. If that's the case, what the fuck were they doing spying on us? Then the worst scenario comes through my mind: they know we're here, and they're baiting us into the house.

It's another moment before Mock advises an all-clear, and then they exit through the rear door.

They hurry back in a much faster trot than when they went up to the house.

"We have something, sir!" Mock says, breathing heavily. "You are not going to believe this. We didn't see it at first, it was so faint, but Kyle has some damn good eyes."

It is good to hear we have something, anything. I'm shocked at what they discovered. I order Raney back to my location and we formalize a plan. We split up the platoon into two teams. Raney will stay outside with twenty-nine men, and I'll take the rest and go inside. I update AWACS with a SITREP, advising them to stay on high alert. We have no idea what we're about to get ourselves into.

My team stays put until Raney has his men in position. They set up overwatch positions on rooftops surrounding the house so they can get a good 360-degree view.

Once in place, my team makes their way to the rear of the house. We follow the same path as Mock's four-person team, climbing over the rubble in formation and then to the rear door. We line up along the back wall of the house. Taking point, I enter first, securing the inside. The back door leads into the kitchen, and I try hard not to step on the trash that is strewn over the floor. It's like a hoarder's house, crap piled up everywhere.

I scan the area, and then, one by one, half of my team starts filtering in, scanning their sectors. The other half stays in position until we're ready for them to enter. Mock signals me to follow him, and I stay on his heels. The smell of musty, mildewed air causes my nose to itch. It doesn't have the same vacant smell that the other houses do. It's almost like the stagnant smell of an athlete's armpit after an intense workout. We tread lightly until we make it back to the bedroom in question. Mock places his finger to his lips, signaling me to be quiet.

Kyle and Martinez also join us in the room. I see Mock raise his night vision goggles, point a finger at his eye, and then use the same finger to point at the ground. I raise my night vision goggles too. I didn't see it at first, and I don't know how Kyle ever saw it in the first place. I wouldn't have fathomed a situation like this, like something out of some spy movie I remember watching as a kid. Right in front of me, a faint yellow glow outlines the king-sized bed. It's a hatch. There's something underneath this house.

The first thing that comes to mind is that each of the houses in this neighborhood is built with a bunker of some sort under it. This is why we couldn't find them. This is why none of our systems ever picked them up. They were hidden underground. I'm even more impressed with this group than I was before. I signal Mock and the others to pause here, and I exit the rear of the building. I advise our eyes in the sky of our current situation and tell them to stand by for further instruction. If each of these houses has a bunker, finding the right one where our guys are being held is going to be painstaking.

How big is this bunker? Is it just the size of the bed or the whole room? Or quite possibly the whole house? If we open this hatch, is there going to be a group of fully armed men pointing their weapons at us? Is it booby-trapped? The questions keep flowing like an endless river of thought.

I really want to see inside, but we must be careful. Mock calls upon Petty Officer Second Class Blake Gifford as he has a fiber optic camera snake. Hopefully we can lift the hatch just enough to poke the snake inside and get a good visual of it without causing any disruption to whomever might be down there.

Gifford arrives and hands me the camera. At the end of the bed, I lay flat on the ground, placing the camera's eyepiece to my right eye. I then nod to Kyle, Mock, and Martinez to lift the hatch slightly. I start slowly feeding the end of the cable through, but only a few inches at first. I scan the immediate area, looking for signs that there might be a trip wire or sensor attached to the hatch or the framing. I follow along all four sides, which is roughly seven feet by seven feet, but there doesn't appear to be anything that would signal or trip an alarm. As I thread out more cable, it shows a set of dirty concrete steps, the same width as the hatch, leading down eight feet into a hall that narrows as it goes deeper. I blink a few times to make sure my eyes are not deceiving me because as the camera goes further, it appears the end of the hall splits off at the end. This is no small bunker. There's an entire tunnel system underneath this neighborhood.

CHAPTER TWENTY-NINE
(Captain Nolan Wilkinson—U.S. Navy)

Sunday, January 26, 2048

The bed is mounted on top of a wooden hatch. Two heavy duty hinges are fastened underneath the hatch at the head of the bed end. On either side of the hatch are two large shocks that will help hoist the foot end of the bed in the air with ease. I signal Mock over. He lets go and kneels beside me, and I hand him the eyepiece. He's just as shocked. He hands it back and I reel in the camera then give it back to Gifford, who stows it in his ruck.

Now that I know what we're dealing with, and know that there is no trap or sensor, I order Kyle and Martinez to grab the end corners of the bed to make the lift. The rest of us stand around the bed with weapons ready.

Slowly and as quietly as they can, the two start raising the hatch. With every inch it rises, the room brightens a little more, the light pours in from below. The hatch's shocks hiss in protest as air fills the cylinders. Damn. These people are more advanced than I would have ever guessed. The engineering required to construct such an achievement is amazing.

With the hatch raised as high as it'll go, several of us kneel, craning our necks low to try and see as far down into the tunnel system as we can. I don't know how extensive this underground system is or how far it goes out, but my curiosity has been piqued. At least the hatch is wide enough for Frank to join us down there.

I return to the backyard so I can speak without being worried that someone below could hear me. I advise Raney and the circling AWACS of our current situation and that we'll be going underground. I'm not sure what we're going to see once we're in, but I request everyone to be on high alert.

I return to the room, passing my team, who are waiting, antsy to go down. My nerves are settled, but I can tell from several tapping fingers on their trigger guards that they are anxious. I go first, and one by one, we enter the sublevel. The house's bad odor only increases. The steps leading down are stacked full of debris and junk, worse than the rest of the house. The construction isn't perfect, as none of the concrete-paneled walls line up evenly, and the ceiling is a bit uneven, but all in all, it's remarkable. This would have taken years to complete, decades maybe, judging from the reports of what these people are like. How could they have constructed something like this without Joscos knowing about it? Especially considering the noise they would have made.

Magazine centerfolds of naked women are plastered on every square inch of the hallway walls. I don't want to know what this hallway is used for. What's visible on the once-white concrete walls is now a filthy, beige color, almost like children with grimy fingers had ran their hands across it every time they walked by.

The lighting dims, humming louder the deeper we go. The flickering lightbulb dangling above my head was by no means professionally installed. Where are they getting their electricity? Some shoddy ductwork pushes heat out of small, rusted vents. When we reach the end of a short hallway, I share a where-the-fuck-did-all-this-come-from look with Mock. No wonder we couldn't find anyone; they are in fact hidden away like cockroaches.

We carefully pile into the twenty-foot-long corridor and line up against either side of the walls. We let our eyes adjust to the light. Mock stands opposite of me at the front of the line, so I signal him to peek around the corner. Our corridor splits off into three directions, straight ahead for what looks like another fifty feet before it splits off to the left and right.

I don't like the idea of splitting up, but we'll cover more ground this way. We have no way of knowing just how extensive this maze is, but we need to hurry. Mock picks fourteen men to go left with him. I get the rest, including Frank, and we go right.

Even through the poor lighting, we can see that a larger hallway ahead has several smaller corridors trailing off from it like a tree root system, probably connecting to other houses in the neighborhood.

Random crap like clothing, furniture, weapons of all sorts, porn DVDs, hustler magazines, stacks of money still wrapped in plastic, and gold bars litter every hallway and corridor we pass. Relics from another time just sitting here collecting dust. Some hallways are so cluttered they are virtually impassable, but if shit hits the fan, they will provide the perfect cover if we need to conceal ourselves.

We continue pushing forward another hundred feet; the tunnel system just keeps going. I click the mic three times to let Mock know we're still alive, and he does the same. A few moments later, someone turns around a corner fifty feet ahead of us. He stumbles along, bouncing off the walls, knocking items over, and making a ruckus. We scatter behind debris and tuck away into one of the many corridors surrounding us. We wait to let him pass, hoping he doesn't randomly stumble upon us from another corridor. He's beyond drunk or high. One fall and I'm sure he'll lie there until he sobers up.

I have two soldiers go ahead of us to make sure he doesn't become a problem. If we can, we need to take him down quietly and find out where our men are located, if they're even here. In his current state, our drunken friend probably wouldn't be much use any way.

The two move ahead in a coordinated approach until we hear a clicking noise coming from one of the other corridors behind us. I glance back and see Frank signaling me, letting me know the sound is coming from the corridor to his left. He shifts back behind some furniture but is pointless with his stature.

Shit! I signal Hall, to go take him out quietly, but as he scuddles back toward Frank, and approaches the corridor to peer inside, another man walks out in the middle of our squad. He makes direct eye contact with Hall, and they both stand there frozen. The man was clearly not expecting to see us, which is a good sign. He's wasted, but obviously he's not as bad as the other guy. He drops the red plastic cup he's holding, and brown liquid splashes out around the edges. He has no weapon on him from what I can see. Without haste, one of my men from behind, covers the man's mouth and slices his knife across the man's jugular. Blood gushes out in pumps as his heart beats its last, saturating the front of the man's filthy shirt. Hall jumps in to help Bradley as the man wriggles violently, grasping his throat as though to stop the blood. It didn't take long for the man's body to go limp, and the two gently lay him down inside the corridor. A few others help hide the body under some blankets and trash sitting nearby. We did our best to cover the pool of blood but didn't get too far before someone spoke out.

"Contact!" a voice yells.

Three suppressed gunshots ring through the tunnels.

"Nolan," Young calls out over the comms. "You need to get the fuck over here on the double."

Young and Moore stand over a massive body, but it's not what I had pictured in my head.

Without any hesitation, I get on the comms, alerting Raney and AWACS. "We have contact! I repeat, we have contact. It's not just humans down here. There are Joscos too! I repeat, there are Joscos down here!"

"What the hell is that?" Moore points his rifle up at the ceiling where orange strobe lights attached to wires running haphazardly flash like a disco nightclub dance floor. I follow the line and notice a camera at the end of the hallway.

"Fuck!" I shout. Things just went from bad to very fucking bad.

"Mock, you guys also seeing this?"

"Yes, sir! What the hell's going on over there?" he asks.

"They have cameras down here. Not in every hallway but down one of the halls we're in," I advise.

"You shittin' me?"

"Nope! Shoot the cameras and anything that comes your way. Stay focused."

"Yes, sir!"

I order Raney and his team to eliminate anything suspicious or threatening they see topside. I also order him to take over the comms with AWACS to ensure our extraction is on standby for an immediate evac and to expect it to be hot. He advised of no current threats, but I'm sure that'll change soon enough.

"Gentleman, we have five minutes to find our men and get the hell out of here!" We don't have the element of surprise anymore, and we sure as hell don't have any time to fuck around.

We pick up the pace, navigating tunnel after tunnel in an offensive forward movement formation. I'm just hoping to see our men around one of the corners—and soon. As we make a turn, we come across a hostile, his back to us, hunched over like he's waiting for us. "Contact!" I blurt out.

He turns around with a rifle in his hands. I put a bullet in his shoulder and one in each of his kneecaps. He cries out in pain, spit flinging from his mouth. I need him alive for the time being. I need to know where my guys are, and I need to know right now.

Moore jumps on top of him, with one foot on his left hand and a knee pushed in his throat. I thrust my knee into his chest with the tip of my weapon pressed against his forehead.

"Where are my men?" I dig the tip of my barrel deeper into his forehead to the point that blood starts trickling down the side of his face.

"Fuck you!" He attempts to scream out through brown, clenched teeth. His face is red and sweaty. "Over Here!" he yells in a muffled voice, but Moore exudes more of his body weight onto his throat.

His eyes well up. Tears drip from the corners of the man's eyes soaking his matted hair. He smells like shit. Probably hasn't bathed in a long time.

"You want the pain to stop?" I slap him in the face to get him to calm down and bring his attention back to me.

"Listen up. You're going to tell me what I want to know. You have five seconds to point in the direction of where my men are! Or it's going to be a quick death." I wave my knife in front of his face. "5…4…3…" He raises his good arm, positioning his hand close to my face. I'm not going to lie. For a moment, I really thought he was going to help us out. He stuck up a finger, but it wasn't the finger I was looking for. He forcefully pushes his middle finger to my face. I grab it and twist it, breaking several of his fingers instantly, and then slam his hand to the ground.

"Alright, have it your way." I pull out my Beretta 92F 9mm and put a bullet in his head, "Let's move!"

"Mock, you got anything?"

"Just a bunch of locals trying to tell us we're not welcome." I hear shots ringing out as he speaks.

"Let me know the minute you have something. We need to find them ASAP! We're on the countdown!"

"Roger that."

We round another corner and come across a large group of well-armed locals who look like a bunch of guerilla-warfare-type soldiers. I spot at least eight of them before backing away. They're huddled up like they're going to hold that point and not let us through. I signal two men to get into position and help me out. "3…2…1. Go." Each of us let out several short bursts from behind the corner. I peek around and see them scattering like the cockroaches they are. Several of them return fire, but their bullets whiz past us. I return fire while sliding across to the other side of the corridor, then tuck away behind the wall. I signal Moore to join me and cover my six, and that's when gunfire erupts.

CHAPTER THIRTY

(Captain Nolan Wilkinson—U.S. Navy)

Sunday, January 26, 2048

Fuck, that escalated quickly. I duck back into the corridor as bullets ping off every wall surrounding us. Pretty sure these idiots couldn't care less if they hit their own people the way they are going about this.

Then, from somewhere behind me, a loud, gurgling voice shouts, "I'm hit!"

I crane my neck around some debris, scanning each of my guys who are in a clear view of my location.

"Who's hit?" I say over the mic, but with everyone taking fire, there's no immediate response.

I repeat it as loudly as I can, but I'm instantly distracted by a group fast approaching from an opposite corridor. I return fire to suppress their advancement. Enemy heads peek out from every corner like targets during shooting practice. From the way they are firing their weapons haphazardly, each man's lack of training is obvious. How they could hit anything is beyond me. My guess? Random luck.

"Jake?" I page for our medic.

With no response, I eye Moore, who's changing out a magazine.

"Moore, where's Jake?" He motions backward. I order Young to take my position, and I inch along the wall, moving in right beside Moore.

"Some welcoming party!" Moore shouts over the noise as he pops several short bursts from his M4.

I jump on the comms, flinching as concrete dust from a fired shot clouds my face. "Jake, you got a copy?"

"Loud and clear, sir," he replies.

"Who's hit?" I ask.

"Cole! Upper right leg. I'm trying to get to him, but I need this corridor safe."

I duck walk back to him, staying as low as I can. Cole is trapped in a hallway that leads up to another house. Eight feet separates us, with a corridor split between us. Moving to the opposite wall from Jake, I get a better view of Cole. Streaks of blood cover the floor beside him. Cole is awkwardly kneeling and raising his rifle over the top of the debris pile, shooting off a few rounds down the corridor to his right. A spray of bullets returns his way, plastering the concrete wall and chipping away large chunks that fall onto his helmet. He tightens his body into a ball as small as he can as bullets continue to pelt the wall behind him.

I turn back to Jake. "Do we have any men down that corridor?"

"No, sir. Cole is the last." His eyes focus on an enemy target, then he fires.

I grab a grenade. "When this goes off, you jump over there and patch him up."

Jake gives me a nod, and I pull the pin then toss it down the hall, then yell, "FRAG OUT!"

The explosion sends bits and pieces of junk toward us. We cower in on ourselves. Once the dust settles, I provide cover fire for Jake with another round of short bursts as he hops over to Cole's aid, popping off a few rounds as he crosses to the other side. I get up and push a dresser along with other debris into the corridor to provide additional shelter while Jake gets to work patching Cole up. I continue to monitor the corridor as well as the access stairs from the house. Wouldn't be good if a group of hostiles tried to flank us.

"Looks like a piece of shrapnel!" Jake yells to Cole.

Needing a SITREP from Mock, I call out over the radio, "Mock, you copy?"

"Yes, sir."

"How are you guys doing?"

"We're under some pretty heavy gunfire, sir. Bit of an infestation problem down here."

"I know what you mean. They're starting to live up to the cockroach analogy. Any injuries to report?" I ask.

"No, sir."

"Good to hear. You guys find any evidence of our men?"

"No, sir. This way is a dead end."

Damn.

"Make your way to our position. We need to regroup and strengthen our forces. The tunnels just keep going from where we're at."

"Already on our way, sir!"

"Roger that." I stay on and give him some brief directions to get to us. Should be easy enough.

While the bastards just keep coming, we throw everything we have at them. Enemy bodies are piling up; at this rate, our exits will be blocked by carcasses.

I call Frank over for assistance. A large group has regained control of the corridor I tossed the grenade down just moments ago. He swings one of his miniguns around the corner, holding down the trigger for a few seconds. The sound reverberates as a slight ringing in my ear closest to the blast. Down the hall, refuse floats through the air like parade confetti.

"Damn. I think you got 'em!"

Frank nods. "Glad I could be of assistance."

I glance back over to see Jake finish wrapping a cloth bandage on Cole's thigh and looks to be taping it up. Once finished, Jake cradles his elbow and hoists him up.

"Good?" I give Cole a thumbs-up, and he hops a few steps to test out his leg.

"I'll survive."

Mock's voice comes over the comms. "Nolan, you copy?"

"Yes, sir."

"We're coming up on your six. Don't shoot us."

"Roger that."

Just as he said that, the shooting stops, like a water faucet being turned off abruptly. We observe the enemies retreat, heading deeper into where we need to go.

"What the heck just happened?" I eye Jake and Cole.

"That's strange," Jake says, echoing my thoughts.

"Yeah. I don't like that."

I jump back on the comms with Mock. "When you make it to that 'T' I was telling you about, hang a left. There'll be signs of grenade damage. I'll have a few men waiting for you. Once you get to them, secure that area. We need to push deeper."

"Roger that, sir!"

We secure our area for Mock's arrival, and I make my way back up to the front of the formation. We fire a few random shots to take care of some unfortunate locals running by.

"Mock, glad you're here. I need you and your team to cover the rear and make sure our exit out of here is clear."

We move further into the labyrinth as we navigate their extensive tunnel system. My mind obsessively considers why they stopped firing at us. Worst case, they are regrouping for a major counterattack. Best case they're getting our men and want to negotiate. In any case, I remind my men to stay alert and focused and to expect the unexpected.

The next corner leads to a large opening. We leapfrog up the corridor, advancing to the large room.

"There!" I point to a makeshift prison cell with two wooden crates sitting in the middle, just big enough to fit a normal-sized human being in them. They must be in there, but why are there only two? I didn't want to think about it, but knowing that he was shot, I'm scared for Nathan.

From the hall, I do another check of the room. Several more corridors split off from the main room. I don't like this. It's quiet and the enemy is nowhere to be found. Maybe they're letting us get our men so that we can leave. That seems farfetched.

I kneel and turn to my team. "Listen up," I say, pointing to Moore, Young, and a few others, signaling them to come forward. "You see those wooden boxes in that cell?"

"Yes, sir."

"We need to get to them but need to make sure it's safe to do so."

"Are they in there, sir?" Moore asks, frowning.

"I don't know, but we're about to find out. If they're not, then we keep moving until we find them. See those three corridors?" Each of them nods. "I need those secure. I don't want anyone to come in. You got that?"

"Yes, sir."

"Once you get those passageways secured, we'll go open them up and see what's inside. Understood?"

"Yes, sir," they confirm again.

We pile into the large room with two guys taking up positions in each of the corridors. I notice a small room cut into the wall off to the side where wall-to-wall computer monitors hang with images of tunnels on them. Well, I have got to give them some credit. They've really built something here. I order several others to start grabbing hard drives and anything else that might be of value.

As we settle into our positions, a loud bang echoes from the hallway we just came from. We turn our heads as a single Josco stampedes in, slamming into the concrete wall opposite us, cracking it in half, and making the top portion fall to the ground. We're momentarily stunned as the eight-foot beast regains its footing.

Shots ring out before the Josco thrusts forward and grabs at the men standing nearby. The three men try to escape its grasp, but the Josco is too quick, and a fight comes to life before our very eyes. The Josco swings around, knocking off two of them, who hit hard against the busted concrete wall and are slow to get up. The third has a choke hold on the beast, doing everything he can to keep hold, like riding a bull. More men jump into the fight. This Josco is not as large as some others but still strong enough to kill us all if not handled properly. The two men who were flung off jump back in, grabbing each of the Josco's legs, but it's far too strong, and the men fling off as easily as a fly gets flicked off an arm.

"Fuck!" I yell out in frustration of not having a clean shot. I make sure the rest of the team stays put and covers their area when a second Josco comes barreling in from the same corridor. Frank turns sharply to find himself face to face with the Josco, who stops dead in its tracks. Frank didn't have time to raise his weapons; otherwise, we would be covered in blood and guts. They stand eyeing each other in a game of chicken.

I'm standing just off to the side of the two, and I see the Josco's eyes widen. It probably doesn't quite know what to think as it looks Frank up and down. Frank stands there unaffected, his composure as solid as a ten-ton boulder. It was like watching a standoff between two gunslingers, one waiting for the other to make a move.

I know what Frank is thinking. If he raises his gun, will he have enough time to disable the threat? Not likely. His reaction time is good but not that good. If he's able to get off a few rounds, who's to say he would be able to stop when the Josco comes for him.

Frank slowly releases his grip on his miniguns and starts to unstrap his exoskeleton. The Josco flinches just the slightest but seems to realize what Frank is doing. Four long seconds later, Frank's miniguns drop to his feet. The Josco stands a good foot taller than Frank, but the fiery revenge illuminates in his eyes. Payback is all Frank could talk about since they took his brother Bryan just a few short days ago.

I'm completely lost for words. I have one standoff taking place in front of me while another fight is currently in progress. I take a few steps back and glance over to see Cole scrambling to his feet with his knife tightly gripped in his hand. Gregg, who has been holding on for dear life, manages to pull out his Springfield Armory 1911handgun and is somehow able to fire a shot into the Josco's thick neck.

The Josco squirms, knocking the gun from Gregg's hand, then bends over, causing Gregg to slam to the ground. The wind is knocked out of him as he gasps for air. I run to Gregg and pull him back away from the fight. Cole stumbles forward with one bad leg, and he, too, is slammed with a quick fist and falls on his back. Cole flips over like a ninja, kicking off the wall, and slides forward with his knife in hand and takes one big swing to the Josco's Achilles tendon.

The beast lets out a torturous grunt of pain as it falls to its knees. It roars and flails its arms violently, striking several men.

"Stand back!" I yell.

Everyone retreats as I walk up with my weapon pointed at the downed and thrashing Josco. I fire three short bursts, hoping to hit it in its head, but they strike its torso instead. Dammit! It squirms harder, and I shoot again, aiming for its head but strike its neck.

"Are you fucking kidding me!"

I step closer to fire one more, hitting it in its left eye. The thing finally stops moving, it's dead.

I turn to Frank just as the other Josco's eye twitches. Perhaps it sensed the death of its friend, but that twitch is all Frank needs. He leaps forward faster than the Josco could react, gripping its throat and slamming its body ferociously against the wall. The concrete splits from the ground up to the ceiling due to the force of their combined weight. Frank releases and swings his double-softball-sized fists in rapid succession at its face. Blood pours from its nose, but the Josco ducks and lunges forward, wrapping its arms around Frank as it slams through a group of men standing nearby. Then, it lands a few upper cuts of its own on Frank's side, but that only infuriates him even more. Frank stops an incoming right hook with both hands while simultaneously turning his body to flip and slam the Josco to the ground. While still clenching the Josco's wrist, Frank stomps on the Joscos chest and pulls while twisting to slowly sever the appendage ligament by ligament. A final, loud snap forces a collective grimace from onlooking soldiers. Frank then beats the Josco with its own arm. Someone behind me throws up.

Frank lets out an ear-shattering roar, a sound I've never heard come from him, but he doesn't stop there. The bloody massacre continues with blow after blow pounding into the Josco's face and chest.

In a fury, the Josco gets up and attempts to fight back but makes a fatal mistake. The Josco slips and falls on its own blood, crashing to the floor face down. Frank jumps on its back and reaches around the Josco's head, placing several fingers in its mouth and pries.

The Josco's head jerks to the side, and Frank puts more muscle and tension into his grip. Like the sound of tearing up a head of lettuce, the ripping of flesh and muscle and cracking of the jawbone make my stomach curdle. Frank separates the lower jaw from its head, then slams it back into the skull of the Josco. The Josco still twitches every few seconds as Frank's eyes glint with satisfaction. Revenge with a taste of justice.

My peers are either winded or staring at Frank in amazement at what they just witnessed. If that didn't motivate everyone to get this shit done, I don't know what the fuck would.

"Damn good job, but we're not finished yet."

"Hello?" We hear a muffled voice coming from the wooden crates.

"That sounds like Jared." I check back with the men who were assigned to get the cell open before our intrusion.

Soldiers start milling about executing their orders. Once we get the four corridors secured as planned, the others frantically grab the hard drives while the rest of us get the cell door open.

"Nolan, you have a copy? Over." Raney sounds urgent.

"Go ahead, Raney."

"You guys better hurry the fuck up. We have hostiles en route from the west and from the south. I have a line of headlights for miles heading our way."

"Fuck!"

CHAPTER THIRTY-ONE

(Captain Nolan Wilkinson—U.S. Navy)

Sunday, January 26, 2048

"Raney, it's time to call in the cavalry! You know what to do."

"Understood, sir! I'll notify the QRF. Let's just hope these bastards don't have air support accompanying the band of misfits heading our way. AWACS is reporting tanks and other improvised fighting vehicles in their convoy coming in from the west. They'll be here in about seven minutes at their current speed."

"Roger that. As soon as we're done here, we're getting the fuck out. Looks like our extract is going to be hot."

"Hot? It's going to be on fire, sir." I can hear a little excitement in his voice.

"Just keep me posted with what's going on topside."

"Roger that. Over."

"Okay men, let's get these crates open now! Looks like we're going to be fighting our way out, so let's hurry." Before we get interrupted again, I order everyone back to their positions.

The sound of flashbangs from down one of the corridors triggers return fire. An exchange of gunfire ensues. Another hallway erupts in a constant frenzy of bullets ripping through the air.

I hear Jared's voice yelling from within one of the crates inside the prison cell, and Frank doesn't hesitate to rip the makeshift cell door off the poorly constructed hinges. He flings the door across the room like a Frisbee, then four of us pile inside.

Both crates are roughly four feet long, two feet wide and two feet tall, with two small three-inch holes cut out from each end of the lid. The area around the holes is stained shit-brown, and flies and other small insects buzz around them. Between the smell of urine and feces and the winged critters, I have a sickening idea of what these holes were used for. In all my years, I've never seen conditions this foul for a prisoner, and I've seen some shit.

"Frank, help hold this point."

"Yes, sir." He raises his miniguns and scans the entire area to provide backup as necessary.

Martinez grabs a nearby crowbar and starts to pry it open with everything he's got.

"Damn thing has a hundred nails holding this lid shut." Sounds of struggle and frustration fill the small space.

Young spots another crowbar sitting behind the farthest crate and starts helping, both men putting every bit of energy they can muster into it. I glance over to the others loading bags of hard drives and documents from the desks. One by one, the CCTV monitors on the wall flicker off as the soldiers rip out cables, destroying everything not of value.

"First one's open!" Martinez announces, bringing my focus back to the crate.

"What the fuck?" I wasn't expecting to see two full-grown men crammed in there like sardines. The sight was worse than the smell. They were covered in urine and feces. Just when I thought these people couldn't be more fucked up in the head, I see this. Those holes were indeed used so they could piss and shit.

"How the fuck are you guys fitting in there? Holy shit?" Martinez says, moving on to the other crate to help Young.

Jared, who is on the bottom, is lying on his back with his knees slightly up. His knees are wrapped around Rob's head. Rob, a member of McCauley's team, is face down, his back covered in fecal matter. They're in there like a yin and yang symbol. Both are wearing nothing but their skivvies. We peel Rob out first, but he's stiff as a board and is shaking like someone who has been sitting in sub-freezing temperatures with no clothes.

He's not in good shape. His face is beaten, and he's almost to the point of death, barely breathing. I call over a few guys to help carry him out; he's not going to be able to walk under his own strength.

Jared, on the other hand, isn't as bad. His furrowed brow and tight jaw indicate pure vengeance and determination; he's pissed. He wants revenge, and he wants it now. We help him out, and he stumbles a few steps as he tries to regain his balance, grabbing the metal bars of the cell tightly. He's shaking, too, and dried blood masks the entire right side of his face, where there is a deep gash over his right eye.

I stay by Jared, giving him water and wiping away the dirt and grime from his face. He relaxes a bit, knowing that we're here and he's safe. I want to ask about his ordeal, but there will be plenty of time for that once we're out of here.

"Second lids off!" Martinez calls out from behind. He and Young fling their crowbars off to the side with a loud clink. Everyone starts helping the other two men out of their coffin.

Both men are laid out in the same manner that Jared and Rob were. Brad was the first out, as he was on top. He looks okay, maybe a little better than Jared, but with the same pissed-off look. Jacob, another one of McCauley's guys, is in the same rough shape as Rob.

"Where's Nathan?" I ask Brad, looking dead in his eyes as he leans against the crate.

A giant boom shakes the sublevel, and dust sprinkles down from the ceiling, ordinance exploding above. I hope it's ours.

"Raney, you have a copy?" I ask, still waiting for Brad to say something.

"Loud and clear, but you better hurry the fuck up."

"What's going on?" I ask.

"Incoming hostiles are at our doorstep, and I don't think they're happy that we're here. Apaches are in place, and the Gunship is raining hell down."

"Roger that. We've secured our package, and we're making our way back now."

"Copy that. Over."

I throw Brad's stiff left arm over my shoulder and carry him out of the prison cell. His stench is so offensive that I let out a small cough.

"Nathan didn't make it." He spoke softly, almost mechanically. "He was shot when they captured us. They knocked me out soon after. When I woke up in this thing, they told me he was dead. Have you found Riley? I didn't see her or hear her voice."

"She's safe and sound back home," I reply. "Scott made it home as well and Gregg is here with us."

"And Frank?" He looks at me, concerned.

"See for yourself." He lifts his head up just as Frank fires down a corridor.

"Good ol' Frank. Damn good to see him." Tears well up in his dark, swollen eyes.

It's a team effort to grab our wounded and get ready to move out. I hand Brad over to another man before walking over to Jared, who is dressing himself with a pair of pants and a jacket he snatched off one of the dead guys. Frank walks up but keeps his distance.

He attempts to fist bump Brad and Jared, but neither return the gesture. "Where's Nathan?" Frank's eyes are filled with concern.

"Nathan didn't make it, Frank. Where the fuck were you guys?" Brad asks.

"Stop." I stand between them before this escalates any further. "Not here. Not now. This isn't anybody's fault, and we got here as fast as we possibly could with what little intel we had."

"You weren't here, and those sick fuckers tried to make us eat him!" Jared points his finger at Frank, clearly angry at him. "Those fuckers said they BBQed him. They ate him in front of us, chewing his flesh and spitting it out on us. Who the fuck does that?" Jared paces with a slight limp, still hunched over from his injuries.

That's some psychological bullshit. I don't know what to say. I wouldn't put it past these idiots to do something like that, but in this case, hopefully it was just a mind game to fuck with their captives. These people are clearly demented and have lost touch with reality.

"I want a fucking gun," Jared demands. "I'm going to kill every fucking last one of them."

I search the floor and grab an M4 that's just lying on some trash and hand it to him, along with a few magazines from the pile. He tucks the extra magazines in his waistband and shoots me a "ready" nod.

"You good?" I glance down at his bare feet.

"Never felt fucking better, sir!"

"Okay then." With that, we backtrack to where we entered this hellhole, encountering only a few stragglers. Jared happily takes one of them out, probably with a few more bullets than needed, but I wasn't going to argue or stop him. You could see it in his eyes. He wants them to pay for what they did to Nathan and everyone else they've hurt. We all want it.

The thunder and pounding of our forces above, raining down with all their might, makes us pick up the pace.

We meet up with Mock and his team who have secured the corridors leading all the way to the hatch where we entered. And one by one, we exit.

After climbing up through the hatch, the line 'bombs bursting in air' from our National Anthem enters my mind. The house shakes like it's about to crumble to its foundation, and the room lights up with bright flashes. It's like watching the Fourth of July on steroids.

"Raney, you there?"

"Yes, sir. Make it fast."

"Talk to me. We're topside, about to exit the house," I announce.

"We have hostiles that keep coming from the west and south. It's hard to say how many, but it's a shit load. The gunship and Apaches are keeping them at bay for now, but we have hostiles popping up from everywhere inside this neighborhood. Over."

"That's because there's an elaborate tunnel system below that connects all these houses. Where you at?"

"I'm up top, on the roof."

"Coming at you!"

CHAPTER THIRTY-TWO

(Captain Nolan Wilkinson—U.S. Navy)

Sunday, January 26, 2048

With the assistance of Frank and Martinez, I climb onto the roof of the house we just exited. Loose granules from the shingles cause me to stumble; it's like walking on marbles. I sure up my footing and continue up a valley between two peaks of the roof. Fires flicker in the distance, casting orange shadows below a smoke-filled sky to the north and west of the neighborhood. Fifty-foot flames shoot into the night sky from a dozen houses.

The peak of the roof offers a perfect 360-degree view, where I come upon Raney leaning against the brick fireplace stack and holding his binoculars up to his eyes. He's talking on his radio, coordinating movements with his men positioned around the perimeter of the very house we're standing on, AWACS, and the QRF. The gunship circles above at seven thousand feet, unleashing its powerful array of weapons, while four AH-64 Apache helicopters buzz around, taking out patches of locals popping out from within the houses nearby.

It's impressive, to say the least. I stand in awe, watching the firepower bombard our enemy. Lights jump and dance across my line of sight. The Gatling gun from the gunship fires a 350-round burst to the north at a convoy of at least a hundred vehicles still heading our way. The bright yellow and orange sparks shower down in a beautiful display of twinkling stars against the dark background. After twelve seconds of that amazing show, they let the Gatling gun cool down, switching to the Howitzer that can fire up to 10 rounds per minute.

The initial thud of the cannon echoes down around us like God himself is pounding his fists together. A second later, the impact of the artillery penetrates the targets, shaking the ground.

Raney finally gets a short break. "How are we looking?" I ask, blinking my eyes hard and moving away from the flames.

"AWACS just reported a large group of Joscos heading our way from the northeast. They're popping out like ants from what appears to be underground bunkers. One of the Apaches is relocating and en route to take care of that mess," Raney explains. "Another line of vehicles is heading our way from the east. The gunship will head that way in a moment to suppress their advancement once they're finished with the incoming problem from the north." He turns his head, looking right at me, before continuing. "We're about to be surrounded. There are a lot more of them than we thought possible. I don't understand it."

Looking west toward the McGregor Airport, I say, "We're not quite in a soup sandwich yet, but our primary exfil is compromised." Hundreds of muzzle flashes from enemy rifles spread out all over the airport, so that's a no-go.

"Right now, our secondary exfil is our only chance of getting out of here. But we need to get moving ASAP. That new convoy is ten minutes out from our location."

"I'll get my team heading there now and secure the area. Have your men fall back." I pat Raney on his back.

"Roger that. Oh, I almost forgot. Ospreys are a few minutes out. I'll let them know primary is compromised and secondary is a go."

"Make it happen!"

Carefully walking to the roof's edge, I yell down to Mock to fall back south, past Highway 84, to secure our secondary exfil. Frank and a few others sit tight with me while Raney gets his men back to our location. Then, we'll all push out together.

"Fuck!" I turn to see Raney red-faced and sliding down the roof on his ass toward me, fragments of brick from the chimney rolling beside him.

"What is it?" I reposition to help stop his movement.

"Sniper, nine o'clock, coming from the west."

"Guys!" I motion Frank to come in close. "We have a sniper to the west. Take cover until we locate and take him out."

"Roger that." He does a two-finger salute.

Raney and I move to the east side of the roof and carefully walk up to the peak, maintaining our cover behind the chimney.

"Hornady, you copy?" Raney calls out to our sniper set up five houses west of us.

"Loud and clear."

"We have a sniper west of us. I need you to locate and terminate."

"On it, sir!"

"Whiplash, Actual? This is Main. Over."

"Go ahead, Main," Raney responds to AWACS.

"Be advised there's a five-vehicle convoy just west of the airport coming in fast to your location."

Damn. Sniper probably called in our position.

"Roger that, Main."

"Where's our fucking break?" Raney asks, taking a deep breath, then jumps on the comms and orders one of the other choppers for assistance. Fourteen seconds later, the Apache launched a Hellfire missile at the convoy a hundred yards from us. Vehicles slam on their brakes, skidding around two trucks that received a direct hit. The other three vehicles don't appear to be deterred by their friends' burning bodies. They regroup but space their line out and continue their same path to our location.

"Got him!" Hornady announces over the comms. "He's at the north end, up on a roof, where the cluster of metal buildings are located, one hundred and eighty yards out." A second later, he fires his weapon. "Target down!"

"Good job. Now get back here on the double!" Raney orders him.

Another sniper round whizzes by our heads, this time from the north.

"What the fuck!" I yell out, grabbing Raney and pulling him around to the south side of the chimney.

"That was close!" Raney adjusts his helmet.

Most of Raney's men have fallen back to our location and set up a perimeter around the house, except for Hornady, who advises us he's twenty seconds out, running south of the neighborhood damn near parallel with the three-car convoy to his south.

Frank takes off toward the road and engages with the lead vehicle twenty-five yards away, helping to distract them from Hornady who's running beside them. The driver swerves right, fishtailing, hitting one of the vehicles that attempted to go around, and the two go into a violent roll, one flipping end over end before coming to a stop on Highway 84 directly south of us.

The third improvised fighting vehicle is positioned directly between my team across the highway and Raney's men on this side, which is unfortunate because it's keeping us from unleashing every bullet we have left in our magazines upon them.

A man pops up from the bed of the truck and shoulder fires a rocket launcher at the incoming Apache. The pilot takes an evasive maneuver, swinging right to avoid a hit, and flies directly over the truck. The driver floors it, fishtailing and swinging it back around to the east in pursuit of the chopper, where the man then opens fire with the .50 cal.

"Oh shit!" I yell out, watching the tracer ammo honing in on the helicopter.

Frank engages, trying to keep the gunner from hitting a friendly, but it is too late. Even though he took out the truck, it wasn't before multiple bullets struck the engines and tail rotor of the chopper. It falls into an uncontrolled spin, with billowing black smoke pouring from the fuselage, and crashes several seconds later north of our location, back inside the neighborhood where the enemy is heading our way.

"Fuck!" I slide down the roof and jump from the edge. "Frank, Martinez, Hornady, my six, now. Raney, get another chopper overhead and protect that downed chopper. You guys stay put and wait for us. Cover our six!"

A collective "Yes, sir" confirms they understand their directive.

Frank hustles back and we head straight into the lion's den. As we're running, two Ospreys, our ticket out of here, get ready to land. Dammit. I give Mock a SITREP and tell them to hold tight.

Fires burn hot around us, and the streets are thick with a fog of smoke. We meet resistance along the way and take out the threats with little effort. We run through the streets as fast as we can while Raney provides us directions with the safest route until we come to the scene. The helicopter crashed on its side into the back of one of the houses that was on fire. The co-pilot is out, but he's trying to get the back cockpit door open for the pilot. Part of the roof is wedged over the top, keeping him from getting in.

"Martinez, Hornady, let's get up there and help Frank hold this position."

Once we climb onto the house, we circle around the co-pilot, who is surprised to see us, and we try to lift part of the roof. The glass in the side door is shattered, so we just need to lift enough so Roger can then attempt to reach in and pull out the pilot. But this section of the roof is too heavy for the four of us.

"Lift with your legs, gentleman!" We struggle to lift it even an inch.

"Fuck!" Martinez spits, and the roof barely budges.

We let go, and it makes a cracking thud.

"Martinez, switch with Frank."

I must be losing my mind to think the four of us could lift this roof. Frank's worth eight of us combined and the only one strong enough. Frank unstraps his gear and leaps up to us in a few jumps.

We get back into position. I crouch down, Hornady to my left, Frank to my right, with Rogers in between us, ready to slide in and grab the pilot the moment the roof gets high enough.

"Ready?" I ask.

"Let's go!" Rogers shouts.

We lift with everything we've got. The wood creaks and cracks.

"Almost there. Keep pushing!" Rogers yells.

We better fucking be there because I'm about to lose my grip. We drop this, and he'll be split in half, becoming a goner along with the pilot. A helicopter zooms overhead, firing its 30mm round from its M230 chain gun. He flies low enough to help clear some of the smoke stagnating around us. The enemy must be nearby. Explosions still erupt all around us. The battle doesn't appear to be lightening up one bit.

AWACS calls for me, but with my hands currently occupied, I can't answer.

"Go ahead, Actual. This is Main," Martinez answers. Thank goodness.

"Be advised, you have three tanks and multiple light armored vehicles to your north, moving in quickly, fifty yards. You need to get out of there. Gunship is thirty seconds out, danger nearby expected."

"Roger that," Martinez replies on my behalf.

Frank is doing ninety percent of the lifting, but we make enough progress for Rogers to start pulling the pilot's ass out.

Rogers slithers out from underneath the roof feet first, pulling the pilot's arms. Soon after, the pilot's head, then his torso, then his entire body emerges from underneath.

"He's out!" Rogers shouts.

We assess the pilot who's fading in and out of consciousness. Blood gushes from a cut on his forehead. It looks like it was caused by a wooden beam puncturing the windshield, striking him in the face. Small spikes of wood are stuck in his skin. Hornady wipes away the red liquid, then places gauze and tape to help stop the bleeding. Where the pilot's right leg should fold back at his knee, it folds forward. *Ouch.*

Shots fire from Martinez's position to the east. A group of locals are yelling from the next street over, and they return fire.

"Rogers, Hornady, you two grab the pilot. Let's go!"

As we descend the house, we do our best to handle him with care, avoiding a cave-in and spots of fire. I provide a SITREP to Raney and Mock and to expect our presence in a few minutes. We fall in behind Martinez, who's taken cover behind a partially collapsed brick wall.

"Take lead." I point to Martinez. "Frank, you and I will cover the rear." Frank makes quick work of strapping his weapons back on.

"Weapons check." We run through our ammo.

"Good!" Martinez says.

Frank nods, and we start our trek south. The ground shakes with one hundred and eighty tons of tanks heading our way, their engines revving near our location.

"We have any more Hellfires out there?" I call out over the comms.

"This is Stag 1," the pilot circling overhead confirms. "I have one Hellfire and a few Hydra 70s left."

"As soon as you have a shot, fire that son-of-a-bitch," I reply to the pilot.

A loud bang from behind puts us on our asses. One of the tanks fires a cannon just yards away. We take cover between two houses, clasping our hands to our ears from the deafening bang.

Through the ringing, I hear, "Actual, this is Stag 1. Take cover, firing away."

We huddle in on each other, staying as close as we can to the brick wall of the house. *Boom*! We feel the percussion from the explosion. My ears sing a high, unyielding soprano, and my vision is nothing but a blurry mess. I stumble to my feet, blinking multiple times to gain clarity.

"Fuck, that was close!" Rogers cries out.

"Yeah, it was." Martinez leans against the brick wall, collecting himself.

"Everybody okay?" Frank asks. He seems to be the only one doing fine. He helps Rogers and Hornady up so they can get the pilot and start moving again. I shake it off and stumble to Martinez.

"You good? Can you get us back?" I ask, talking loudly over the buzz in my ears.

"I'm good." He shakes his head and then gives a thumbs-up. "Yes, sir."

The gunship then jumps on the comms, warning us that they are about to light up the remaining tanks and vehicles with the Bofors 40mm cannon, expressing the urgency for us to vacate the area. Didn't have to tell us twice. Within seconds, we round the corner and yell "Friendly" so Raney and his men don't mistakenly take us out. Two of his men greet us and kindly take over handling the pilot.

The gunship's cannons thunder in the air as we continue our way south of Highway 84, where the two Ospreys have been waiting for our arrival. The three remaining Apaches circle the outskirts, taking out anything alive.

We cross the highway just as two of Raney's men cross my path, carrying someone over their shoulders.

"He okay?" I ask Raney, who's trotting beside me.

"I have no fucking idea. He's not one of us," he says. "A couple of my guys picked him up. I'm sure you and the Major are going to have questions."

"Didn't realize we were taking prisoners on this mission," I say, to which Raney shrugs his shoulders.

Raney pulls out his sidearm and caulks an eyebrow. "We don't have to."

I thought about it for a moment. "Keep him alive."

"You sure?" He waves his gun.

"No. But yes."

"You're the boss."

We reach the Ospreys, and load up, me being the last to step on board. We do a headcount, making sure everyone is accounted for, and once I have confirmation, I signal the pilots to get the hell out of there.

I watch from the rear of the Osprey just as the sun starts to rise in the east. Fires burn and smoke fills the air to the west. Jared walks up, stinking to high heaven.

"Dude, you reek." I smile and punch his shoulder. "You want to give the order?"

He smiles. "With fucking pleasure."

I hand him my radio. "Fucking level this place."

We watch the light show as everything within a mile radius of the neighborhood explodes under the relentless bombardment of every artillery we have left in our arsenal.

CHAPTER THIRTY-THREE
(Major Oliver White—U.S. Marines)

Monday, January 27, 2048

The glare of the sun on the windshield blinds me as I turn the corner and make my way to the north end of the base. The sun seems brighter this morning. Maybe it's just me, or maybe it's the fact that Operation Search and Rescue resulted in better news than I was expecting, and my mind is trying to find the happiness of it. I was heartbroken to hear that we lost Nathan, but on the positive side, they rescued Jared, Brad, Jacob and Rob, who were assumed dead when the Joscos stormed their base camp during Operation Texas Bandit. It was an even bigger shock to hear that the Joscos didn't kill them or eat them in the ordeal. Instead, they captured them, and then took them to this Serpent's Head outfit. With all the computers and data we've been able to recover, this tangle of webs keeps getting more complex with each passing day.

A line of unorganized parked cars leads the way to where Nolan and his team landed five minutes ago. Families run and kids skip along the tarmac to see their loved ones.

Seeing an opening, I swing in and park. A gust of cold air strikes my thinly clothed body and goes straight to my bones as I exit the jeep. After hearing the good news, I didn't bother grabbing my jacket or the necessities for the thirty-degree weather. I'm sure I'll be paying for it later, but I'm too eager to catch up with the team to care.

I notice Nolan and his team lined up on either side of one of the Osprey's rear cargo bay doors. My heart sinks, and what follows makes me even more sad. Inside the Osprey, I see several men carrying a body on a stretcher covered in an American flag.

"Jacob didn't make it, sir," Frank says.

We stand in silence and salute our fallen brother.

So long as men roam the Earth, there will always be war. This war has taken so many lives, and even with the absence of humans, there will be more. War has been and always will plague this world. We may not be here to see it through, but there'll be more, even if only between the two distinct groups of Joscos with different goals.

The ambulance takes Jacob's body away, his family right there with him.

"I was hoping he'd pull through, but those bastards did a number on him," Nolan says as he walks up from behind.

"Glad to see you, Nolan!" We shake hands.

"Likewise."

"From all accounts, it seems their outfit is more capable than what any of us could have imagined."

"You'd have to see it to believe it. They are more than capable. It was extraordinary, which concerns me."

"How so?"

"Retaliation."

"Really." I suck in a deep breath and pay attention.

"We may have won this little skirmish, but I fear this was just a small encounter compared to what we might see once they regroup. We may have destroyed some of their vehicles, tunnels, and infrastructure, but we have no idea how deep it goes or how many communities have the same setup."

Hearing that assessment wasn't comforting, and now I fear something big that I hadn't ever considered is coming our way.

"In the chaos, we did snag you a present that might be able to help answer some questions."

"We took a prisoner?" I'm genuinely intrigued.

"I wasn't keen on bringing him back here but thought he could be useful."

"Has he said anything?"

"Nothing yet. We had to duct tape his mouth shut because he kept blabbering on the way here, just stupid shit. How much he is going to enjoy eating our bodies and shit like that."

"How about we go remove that duct tape?" I ask, to which Nolan nods.

***

Nolan and I wait in the room opposite the interrogation room, looking through the double-sided glass. The door opens and two MPs, both wearing face masks and gloves, escort the guy into the interrogation room, trying to seat him at the table. The dinky man curses and takes swings with his cuffed hands at the two MP's heads. They subdue him with force and chain his hands to the table, where a thick metal "D" ring is fastened.

"Jeez. Your guys really know how to pick 'em."

Nolan laughs. "Yeah, well, surprisingly, this is about as good as it gets."

The man's eyes are bloodshot, left one slightly crossed. His hair is partially matted with clumps of dirt and grime. His face is pitted with acne scars, and small growths sprout from his neck. His teeth are stained a dark color somewhere between deep yellow and gray. His ratty clothes are in no better condition than his hygiene.

"Could be worse, I guess." Nolan shrugs.

"Worse than this?" I turn to Nolan. "How in the hell have these people lived all these years in those conditions?"

"No idea, but I assume they are second-class citizens to the Joscos, which may explain their cannibalism," Nolan says.

"Second class? More like third class," I reply. "Let's get to it. I have a feeling this is either going to go badly or very badly."

We enter the room. "Well, hot damn. It's Major Oliver White," he says in the deepest hick voice I have ever heard, placing his cuffed hands on the table. The chain causes a loud clank that echoes throughout the small room.

Surprised is an understatement.

"So, you know me?" I ask.

"I do know ya." He jiggles from side to side in his chair, all excited, like he's about to sit on Santa's lap. "And I know ya, too, Mr. Nolan." He points to Nolan, who quirks an eyebrow. "Can't believe I'm seeing it wit my own two eyes. Never figered I'd be sittin' right her." He smiles bizarrely with only half his mouth.

"And why is that?" I take a seat across from him.

"Yur famous. A savior to yur people." He puts his hand in the air like he's praying, spreading his hands out as far as the cuffs allow.

"A savior?" I reply. "That's a bit of a stretch."

"Well, ya sure." He slams his hands on the table. "You saved all of dem lost people up her. Creatin this sanc-tu-ary behind a river."

"I guess we need to start praying to the Aw Mighty Oliver," Nolan says in a serious voice, giving me a wink, but I'm not amused.

The man laughs cynically.

"Let's move past my deity status for a moment because we have a lot of questions."

"Yes'ir. I'll do ma best to answwa yur ques-ti-ons, Aw Mighty Oliver." I turn to Nolan, giving him a look, irritated that the nickname stuck. "Immall ears." He points to his ears, laughing.

"Since you already know who I am, what's your name?" I start off with something easy, placing my left hand on the table and crossing my legs to get comfortable. This promises to be good.

He observes my taped-up hand. "Oh! A lil' battle scar." He smiles, licking his lips. "Them wolves are mean-uns, aren't dey?"

I maintain my composure because him knowing that is very odd. How would word of something like that have traveled down to their community when most people here don't even know? My mind spirals out of control thinking we have moles, spies roaming around our parts. I keep it together and focus for now.

"You have a name?" I ask again.

"Bill," he replies with too much emphasis on the "B."

"Just Bill?" Nolan asks.

"Jus Bill."

"How are you alive right now?" I ask.

"Uh?"

I could tell he was a bit confused by the question; my inner monologue of questions got away from me.

"Let me rephrase a bit. How is it that you and your people are alive and, by most accounts, appear to be doing well?" I suppose "well" was subjective. "And living with Joscos? I mean, I haven't met a Josco that hasn't tried to kill me when face to face with it."

I thought about that question as it came out, thinking about the rogue group up north, but I left it alone.

"I can see ha dat might be confusin' to ya. Ya see, there's a kind of ag-ree-ment 'tween us." His words are slow and thick like dark molasses.

"An agreement?" Nolan chimes in.

"Yup ag-ree-ment. We look after dem Joscos, dey pro-tect us. Dey were sposed to protect us from da likes of you, but we sees how dat went las night." He smirks. "But ya weren't sposed to find our hiding spot." He points at us, shaking his finger. "How'd ya find us?" He gives us a look almost as if he is proud of us.

"Got lucky," Nolan says.

"Wull, no doubt 'bout dat, Mr. Nolan. Shit…luck." He rolls his eyes using his entire head.

"What about the tunnel system, you guys created that? It's impressive. How did you guys pull that one off?" I ask.

He looks at Nolan. "Got lucky." Touché, Bill.

"Do you know this man?" I pull out a small photo of Dr. Anderson from my chest pocket and slide it across the table.

Bill looks at it and smiles, then tries to stifle it by pursing his lips as he throws the photo back on the table.

"Judging by that look, you do know him," I say.

"Not met 'im, know of 'im." His voice changes to a more serious tone.

"Okay, sure. What do you know about him?" I stuff the photo back into my pocket.

He sits there quietly, just staring at the shackles around his wrists like he left consciousness for a minute.

"Hey, I gots a qes-tion for ya," he asks, perking back up.

"Okay, go ahead," I reply.

"Wus the dif-fer-ence 'tween ya n me?"

There are so many answers I can give, but I feel this wasn't a question but more of a joke.

"Besides the obvious?" He's starting to get annoying, and I probably could have been a little more tactful.

"Be-sides the ob-vious?" He sits up straight, trying to repeat my words to impersonate my voice. "The dif-fer-ence"—he pauses and leans back in his chair—"is dat I'll still be livin when dis ends." He lets out another one of those cynical laughs.

Nolan and I exchange a look. "And what exactly does that mean?" I ask, uncrossing my legs, leaning in closer to the table.

"It means"—he leans forward, looking directly into my eyes, his stench invading my nostrils—"I hope ya've made yur peace with God, Mr. Oliver, cause ya have no idear what ya've started."

(Petty Officer First Class Jayce Brock—Navy SEAL)

Monday, February 10, 2048

I sat for a good ten minutes, watching the snow melt away on the windshield before I put the jeep in reverse. Ever since tracking down the rogue group of Joscos, my mind hasn't been the same. Flashes of someone else's visions creep in randomly throughout the day and in my dreams…well, nightmares. This can't be normal, but I won't be able to rest until I know why the heck scenes of Joscos play out in my mind. And why now? Am I turning into one of them?

Hawkeye must have sensed my conflicted emotional state as he nudged me with his wet nose, his worrisome eyes staring deeply into mine.

"I gave you a choice, and you jumped right in, so don't look at me like that." His head tilts to the side. "We're just down the road." I shrug my shoulders but keep both hands on the steering wheel at ten and two. "I can turn around and drop you off." He responds with a shallow growl. "Just sayin'."

He whimpers as if he's trying to console me. I can't say that I blame him. This isn't my smartest idea. It's been a little over a week since our new neighbors stopped roaming around and created a sanctuary of their own just north of our territory in Canada, near Horseshoe Bay. Drones have been flying nonstop 24/7, monitoring their every move since we tracked them down two and a half weeks ago. But since they seem to have settled down for the time being, I figure this is my one and only opportunity to visit them.

I'm sure I'll regret this. The area is prohibited, and as soon as I get within several miles of the place, the Major and whoever else is monitoring Them is going to know. No one other than Hawkeye knows my condition—his lips are sealed—but after this trip, the higher-ups are going to have a lot of questions that I'm going to have to answer. And as sure as the sun rises in the east, I'll be reprimanded and quite possibly punished somehow for this act.

This new breed of Josco is quite the opposite of what we've understood them to be. Their knowledge and evolution have been impressive, to say the least. Over the past two weeks, video from the drones has captured campfires with what looks like families sitting around them to keep warm. Kids of all ages have been spotted playing. Huts have been built out of trees and other materials from nearby towns. We even have footage of them hunting wildlife like packs of wolves…tracking and stalking them until they make their kill. As captivating and surprising as that all is, they're still animals, and we can't trust them. There have been a lot of complaints from the locals as to why we haven't bombed the hell out of them already. The lack of action from the Major has put everyone on edge and put him in the hot seat. Rumblings of removing him from his position are gaining speed every day that nothing is done.

I have mixed feelings on the matter. I understand where he's coming from since, like me, he has first-hand experience with Them. They didn't attack when either of us were face to face, but could they? Could they be easily triggered and then go on a rampage? Or are they capable of more? Can they be trusted? Is there a way for us to coexist?

Hawkeye jumps in the back seat to lie down, distracting me from my thoughts. It's a long journey to where we're going, so I guess he's going to sleep the time away.

***

It took a full day's drive, and halfway through it, the sun peeked out of an otherwise dreary sky, but we made it to the Sault Ste. Marie bridge post that will take me to Canada. One of two things is about to happen. I'm either going to get turned away and this day is a waste, or I will be able to sweet-talk my way in and they'll be none the wiser of my intentions.

Hawkeye perks up when I apply the brakes and the jeep starts to slow. He jumps back up front. I turn to him with a finger pointing at him. "Keep cool." He licks my finger. "Don't say a word. Let me do the talking. I know how you can get flustered in these situations, so…just sit there."

A guard exits the small ten-foot by ten-foot cinder-block shack with his M4 in an off-side drop position and looking curious. His thick neck and jaw show more muscles than I have on my entire body. Shit. He looks like a hard ass. I'm gonna have to do some major butt-kissing. Through a large window, I see movement inside the shack. Another Marine stands up and walks toward the exit, donning his helmet. He emerges wearing a thick jacket with his weapon in a military patrol-ready position, that same raised eyebrow.

I drive up at a crawl while rolling down my window, ready to hand the guard my ID. Hawkeye ducks his head to inspect the men as we close the gap. "Remember what I said. Just keep cool and everything will be okay." I pet the top of his head.

"Can I help you?" The guard's deep, raspy voice struggles. He must've been a drill instructor with a voice like that.

"Yes, sir." I hold out my ID as I read "Rogers" on his name tag. "Just coming up here to get away and do a little dog training."

He takes my ID but doesn't inspect it right away. "I'm sure there are plenty of other places south of here you could do your dog training"—he raises my ID so he can compare it to my face—"Petty Officer First Class Brock."

"That is true, but I've always wanted to come up here and do a little camping in my off-time and figured why not do both right now, you know, while I'm still young. Oh, and maybe do a little fishing." I feel like an idiot, trying my hardest to give a compelling smile. I might as well have a tattoo across my forehead that says 'guilty'.

"Where you headed, Brock? It's going to be dark soon and we have orders not to let anyone pass right now." He hands my ID back.

"Yeah, I know about that, but I'm headed east, Whitefish Falls. You heard of it?" I say in my most convincing voice. "Saw pictures of it in a magazine…looks like a nice place to relax."

"Can't say that I have, but I can't let you pass. You're gonna have to turn around and go somewhere else to relax," he says sternly.

Dammit. I look to Hawkeye for advice. He just stares back doing what I ordered him to do: stay quiet. What the heck can I say that'll get this guy to budge? I can feel sweat threatening to break out of the pores on my forehead. Please no.

"I drove all this way, Corporal. A day's drive. Cut me some slack this once?" I plead with him. "Just a day? I'll come back tomorrow evening, and you'll never know I was here."

"Sorry, sir, you should know better than anyone. I have orders to follow."

I'm about to give up when another person rises from inside the shack, sauntering over to the other guard who has been standing deathly still as if he was waiting for me to do something stupid. They talk for a moment, then the guard points at me, and guy number three makes his way over. As he gets closer, his round, bearded face becomes more visible with each step. I know him. Couldn't tell at first with the full beard, but that's First Sergeant Pete Worth. I think I may have an in. My hope rejuvenates.

He pulls Corporal Rogers to the side and starts asking him questions, but I can hear them as clear as day. I hear him ask who I am, and the Corporal gives him my name, to which the First Sergeant does a double take at me and heads straight for me.

"Holy shit! What the hell are you doing way up here?" We salute each other, and then I open the door to step outside so we can shake hands properly. I should have grabbed my jacket; it's freaking cold with the heater not blowing on me.

"Well, I thought I would come up here to do some dog training and, honestly, just get away for a bit with everything that's been going on," I offer.

"Man, I hear that. The Major put this place on lockdown after that hostage, Waco guy was assassinated in his own cell. Shit's been as tight as an elephant's ass." I smirk at his comment, genuinely entertained.

"Where are you headed, and for how long?" His voice sounds promising, unlike Corporal Rogers.

"Whitefish Falls." Hawkeye moves to the driver's seat.

"Whitefish Falls, huh?" He reaches over and pets Hawkeye through the door. "That's the only place you're going?" His voice shifts with the downward tilt of his chin.

"Yes, sir." *Don't look away. Act confident.* I stand a little straighter.

Pete looks over his shoulder. "Man, I really shouldn't be doing this." He lowers his voice. "If we didn't know each other, your ass would be turning around to go somewhere else."

"I completely understand." My heart beats with excitement that I'm getting away with my master plan.

"You have two days! Your ass better be back here by mid-day Wednesday, or we're going to have problems," he says sternly.

Damn. Maybe I should have stayed home. All I can think now is that I'm about to burn this bridge…metaphorically of course. Guilt hits me; he could get in a lot of trouble for this. But I need to know what's happening to me or I'll lose my mind.

I nod, jumping into the jeep, and Pete waves me forward. The other two guards lift the gate to let me pass, glaring at me with displeasure. I raise a finger from off the steering wheel letting them know I appreciate it, but their scowls don't budge.

"That's one obstacle down, now one to go." Hawkeye paws at me with what feels like a warning. "Don't start. I know this isn't a smart idea. Any sign of trouble and we're out of there faster than you can eat your dinner. Deal?" He whimpers and groans.

Not even five minutes later, I am on the outskirts of the city. I pull over and grab my map to make sure I'm following the correct roads to Horseshoe Bay. There's one main road, but as I get closer, I notice a few side streets that aren't marked on the map. If I'm lucky, maybe signs will still be posted to guide me in.

"It's now or never, Jayce," I whisper to myself and hesitantly let off the brakes. I'm trying to picture how all this is going to go down, but I'm at a loss for anything reasonable. How the heck am I going to communicate with them? Are we going to draw pictures for each other? I laugh at the thought. Is that one dude who was holding the baby going to remember me? Should I walk up holding a white flag to let them know I come in peace? Do they even know what that means?

Crap. My hands sweat as I grip the steering wheel harder, thinking about every scenario of what could go wrong. But on the flip side, what if it goes right? How am I going to explain this to the Major and everyone else? My heart races even more thinking about confronting him.

Close to the sanctuary's entrance, my head aches for a split second as if hit by a lightning strike, then it goes away. A child's voice intrudes on my thoughts.

What are you doing here?